Enjoy the Journey!

Brian W. Ratty

Destination Astoria

—⁓—

Odyssey to the Pacific

Brian D. Ratty

Sunset Lake Publishing
89637 Lakeside Ct.
Warrenton, OR 97146
503.717.1125
#93-1015196

First Edition published in March 2014

ISBN-10: 0615940773
ISBN-13: 9780615940779

Create Space Title ID: 4244100
Printed in the USA

Sunset Lake
Publishing

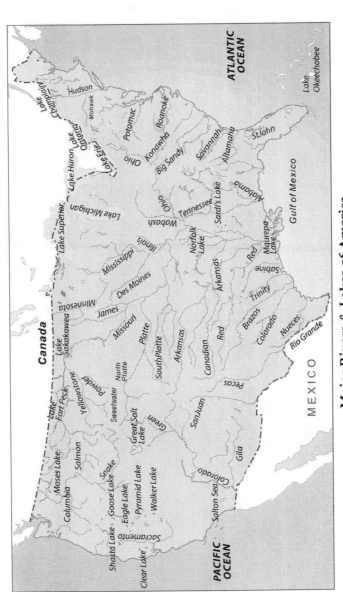

Major Rivers & Lakes of America

Tess
Always… Forever

Introduction

—ᨠ—

*A*t my best, I'm only a storyteller. My novels are mostly yarns about history, events, and the people who came before us. I depend on vivid descriptions, bold characters and a strong story-line to keep my readers engaged. So it is with <u>Destination Astoria, Odyssey to the Pacific</u>. One could search the annals of American history and not find a story with more danger, despair and missteps than the Astor Overland Expedition of 1810. At the time, John Jacob Astor was believed to be the richest man in America. He had made his fortune in animal fur and had visions of controlling the fur trade worldwide. Astor's idea was a grandiose scheme: to send a brigade of thirty men across the uncharted continent, while sending a ship full of trading supplies around the Horn to meet up with the troop and build a trading post on the Columbia River. It is this plot that becomes the backdrop for <u>Destination Astoria</u>.

Writing historical fiction can be a tricky enterprise. The storytelling presented many challenges, such as working with Eighteenth-Century language and the many jargons of the day. Research information about the true culture and faith of the early frontiersman was quite sketchy. And finding resources that could shed light on the civilization and societies of the local Indians was an even more daunting task.

So the true storytellers take liberties: they embellish, they animate, and they entertain. The history of storytelling is a complex form of tattooing. Before man learned to write, he had to rely on his memory. To survive, he had to become a successful hunter and a good listener. Early aboriginal people painted symbols for stories on cave walls. Most early cultures depended on storytelling for education and entertainment. The North American Indians told stories using a combination of oral narrative, music, rock art and dance. Traditionally, these oral stories have been handed down from one generation to the next. The early seafarers and frontiersmen who made contact with the Indians were also mostly illiterate. They, too, depended on visual and animated ways of communicating with the natives. Today, storytelling is an intrinsic part of our culture. In our movies, books, music, architecture and art, we find the influence of storytelling. But much of what we see and read today is what I call 'brash and dash' story development. Often the characters are weak and the descriptions vague, while the stories are filled with gratuitous violence and lewd language.

I write what I like to read, so I shy away from salacious stories. Instead, I hope to propel my reader back in time while making my characters so lucid that they become part of the reader's family. <u>Destination Astoria</u> is held together with the glue of history, while the powerful descriptions and genuine characters move across the pages with the fury of a prairie storm. With thoughtful and brutal twists, my story portrays a lost breed of adventurous frontiersman who helped blaze the Oregon Trail. Enjoy the journey!

Contents

—ɯ—

I
Reflections

—⚶—

A husky gray-haired man, dressed in a blue felt waistcoat and tan woolen trousers, slowly descended the dark staircase of the Astoria Hotel. Once on the main floor, he used a silver-tipped cane to amble across the dim, empty lobby. His weathered hand pushed open the frosted-glass saloon doors, and he entered a smoky barroom.

On one side of the room was an ornate mahogany bar with a brass footstool. On the other side were numerous wooden tables and chairs. With the *tap, tap, tap* of his cane, he shuffled down the long bar and looked out through one of the nine-paned windows that fronted the hotel. The sky remained a gray shroud, and the rain continued in earnest.

Astoria Oregon, in 1860, boasted broad boardwalks, with businesses on both sides of a timber planked street built on log pilings high above the river shore. Across the way, between some buildings, the old man had a view of Scowl Bay. There, resting at the end of a wharf was the steam schooner *Rachel*, the ship he and his wife had arrived on. Forty-five years had passed since he last stood on these shores. During those years, this little settlement had sprung up around the old fort, and it now had a population of nearly a thousand souls. Other things had changed as well. Most of the Indians were gone. They had either died off or been forced to move to reservations. The Columbia River without Indians was like the night sky without stars.

"What's your pleasure, mate?" a voice rang out from behind.

Turning from the window, the old man faced a burly, white-aproned bartender with black, slicked-back hair. "Mug of coffee, sweetened with a spot of brandy," he answered with authority, and moved to the end of bar.

The barkeep smiled and took up his position behind the counter. It was still early in the morning, and the barroom was almost empty. One table in a far corner, closest to the woodstove, held three men, loggers by the looks of them, and a few tables over was another table with two men who looked like fishermen.

As the old man's mug of coffee arrived, the glass doors opened, and the third mate from the *Rachel* stepped inside the saloon. Moving to the other end of the bar, he recognized the old man and nodded his way. The old man's expression brightened and he tipped his mug to the mate.

The barkeep approached the sailor. "What's your pleasure?"

The lanky third mate removed his hat and set it on the bar. "Whiskey," he answered. As the bartender turned for the back row of bottles, the mate continued, "Do you know who that old bloke at the end of the bar is?"

The barkeep turned back to his customer, "Nay."

The sailor smiled. "He's one of the old-timers. He came in on my ship. They say he knew Astor, opened the Oregon Trail, and settled out here before the Astorians came. If you get him talkin', he spins a great yarn."

The bartender gave the mate an approving nod and poured his drink.

From across the room, the boss of the loggers called out for more drinks. When the bartender delivered the order, he told the table what he just learned about the old man at the end of the bar. "I understand that if you get him talking, he spins a good story about the old days," the bartender said.

With a few coins, the timber boss paid for the drinks, and then turned to the bar and shouted, "Hey, old-timer, come join us. We won't bite." The boss was a giant of a man dressed in a plaid wool shirt with dirty blue overalls. Next to him were two younger blokes, one with bright red hair and the other with a full head of blonde locks.

The old man turned toward their table, picked up his mug, and shuffled his way across the room with a *tap, tap, tap.*

As he approached, the big fellow stood with an extended hand. "They call me Swede. I be the bullbuck for these boys."

The old man shook his powerful, rough hand. "I be Clarke. Dutch Clarke." He pulled up a chair and took his seat. "Thanks for the offer. It's been years since I drank with woodsmen."

"What brings you to our little town?" the Swede asked.

Dutch glanced down at his coffee mug. "Got some family that's buried around here, and I came to pay my last respects."

The Swede smiled. "Understand you were friends with Astor."

Dutch looked up at him with a scowl on his weathered face. "Nay, not friends. Didn't trust the man."

"Did you really open the Oregon Trail?" the fair-skinned blonde fellow asked.

Dutch turned to him. "Had a hand in it. Not much more than that."

"Is your name in the history books?" the redheaded lad asked.

Dutch chuckled. "Reckon not, seeing how when I crossed the divide my last name wasn't Clarke."

"How the hell did your name get changed?" the Swede asked, openly curious.

Dutch took a long look at his three new friends and shook his head slowly. "Nay, it's a long story, and I don't want to bore ya."

The Swede pointed to the window. "Look outside, mate. It's pouring out there, and we don't have to be back to camp until tomorrow. We've got a warm fire, a bar full of booze, and nothing to do. So please, enlighten us, sir."

Dutch grinned at him and nodded. "Alright, but you stop me if I ramble on too long. Now where should I start? Hum, how about with that scoundrel, Astor?"

Crossroads ————————

Dancing upon a warm breeze, a bald eagle with a wingspan the size of a man flew effortlessly high above a placid blue lake. Hunting for fish the eagle seemed to sleep, wing wide and silent seen.

On the lake below, a small birch canoe with a curved prow fore and aft glided to a halt. As the rower rested his paddle across the gunnels, he watched the regal bird instinctively quest the water. The man, dressed in fringed buckskins, with long flowing auburn hair, held one hand above his eyes to shade them from the brightness.

In front of the man, in the bottom of the boat, were a stack of animal pelts, his traveling pack and a long rifle. In front of this lump, at the bow, a dog sat on its rump watching the same scene with its head cocked in a curious twist.

"Our Indian friends use eagle feathers on their war shields," the man said to his dog. "If I kill that bird, he would be worth many skins."

At that instant, the eagle's wings awakened and he swooped down upon the lake with outstretched talons, snatching up a fish in his claws. The fish was big and squirmy, but the eagle's grasp was firm and his wings powerful. Within a few seconds, the white headed eagle rested in a nearby treetop, ripping the flesh from his fare.

"Nay, King," he said to the dog again. "That's a wretched idea. I won't kill him today or morrow. He be too majestic. Be a sin for him to be a feather within some Indian lodge."

With a whistle on his lips, the mountain man took the paddle in hand again and began gliding the canoe across the tranquil water. Each deliberate pull from the young man's lean and muscular body slid the boat forward, while his keen blue eyes searched the shoreline for landmarks, game or trouble. The prow of his birch canoe was painted with a human handprint, a symbol that marked the boat as being a Seneca canoe. The Seneca Indians were one of six nations living in western New York State in 1809. Frenchie, the man who ran the local trading post, had traded a rifle for the pirogue, a few years back. Now it was used by Dutch Blackwell for his trading travels up and down Lake Ontario.

Dutch, a twenty year old trapper and trader, was born in a Tillamook Indian village on the coast of the Pacific Northwest. His mother had been a Tolowa Indian slave, his father a Boston man, Joe Blackwell, who arrived at the Tillamook village with Captain Robert Gray on a ship, the *Lady Washington*, in 1788. During a skirmish with the Indians, the ship had made a hasty departure, leaving Dutch's father marooned with the Tillamooks. A year later, Dutch was born and for seventeen years was raised by his family in the Pacific Northwest wilderness. From his lineage and swarthy complexion, he knew himself to be a breed, but he bristled when anyone used that word. He was in fact, a fearless trader and trapper who knew the Indian cultures well, and he had an ear for their many different tongues. Between signing and talking, he could powwow with almost any tribe.

"There be our river," Dutch shouted to his dog, while turning the canoe into a small cove. "Be drinking whiskey and eating Frenchie's gruel before the sun is gone."

Dutch had made his mournful journey to Boston after the tragic death of his family out on the Pacific. His purpose had been to find his Grandfather and an uncle named Fredric. But, when he arrived at Boston Harbor in July of 1807, he found that his grandfather had died and his uncle had gone west in search of his brother. Dutch was without a family again, and this fact weighed heavily on his soul.

When a man from New York read in the Boston newspaper of his adventures out west, he offered Dutch a two year contract to trade and trap for his fur company. John Astor was to pay Dutch $400 for this contract, and now that period had expired.

The two years he had spent working with the Six Nation Tribes had been an arduous adventure. In the bitter cold winters, he had trapped; in the hot humid summers he had traded. He had grown to dislike Astor's policy of trading arms and whiskey to the Indians.

With the contract now complete, he was returning to the trading post to collect his wages and then, somehow, take his heart back to the Pacific Northwest. An old Tillamook squaw had once told him, *"The past is the best road to the future."* Dutch had a restless desire to return to the Columbia River and his only remaining family, the Northwest Coastal Indians.

After turning the boat into the cove, he maneuvered around some rocks and entered a small, lazy green estuary that flowed from the east.

"Less water than we had a few weeks ago. Keep an eye out for rocks."

The dog in the front turned his head back to Dutch, his nose twitching.

"Okay, then, I'll watch out for the rocks. You tell me if there be any Indians about."

King, the dog, was a curious animal, with a shiny black short-hair coat and a light tan belly. His two front legs ended in white paws, while his powerful haunches were as black as burnt wood. He weighed about forty pounds, with bright, clear eyes, small pointed ears, a short brown shiny snoot, and teeth as sharp as lightning. His disposition was both bitter and sweet; vicious if surprised, submissive when trusting. The dog was surely a native cur and, Dutch suspected, had been poorly treated. He had found him wandering a trail outside a Cayuga village. The dog was skittish, underfed and standoffish to his first approach. But when he turned away to return to his canoe, the mutt tagged along. Dutch figured he was the first white man the dog had ever smelt. He must have liked the scent, as they bonded quickly, and the two had been together ever since. When needed, the dog hunted his own fare and found his own bed. They made good companions, as both were as independent as the breeze. But King didn't much care for Indians and could smell them half a mile off. Dutch liked that; the dog's nose was his blade against any approaching trouble.

His name had come about in an unusual way. During the Revolutionary War, the tribes of the Six Nations had sided with King George. After the British defeat, however, the Crown deserted the tribes. Many years later, the Indians were still blabbing about being forsaken by King George. Dutch figured that the dog had abandoned them, as well, so why not name him King George? It seemed only fitting.

The way up the small river was much slower going than on the lake. It was late in the season, and the water depth and flow were slight. After a few miles, the stream cut through a small gully with trees on each side. It was the middle of September, and the forest was in the midst of changing colors. Long gone were the wonders of summer, replaced with cool crisp nights, and short warm days. The journey up this twisting river was like riding inside a fire pit, with the walls of the canyon ablaze with crimson, yellow and orange foliage. Dutch marveled at the spectacular beauty of Mother Nature's palette.

Moments later he came to his first obstacle, a small waterfall that blocked his way. Here he pulled ashore. Three times more, the boat and all the pelts had to be portaged around various water hazards, making for a slow passage.

It was late afternoon when they reached the confluence of three rivers. Here Dutch turned east once again. An hour later, the canoe slipped onto a large inland lagoon that the natives called Oneida. The lake was about twenty five miles long and five miles wide. With the sun low in the sky, the tranquil blue water glistened with a thousand winks of light.

Treachery ————

The long, forested lake ran almost due east and west. Dutch turned to the north and rowed into a large cove where, high upon a sandy beach stood a log house with smoke rising from its stone chimney. Paddling for shore, he noticed Frenchie's canoe resting on the beach. But in the shallows next to it, was another. Frenchie had customers. As Dutch glided ashore, he saw the marks on the canoe and knew it was from the Kickapoo nation.

Bloody strange. The Kickapoo roam hundreds of miles west of here...

As the canoe came to rest, King jumped out, ran for his favorite bush and promptly raised his leg. Pulling the boat to higher ground, Dutch removed his knapsack and put it on his back. Then grabbing his rifle and bundle of furs, he stumbled towards the front porch with the heavy load.

Moving slowly up the log steps, he found a new wooden sign above the doorway. In white letters, it read simply, *'American Fur Co. Post 9.'*

Dutch chuckled to himself. *Foolish. Indians can't read.* As King joined him on the porch, the dog immediately started to growl and work his nose.

"Ye smell em, don't you boy? No worry. I'll shoo em off."

As the dog backed away from the entry, Dutch used his knee to unlatch the door and swing it into the room. Crossing the threshold, he moved to his left and dropped the heavy pelts onto a wooden trading table with a loud thud.

Frenchie was at the rear of the room, restocking wool blankets on the tall shelves. The French Canadian was burly. His belly jiggled over a beaded Indian belt nearly forty five inches long. He wore buckskin trousers and a linen shirt that was soiled with blood and grime. His chin was covered by a weedy brown beard, stained black around the mouth from his constant chewing of tobacco. Frenchie's eyes were as gray as his long matted hair.

"How did you do, mate?" the fat man asked in a heavy French brogue.

With a scornful glance, Dutch spotted two young Indians across the murky room next to the fireplace. They both were standing in soiled buckskins by a planked bar held up by large casts, drinking from a brown earthen jug. One brave was tall and rawboned, the other dirty faced and pudgy. Both were copper skinned, with wide fleshy noses and black hair.

Turning back to Frenchie, Dutch replied, "Twenty six prime pelts. From your fresh supplies and new sign, I reckon the barge came while I was gone."

"Aye," the fat man answered, moving to the trading table to inspect the pelts.

The room was smoky and smelled sour, so Dutch left the door open and moved to the fireplace, where he took off his pack and rested his rifle against the stones. "Did Astor send my pay?"

"Nay."

Going behind the planked bar, Dutch grabbed a red-clay jug and poured a splash of whiskey into a tin cup. After taking a swig, he replied, with a bitter face, "Sent him a letter on the spring barge, telling him of my needs. You sure he didn't send any money?"

Just then, the two Indians started squabbling about sharing their jug.

Dutch turned angrily to them and said in their tongue. "Take your damn argument outside Kickapoos. Don't want to hear any more gibberish." Then, turning back to Frenchie, he continued in English, "I'm not spending another winter in this god forsaken hell hole. My contract was up last week, and I want my wages."

"Don't have that kind of money Dutch," Frenchie answered.

"How much do you have?"

The fat man moved to the bar and poured himself a drink from the same red-clay jug.

"They sent me fifty fresh minted Continental dollars. But that money is for buying trade goods from the Canadians, come spring."

The two Indians started arguing again.

Dutch reached to his belt, pulled out one of his pistols, and lay it with a loud thump on the bar's wooden planks, pointing in their direction. "Take your jug and go. I'm not asking again."

Their gallon jug was brown clay, which held Indian whiskey or 'firewater.' Frenchie made the concoction by diluting whiskey with water and kerosene, then adding peppers and gunpowder. It was an awful swill. The red-clay jugs held the white man's whiskey.

The tallest Indian, dressed in soiled buckskins, mumbled something to the other brave, glaring hatefully across the bar.

Dutch reached out and put his finger on the pistol trigger, returning the Indian's glare.

Tension filled the stale room. The only sounds came from the crackling fire. Frenchie slowly put his hand on his hip knife.

"Have they paid for the jug?" Dutch asked.

"Aye, a fine beaver skin," the fat man answered.

"Well, Kickapoo's, Are you drinkin' or fightin'?"

After a few seconds, the bigger brave grabbed the brown jug and motioned with his head toward the door.

As the two Indians walked out, Dutch called, "Stay clear of the dog. He don't much like Indians."

Once the braves had departed, Frenchie returned to the trading table and continued inspecting the hides. Dutch fetched a new log for the fire and then stood silently, staring at the flames while sipping his whiskey.

Holding up a large pelt, the fat man asked, "What the bloody hell is this?"

Turning his way, Dutch replied, "The skunk skin is mine. It will make a proper winter hat."

"Good," Frenchie said with a sour face. "We don't trade in skunk skins."

"It's well cured, and the biggest skunk I've ever seen." Dutch poured himself another cup of whiskey. "Why is Astor trying to cheat me out of my wages?"

"Don't know, lad. Maybe he thinks you're staying another year."

Taking a big swig, Dutch replied, "Reckon I'll have to paddle down to the city and ask him myself."

"That be a long paddle, 350 miles or more. Why not winter here and go back with the barge, come spring?"

Just then, the dog entered the room and curled up in his favorite spot in front of the fireplace.

"Nay," said Dutch, "won't be wintering here. The dog and I will leave 'morrow."

"Suit yourself, lad," Frenchie replied with a strange look on his face.

Mid-morning the next day, under a cloudy sky, Dutch loaded the small canoe and noticed that the Kickapoo boat still rested on the shore. He warned Frenchie, who didn't seem concerned.

"Not to worry, lad. They be sleeping it off in the forest. They mean no harm."

With King in the canoe, Dutch shook the fat man's grimy hand and said farewell. As he paddled off, he shouted back, "I'll leave the boat at the company warehouse. The barge will bring it back next spring."

"Aye," Frenchie answered. "Have Astor send me another trapper."

With the wave of his hand, Dutch plunged his paddle deep into the water and mumbled to himself, "So long, fat man."

The canoe headed south across the lake and then turned east, hugging the southern shore. As Dutch worked the paddle, he thought about Astor and cursed him for forcing him to make the long trip. But he had learned much in the past two years, mostly of the culture of the Six Nation Indians. They were, in many ways, superior to the Pacific Indians. They cultivated the land, were gifted artisans and had learned to use iron tools. Some had even taken to the white man's religion. But it wasn't all good; many of the Indians were thieves, still more were drunks, and all were warlike. Dutch vowed that when he returned to the Pacific he would teach the tribes how to work the soil and better care for themselves. But would he trade muskets and whiskey, or speak to them about religion? No dammit!

After a few hours of rowing, the sun showed itself, and Dutch paddled to the leeward side of a small forested island, where he came to a halt. Taking some venison jerky from his pouch, he put a piece in his mouth and tossed a second morsel to King.

Watching the dog chew the tough meat, he asked, "How about fish for dinner?"

Taking a short piece of deer sinew from his rucksack, he fastened a small hook on one end and slipped a chunk of jerky onto it for bait. Then he took his sea knife, sliced half through a lead bullet, and fastened the ball to the line as a weight.

Within the hour, they had three nice perch in the bottom of the boat. After cleaning the fish, Dutch rolled them in a wet cloth and stuffed them in his pack.

As he was doing this, the dog's nose started twitching.

Looking across the water to the shore of the island, Dutch asked, "We got Indians over there, boy?"

The dog raised his nose high, sniffing quickly, and started to softly growl.

"Don't worry. We're done. Got more than enough for supper."

For the next few hours, Dutch rowed the canoe due east. All the while, King kept looking back at the boat's wake, with his nose twitching.

With one eye on the dog and the other onshore, Dutch stayed alert for trouble.

Around his neck he wore two strands of animal teeth. One necklace had been his father's, and the other his brother's. The teeth had been taken from a dead cougar that had tried to kill his father. His Indian blood brother had saved his life and crafted the strands as a trophy.

Tucked into his belt were two British flintlock pistols. Resting next to him lay a Kentucky long rifle inside a buffalo sheath. These also had belonged to his father. On his belt was a twelve inch sea knife that his blacksmith Grandfather had crafted and given to his father when he departed from Boston Harbor with Captain Gray in 1787.

A Bible, a metal flute, a corncob pipe, a leather pouch, and these weapons were all that remained of Dutch's family legacy – a sad thought. But he had other God given gifts, as well. His sense of direction was that of a hawk's, and he could recall almost anything he read. But his biggest prize was that, at times, he could hear his dead father's voice inside his ear. The man's spirit often talked to Dutch, and Dutch listened.

With the sun slipping low in the western sky, they finally reached the headwaters of the Mohawk River. Like a snake, this long twisting tributary drained down to the Hudson River, which then flowed to New York City. Here, Dutch beached the canoe and set up camp in a maple grove next to the sandy beach. The site had been used before by many travelers and had a stone surrounded fire pit, a large log snag that could be rolled into position as a backrest, and a dense forest for fuel. The ground cover, up from the sandy beach, was mostly dried grass, scrub brush and twigs.

Normally, when Dutch camped next to a lake, he would conceal his campfire from being visible out on the water. But this day was different; he'd had a feeling all afternoon that something was dogging them. On this night, he would build his fire big and bright so that it might welcome any intruders.

Rolling the log snag into position, Dutch started a fire. Then, as it took hold, he walked to the lakeshore. With King squatting in the sand next to him, he cupped his hand into a make-shift spyglass to scan the lake's water, but he saw nothing other than the makings of a dramatic sunset with puffball clouds.

Returning to camp, he cooked the three fish slowly in an iron skillet, while watching the pink and amber horizon. Once they were cooked, he gave one fish to King on a tin plate, and set out the other two for himself in the same manner.

"We be the bait tonight, boy," he said to the dog while his steel blue eyes searched the crimson horizon. "They will think us tenderfoots."

After dinner, Dutch lit his corncob pipe and set about arranging the trap. On the ground next to the log, he spread out his camp canvas and emptied the contents of his rucksack onto it. Then he rolled the contents into a blanket, to create the appearance of a bedroll. At the top of this roll he placed his hat, and set his rifle against the log snag. At the foot of the roll was a small bush, which he draped with a dark blanket to make it look like a sleeping dog. Using the firelight, he double checked that his pistols were primed and loaded. Then he moved his coffee pot to the pit stones. Finally, he added more fuel to the fire, and surveyed his work by the light of the dancing flames.

The ruse was set.

Moving a short way into the maple grove, he found a place in the shadows that offered a good view of the camp. Crouching by a tree trunk, he whispered for King to join him.

Moving through the underbrush, the dog soon arrived at his side.

Using hand signals, he instructed the dog to sit, then whispered in his ear, "We want no trouble, so we have to be quiet. We will see if my gut is wrong or right."

Taking the two pistols from his belt, he cocked each gun once and placed them on the ground in front of him. Then he came to rest on his butt, with the tree at his back.

From where they lurked, he could see the entire campsite with the moon lit lake in the background. He heard an owl hoot in the distance, the crackling of his fire and some small critters in the woods. After a few minutes, King curled up on the ground and fell asleep.

Time dragged on…but waiting was a hunter's game. Soon, Dutch's eyes grew heavy. He cursed himself for drinking a cup of whiskey with dinner. He should have made coffee. As the fire burned down, his mind began to wander with the breeze in the trees. His thoughts blurred, and his alertness dimmed. Time was now his enemy.

Fizz…Bang!

The flintlock rifle shot jolted Dutch from his slumber. When his eyes snapped open, he saw gun smoke rolling above his camp site. Grabbing his pistols, he stood quickly.

In the dim light to his right, he spotted the two Kickapoos from the post. The tall one had just fired his rifle into the bedroll, while the pudgy one was charging the dog-bush with a spear.

Cocking the pistols all the way back, Dutch took aim at the tall Indian.

At that instant, he heard his father's words: *Just nick him.*

He aimed for the Indian's legs, but as he pulled the trigger and the flash pan burned, *fizz...*, King jumped up, jarring his arm.

Bang!

The ball sped wildly across the camp, hitting the tall Kickapoo directly in the chest. The bullet instantly exploded the Indian's buckskin top, blossoming blood red, and he dropped to the ground with his rifle.

Quickly glancing to his left, Dutch found the second Indian pulling his spear from the bush and pointing it at his growling, charging dog.

Pulling the trigger of the second pistol, Dutch heard the *fizz...* but no bang. Misfire.

The Kickapoo threw the spear at the leaping dog but missed. King landed on the pudgy Indian, and they both rolled to the ground.

Rushing from the thicket, Dutch saw that the dog had a vicious hold on the forearm of the Indian. Growling, jaw locked, King tried to drag the Indian across the ground, while the Kickapoo screamed and tried the stab the animal with his knife.

Dutch ran up and kicked the blade from the Indian's hand. "Let go, King. Let go!"

Reluctantly, the dog released the Indian's arm and backed off, still growling.

The pudgy Indian had hit his head on a rock in the scuffle and was bleeding from his forehead. The bites on his arm reached almost to the bone, and were squirting blood.

Dutch dragged the wounded Indian to the log snag and retrieved a cloth, which he tied tightly around the tooth marks. Then, summoning King to stand guard over the half-conscious brave, Dutch hurried over to the tall Indian. Kneeling by the man's blood soaked torso, he felt for a pulse.

The Kickapoo was dead.

Shaking his head, Dutch stood up and called, across the camp, "Your friend is dead. Didn't want to kill him." Looking down again at the blood soaked body, Dutch saw something glint in the flickering firelight – a coin on the ground. Bending down, he picked it up, then found two more that had apparently dropped out of the dead Indian's poke. Weighing them on his palm, he examined the bloody coins, and saw that they were fresh minted Continental dollars.

Thoughts roared in his head. *An Indian with cash money is rare, and silver dollars rarer yet. Did they kill Frenchie for these coins?*

Building up the fire, Dutch returned to the wounded Indian and slipped off his shoulder pouch. Inside, he found three more coins.

Shaking the Indian hard, he yelled, "Where you get this money?"

The Indian only moaned softly, shrinking from his rough touch.

Dutch snatched up his canteen and poured some water over the brave's head, rousing the Kickapoo. Holding the coins out to the Indian, he asked his question again. "Where you get this money?"

The Kickapoo's frightened gaze shifted from the coins to Dutch's angry face. Looking away, he mumbled something.

"Louder!" Dutch demanded. "You kill Frenchie?"

The Indian shook his head in denial and mumbled, "He give us money."

"Why?"

"He need you dead," the Indian whispered, his face a mask of fear.

"You lie. There's no profit in that for him."

"Chief in city tell him to do. No pay you. My arm on fire!"

Taken aback by the news, Dutch reached for his jug of whiskey and gave the brave a swig.

"I'll fix your arm or cut it off. You tell the truth. How much did he pay?"

"Coins and red jug. We bring back your ears for more."

Dutch took a swig from the jug, as well, trying to think it out. Astor paid six dollars and saved four hundred. Hmm. The unexpected tale somehow had the ring of truth.

Handing the Indian the jug again, he said, "You drink. Where's your canoe?"

With his good arm, the Kickapoo pointed with the jug and murmured, "Up beach there."

"The dog will watch. I'll be back and fix arm."

Dutch stomped up the beach in the moonlight and found their canoe. Wading in the water, he towed the boat back and placed it next to his. In the bottom of their boat, he found some blankets and a half full red-clay jug.

The Kickapoo was telling the truth.

Walking back to camp with a blanket and the jug, Dutch set them next to the fire, then slipped his sea knife into the hot coals. Returning to the dead Indian, he lifted him onto his shoulders and carried him to the Kickapoo canoe, lowering him gently to sprawl in the bottom of the boat. He hated having killed this Indian, and knew that the death would haunt him. Bowing his head, he said a silent prayer.

Returning to camp, he found the wounded Indian sufficiently numb from the whiskey, and set about cleaning the wound with alcohol and wrapping his head with a cloth.

As he worked, he said loudly to his half-conscious patient, "Take your friend home. Tell his family the truth. If you don't, my dog will find you again."

For the deep teeth bites, he scorched each one shut with his red hot blade. The smell was dreadful and the Kickapoo screamed, and then passed out again.

When the job was finished, Dutch slumped next to the unconscious Indian, resting his back against the log. Taking the Indian jug to his lips, he drank a large mouthful and screamed angrily to the moon, "Astor, you bastard, you'll pay for this treachery!"

At first light the next morning, Dutch broke a cold camp and packed his belongings aboard his canoe. All the while, the wounded Indian still slept beneath a blanket, next to the log snag. The day was cloudy, the morning cold, and Dutch's mood was gloomier than both. Dark and angry thoughts filled his mind, one of which was the temptation to kick a hole in the side of the Kickapoo canoe so there would be no temptation for the injured Indian to follow him. But he resisted the idea; with only one good arm, the Kickapoo would never be able to keep up the pace.

Instead, Dutch walked to the blanketed mound and kicked at it. "Wake up," he demanded.

The mound moved slightly, and a head with sleepy eyes popped out of the blanket cocoon.

"Let me see your wounds."

Still dazed from sleep and hung over from whiskey, the wounded Indian sat up and gazed around the empty camp, clearly trying to collect his thoughts. Dutch bent and removed the dressing from the man's head. The scab was free from any fresh blood, and a large welt could be felt.

"Got a headache, I'll bet. Suits you fine."

Removing the cloth bandage from his lower arm, Dutch found the bite marks also free of fresh blood. Although, cauterizing the bites with his hot knife had caused the arm to swell, and it looked painful to the touch.

Standing, Dutch angrily talked and signed to the young Indian. "I've taken your money and your whiskey. Your friend died for nothing! Take him home. Powwow truth to Council. If you speak with forked tongue, I will return and kill you."

The wounded Kickapoo's bloodshot eyes widened, and his face filled with fear, but he said nothing.

Dutch glared down at him, turned, called for King and moved toward the lake. On the beach, he looked down at the dead Kickapoo in the bottom of the Indian canoe and shook his head, one last time. Cursing the morning, he got the dog into his boat and paddled off.

The King of the Skins ————————

With the first signs of a hazy sun in the east, Dutch turned his pirogue, into the green Mohawk estuary. There, he dug his paddle deep in the water. It would be well over 150 miles, as the river flowed, before he reached the Hudson, and so he paddled with a steady rhythm, keeping up his quick pace.

His teeth had been set on edge by the events of the night before. He was angry with the Kickapoo's, and madder than hell at Frenchie, but his greatest wrath was reserved for Astor. Two years before, he had met this German born fur merchant at the man's home in New York City. There were those who said he was rich, while others called him a miser with no love for his adopted country. Dutch had found him pleasant enough and knowledgeable of the fur trade, with operations in both America and Canada. Surely a man with those means would not waylay a trusted trapper for the sake of a few hundred dollars. And yet he had!

Now Astor would pay.

The upper reaches of the river were narrow, with a strong current. But as the Mohawk bent and twisted through the landscape, the green run widened and the flow slackened. Soon it started to rain, gently at first and then in earnest. Dutch reached into his knapsack, drew out his sealskin coat and put it on. Then, reaching into his pouch, he retrieved a few rounds of hardtack, and tossed one of the biscuits to King.

"The rain will soften them, boy," he said to the dog.

Keeping his gaze on King's nose, Dutch took paddle in hand again and moved on. With the pace challenging his strength, he rested every few hours, carefully bailing the boat with a sponge. The bark hull was thin and delicate, so nothing other than a cloth or sponge could be used for bailing. He wished he was rowing in a Tillamook dugout, as their boats were stronger made and more reliable in faster waters.

As they moved down the crooked river, Dutch recalled hearing Frenchie talk of a small village on the north shore at the confluence of the Mohawk and Hudson Rivers. There, with any luck tomorrow, he might find a hot meal and warm bed. That goal and thoughts of revenge filled his head. Unfortunately, he had killed Indians before. Astor would be his first white victim. Or maybe a living but maimed Astor would be better. After all, the Kickapoo's had been instructed to take his ears back to Frenchie, so he had every right to take one of Astor's. Or not. If Astor loved money so much, he could rob him...

But Dutch wasn't a thief, and he did not see how he could live with such a deed.

Soon, his mind turned to his own faults; he was young and dumb and had much to learn. Often stubborn and wrong-headed, he trusted too much, talked too much and didn't have the bloodlust of his father. Yes, he had killed countless animals, but God had put these creatures on Earth for man to use. It was the killing of humans, Indian or not, that pulled at his soul.

These dark thoughts and many more consumed his rowing until darkness beckoned. Exhausted, wet and cold, Dutch searched out a suitable camp site on the river shore. Using his camp canvas, he soon had a small tent set up. But search as he might, he could find no dry tinder for a fire. A cold bivouac on a rainy night was a miserable place, but he and the dog were soon snuggled under the tarp, eating jerky.

Once the meager meal was done, Dutch poured a cup of whiskey and listened to the whisper of the rain. The sound had always been soothing to him, and soon his mind was dreaming to its rhythm. The last thing he remembered, that night, was his father's voice in his ear: *Revenge is for fools. Life is for living.*

At first light the next morning, they continued their seemingly endless journey down the river. With brighter weather, Dutch found that his thoughts were sunnier, as well. He still had anger and disappointment in his heart, but the sharpness of his appetite for revenge had waned with the rain. Now his thoughts turned to a hot meal and a warm bed… and to his home on the Pacific.

By noon a promising sun was out, so they stopped to rest and to dry their camp gear in a warm breeze. Dutch also made a small fire and brewed some hot coffee. Being warm inside and out was a luxury. After eating some hardtack and jerky, they were off again.

Digging deep with his paddle, Dutch watched the autumn countryside slip by. His gaze was wedded to a land that was a kaleidoscope of colors, rich hues of reds, yellows, oranges and browns. It was a delicious sight. This was an endless land worthy of the name Empire State. But then, much of what he had seen of America was the same; a place where a man had elbow room. Would he call himself American? His father was a Boston man and his mother Tolowa and Spanish. Well, the Indian part made her a true American… so yes, he decided proudly, he was an American.

Late in the afternoon, Dutch stopped his paddling to rest. This time, however, when he stretched out his legs and dropped his head back and closed his eyes, he fell asleep.

After only a few minutes, he awoke to King's barking. Becoming aware again, he found that his boat was being pulled by a strong current directly toward the confluence of the two rivers. Try as he might, he could not navigate the unstable canoe toward the village on the northern shore. In just a few heart beats, the boat shot through the lower river gap and onto the Hudson River. He had gone a mile more downriver before the currents would give the canoe's control back to Dutch.

With the hot meal and warm bed now in his wake, he cursed himself for falling asleep. How could he return to the Pacific if he couldn't even navigate two lazy rivers?

That night, he camped on one of the many islands on the Hudson. The next morning, he paddled by the gable roofs of Albany and, much later, with darkness approaching, found shelter in some farmer's barn.

It was in the afternoon of the fourth day when he arrived, with seagulls screaming, at the waterfront of New York City. Dwarfed by the tall ships, he paddled down the long lines of docked vessels until he found the company wharf. There he unloaded the canoe and then turned it upside down on the dock. Sliding the pack on his back and carrying his sheath rifle, he and the dog walked up the steep gangway to the fur warehouse. Through a dirty window, he saw a clerk working at his desk.

Opening a small door, he stuck his head in and asked, "Is Astor in town?"

"Aye, I think so," the older man replied from his journals.

"Good. You'll find a Seneca canoe on your dock. It belongs to Post Nine. Frenchie wants it back, come spring."

"Aye," the man answered.

Closing the door, Dutch confronted the most fearful part of his entire journey, walking the cobblestones of a big city. New York City was roughly twice the size of Boston, with 80,000 citizens. Dutch had hated his time in Boston because of the crowds, and here he was again, lost amid hordes of strangers. The people in the cities reminded him of ants, scurrying about in every direction with no regards for each other. And the noise and smells were as spooky as those in a forest on a moonless night. He would finish his business with Astor and then retreat from this city, as quickly as he could.

It was a long walk from the waterfront to the company offices on Liberty Street. All along the way, the people he passed stared at him with scorn. He could feel their prying eyes and heard their snickers. Dutch was out of place and out of step with the 'civilized' people of a city.

When he finally arrived at the company offices, he was informed that Mr. Astor was working from his home. That residence was another ten blocks uptown, and Dutch decided to rest himself and clean up first. Relieved that the long trip was over, he walked to the public house where he had stayed two years before.

The Running Fox was one of the many pubs that dotted the waterfront area. Walking into the three story stone building, Dutch crossed a small lobby, with the pub and dining room on one side and the staircase and baths on the other. At the back wall a man stood behind a tall desk. Older and rawboned, he wore a pair of tiny, square spectacles on his long, skinny nose. With a sour expression, the man gave Dutch and King a long look as they approached.

"May I help you?" he asked in a deep British accent.

"Aye. Need a private room. Oh yes, and a bath and a wet shave."

"Indeed you do," the clerk said with distain. "One dollar."

Dutch was shocked by the amount. "Your prices have gone up."

"Nay. Four bits for the room, two bits for the bath and shave, and..." He peered down at King "...two bits for the dog."

"That's twice what I paid two years ago."

"I remember ye. You're one of Astor's men. Didn't have a dog then, and you were freshly bathed. The maid can wash out your filthy togs for a dime more."

Dutch was too tired to haggle with the surly clerk. He reached into his poke and paid the man with small coins, right down to the extra dime.

"Tell the bath-man I'll be down shortly. What are your meal hours?"

Reaching for a room key, the clerk slid it across to Dutch. "Room 207, second floor at the end of the hall. Dinner is served from six to nine, and the maid will have your bath drawn within the half hour."

"You have a maid as a bath-man?"

"Aye. Daisy runs our baths and is good with a razor. You be in good hands."

Dutch had taken a few fancy baths in Boston, but they had always been tended by a man. Having a woman in his bathroom seemed as strange as the city itself.

Upstairs in a drab room, Dutch lit a small fire in the coal fireplace and then poured himself some whiskey. As the room warmed, King curled up in front of the flames and was soon snoozing.

Glancing across the room, Dutch saw his image in a wall mirror. What glared back was a shabby looking bloke with a dirty face and two weeks of red whiskers, dressed in buckskins that were sweat stained. His auburn hair was tangled, and he had dark rings around his tired young eyes. What he saw was frightening, and he suddenly understood the reaction he had received from the people on the street.

Half hour later, Dutch walked into the baths. The long, narrow, oil lit room was devoid of windows, and had a black marble floor with white tiled walls. There was a warm dampness in the air from the coal fired water heaters, and the room smelled sweet from bath oils. On his right were four bathing booths, with cloth curtains for privacy.

From the stall farthest down, a woman appeared and greeted him, walking his way.

"You must be Mr. Blackwell," she said with an Irish brogue.

She was young, with a pretty face and bright red hair. A green skirt covered her lower body while a white blouse with a low neckline accentuated her full figure.

"Aye, and you must be Daisy."

She eyed him from toe to top, shaking her head. "You be a stinker! What bilge did you crawl out of?"

Annoyed Dutch replied, "Been in the western wilderness for the last two years."

"I can smell that. You will be me challenge," she said, with a face full of purpose. "Your tub is waiting."

The small candlelit booth had a dressing area on one side and a sideboard full of soaps and bath oils on the other. On the floor, in between, was a large copper tub half full of steaming water.

"Off with ya clothes," she said with a twinkle in her green eyes, and pointed at the dressing area. "I'll get them washed and drying before I bath ye."

Dutch removed his buckskins and stood before the maid in only his long underwear.

"Need the small clothes, as well," she said, with outstretched arms.

"In that case, I'll need a towel."

A grin chases across her lips, "No modesty here, lad. Got five brothers, and I've seen it all."

Red faced, Dutch turned his back to her and removed his remaining clothes.

"Ye slip into that hot water and soak," she said. "I'll be back shortly."

The steamy water was luxurious, reminding Dutch of the many hot springs back home. As his mind slipped back there, his body relaxed like a blade of grass in a summer breeze. Soon, his anger and stress ebbed away. He was in his mother's womb, a safe, warm place to be...

Ten minutes later, Daisy returned, carrying a bucket of hot water, which she added to the copper trough. Then she set about bathing Dutch, scouring him with soap and brush, all the while chattering like a squirrel. She gave him no chance to reply; she simply talked – about herself, her brothers and her Irish homeland. As she moved around the tub, Dutch noticed her soft, creamy skin, and how revealing her blouse was. Her touch was firm but gentle, and always on the move. Quickly, he shook off those thoughts, determined not to be aroused.

Finally, she washed Dutch's hair and scraped his face clean of the red whiskers. Her hand with the razor was steady and sure. After rinsing his face clear of soap, she peered down at him with a strange look on her face. As she talked, she let her gaze rove slowly down to where his naked body was submerged in the soapy water.

"Ain't you a fine lookin' lad... and, from appearance, all man."

Dutch felt his face heat with a blush, while his mind stumbled in a search for words. He had seen that strange expression before, on the faces of young Indian maidens around the council fires. But he had paid them no heed.

"Trim your locks for a dime more? Then you be truly a handsome gent."

"Aye," Dutch answered, still feeling awkward.

After Daisy had finished the trim, she stood and held out a hand mirror for Dutch.

As he viewed her work, she said, "I'll check your clothes. Sure the small ones are dry, but the rawhide will take longer. While you wait, I've got some nice cigars, if you like. Only a nickel more."

Dutch agreed, and she offered a wooden box for his selection. Then she cut his cigar with a small pair of scissors and lit it for him from a candle.

As he puffed out blue smoke, she said, "How about a brandy? Just a dime more."

A smile crossed his lips. "You've got quite an enterprise going on here."

"Aye," Daisy replied. "Lassies like me have to make it, anyway we can."

"Fine. I'll take the brandy. Do I pay you or the desk clerk?"

With a sly grin on her face, she answered, "Reckon I did the work, so why not me?"

Half an hour later, Dutch left the baths feeling and looking like a new man. Even the sullen front desk clerk gave him a nod and a smile.

Later that evening, Dutch and King went downstairs for dinner, and their barmaid was...Daisy. He learned that she cleaned rooms in the mornings, ran the baths in the afternoons, and worked the barroom for both the noon and evening meals. She was one resourceful wench.

In the smoky, crowded pub, Dutch ate beefsteak, potatoes, cheese and bread while downing two flagons of wine. As he devoured the meal, he fed scraps to the dog curled up under the table.

At one point, Daisy returned with a soup bone for King. "He be like you, young and fresh," she said with a wistful look. "You are a handsome lad...but a bit shy for the likes of me."

When Daisy finally came to collect for the meal, she said loudly, "Two-bits for dinner, a dime for the wine." Then she put a hand on Dutch's shoulder and whispered in his ear, "For two-bits more, I'll come to your room and tuck you in."

Dutch was baffled. "Don't know the meaning of 'tuck.'"

"You know. We could...share each other." She smiled bashfully, and whispered, "I be a good tucker."

Her meaning hit Dutch like a musket ball. Red faced again, he was lost for words.

Opening his poke, he paid his tab with small coins, then looked up at the wench.

"I'll bet you are," he stammered. "But I'll take just the meal. It was delicious!"

The next morning, Dutch dressed in trousers and a waistcoat he had purchased in England. Underneath the jacket, he wore his clean buckskin shirt with two strands of cougar teeth. On his hip was his sea knife, with one pistol snug in his belt. The last items he dug from his knapsack were his sea boots. Those would replace his moccasins, which didn't fare well on cobblestones.

With thoughts of revenge swirling again, he locked the dog inside his room and departed to confront Astor.

But while Dutch was walking the tree lined cobblestones towards uptown, his musing, like a shifting breeze, turned to the coming winter. It was too late in the season to go west. And it would be too expensive, as he had found out yesterday, to winter in a city. He could sign on with a ship going to the Pacific, but his father had warned him many times not to double the Horn.

Still, he had to do something. A decision would have to be made.

Shaking off those thoughts, Dutch reminded himself of the business at hand.

He had visited Astor's luxurious brownstone at 223 Broadway two years before. It was a beautiful home, three stories tall with a marble stoop that lead to a massive mahogany front door. Climbing the short stairway, Dutch used a brass knocker against the iron guard.

Moments later the door opened, revealing the pretty, well-dressed woman that was Astor's wife Sarah.

"Good morning ma'am. Is Mr. Astor at home?"

She had soft delicate features that he had remembered from before, but she gave him a stern look.

"Maybe... may I say who is calling?"

"Aye. I'm Dutch Blackwell, and I work for your husband."

"I'll see if he's in," she said, and then slammed the door shut.

Dutch waited on the stoop, muttering his outrage.

After a long minute, the door opened again...and there stood John Jacob Astor. "Didn't expect to see you, lad. Come in," he said.

Astor showed Dutch through a marbled foyer and into a stuffy wood paneled library. Moving across the spacious room, Astor took a seat behind a large, hand carved oak desk stacked with papers. He had a rugged physique and was clean shaven, with long, straight, fair hair. His jaw was square and his mouth firm, but when he talked, his speech was marked by a German accent. All in all, he was just as

Dutch remembered him: thick-necked and strong-faced, with deep-set eyes that were almost black.

Coming to rest in his seat, he asked, "How'd you get here, lad?"

"Canoe," Dutch answered, standing in front of the desk.

"That be a long paddle. I'm surprised as hell to see ye."

"I'll bet you are...as you thought me dead," Dutch answered angrily.

Astor looked amazed, "Dead! What the blazing hell are ye talking about, lad?"

Dutch reached into his poke, pulled out the six bloody dollars, and slammed them down on Astor's desk.

"When you didn't send my wages, I figured I'd come here and find out why. But along the way, two Kickapoo's tried to waylay me. It didn't work. One is dead and the other badly mauled. The Indian that lived told me Frenchie had paid them these coins and a red jug to kill me. And he said that you, the big chief in the city, had told him to do so. Oh, and let's not forget...they were told that if they brought my ears back, Frenchie would pay more."

Astor listened to Dutch's story with a wide eyed look of bewilderment. "Halt," he finally interrupted, waving a hand. "I had no part in this affair. It makes no sense. Why would I want ye dead?"

"You'd save my wages."

A grin chased across Astor's face. "Look around you, lad. Would I worry about your meager money?"

"Some say that it's your way," Dutch replied bitterly.

Astor shook his head, "You disappoint me Dutch, bursting into my home and repeating accusations from the lying lips of an Indian. I did send a letter to Frenchie, telling him to dissuade you from returning until the spring. But it made no mention of any threats."

"Rubbish. You lie!" Dutch shouted, full of fury at the man's claims of innocence.

The room fell silent for a moment as the two men glared at each other. All that could be heard was the ticking of a clock. With eyes blazing, Dutch slowly moved his right hand to the grip of his pistol.

"Don't trifle with me, lad. You're threatening the wrong man," Astor said firmly, with a small bead of sweat rolling down his brow.

Dutch hesitated. He could stand here and call Astor a liar all day, but that wouldn't change a thing. Suddenly, he heard his father's voice: *Leave it be, son.*

Slowly pulling back his hand, Dutch said, "Then I will take my wages and be gone."

His words broke the tension, and he felt the anger drain from his body.

Astor dried his forehead with a pristine hanky and smiled up at him. "Aye, I'll write you a bank draft. Let me see, that was...three hundred dollars."

Dutch shook his head. "You are a miser. It was four, and I'll take gold."

Astor stared at him for a long moment, then lifted a strong box from his desk drawer. Unlocking the lid, he counted out twenty Spanish gold pieces. Finishing the count, he slid the coins across the desk to Dutch.

"And the letter."

"What letter?" Astor asked.

"The letter you promised, declaring me a free trader."

Nodding his head slowly, Astor replied, "Aye... aye, I remember now." With hands that quivered slightly, Astor took quill in hand and began to write on the parchment. As he did, he commented in a steady voice, "I've formed a new enterprise, The Pacific Fur Company. Come spring, I'm sending a regiment of thirty men across the continent to build a trading post at the mouth of the Columbia River. I'm also sending a ship around the Horn, with enough supplies to stock the post for two years. I'd like you to be part of that venture. You know the Pacific Indians and their ways. Winter here in the city and, come spring, make your way to Saint Louis. Be a five year contract at two hundred a year. What say ya, lad?"

Dutch was surprised at the news and shocked by the offer. "What route will they take?" he heard himself ask.

"Same as Clark, up the Missouri."

With a small grin, Dutch replied, "That be a long paddle."

"Aye. What say ya then? Will you join the brigade, come spring?"

After putting the shiny gold coins and the six silver dollars into his poke, Dutch stared back at Astor for a long moment. "I came here to kill ya, or maybe take an ear, and ye offer me gold. An old Tillamook squaw once told me that life was about a voyage home, not a journey of hate. I'll reflect on your scheme during the winter… but it won't be here. I'll return to Boston and stay the season at the Sea Witch. Come March, I'll let you know."

"Fine," Astor replied, then stood and extended his hand. "I'll send ye whatever news I receive from Montreal. This enterprise will be quite an adventure, and we all will surely profit."

After shaking the man's limp hand, Dutch turned to leave, then stopped at the library door.

Looking back at John Astor, he said, "That Kickapoo died for nothing, but I believe his friend was telling the truth. I don't trust you…but I do like taking your gold."

II
John Jacob Astor

—ɷ—

*T*here were those who called him a dishonest scoundrel, while others called him an empire builder and business genius. Whatever opinions one had, if you were in the fur business early in the nineteenth century, you knew of John Jacob Astor.

Born Johann Jakob Astor on July 17, 1763 in Walldorf, Germany, he was the third son to the local butcher. His mother was a hard worker but frugal to the point that the family often went in rags. All the siblings did odd jobs for their father; at one point, John Jacob was a milk salesman. Then at 16, the eldest son, George, left home for England, where he found a position in the musical instrument business. The next son, Henry, soon departed for New York City, where he became a butcher like his father. In 1780, after their mother's death and their father's remarriage, John Jacob booked passage to London. There he went to work with his brother George, learning to make musical instruments. During that time, he mastered the English language and began to read, with great interest, about the rebellious American colonies. By the end of the American Revolution, John Jacob Astor had saved enough money for passage to the United States. He sailed in November of 1783 with $25 in his purse, a ticket for a crew's berth, and seven flutes as the seeds for a new business in the New World.

On that passage, he met another German emigrant, one who had been to North America before and had worked successfully in the fur trade. Astor questioned the man extensively and by March of 1784, when they finally reached New York City, he was convinced that the fur trade was for him.

No young man had ever reached the American shores more determined to make his fortune than John Jacob Astor. Early on, he married Sarah Todd, who brought to the union a dowry of $300. She was a handsome lady with a keen business sense and an expert eye for furs. It was her dowry that enabled Astor to set up a shop where they sold musical instruments and bought furs. Astor wasn't as frugal as his mother and, when profits were made, he spent some of the money on improving his family's position.

For a few years, Astor traveled the frontier, learning the fur trade and making contacts throughout the Great Lakes Region and also in Montreal, which was at the heart of the trade. He was always welcome around the wilderness camp fires, as he had a pleasing personality and played a lively flute.

By 1800, Astor was recognized as the leading American merchant in the fur business and was thought to be worth a quarter of a million dollars. But he was only just beginning.

Some thought the Louisiana Purchase of 1803 was an act of folly for the young republic, but Astor was not one of them. With that immense territory under United States control, it became possible to envision the fur trade extending all the way to the Pacific coast.

In 1808, Astor incorporated as the American Fur Company, a move that consolidated his personal holdings in the East and prepared him for an all-out assault on the far West. But he was not without competition, as the Hudson Bay Company and the Northwest Fur Company, both Canadian enterprises, were slowly making their way to the far West, as well. Then there were the regional companies, like the Missouri Fur Company, who also realized the great potential profits of the Oregon Country. But Astor's idea was a grandiose scheme: send a brigade of thirty men across the continent while sending a ship full of trading supplies around the Horn to meet up with the troop and build an outpost on the Columbia River. To accomplish this task Astor founded another enterprise, the Pacific Fur Company. By doing so, this newly formed venture would control all the fur trade of the far West. The Astor Expedition would be to the fur business what the Lewis and Clark Expedition was to America.

—ᙡ—

The Sea Witch ——————

Bang!

The ship's bow slammed through the curling waves as it sailed north in stormy seas. At 120 tons, the *Hampton Roads* was a seasoned schooner plying the Eastern Seaboard, delivering mail. She also made herself available to a handful of passengers, offering a cramped salon that had once been the aft hold. Skylights and a gangway had been installed where the hatch cover had once been. The salon was bright and offered seating for a dozen passengers. On each side of this parlor were four tiny sleeping compartments with double berths and small portholes. The larger forward hold carried the mail and other government freight. While the accommodations weren't luxurious, the schooner was well maintained and manned with a skilled and disciplined crew.

When Dutch had paid his fare, the purser had told him, "With favorable winds, it should be thirty hours to Boston."

Dutch and King endured the first few hours of the cruise in their cramped compartment, twisting and rolling with the seas. Dressed in his buckskins and sea boots, Dutch used this time to carefully cut up the skunk hide for his new winter hat. Then, with the seas moderating, he started sewing the hat's parts together. But he soon found the dim light from the small porthole not to his liking. Locking the dog in the cabin, he went into the empty salon to take advantage of the better light. After pouring himself a fresh mug of coffee at the sideboard, he settled into one of the overstuffed leather chairs. Taking needle and thread in hand again, he went back to work on his hat.

A few moments later, a lady passenger entered the parlor and poured herself a cup of hot tea. After adding milk and sugar, she moved to another of the overstuffed chairs, close to Dutch.

"What'cha sewing, lad?" she asked in a voice with a heavy British accent.

Dutch looked up from his work and saw that she was a middle-aged woman, dressed in a plaid woolen skirt and white silk blouse, with a black cloak on her shoulders. She had a chalk-like complexion, with painted red lips. Around her neck she wore a pearl necklace with matching earrings. But there was nothing dainty about this lady; she was big, with a bold, fleshy nose and a stubby neck. Her short brown hair was streaked with strands of gray, and her booming voice was fearsome.

"Making a winter hat, ma'am," Dutch answered politely.

She glared at the skin in his hands. "In London, we are British, don't you know. We use only beaver for our hats. Didn't know you folks here in the Colonies were using skunks hides… but then, sadly, this is a poor country."

She paused for a sip of tea, with her stubby little finger high in the air. "My husband and I – he would be Lord Rudolf and I'm Lady Rudolf – are just completing a three-year around-the-world trip. We were on safari in Africa, rode elephants in India, and went hunting for kangaroo in Australia. It's been a delightful time. You know the sun never sets on the British Empire…"

Dutch smiled and nodded his head as this lady babbled like a brook. Reflecting that she was typically English, with high opinions of herself and all things British, he returned to his sewing and let Lady Rudolf ramble. She never asked another question of Dutch or tried to include him in the conversation. She just talked! Luckily, after nearly an hour, a short skinny older gentleman wearing a tweed waistcoat joined them, and Lady Rudolf introduced Dutch to her husband.

Standing, Dutch shook his outstretched hand while Lord Rudolf asked, wide eyed, "Is that a skunk-skin hat? Would you sell it to me, lad?"

"Sorry, sir I'll need it, come winter."

"You have a look of the outback. Would you be a frontiersman?"

"Aye, I've been trapping out West and trading with the Indians."

"When we were in Australia," Lady Rudolf inserted with excitement, "we saw many Aborigines. They are a backwards lot, and they run around the countryside naked, speaking a gibberish no one understands. Have you killed any Indians out West?"

Slipping his nearly completed hat onto his head, Dutch turned to Lady Rudolf with a scornful glance. "That would be like killing myself, ma'am, as I be part Indian." Then, turning back to the surprised Lord Rudolf, he continued, "Nice meeting you folks. While you're here in the Colonies, stay close to our towns. You never know what might be lurking in our forests."

Dutch gave the British couple a wide berth for the rest of the trip. His father had talked many times about the arrogance of the English, and now he had experienced it. He saw the Rudolf's only once more, when they were departing the ship in Boston Harbor. Apparently during the night, Lord Rudolf had come down with a fever, and he was being helped down the gangway to a waiting carriage. Dutch felt sorry for the couple, as they had come so far and now Lord Rudolf looked so sick. He wished them well and hoped that Lady Rudolf would learn to keep her mouth shut.

Robert Hayes, or Sandy, as everyone called him, was the owner of the Sea Witch. He had purchased the public house a few years earlier, after spending nearly forty years as a merchant seaman. On one of his many trips, aboard the sloop *Lady Washington*, he had departed Boston Harbor for the Pacific Northwest in 1787. It was on this voyage that he met and befriended Dutch's father, Joe Blackwell. He had helped the young sailor find his sea legs, and had taught him how to climb the rigging like a spider. Over their many months at sea, they had become good mates. When Joe went missing during a skirmish with the Tillamook Indians, it was Sandy who wanted to return to the village and try to find him. But Captain Gray and the crew believed that Joe had been killed during the fray, and they refused to put the ship in jeopardy again.

Twenty years later, when Dutch first walked through the doors of the Sea Witch, it was Sandy who recognized his old friend's sea knife on Dutch's hip. It had been an emotional revelation to hear of Joe Blackwell's life and death amongst the Pacific Indians. That tragic event made Sandy feel guilty for deserting his old mate, and he had pledged to treat Joe's son as his own.

Two years before Dutch had spent a few months with Sandy. It was he who got Joe Blackwell's adventures published in the local newspapers. After the story was printed, Dutch became the son of a famous Bostonian, with many people coming to the pub to meet him. Dutch hadn't like that; it involved too many foolish questions from too many strangers.

It was early afternoon when Dutch and the dog stepped off the *Hampton Roads*. With a warm sun in the sky, they moved through the hordes on the dock and turned up Commercial Street. King had been skittish in New York City because of the crowds, and Dutch had taught him how to heel. Now, on the cobblestones of Boston, they walked almost in lock-step.

Soon, they came to the pub, and stopped across the street from it. Nothing appeared to have changed since his last visit. The tavern was a typical waterfront pub, a two-story red brick building on a small but deep lot. The hand-carved sign above the doorway was badly weathered and the few windows facing the street were smudged and dirty. The Sea Witch was a waterfront dive.

Reaching into his knapsack, Dutch retrieved his winter hat and put it on. Pulling the skunk skin down low on his forehead, he tried to conceal his eyes. Then he swung the rucksack back onto his shoulders and crossed the busy street.

Just before opening the front door, Dutch knelt to King's level and gave him pat on the head. "Sandy be a good mate, so no trouble. We want to winter here, not in some farmer's barn."

King looked back at him with a cocked head and bright eyes. Satisfied, Dutch straightened again, and they walked into the pub.

The stale smells of the tavern brought back a flood of memories. The pub was a long narrow parlor with low ceilings and a wide pine plank floor. On the right were wooden booths against a brick wall. In the middle of the room was a row of small tables and chairs, and on the left a long mahogany stand-up bar. That bar was the damndest thing Dutch had ever seen. There was a long brass foot shaft running the length of the counter, under which, was a tilted urinal that drained outside to a small trough in the street. He had never seen such an indoor urinal before, and marveled at its purpose.

The kitchen was at the rear of the room, with a storeroom, staircase and a door that opened to the backyard and the outhouse. Sandy lived upstairs in a one-bedroom apartment that faced the street. In the rear of the building was a second bedroom, with a covered back porch and outside stairway leading down to the privy.

Dutch moved to the front of bar, with King on his heels. Looking down the mahogany planks, Dutch spotted Sandy talking with two customers.

"Can a bloke get a pint in this flea-infested pub?" Dutch shouted down the bar in a deep, disguised voice.

Sandy turned from behind the bar and started walking his way with a sour look on his face. He was bald, short, skinny and bow-legged. His wrinkled face looked tired, and being in his early sixties had slowed his gait.

Stopping at the end of the bar, he said in his squeaky voice, "No need to scream, mate. I ain't deaf. What's your pleasure?"

Clearly, he hadn't yet recognized Dutch. "How about a free pint for a man down on his luck?"

Sandy's face turned crimson with anger. "The pint's a nickel, mate, or take your hard-luck story somewhere else."

Dutch fumbled for his poke and then slapped a twenty-dollar gold coin on the bar top. "Guess I've even got enough to buy an old jack-tar like you a pint."

With wide eyes, Sandy's mouth dropped open. Then Dutch slowly slid off his skunk hat. "Like the British, I've returned."

Sandy's face instantly lit up with a smile, and he leapt across the bar to give Dutch a hug. As they embraced, he whispered, "Good Lord, lad, why didn't you write me? I would have met you at the dock."

Dutch bristled at this public show of affection and tried not to show his embarrassment.

Finally, Sandy pulled back and shouted down the bar, "Kate, get the hell out here! Got a mate for you to meet."

They quickly moved across the room to one of the large wooden booths. Then a middle-aged lady in a plain muslin dress and pale blue apron joined them. As she sat, Sandy introduced her as his kid sister, Kathleen. She had raven hair with strands of gray, and wore a gold cross necklace around her thin neck. Her aged face had delicate features, and there was a twinkle in her dark brown eyes.

She extended her hand across to Dutch. "Everyone calls me Kate. I've heard much about you."

Dutch shook her hand just as the dog, sitting on his haunches and staring up at the table, let out a whimper.

"This be your dog?" Kate asked with a broad smile, looking down at King.

"Aye. Found him on an Injun trail, last year, and we've been mates ever since. I named him King George because he, too, has forsaken the Indians."

"Will he bite?" Kathleen asked.

"Nay, he's only vicious to Injuns," Dutch answered with a grin.

"Can I pet him? I love dogs."

Dutch nodded, liking Kate. "Should be okay. Just move slowly. He belongs in the wilderness, not here in a city."

Just then, a customer called out, and Kathleen slid out of the booth to take care of business. Sandy and Dutch talked awhile, mostly about Astor and his operations. When Kate returned, she brought a bottle of Spanish brandy and three glasses.

"I've been saving this for a special occasion," she said with a warm glow on her face.

With King curled up on the planks under the table, they drank the tasty brandy. Every now and then, one or the other would have to get up to take care of costumers. They made a fine barroom team. Dutch answered their many questions and even told them about being ambushed by the Kickapoos, and about Astor's offer of a new five-year contract. He also talked of the British couple on the schooner and then of his plans for the coming spring.

"Reckon that's why I'm here," Dutch said, sliding a Spanish gold piece across the table to Sandy. "I was hopin' King and I could winter here. If twenty dollars ain't enough, I've got more."

Sandy and Kate looked at each other with a strange expression on their faces. The table went silent, and Dutch knew there was something amiss.

Finally Kathleen said, "We can do that. I'll bunk with Sandy. We did that often when we were kids."

Just then, another customer called out, and she jumped up again.

With her departure, Dutch said, "I'm so sorry. I had no idea she was living here."

"Why would ye?" Sandy replied. "Her husband died a little over a year ago, and then her only living son ran off and joined the Navy. She's was having a hard time. So I asked her to move in here and help me out."

Sandy was a warm, generous man, and his love for his sister showed on his face.

"In any event," Sandy continued, sliding the coin back to Dutch, "I would never take your money. I owe you too much."

"You owe me nothing, mate. I'll find a room at a boarding house. Tell me more of Kate's family."

Over a second glass of brandy Sandy gave Dutch the details. For almost twenty years, she had been married to a seaman named Henry Wilson. They had four children, but one of them was dragged to death by a runway horse. Two others died of the pox at early ages. Her last-born son had taken his father's death poorly, and ran off to sea. She had no income, only a small farm on the outskirts of town. She sold that homestead for a mere fifty dollars and moved in with

Sandy to find a new life. Her story was all too common, and a tragedy to hear.

When Kate returned, she placed a bowl of beef stew in front of Dutch and gave a soup bone to King under the table.

"Thought you boys might be hungry," she said with a warm smile. Then, turning to Sandy, she continued, "Supper crowd is about to start. I'll need your help."

"Aye." Sandy moved to get up.

"Thanks," Dutch said to Kate. "It smells delicious. After we've eaten, we'll go find a room and come back later for a pint."

Kathleen gave Dutch a sly grin. "Nonsense, your room is waiting. I've already moved out."

"That's just not right," Dutch answered, shaking his head.

"I'm not asking, I'm telling. It's done. After you get your traps upstairs, come back down and lend us a hand."

"Don't argue with her mate," Sandy said with a grin. "She's a bull-headed woman who always gets her way."

Dutch and Kate smiled warmly at each other for a moment. Then he slid out of the booth and did something totally out of character: he hugged her.

As he did, he said, "I love strong women. My mother was one."

"Aye," she replied. "And I'll love having a young lad around again."

Turning to Sandy, Dutch said, "One last favor mate. No news stories about me or Astor or anything. I want a quiet winter."

Sandy flashed a toothy smile, "Aye."

Late that night, as brother and sister prepared for bed, Sandy asked Kathleen, "Can you stomach having Dutch around? He can be as rough as a barnacle."

"I can smooth his edges," she answered, brushing her hair. "There's sweetness in his eyes. And," she admitted, setting aside her brush and slipping beneath the covers, "he's made this old wench very happy again."

Sandy reached to the night stand and turned down the oil lamp.

With the room in darkness, Kate said from her side of the bed, "Fair warning. The one thing I can't stomach is snoring."

Demons ————————

At dawn the next morning, Kathleen went downstairs to light the stove. When she looked up from the kindling, she spotted King pacing the floor planks. As soon as the fire had taken hold, she moved the coffee pot over the heat and opened the back door for the dog. As he shot out for the bushes, Kate walked towards the privy. Looking up at a cloudy sky, she felt the first cold breeze of October and knew rain was beckoning.

On her way back, she called out for the dog. Waiting for him on the back porch, she yelled up to Dutch's room, "Breakfast be ready in an half-hour. You'll love my biscuits."

As the dog joined her on the porch, she heard some movement upstairs and went inside.

Just as the coffee pot was about to boil over, Sandy appeared. Watching Kate at the stove, he sat drinking his coffee and reading a newspaper. Twenty minutes later, the biscuits were done...but no Dutch.

"I'll go fetch him," Sandy said.

Pushing the partly open door all the way, Sandy found Dutch still in bed. He looked dead to the world, and there was a foul smell in the room.

"You okay, lad?" Sandy asked, shaking his shoulder.

Dutch let out a soft moan and slowly opened his blood-shot eyes. His face was beaded with sweat, and his right hand trembled slightly on the bed covers.

"...be alright... jus'...need some rest," he babbled under his breath.

"You don't look good, mate," Sandy said. Walking to the door, he called out for Kate. Then, taking a glass of water from the nightstand, he tried to get Dutch to take a drink, without success.

Kathleen came into the room with King. As the dog jumped up on the foot of the bed, a concerned Kate felt Dutch's forehead.

"He's burning up," she said.

"Bet it's the same bug that British prick had on the schooner. Bloody foreigners... curse them all!"

"We don't know that. It might be just a cold. Let's get some wet towels and see if we can bring his fever down."

"Should I send for Doc Bates?"

Kathleen turned to her brother with a frustrated frown. "That bloody quack that drinks his lunch everyday? I wouldn't let him touch the dog. I'll care for this lad. You call in some help for the pub."

With Sandy downstairs taking care of business, Kate stripped off Dutch's night clothes and placed damp towels across his naked body. She had no qualms about his nudity; Dutch was now one of her brood. He moaned a few times, but was mostly unresponsive to her actions, which frightened her even more. Kathleen repeated the treatment for a number of hours until, realizing that it wasn't working, she went to the bar and brought back a bottle of grain alcohol. This she rubbed across his sweating body.

In the afternoon, she tried to get some chicken broth down him, but he swallowed very little. His fever remained dangerously high into the night. Finally, in desperation, Sandy and Kate got Dutch out of bed and stood his nude body out on the second-story porch in a pouring rain storm. The cool rain seemed to help, as he was soon conscious enough to mumble something about being cold. Taking him back inside, they dried him off and returned him to his bed. In the kitchen Kate made up a pitch cloth with mustard weed and dill. She spread it across his chest and prayed that his fever would soon break.

At times, Dutch was semi-conscious, babbling words that made no sense. At other times, he would cry out clearly about his life amongst the Indians, his mind at the mercy of his inner demons.

The rabbit hole that pulled him along had no beginning or end. As he tumbled around this whirlpool, he had ghostly visions of the Indians he had killed. In a flood of gruesome memories, they screamed at him in their native tongues with a horrible wrath. Then, after a flash of light, he was stumbling down a pitch black trail with thunder crackling across an unseen sky. With each quiver of lightning, he saw the shadows of the giant Redwood trees towering high above his way. Where was he going? Where had he been?

In the blink of an eye, he was walking in the sunshine, with a warm breeze on his face. Rounding a bend, he came out of the forest and spotted a herd of elk grazing on a grassy knoll. He walked among them, and they paid him no heed.

His trail stopped at the edge of a great gray bay. There, standing knee deep in the water, was his mother. She held a basket of clams with one arm, using her free hand to pick more from the shallows. Her white buckskin dress and her shiny black hair glistened in the sunlight.

She looked Dutch's way and held out a fat cockle. "These be our ancestors. They are the flavor of our yesterdays. Help me gather more, my son."

From the shore, Dutch called out to her, "Mother... Mother, I will help."

But just as he prepared to step into the shallows, his father's voice was in his ear. "This be not your time, my son. We will all be together again, by and by."

Then the vortex swept Dutch away once more.

It was just dawn, with a dim gray light streaking across the room, when Dutch next opened his eyes. He stared blinking at the bedroom ceiling for the longest time, collecting his thoughts. What had happened? What had his visions meant? He was here, but parts of his soul wanted to be back there.

Soon, he was aware of the dog on the blankets, curled up against his legs. Slowly looking down at King, Dutch saw Kathleen sleeping in a large rocking chair. She had a blanket around her shoulders and a Bible in her lap.

He nudged the dog gently with his leg. King raised his sleepy head and looked up the bed. When Dutch gave him a small smile, his eyes came alive, and the dog crawled on his belly up the bed whimpering.

The sound woke Kate with a start. When she bolted from her chair, she found a tail-wagging King licking Dutch's face.

"Praise the Lord. You're back!" she said with a bright, surprised face. "Thought we'd lost you. How do you feel?"

In a weak voice, Dutch mumbled, "Like a mule kicked me. How long have I been out?"

"Three days, more or less. Are you hungry, lad?"

Dutch licked his dry lower lip. "I taste chicken soup, and it's delicious."

"I'll go warm some up," she said, smiling, and bent down to give Dutch a hug. "God bless you, boy."

With prayer and deeds, Kathleen had saved Dutch's life. She continued to hover over him with bowls of chicken soup for another week. During this recovery, Sandy brought Dutch two journals. One was on the Lewis and Clark Expedition, and the other on the exploits of Captain George Vancouver and his discoveries on the Columbia River. Dutch devoured each word and studied every map. He made notes on the pages and redrew the charts from his own memory. By the time he was finished, Dutch had a detailed map of the mouth of the Columbia River, using both native and English names.

Each night, after the pub was closed, Sandy and Kate would sit around Dutch's bed, and he would read to them from the journals. Often he would insert his own words, as well, and tell short stories of his life in the untamed Pacific wilderness. They were enthralled and made many queries.

Towards the end of the week Kate made a request that Dutch struggled with. "Will you speak to my church congregation of your Pacific adventures?" she asked.

It was something Dutch had no stomach for. But what could he say? She had saved his life; now it was time for him to repay her kindness. He reluctantly agreed.

Dutch escaped his bed the very next day. The fever had taught him many things, chief among them the loving care of Kate and the generosity of Sandy. Had this sickness struck him while he was living in the outback, he would surely be dead.

During Dutch's slow recovery, Sandy and Kate became aware of the many barnacles that grew upon their friend's soul. His home had been around wilderness campfires, not the domestic hearths of the big cities. As a result, shortcomings were displayed in many ways, from the manner in which he ate his food to his offensive utterance of vulgar words and his cocksureness. But then, what could be expected? He was a half-breed, born and raised within the cultures of the savage Indians of the Northwest.

Kate took his imperfections as a challenge, and became determined to refashion him into a man with a modicum of social graces. This she hoped to do by teaching him some etiquette, appealing to his inherent good nature, and applying a strong dose of religion.

Kathleen's mission of atonement started on the third morning, when Dutch joined his adopted family at their kitchen table for the morning meal. The windowless room was dim, lit only by the stove fire and two oil lamps. Dutch sat at the wooden table, wearing a calico shirt and homespun britches given to him by Kate, while Sandy sat across from him in a red flannel shirt and blue canvas trousers. The two men were drinking coffee from porcelain mugs, and reminiscing about their yesteryears, while Kathleen worked the stove.

"I tell you, Sandy," Dutch said in a determined voice, "your Captain Gray was a goddam coward for abandoning my father out there in the wilderness."

At the stove, Kate bristled with his vulgarity, while Sandy's expression soured at the harsh words about his old shipmate, Captain Gray.

"You don't know what the hell you're talking about, boy," Sandy responded angrily. "The whole damn crew believed your father was dead. And the Captain had the welfare of his ship to think about, so we reluctantly moved on."

"Just a bunch of bloody cowards," Dutch retorted. "I'd never leave a mate behind."

Turning from the stove with a plate full of biscuits and bacon, Kate spoke before Sandy could reply. "Let's have no more talk about such matters. The past is the past, and we can't do much about it."

Placing the platter loudly on the table, she returned to the stove and fetched an iron skillet filled with scrambled eggs. These she spooned onto the three empty plates on the table. Then she sat down, and the three friends began consuming their repast.

As usual, Dutch removed his sea knife from his hip, sliced open a biscuit, and slathered it with jam. With the fingers of his right hand, he began scooping up and devouring the eggs, after which he wiped his greasy paw on his pants.

Kate had seen this behavior before, and could stomach it no more. With her left hand, she quickly reached out and grabbed Dutch's right hand, just as he reached for more eggs. Squeezing his paw hard, she said, "You will find a knife, fork, spoon and napkin next to your plate at every meal. These utensils you will use when you're at my table. And, in my kitchen, the Lord's name will not be taken in vain. These are my house rules, for both you and Sandy."

In the dim light, Dutch looked into her earnest brown eyes and felt anger swell up inside of him. *Who the hell made you queen?* He wanted to ask, but then thought better of it. Instead, he swallowed and replied, "Yes, ma'am. Sorry if I offended."

"And, Dutch," Sandy added, "don't be short on listening and long on talking. That's why God gave us two ears and one mouth. This be the same forecastle advice I gave your father."

Picking up a fork, Dutch smiled ruefully at his two friends. "Guess I've been taken to the woodshed this morning! Well, it's good to know one's faults. Now I can correct them. Reckon a little Boston wisdom be good for my soul."

Over her breakfast, Kathleen rejoiced silently, that some real progress had been made. Glory be to God!

In the early afternoon on the first Sunday in November, Kathleen and Dutch walked to the church meeting with snow flurries flying. The white church was a large wood-framed building just a few blocks up from the waterfront.

Dutch paused for a moment by an outside sign. "Kate, what does the word 'Methodist' mean?"

"It's a religious order that broke away from the Church of England. We are Christians doing missionary work and serving Jesus Christ."

Inside, they found a crowd of almost a hundred people. The congregation sat on wooden pews, facing a candle lit altar, and a large stained-glass window dominated the back wall. With its different colored glass, the window seemed to glow. Next to the altar was a tall wooden pulpit with a carved stone cross on the front. This was the most inspiring church Dutch had ever seen, and he marveled at its beauty.

The room echoed with their footsteps on the stones as they moved down the pews to the front of the church. There, Kathleen introduced Dutch to the minster, Reverend Hathaway. He was a small man, dressed in a black tunic with a white fluffy shirt. His handshake was as limp as a noodle.

The good Reverend started the meeting with a prayer and a welcome, then introduced Dutch to the congregation. Dressed in his buckskins and winter hat, but without his pistols, Dutch stood nervously and walked to the altar, where he turned to face the pews. All of the parishioners seemed to be glaring up at him indifferently. Why had he agreed to do this?

He started meekly talking about the Pacific Northwest. Soon, some of the congregation shouted for him to speak up. Clearing his throat, he pulled a booming voice from within and started over again. This time his voice echoed off the rafters. He talked of the Fir trees of the Oregon Country and said that they were more numerous than grains of sand. Of the giant Redwood trees and how their tops were always in the clouds. He spoke of the different Indians cultures and their rituals. Dutch concluded by telling the crowd about the fur trade and the simple trinkets he traded for pelts. In the end, he found that he had rambled for almost a half-hour.

Reverend Hathaway raised his hand and asked a question. "What faith are you, lad?"

Another from the crowd asked, "Where did you go to church?"

And another voice added, "What faith will you teach the savages?"

Not one question about the Indians themselves! Dutch was surprised by their silly concerns. "I'm a Christian. That is my faith. My church is found in the wilderness forests. And as far as teaching a faith to the Indians, I be no preacher. Their own rituals have worked just fine for millennia."

There was a loud murmur from the congregation, and many angry faces.

"Do you even read the Bible?" one man shouted.

"Aye," Dutch answered, and pulled his bible from his pouch.

"What kind of bible is it?" a woman called out.

"I know not what 'kind' it is… It's the bible given to me by a Franciscan monk, many years ago."

"Catholic!" Reverend Hathaway shouted. "They aren't a Christian religion. They are a cult controlled by the Spanish government."

The murmur in the crowd got louder, with some members raising their fists in anger while others started booing.

From the back, someone shouted, "Blasphemy!"

At the altar, Dutch heard their wrath and felt his own fury well up. Why had he agreed to this?

Red-faced with anger, he addressed the parishioners again. "The Pacific Indians be friendlier to strangers than thee. I was told you were a Christian lot. Reckon not." Then, holding his Bible high over his head, he continued. "I learned to read from this black book, and I don't recall ever reading the word Catholic or Methodist in it. But I do remember these words from John 3:16.: 'For God so loved the world that He gave His only begotten Son, that whosoever believeth in Him should not perish, but have everlasting life.' That is the true Christian way. Your petty religions are rubbish. And I need no sticks or stones of a church to confirm my faith. Nor do I need to stand on a stump and bellow my beliefs. My salvation comes from this book and from my heart. You people should worry about souls, starting with your own. May God forgive your closed minds."

Then, with the congregation as quiet as the dead, Dutch strode out of the church, with his head high and Kathleen on his heels.

Silently, they walked shoulder to shoulder back towards the pub.

Finally, a fuming Dutch said, "Sorry if I embarrassed you with my homily. Those Methodists got under my skin."

Kate walked a few more steps and then stopped and turned to Dutch. With an adoring look, she replied, "Best sermon ever given in that church. I be proud of you, lad."

Boston winters could be hard as a rock. With Dutch's sickness and the church debacle now behind him, he wanted to establish a rhythm of helping out around the tavern. He loved and respected his friendship with Sandy and Kathleen, and he dreamed of spending the rest of the winter quietly.

But that was not to be. Two mornings after his bellicose presentation at the Methodist Church, Kathleen showed Dutch a local newspaper. With a long, sad face, she pointed to a headline on Page Three:

Wilderness Preacher Calls Methodists Narrow-Minded

Reading the short article, he found that the truth had been greatly embellished. Dutch was portrayed as a fire-eating mountain man with a tomahawk in his belt and a rifle in hand. Among other things, it stated that Dutch had scolded the parishioners because of their faith and had warned the good Reverend Hathaway to watch out for his soul. All in all, the article was a pack of lies and half-truths.

Dutch was disappointed and angered by the story. "The scoundrel that wrote this should be horse whipped. I wanted none of this."

Kate was apologetic about the article, but there was nothing she could do. Sandy took a more humorous view. "They spelled your name right, lad. And fame always follows the famous," he proclaimed with a grin.

Boston Society ───────

Early the next afternoon, Sandy handed Dutch a small envelope. "This came by messenger just before noon."

Looking at the message Dutch found the address written in a delicate hand.

Dutch Blackwell
c/o Sandy Hayes
Sea Witch Pub

Inside the envelope, he found a short handwritten note.

Glad to hear of your recovery. Please join me for a luncheon at my home on Friday at noon. Sandy knows the way. Look forward to seeing you again. Regrets only.

Warmest personal regards,
Becky Barrel Hanson

Bewildered by the message, Dutch stuffed it into his pocket. Miss Becky had been Dutch's father's first sweetheart. They had said their farewells aboard the *Lady Washington* on that fateful day in 1787 when Joe Blackwell sailed for the Pacific Northwest. She had waited for Joseph to return for over three years before hearing the wrongful news of his death. Dutch had met Miss Becky only once, two years before. They had exchanged some family trinkets and talked of Joe's life amongst the Indians. Dutch remembered Becky as a pretty, soft-spoken lady with green eyes. But how did she know of his sickness, or that he was even in Boston?

That evening, after the pub had closed, the three friends stood at the end of the bar, enjoying a drink and talking of the day's events. Here, Dutch showed the note to Kathleen and read the message out loud.

"Who is Becky Barrel Hanson?" Kate asked curiously.

Sandy answered, "Her father was Old Man Barrel. He owned the biggest import company here in Boston. When he died, Miss Becky inherited the business. She struggled with the company for a few years and then married one Hubbard Hanson. He had been in the import business in Holland. Some say it was a marriage of convenience. Anyhow, Mr. Hanson saved the Barrel House, and they are now the crust of Boston society."

As Sandy talked, Dutch took a mouthful of brandy and let it slowly trickle down his throat. This was all news to him. But then, when Becky and he had met two years before, he had not asked her any questions about herself. He had just talked about himself. *Typical me*, he thought with regret.

"What I don't understand," Dutch finally asked of Sandy, "how did she know of my fever, or that I was even in Boston?"

Sandy looked carefully at Dutch. "That would be because of me, mate," he answered.

"Why?"

"Two years ago, I gave her my word to share any news of you. For some reason, she has taken a liking to ya. I figure she's still moon'en about your father, and you're the closest thing to him."

Dutch shook his head in disbelief. "I had no idea... Is there anything else I should know?"

"Aye. That chicken soup I gave to Kathleen each morning, during your fever, was cooked in Miss Becky's kitchen. Her butler Bentley brought it by, each day, and I would tell him of your condition."

All this news was a revelation to Dutch, and he moved behind the bar to pour another brandy.

"Will you go to the luncheon?" Kathleen asked eagerly.

"Hadn't reckoned to. Now, though, I feel obligated. But I worry of my shortcomings."

"Ever eaten at a rich man's table?" Sandy asked.

"Haven't had the occasion," Dutch responded with a foolish grin.

"You have any togs other than hand-me-downs and buckskins?" Kate asked.

"Got a pair of britches, a white ruffled shirt and a waistcoat I bought in London."

"You give 'em to me," Kathleen said. "I'll get them cleaned and pressed. Then I'll teach ya some more etiquette."

"Etiquette! What kind of word is that?"

Kate smiled. "It's the opposite of wilderness. You'll see."

Kate had worked as a maid, in her younger years, and knew the rich folks' ways at what she called soirees. The next day, she cleaned and pressed Dutch's store-bought clothes until they looked like new. Then she shined his sea boots with lamp-black until he could see his reflection in the toe.

The Sea Witch's kitchen wasn't fancy. The plates, cups and utensils used each day were a mismatched lot of items. But Kathleen did her best to scrounge up enough different tableware to make up one crude formal place setting. The setting included four different types of plates, three types of forks, three kinds of spoons, two types of knifes and four different sizes of glassware. She drilled Dutch for hours on how to use each item correctly.

"The soup will come first, then the salad, next the entrée and finally the dessert. Your water glass is the big one at the top, and next comes the champagne glass and two wine glasses. Your forks will be on the left of your plate. Use them in order, salad and dinner. Your spoons and dinner knife will be on the right of the plate. Use them in order: Soup spoon, dinner spoon and dinner knife. Your butter knife will be on the butter plate at the upper left. Just above your plates will be a dessert fork and spoon. This is very important, Dutch. You must memorize all this tableware."

Dutch looked down at the setup, scratching his head. "This be silly. Why do rich folks make such a fuss over filling their bellies?"

Kate looked at him with displeasure. "A formal meal is not 'filling a belly.' It's an experience of fine dining, suited for kings and queens. You must not insult your host!"

That night, Dutch went to bed and dreamed of tableware. Which was which and what was what…?

The next morning, over breakfast, Kathleen gave Dutch instructions on basic table manners. "Don't slouch, don't talk too much, and no profanity when the ladies are around." Then she filled the tub in the storeroom with hot water, and told Dutch to bathe. After which Kate trimmed his hair and gave him a shave with a razor as sharp as her tongue. As she watched him dress in his clean togs, she spouted out more do's and don'ts. By mid-morning, he was ready and nervous as a bride groom.

When Dutch went upstairs to fetch his pouch, he also slipped on his sea knife and cougar necklace. Then, putting his winter hat on, he returned downstairs. He was standing at the end of the bar, watching the clock and drinking coffee, when Kate came out of the kitchen with a box. Reaching up, she slipped his hat off.

"You'll be wearing no skunk skins today, lad," she said with a twinkle in her eyes. She opened the box and brought out a black bowler hat. "My husband wore this only once... the day we were married. It will help you look like the proper gentleman you are."

Dutch slipped the hat on and looked at himself in the back bar mirror. It felt funny and it looked funny. But, after all of Kathleen's work, what could he say?

"Thanks for all your help," he said, giving her a hug. "I won't let ye down."

Pulling back, she looked carefully at Dutch in all his finery. He was a handsome lad with his dimpled chin and youthful face. But then she noticed his necklace.

"Wish you wouldn't wear those cougar strands. They are so out of place."

"They go where I go. This is my house rules," he answered with determination.

"Aye," she replied with a grin. "Well, they will make for interesting table chatter."

When Sandy returned from helping some customers, he poured a shot of brandy into Dutch's coffee. "That will take the edge off. Are you jittery, lad?"

"Aye. I hope this doesn't turn out to be another Methodist fiasco."

Reaching into his pocket, Sandy produced a slip of paper and handed it to him. "Here's Miss Becky's address. Give it to the coachman. You should have no problems finding a coach back, in her neighborhood. But remember this, Dutch – don't let the rich folks intimidate you. We live with fear or faith, so trust in yourself."

The day was crisp and bright as the carriage high-stepped though the city and out into the countryside. With his head swirling with instructions and his mind full of doubts, Dutch sat back on the leather seat, watching the sights go by. Kathleen's words still rang in his head: *You must not insult your host!*

When finally the coach pulled up to Becky's home, he could not believe his eyes. The building was an immense, three-story stone mansion, with manicured gardens all around and the architecture of a summer palace.

Nervously, Dutch paid off the coachman and walked up the tall steps to the massive double front doors, where he rang the brass bell. As he waited, his mind again filled with doubts.

Finally, the door was opened by a Negro girl who wore a black dress with a white apron and bonnet. "Yes, sir," she said.

"Dutch Blackwell to see Miss Becky."

The girl's black face seemed frozen for a moment. Then she smiled. "Yes… Mistress Hanson. Please, come in. I well get Madam."

Dutch walked through the doorway and into a large marbled foyer. Standing with hat in hand, he gazed at the grandest home he had ever seen. The walls were covered with artwork of all kinds. The furniture was made from rich-looking woods, with a glossy shine that reflected the light. High on the ceiling, a giant crystal chandelier held dozens of unlit candles. It was as if he had stepped onto the other side of the world, the rich side.

Then a pair of sliding doors opened, revealing Miss Becky, accompanied by an older gentleman dressed in black formal attire. Quickly, she crossed the foyer with a warm smile and gave Dutch a hug. Her blue dress and soft skin smelled of spring. Now middle-aged, Miss Becky was still as radiant as sunshine.

"I'm so pleased you are well and could join me," she said in her sweet, soft voice during the embrace. Pulling away, she continued, "This is my butler, Bentley. He will take that fine-looking hat."

Handing the bowler to the butler, Dutch said, "I've heard of thee. You brought me chicken soup during my fever."

"Yes, sir," he answered, with a stoic expression.

"The soup was a wonderful elixir. I thank you both."

"Bentley told me you had a run-in with the Methodists," Becky said with a grin.

Dutch was embarrassed that they knew the news. "You must have read of it in the newspaper."

"No, sir," Bentley answered. "I was in the congregation."

Dutch was astounded that his Methodist adventure just wouldn't go away. "I hope I did not offend thee."

"No, sir," Bentley answered, a small smile finally appearing on his lips. "Best sermon I've ever heard. Short and to the point."

"Bravo, Dutch," Becky said in a playful tone. "If the fur trade doesn't work out, you can always become a wilderness preacher! Let's go into the library. I have someone for you to meet."

The library was the most impressive room Dutch had ever seen. The walls were full of bookshelves containing hundreds of volumes. And everywhere he looked there were seafaring knick-knacks and artworks of all descriptions. The room was large, with a high ceiling and three bright windows that faced the front of the house. Opulent furniture of all sizes rested on imported plush rugs that covered the highly-polished wooden floors. He had the urge to rush to the shelves and peruse the books, but he didn't.

At the far end of the room was a large, crackling wood-burning fireplace, where an older man stood next to the ornate carved mantel. He was a tall, lean, distinguished-looking gentleman, with silver-gray hair, rust-colored eyebrows and a bushy mustache. He wore a brown velvet waistcoat with riding breeches and boots. His weathered face told of days gone by, while his broad, square shoulders spoke of authority.

"Commodore Clarke," Becky said as they approached, "I'd like you to meet Dutch Blackwell, the fur trader I told you about."

Extending his hand, he answered warmly, "With a name like Dutch, would ye be a Dutchman?"

Shaking his firm grip, Dutch smiled. "Nay, the Indians gave me that name. In their tongue, Dutch is *Dutcu*, which means 'badger.' Would you be Clark like Captain Clark?"

"Nay, I'm Clarke with an 'e.' It be the Scandinavian way."

Dutch had once before read the name Clarke with an 'e,' but he could not place it.

"Many years ago, Dutch's father, Joseph Blackwell, was my first sweetheart," Becky said with a proud smile.

The Commodore's eyes flashed a strange look as he stared intently at Dutch for the longest moment. Just then, Bentley appeared with a silver tray, three glasses and a crystal decanter of red wine. Each took a glass, and Bentley poured out the nectar. Leaving the tray, he then departed the room again.

Holding his glass high, the Commodore made a toast. "Here's to your father, Dutch. Where is he now?"

Sipping the wine, Dutch told the Commodore of his demise, out in the Oregon Country. The man seemed genuinely sad to hear of the deaths of Dutch's parents, and he asked a few odd questions about their final resting places. Dutch considered this to be nothing more then morbid curiosity. As they talked further, Dutch learned that the Commodore was an old family friend from Amsterdam. He was an import/export merchant in the Netherlands, just like Becky's late father and current husband.

"Will Mr. Hanson, be joining us?" Dutch asked respectfully.

"Sorry, no. He is in Philadelphia on business," Becky answered with a flash of sadness.

The conversation then turned to commerce. The Commodore owned a fleet of merchant ships. He was in America to oversee the refitting of a ship he had recently purchased, an aged brigantine named *Queen's Revenge*.

"She should be as good as new, come the spring. Then we'll sail her home and put her into service," he said proudly with impeccable English.

"Tell us about Astor, Dutch," Miss Becky requested. "I want to hear of your adventures with him"

"Aye," the Commodore added, "we hear he is becoming a very wealthy merchant."

Dutch told the brief story of his past two years: of the Indians, the trading and the furs. He did not tell them of the ambush, but did talk of Astor's plan to send a brigade across the continent.

"Will you join him in this venture?" Becky asked.

"Aye. I will return to the Columbia River. I've been far away, far too long."

Just then the double doors from the foyer opened, and a young lady and a square-jawed man with broad shoulders entered the library. The gentleman was wearing a light blue sea-coat with gold epaulettes. The young woman was dressed in a black skirt with a yellow silk blouse, and around her shoulders she wore a delicate white shawl. As they walked across the room, Dutch felt as if he were frozen in place, ogling the beauty of the young lady.

Becky introduced the couple to Dutch. The gentleman was Captain Eric Jacobson, the son-in-law of the Commodore. The young woman was Mary Jacobson, the daughter of the Captain and the Commodore's granddaughter.

Dutch shook the firm grip of the Captain. "A pleasure meeting you, sir."

He turned to Mary. She curtseyed and extended her white-gloved hand to Dutch. For a split second, he hesitated. Then he heard Kathleen words: *If a lady offers you her hand, don't shake it. Kiss it.* Reaching out, he did so, with a slight bow.

"Nice meeting you, Miss Jacobson."

"Likewise, Mr. Blackwell," she answered shyly.

There was something about her that tied his stomach in knots. As the group talked, he kept stealing glances at her. She was young. Very young. Mary was no longer a girl, but not yet a woman. Nevertheless, she was the most beautiful female Dutch had ever seen. Her golden hair framed a sweet face, with full pink lips, high cheekbones and deep-set blue eyes. She had tight, pale skin, and a petite figure that was still developing. Each time he gazed at her, he had to remind himself not to stare.

Just then Bentley proclaimed from an open doorway, "Lunch is served."

The long dining room table could easily seat twenty guests, so their small group had been set up at one end of the board. Miss Becky sat at the head of the table, with Captain Jacobson and Mary on one side and the Commodore and Dutch on the other side. The large narrow room had velvet-draped windows on one wall, with a long wooden buffet on the opposite wall. At the far end of the room stood another fireplace, which held the warm glow of a fire. On each side of the fireplace were swinging doors.

Dutch anxiously looked down at the table setting before him. He found that the setup looked just like what Kathleen had taught him. Thank God!

As Bentley poured champagne around the table, Mary said quietly, "I've been admiring the strands around your neck, Mr. Blackwell. Would they be ivory?"

Surprised by her question, Dutch held his necklace out for the others at the table to see.

"Nay, they be cougar teeth, Miss," he responded proudly. "Long ago, when my father was hunting, this cougar tried to kill him. My blood brother, Mole, killed the cat with a single arrow and made these strands as a trophy."

Mary and Miss Becky appeared enthralled by his story, while the rest of the table seemed only mildly interested. "How quaint," was Captain Jacobson's only reply.

Once the champagne glasses had been filled, the Commodore toasted the host, thanking her for her generosity. The champagne was the first that Dutch had ever sampled, and he found the bubbly drink outstanding.

Shortly, soup in a large tureen was served by a Negro footman. Each guest was served a portion of bean broth in their soup bowls. While this was happening, another black footman placed small rolls of bread on the butter plates. As the servants worked around the table, they were silent, the only conversation coming from the guests. Dutch felt out of place, but he was comfortable in his chair, as he knew which spoon to use.

Over the soup course, Dutch learned that Captain Jacobson would take command of the *Queen's Revenge* when the refit was completed, and would sail her back to Holland. The handsome captain was in his prime, with short brown hair and deep-set hazel eyes with a piercing stare. His stout body was muscular, with hands twice the size of most. When he talked, his deep voice bespoke authority. Clearly, Captain Jacobson was not a man to trifle with.

Dutch also learned that Mary would remain in Boston, attending a finishing school until the spring. As she shyly talked of her education, Dutch and Mary made eye contact a few times. Her English was near perfect, and her voice was as sweet as spring. Dutch was smitten with her, and kept looking away so as not to embarrass himself.

Then disaster struck. The footmen took away the soup bowls *with* the salad plates! *This isn't right*, Dutch thought, *Kathleen said the salad would be next.* Moments later, a shelled lobster in a long, narrow bowl was placed on his dinner plate. He had eaten lobsters before and found them delightful. But they were a messy crustacean to eat. What would be his plan now? Use the dinner knife to break the shell? Or maybe use his sea knife? As these thoughts filled his head, the other footman delivered small silver bowls to each guest. The smaller bowl looked to contain melted butter, while the larger one held a clear liquid with a curl of lemon peel floating on top. He was lost!

Dutch felt a gentle nudge from under the table. Looking up, he found Mary watching him with a shy grin. She looked across at him and then gathered up the small silver utensils that rested on the tablecloth at the very top of her plate. Dutch had not even noticed the tools until that moment. One of the items was a small pair of silver scissors, engraved with a design of grapes. She used this utensil to cut away the thin shell from the underside of the lobster tail. Dutch did the same, with his eyes focused on her and his ears attuned to the table conversation. Next, she used a little silver spear to remove the meat from the tail. Cutting up this soft meat with her dinner knife, she used her outermost fork to dip the meat into the melted butter. Dutch got the idea and smiled across at her with a silent nod. She returned his appreciation with fluttering eyes.

The conversation turned to the Pacific Northwest and the fur trade. The Commodore and Captain Jacobson asked Dutch many questions about Indian culture, the Columbia River and what trade goods were the most profitable. He answered their inquiries as best he could.

Then Captain Jacobson asked about Astor and his operation. Dutch told them about his experience with the American Fur Company and how they had traded whiskey and arms for pelts.

"This I do not hold with," he told the table.

"What do you think of Astor as a man?" the Commodore asked.

Dutch thought a moment. "He's part scoundrel and part empire builder. But I don't trust the man."

"Explain to Captain Jacobson what you were telling me about Astor's plans," the Commodore requested.

Dutch obliged, describing the plan to send a thirty man regiment across the continent in the spring to open a trading post on the Columbia River, and about the ship he was sending, filled with trading supplies.

"Will you be joining Astor in this venture?" Captain Jacobson asked.

"Aye, more than likely, a lone rider crossing the continent would be a foolish adventure."

"But, sir," Mary asked with a shy look, "if you don't trust this Astor... why join his venture?"

Dutch was pleased by her question. "I will be taking my own trading supplies across country. Once we are on the Columbia, I will quit his employ."

"He will not tolerate your competition," the Commodore said with a firm voice.

Smiling, Dutch replied, "I have a letter with John Astor's signature, declaring me a free trader. And, best of all, I'll have the local tribes with me."

"Aye," Captain Jacobson said, "until Astor starts trading whiskey and rifles with them. Then your alliance will fall apart."

Becky interrupted, "I asked Dutch here for a pleasant luncheon, and we pepper him with questions! Please forgive us."

After the lobster course, Mary cleaned her fingers in the bowl with the water that held the lemon peel. Dutch did the same. Then came the salad and, after that, a dessert he had never tasted before: ice cream. It was marvelous! He talked of his delight at the ice cream repeatedly to those at the table, and they enjoyed his enthusiasm for a treat that was common fare for their meals.

With the luncheon over, Becky ordered her carriage to be brought around to take Dutch back to town. As they waited, they shared more wine, talking of Sandy and the Sea Witch. Then, as Mary and her father rose from the table, Dutch stood and shook the Captain's hand once again.

Turning to Mary, he took one last, fond look at her. "I hope our ways might cross again, Miss Jacobson," he said with a nervous heart. She shyly smiled in reply.

As Becky and the Commodore walked Dutch to the front door to say their farewells, Dutch thanked Becky for the luncheon, "Never been to such a fancy affair. Thank you. I will not soon forget this soiree."

Miss Becky hugged Dutch, "Once you arrive out West, write to me so that I know you are well."

The Commodore clasped his hand again, and his final remark rang in Dutch's ears all the way back to the city: "It's a pleasure meeting a young lad with great expectations."

Back in a wooden booth at the Sea Witch, Dutch told Sandy and Kathleen of the day's events. He described the mansion, the servants, the guests and, of course, the food with all the wrong utensils.

They laughed at his predicament. "Grape scissors and lobster spears! I should have warned ye," Kate said with a grin.

He then explained how Mary, that mysterious and beautiful young lady, had saved him from embarrassment. With great excitement, he went on to describe her in every detail.

He concluded by saying, "She has stirred my heart like no other. I can see a life with her."

Sandy and Kathleen looked at each other with surprised expressions. "That be a fine thought, mate," Sandy finally said with a serious look. "But rich ladies of privilege only know of luxury and leisure. People like us, who work with their hands, have no place in their worlds."

"But it be a nice notion," Kate added with a forced smile.

Dutch looked carefully at his two friends. Deep down, he knew their words were true. But the knot in his stomach still remained.

III
The Tale of the Tonquin

—ɯ—

A fictional story could not have been written with more intrigue, tragedy and drama than the true tale of the ship Tonquin. This three-masted bark was a 290-ton American merchant ship built in New York in 1807. John Jacob Astor's Pacific Fur Company purchased the ship for $37,860 in August of 1810. He then hired United States Navy Lieutenant Jonathan Thorn to command the ten-gun vessel.

After securing a crew comprised mostly of Brits and Canadians, the ship departed New York harbor on September 8, 1810 bound for the Columbia River in Oregon Country as part of the Astor Expedition. The cargo on board the ship included fur trade goods, seeds, building materials for a trading post, tools, and the frame of a schooner to be used for coastal trade. These provisions had been carefully selected and purchased under the watchful eyes of four partners of the Pacific Fur Company who would make the voyage with Captain Thorn. The crew consisted of thirty-four people, including the partners and the captain. Additionally, there were twelve clerks and thirteen Canadian voyageurs plus four tradesmen aboard the ship: a blacksmith, a carpenter, a boat builder, and a cooper.

With tension already brewing in the ranks, the *Tonquin* sailed for South America. Just before rounding Cape Horn, the ship put in at the desolate and deserted Falkland Islands to make repairs and take on fresh water. Upon leaving a few days later, Captain Thorn set sail without eight of his crew. He only stopped to retrieve them after another crewmember threatened to shoot the Captain. On December 25, the troubled ship rounded Cape Horn and sailed north, reaching the Sandwich Islands on February 12, 1811, where they traded for sheep, hogs, goats, poultry, and vegetables. The *Tonquin* also took on twelve native Hawaiians, who were recruited for the fur venture in the Northwest.

On March 22, 1811, the *Tonquin* reached the Columbia, where dangerous bar conditions blocked the ship from accessing the river. Anchoring off Cape Hancock (Cape Disappointment), Captain Thorn sent five men out in a dinghy to locate a navigable channel. However, their small boat was lost in the towering swells. The next day they tried again, with another five men in a longboat. This attempt was also unsuccessful, and their boat was nearly lost. On the third attempt, a skiff with five sailors aboard located the channel. But as the boat was returning to the ship, it was swamped and also lost. Finally, on the 24th of March, the *Tonquin* was able to cross the bar and enter the Columbia's estuary, where they anchored in Baker's Bay and began searching for the lost men. Only two of the ten crewmembers were found alive.

After the rescue mission, the ship proceeded upriver fifteen miles to where the present-day city of Astoria, Oregon, is located. There they anchored and began the construction of an outpost they named Fort Astoria. As the trading post neared completion, much of the ship's cargo was unloaded into the fort. The ship remained at Fort Astoria for 65 days before moving downriver with a crew of twenty-four. On June 5, 1811, the ship left Baker's Bay and sailed north to trade for furs. Once off of Nootka Sound (Vancouver Island), the tragic tale of the *Tonquin* would continue.

—⚒—

Boston Winter Camp ————

On brisk fall mornings, there was no cozier place to be than Kate's kitchen. Dutch and Sandy would sit at the large kitchen table, drinking coffee, reading the Boston Gazette and bantering with each other while Kate plied her magic at the stove. Even King had a special spot on an old blanket, where he would curl up and dream of the scraps he would soon receive. For Dutch, those early morning hours reminded him of the family time he had long lost.

Soon, the aroma of Kate's biscuits and homemade chutney would seep through the neighborhood like a spring breeze. She had a knack for cooking, and worked hours at her woodstove. The meals she prepared were always simple, like corned beef and cabbage, chicken and dumplings or cod chowder. She and Sandy knew what their customers wanted and how much they would pay. While the tavern was a waterfront dive, the food served was always hot and hearty and the spirits poured, always generous.

With dreams of Mary still weighing heavily on his mind, Dutch pitched in around the tavern, helping anyway he could. Long ago, his father had taught him that work was the best elixir for an idle mind. The pub was open from ten in the morning until midnight, so the days were long and the work burdensome. Dutch swept the floors, cleaned the spittoons, chopped wood and washed the pots and pans. Each morning, he filled the barroom jugs from the 40-gallon wooden barrels of rum, whiskey and brandy in the storeroom. He also filled the smaller drums of beer, ale and wine that rested on the counter behind the bar. He then helped Sandy tend bar, serve the food and collect the money. On weekends, he would sometimes play his flute for the late-night drinkers, and found that he enjoyed these rare prospects to share his music and learn new tunes from others.

From Sandy he learned that the best traits for a bartender were to be a good listener with keen eyes and fast reactions to prevent any problems. "Run no drink chits," Sandy had told him. "Always collect first and be alert for trouble." At times, the pub was a cesspool of quirky characters ready to cause problems at the drop of a hat. As part of Sandy's campaign against troublesome patrons, he had strategically placed three iron-tipped belaying pins along the back bar. These sticks could knock out any rowdy sailor with a single swing.

The colorful clientele of the Sea Witch was as diverse as the ships in the harbor. Half of the customers were boisterous seamen who spoke many different languages. There were Scandinavians, Europeans and Asians all talking a gibberish of tongues only they understood. Dutch found this diversity fascinating, and soon learned to converse with most of the pub's foreign patrons using Indian-style sign language. The other customers were the local merchants. They were all men; no women other than Kathleen ever set foot in the pub. Not even the ladies of the evening dared venture into the tavern, as Sandy would run them off with profanity Dutch had never heard before. Sandy said this practice was for honorable reasons, as the ladies would beguile the sailors and fleece their purses. But Kate was different. The regular customers loved her cooking, and many patrons showed up almost every day.

One such customer was a teamster and horseman named Tony Rawlins. Sandy called him the Spaniard. He owned a freight company that roamed all over New England, bringing wagon loads of crops and dairy products into Boston, then distributing mail and dry goods to the countryside. His warehouse was down on the docks, and he was a regular for lunch. His fare was always the same: three tankards of ale and Kate's special for the day. Tony was a stout, middle-aged man with a crowned bald head, with big ears and hands twice the size of most. He claimed his huge paws were from driving eight-up horse teams all of his life. The Spaniard often talked of the poor country roads, the dangerous river crossings and his run-ins with highwaymen and renegade Indians. Tony knew the lay of the land and how to get anywhere with a wagon full of freight. Dutch took a liking to him right away, soon learning that he had been born in Western Pennsylvania and had been to Saint Louis in his younger years. Dutch told the Spaniard of his plans to travel there, come spring. "There ain't much out there, lad," Tony had replied, with a flagon in hand. "It's the middle of nowhere, with just a few folks and breeds trying to scratch out a living."

"Could I buy some good horses and supplies there?"

"Nay," the Spaniard had answered, shaking his head. "Whatever horse flesh is out there is wild Indian ponies or tired plow plugs. And whatever supplies you might find in town will cost you three times more than here in Boston. If you're going that way, lad, take your own steeds and provisions."

"But how the hell do I get there from here with horses and trail supplies?" Dutch had asked with a frustrated scowl.

Tony smiled. "That's simple, lad. I know the way. You give me a list of your trail needs and I'll outfit you, right down to the horse flesh."

The Spaniard was a good mate, and he knew the pitfalls of traveling across the hinterlands through a country side of few roads and many rivers. Over the coming weeks, Dutch and Tony worked out a detailed account of his needs for crossing the continent.

Strangely enough, another customer, Doctor Bates, would also play a role in Dutch's upcoming odyssey to the Pacific. Kate had called him a quack, and had little regard for the man's medical skills. After all, he was a drunk and a consumptive, but as Dutch got to know him better, he found the old sawbones to be an intriguing physician. He had been a Navy doctor in the Revolutionary War and told many stories about tending wounded sailors during great sea battles. "With canon fire bursting and the decks slick with blood, I stood for hours, sawing off body parts like so much cordwood. As soon as I finished one chap, another would be dropped on my table. It was a nightmare of human agony, mangled bodies and broken dreams."

After the war, he became the quarantine doctor for the Port of Boston. Now he and his staff met every foreign ship before it was allowed inside the harbor. They checked the crews for diseases, and tended to the sick and injured. After his war-time doctoring, being a quarantine physician was as mild as a spring day.

Bates was a thin, older, quiet man with a blank stare in his deep-set brown eyes. His face showed his age, and when he talked his voice was low and raspy. His daily lunch habit was to eat half of his food while downing three or four flagons of rum. Over the months of that winter, he and Dutch became mates, and they often talked of Dutch's plans to trek to the Pacific.

Then, one day in November, Dr. Bates came into the Sea Witch carrying a small brass-hinged wooden box. As Dutch served him his first rum, the good doctor opened the box and showed him the contents.

"This is my first healing kit," he said, opening the lid. "It's got all the basic tools needed for medical care aboard a small ship. I want you to have it, Dutch."

Inside the case was a booklet on doctoring. Underneath it were tiny wooden compartments with shiny steel instruments. There were also rolls of cotton bandages, twine and four bottles filled with liquids.

The doctor pointed to these vessels. "The clear liquid is grain alcohol for cleaning wounds, not for drinkin'. The next bottle is cod liver oil; use it for pleurisy and fevers. The next is calomel; use it sparingly as a cathartic. The last bottle is laudanum; use it for pain or anything else that might ail ya. Anyhow, lad, the kit's small enough for a saddle bag, and it might be useful on your trail."

Dutch was surprised and pleased with the gift. "But, Doc, don't you need this kit for your work?"

"Nay," Bates answered with a pitiful face, "my depravities are getting worse, so they are putting me out to pasture, come the first of the year. You'll need it more for your journey than I will where I'm going."

Dutch heard the sadness in Doc Bates's voice, and felt sorry for him and the bleak future he faced. After a second flagon of rum, they spent an hour going over each item in the kit. Bates was a good man and, drunk or sober, he knew doctoring inside and out.

Then there was the bee man. His real name was Vergil Hampton. He and his three sons owned one of the local livery stables. He was an old fellow well into his seventies, and he came into the pub almost every afternoon for rum and tea. Vergil was a short man with a face full of wrinkles and a head full of stories. He could talk for hours, to anyone that would listen, about the old times of Boston and what it had been like to live with the local Indians. His favorite story concerned how he became a bee herder.

"My family arrived here in the early 50's. I was just a boy then, don't you know," Vergil would start out, with a mug of rum in hand. "Papa found the land sterile. The Indians told him the land had gone bad after all the bees had died off in the deep freeze of the winter of '49. Papa planted vegetables and fruit trees for years, but nothing would really grow." He paused a moment, taking out the makings for a cigarette, with his old face aglow. "Then the local chief told Papa to find new bees so the land would be fertile again. So my father turned to me – I was just fifteen at the time – and he told me to walk south until I found some big, healthy bees, and to bring them back to Boston. Well, I walked all the way to the Carolinas before I found them bees. Then I had a hell of time herding them damn bees back to Boston." He'd pause again, rolling and lighting his cigarette.

"How did ye herd them bees?" someone would always ask.

"I found me a Leprechaun. He told me to catch the queen bee in a jar, and then he taught me a tone that sounded like nectar to them bees. So I whistled myself all the way home to Boston with a dark cloud of bees following. Reckon it be me and my bees that turned New England fruitful again."

Vergil was like that, one tall tale after another. He was indeed a quirky and colorful customer.

When Dutch first arrived in Boston, two years before, he had gone searching for his grandfather's blacksmith shop on North Street. When he finally found it, he was sad to learn that his grandfather had died a few years before. A new smithy, John Cornwall, had purchased the business from his Uncle Frederic. Dutch never met this uncle, as the man had moved away before Dutch arrived in Boston.

Now John Cornwall was a patron of the Sea Witch. He was a pipe-smoking, robust bloke who frequented the pub a few times each week. John drank beer and loved telling lewd jokes and poking fun at the other customers. He was a good-spirited chap who had a belly laugh that was contagious.

Over the months, John and Dutch often talked of his grandfather, Samuel Blackwell, and his Uncle Frederic. From these conversations, Dutch formed an image in his head about what his uncle might look like, right down to a jagged ruby scar on his right forearm. Frederic had told Mr. Cornwall about the forge accident that marked him for life. It was after this injury that he had sold the shop and moved West, in hopes of finding his brother Joseph. The smithy was a good soul with a big heart and a talent for always looking on the brighter side of life.

As fall waned and winter bit, the Sea Witch crowd thinned. With the North Atlantic now blowing and rolling beneath inky skies, few ships dared to make sail, and the harbor soon dwindled to only a few hearty boats. It was during this time that ships looking to sail had trouble finding crews. To remedy this problem, a hundred-dollar bonus was paid by the captains for any new crewmembers. When this didn't work, the captains walked the waterfront pubs, offering two hundred dollar bounties for any shanghaied sailors the innkeepers could provide.

Sandy hated this long established practice, and refused to have anything to do with hijacking sailors. "I be no crimp. Reckon you can keep your blood money," he told the captains. "The Sea Witch be a safe harbor for sailors, not a scandalous snatch house."

On the Pacific Coast, the local Indians held winter celebrations for the salmon harvest. This was a special time of feasting with family and friends. Bostonians did the same, but they called it Thanksgiving. Just like the salmon harvest, this unique day was filled with ceremonies and traditions. Early on, Sandy announced that Kate would be cooking a rare Thanksgiving meal for the pub's patrons. With King curled up on his blanket, the dog watched Kate work for two days as she prepared her special feast. And what a savory meal it was: wild turkey, potatoes, gravy, yams, corn on the husk, and sweet treats Dutch had never tasted before, pumpkin and venison mince meat pies.

Late Thanksgiving evening, after the doors were locked and the lamps turned down, Sandy, Kate and Dutch sat at the kitchen table, eating the gratifying leftovers.

"This Thanksgiving is a marvelous thing. How did it come to be?" Dutch asked, with a turkey bone in hand.

"The way it's told, it started with the Pilgrims, many years ago," Kate answered. "They were starving and the local Indians fed them from the bountiful land. For this kindness, the Pilgrims called it the celebration of Thanksgiving."

"What happened to the Indians?"

Sandy stared at Dutch with a blank look and then said, "Don't really know. Reckon they died from the white-man's diseases...or his lead balls."

"How sad," Dutch replied shaking his head. "The Pilgrims got the corn, while the Indians got the husk. But then, that ain't new. The white man is always cheating my red brothers."

The Saturday night after Thanksgiving, Dutch and Sandy had problems with two drunken Irish sailors that had come into the pub. The jack-tars had staggered through the front door with their sea boots and coats covered with snow. After shaking off the dampness, they had taken a booth and loudly ordered Irish whiskies and coffee. Sandy patiently explained that he sold only Tennessee whiskey. Their reaction was boisterous and profane, but after some talking amongst themselves, they agreed to try the American whiskey. When Sandy returned with the fortified coffees, the redheaded lad took one sip and started yelling. "This swill tastes like horse piss, old man. I said Irish whisky."

Sandy stared at the young bloke for a moment and then replied, in his squeaky voice, "I told ya, I sell only Tennessee whiskey. That will be two bits."

The redheaded sailor bolted out of the booth with his mug in hand. Confronting Sandy, he screamed, "I'm not paying for this rubbish. You can go to hell." Then he threw his hot coffee in Sandy's face.

The pub went silent.

From behind the bar, Dutch witnessed this ruckus, grabbed a belaying pin and leaped over the bar. Wide eyed, Sandy stood his ground, calmly using his shirt sleeve to dry his face.

"What'a you gonna to do about that, old man? Ya lily-livered varmint, ya don't know nothin' about good whiskey," the redhead slurred to Sandy.

"Did he burn ya, mate?" Dutch asked, rushing to Sandy's side with the belaying pin in hand.

"Nay," Sandy answered with a fiery voice, "but he's put my bristles up. I think these scoundrels should leave."

At that, the redheaded sailor dropped his porcelain mug to the planks, where it shattered as he swiftly pulled his knife from his hip. "I ain't afraid of ye Yankee pricks. I'll show you how an Irishman fights."

His stunted mate quickly slipped out of the booth, with fear on his face. "Colin, we want no trouble with these blokes. Let's go back to the ship."

Dutch handed the belaying pin to Sandy and pulled his sea knife from his hip. "Now, this be a proper shank, big and sharp enough to spoil your guts," Dutch said to Colin, with anger in his eyes.

"No problems, Colin. Let's get the hell out of here," his friend pleaded.

The redhead returned Dutch's glare for the longest moment, all the while holding his blade at the ready. Then he blinked, turned away and started to leave, with his pal on his heels.

"That'll be two bits for the drinks and a nickel more for the mug," Sandy shouted firmly at them.

The friend stopped and turned back to the booth. Fumbling in his pockets, he pulled out some coins and slapped them on the table. "Sorry, mates," he whispered, looking at Sandy. "He's always been an ugly drunk."

With the two sailors out the door, Dutch turned to Sandy. "Gutsy call, asking for your money."

"Reckoned they owed it to me," Sandy said, smiling proudly, "and ye had my back."

A few hours later, Dutch bolted the front door and turned down the lamps. He then went upstairs with King to read, while Sandy and Kate stayed behind, cleaning up from the day's business. With the dog resting on the foot of the bed, Dutch lit a fire in the stove and took off his belt. Waiting for the room to warm, he rubbed his hands together and thought again about the scuffle with the Irish sailor. It had lasted just a few heart beats, and he was pleased that he had been able to defend Sandy. But what of the future? What would Sandy do after Dutch was gone? Sandy was too old and too small to put up with jack-tars like those. Dutch would have to talk to him about having more protection behind the bar…

The sound of whimpering shattered his thoughts. Turning, he found King whining and pacing by the back door.

"You were just out," Dutch told the dog. "Alright…alright, I'll let ye out again, but make it quick."

As Dutch opened the back door, King shot out onto the porch and down the snow-covered stairs. The blast of winter air hit Dutch's face with a cold sting. Closing the door, he turned back to the stove.

Thud, something fell downstairs. Dutch didn't think much about the loud noise until he heard Kate scream out with a deadly cry. Instantly, he grabbed his knife and bolted down the inside stairway. When he got to the bottom, he saw the open door to the darkened storeroom and beyond to a glowing kitchen. As muffled screams came from that direction, Dutch ran into the dim storeroom, where he found Sandy face-down on the floor, with parts of a broken clay jug next to him on the planks. Dutch paused a second, fearing him dead, then quickly crossed the room towards the lit doorway.

Pushing the door all the way open, he saw Kate sprawled on the kitchen table, with the redheaded Irish sailor on top of her. His right arm was holding her down, with his hand over her mouth. His left hand was up her dress, while his shoulders were fighting off her desperate struggle.

Instantly, Dutch leaped across the room and brought the butt end of his knife down hard on Colin's head. The two men rolled off the table and fell with a thud to the floor. With arms and legs flying, Dutch got a second blow to Colin's temple. This stunned the drunken lad for a second, and a third butt blow to the head made the Irish sailor crumple on the floor like a furled sail.

Scrambling to his feet, Dutch rushed to Kate, who was still sprawled on top of the table. Her eyes were filled with tears, and she was sobbing and shaking her head. The bodice of her dress had been ripped open, exposing her breasts. Dutch reached to a hook on the wall and covered her with an apron.

"You hurt?" he asked, out of breath.

She blinked several times before responding in a near whisper, "Nay... I don't think so. He just scared the hell out of me. Thank you... thank you, I'll be alright."

Dutch turned quickly back toward the storeroom. "Sandy's down."

With the dog scratching at the back door, Dutch returned to where Sandy lay, dazed and half-conscious on the deck. In the dim light, he could see blood on his friend's head from a gash where Colin had knocked him out with a jug. Dutch helped Sandy to his feet and guided him, staggering, into the kitchen, where he fell into a chair. Kate had slipped the apron on and sat in another chair, still dazed. Lamp in hand, Dutch quickly examined the gash on Sandy's head. The cut was nearly two inches long but not very deep. Finding a cloth by the stove, Dutch dampened it and placed it on Sandy's gash and placed Sandy's hand on it. "Hold it there. I've got to let the dog in," Dutch said to his unresponsive friend.

Once he had brought King inside to stand guard in the kitchen, Dutch went out to the bar and poured two large glasses of whiskey. These he gave to his stunned friends. Then Dutch knelt beside Colin, binding his hands with rope while Kathleen and Sandy sipped the liquor. Soon, the brother and sister recovered their wits and started to ramble about the attack, turning their shock into words.

As soon as the Irish sailor was tied securely, Dutch poured water on his face. His eyes slowly opened, and he became aware of King's snarling muzzle, and of the three angry friends watching his every move. His eyes filled with fear, and he struggled, trying to loosen his ropes.

"That Irish prick caught me off guard. What do we do with this bloke?" Sandy finally asked.

Dutch stood over the Irishman, looking down at his frightened face. "Reckon I could let the dog have a crack at him."

"Nay," Kate firmly said, getting to her wobbly feet and snatching Dutch's sea knife from the table. "Give him to me. I'll make him a gelding, right here in my kitchen."

At Kathleen's angry words, Colin's eyes bulged, and sweat began running down his temples. "Please," he begged, "I meant no harm. The whiskey made me do it."

Dutch held out his hand as if to stop Kate's approach and looked down at Colin. "She's just the wench to do it, lad. She loves butcherin'."

"Please...have mercy on me," the redhead sobbed with quivering lips.

"Gag him," Sandy responded, spitting fire. "Then go find a ship that's shorthanded. We'll send him on a winter cruise."

This was the first and only time that Sandy shanghaied a sailor. He didn't like doing it, but the Irishman had tried to have his way with Kathleen and that made all the difference. Before the sun was up, a shackled and gagged Colin was escorted out of the pub and down to the docks, where an embargo-running slave ship was waiting. The cruise would be to Africa and back, a good year or more. Sandy hoped the redhead would use the time to repent of his sins and mend his ways.

As for the bounty, Sandy gave the two hundred dollars to Kathleen. After all, she had gotten the worst of it. After the installation of a new dead-bolt on the backdoor, and a few jokes about Colin's winter cruise, the incident of the Irish sailor was soon forgotten, although

Kate never again worked alone in the kitchen after the pub closed, preferring to ask Sandy, Dutch or King to remain with her in those late hours.

The Northwest Indians had a tradition of Potlatch, a ceremonial festival where gifts were bestowed on their guests. Bostonians did the same, and called it Christmas. Dutch's wilderness family had always celebrated Christmas, but rather than using it as an occasion for gift giving, it had been a day of Bible readings and reflection. When Kathleen told Dutch of the American tradition, she told him that he wasn't to worry about giving any gifts. "You are a stranger to our customs," she said. "So let Sandy and I bestow presents on you."

Dutch thought her proposition over, but would have none of it, so he hired the blacksmith to forge gifts for his two friends.

Christmas was the only day of the year that the pub was closed. Early that morning, Kathleen rousted both Dutch and Sandy from their warm beds. Then, with promises of champagne, roasted goose and sweet pies, she persuaded them to join her at church. Once again, Dutch found himself at the Methodist church he had come to distrust. But this time, to his surprise, the Reverend Hathaway gave a rousing sermon which included holiday songs and music that Dutch had never heard. He enjoyed every moment of the worship, and even shook hands with many of the parishioners after the service.

Later that afternoon, the friends sat at their favorite booth, drinking champagne and talking of Christmases past. After a few glasses of the bubbly wine, Sandy excused himself, then returned to hand Dutch a pair of boots.

"I asked the Spaniard what ya might need for the long journey, and he said good riding boots. So I had him find ya these. They ride high over your calf, and there's a steel plate in the toe, and the heel is taller than normal, to help ya stay in the stirrup. He calls them trail boots."

Dutch examined the footwear closely. The boots were crafted in brown leather, with detailed scrolling and silver rivets up the sides. The heel and soles were custom stitched and tacked to the upper leather, and the toe was pointed, with a steel plate inside. With excitement, Dutch pulled on the boots and walked around the planks for all to see. The trail boots fit perfectly and were splendid to wear. By the time he finally looked up from his feet, Kathleen was standing by the booth, holding her hat box.

Opening the box, she said, "The Spaniard also told us that you would need a good hat. One with a brim to keep the sun and rain off your face and with a crown that would let your head breath. My husband's old black bowler fits that bill, and I've added a turkey feather to it so it won't look so formal out on the trail. You'll look dapper in this hat, Dutch, and I'd be pleased to have you wear it West."

Dutch was stunned with her gift as he hated the hat. A frontiersman wearing a bowler with a turkey feather would look silly. But what could he say? With a smile on his face, he put the hat on.

She dug deeper into the box. "He also said strong breeches would be needed, so I sewed you a pair out of sailcloth." As she pulled the dyed blue trousers out of the box, her face beamed with pride. She held the pantaloons to Dutch's torso and checked the fit. "They'll just need a little final adjusting."

Dutch loved the trousers; they would be snug and warm on the trail, and would wear well. He hugged Kate for a moment and then excused himself, returning as quickly as he could with his own two gifts, which he offered shyly.

For Sandy, the blacksmith had made an identical copy of Dutch's sea knife. "My father's knife brought us together, mate, and I thought you should have one for your hip."

Sandy glowed as he examined the well-crafted blade. "Bloody wonderful," was all he could say.

For Kathleen, there was a deep iron skillet with a bone handle. "You're always burning your hands with your old pan. Mr. Cornwall said this bone handle will protect ya from the heat."

A surprised Kate held the heavy skillet; it was indeed a superior pan that would service her well. "I told ye, no gifts...but now, each time I use this pan, I will think of ye. I love your gift," she said with watery eyes.

That night, before their Christmas dinner, Dutch spoke the blessing while holding hands with Sandy and Kate: "Family and friends are special spirits given to us by angels. God bless this food and my glorious friends."

The Golden Offer ————

The New Year came cloaked in a nor'easter that dumped more than a foot of snow on Boston. It was miserable weather that reminded Dutch just how lucky he was to be making his winter camp inside the warm pub. But he worried about gaining weight and getting camp-soft during the inactive winter months. Even King had put on a few pounds, eating Kate's discarded vittles. So Dutch chopped wood every day and redoubled the chores he performed to help out around the tavern. And through it all, as always, he longed for a wilderness trail with the warm sun on his face and a cool breeze at his back.

With the worsening weather came fewer customers. Only the hearty or foolish dared to walk the icy streets in the blowing snowstorms of the first few weeks of January. On the first Monday of the New Year, the pub had fewer than ten patrons all day. But in some ways this was good, as Kathleen couldn't get out for her supplies and the liquor wagons had to remain in their stables. Boston had slowed to a crawl.

To help pass the time, Kate and Sandy decided to make improvements in the kitchen, while Dutch cleaned every nook and cranny of the pub. One afternoon, dressed in old denims and a dirty apron, Dutch was on his hands and knees cleaning the stand-up urinal at the bar when he heard the front door open. Looking up from the tiles, he saw two men with tricorne hats and gray wool coats stomping through the pub's snow-swept doorway. As they shook the snow off and removed their headgear, he recognized them as Commodore Clarke and Captain Eric Jacobson.

Surprised, Dutch stood and greeted them, "Welcome to the Sea Witch, gentlemen. It be a quiet place, today, but the food is hot and the drinks are strong."

Captain Jacobson turned his way with a grin and, in a heavy accent, said, "Ye don't look much like a frontiersman, dressed in scullery clothes."

The Commodore approached Dutch with an outstretched hand. "We came to see you, lad. Hope we are not pulling you away from an important task."

Dutch, embarrassed by his attire, returned the Captain's grin with a nod. Then, after wiping his palm on his pant leg, he shook the Commodore's hand. "Surprised to see you again, sir. With this weather, it's been a little lonely around here. What can I get you?"

"It's colder than the North Sea out there. How about you join us for some brandy and coffee?"

"Aye, guess my customers won't miss me," he agreed with a smile. As Dutch showed the two men to a booth, he wondered at their strange visit. Why would they want to venture out in this weather to see him? "I'll be back right back," he said, once they were settled.

Opening the kitchen door, Dutch poked his head in. "Sandy, I've got two blokes I'd like you to meet – that is, if Kate can do without you."

Kathleen smiled from the stove. "You can have him. He's all thumbs today."

Stepping behind the bar, Dutch poured four mugs of coffee and spiked the brews with brandy. Then, with Sandy on his heels, carrying the coffees on a tray, he returned to the booth and slid the mugs across the table.

"Gentleman, I'd like you to meet Sandy Hayes. He's my mate and the proprietor of the Sea Witch. Before being the owner, he spent nearly forty years at sea."

They grasped his hand warmly and invited him to take a seat. While they sipped at the hot drinks, Sandy told them the story of rounding the Horn aboard the *Lady Washington* in 1789, and sailing for almost six months to the Pacific Northwest coast. They asked many questions about Captain Gray, the crew and his ship. The Commodore was most interested in his account of the skirmish with the Tillamook Indians, and how Dutch's father and the African cabin boy had become marooned with the tribe.

"They were just lads at the time," Sandy said sadly. "I wanted to go back for them, but Captain Gray couldn't put the ship in jeopardy again."

"That's a bloody hard call," the Commodore answered while stroking his rust-colored mustache. "It be a crying shame to leave shipmates behind."

The Commodore seemed impressed with Sandy, and they talked more about the sea and different ports of call. After the coffees were consumed, Sandy excused himself and took the mugs back to the bar for refills.

As Sandy left the table, the Commodore turned to Dutch. "After hearing of your adventures in the fur trade on the Pacific Coast, Captain Jacobson and I started talking about opportunities out there. But we have many questions. Would you be so kind as to answer a few inquiries?"

"Yes, sir," Dutch answered politely.

Their questions were simple enough; how many hides could a ship expect to trade for in one season? Would the Indians be friendly or hostile? What kind of trade goods would a ship need, and what value would those goods have?

"If we paid you twenty dollars, would you write out a list of the trade goods needed, with an estimated value of each item?" the Commodore asked, his bushy red eyebrows raised.

"Aye," Dutch replied, "but it is a task that will take some time."

"You told us that you would join Astor's brigade to cross the continent and that, once on the coast, you would quit his employee. Is this still your plan?" Eric asked, with his customary piercing stare.

"I reckon so," Dutch replied. "While Astor be a man not to trifle with, I just don't trust him."

"You talked about packing in your own trade goods, but what kind of goods could a lone rider carry across the continent?" the Commodore asked.

Dutch smiled at this query. "I'll take mostly vegetable seeds, metal arrow heads, fish hooks and iron files, and enough molasses to make spruce beer. The Indians love this brew."

"Iron files? Why?" the Commodore responded, his leathery face ablaze with curiosity.

"They are worth their weight in pelts. What few iron tools the Indians have soon begin to rust, and they have no way to refurbish or sharpen them. Thus the iron files."

With a broad smile, the Commodore said, "You do know this trade."

"What of flintlocks?" Captain Jacobson asked.

"Aye, I have thought about what you said at lunch. It is true that, if I don't trade muskets with the Indians, others soon will. So I'll take as many as I can carry. But I'll only trade those rifles for Indian land."

"You sound like you're making a home out there. Is that so?" the Commodore responded, sounding surprised.

"Aye. The Indians are the only family I have, and I intend to plant my roots there."

"Why not here in Boston? A young man like yourself could flourish here," the Commodore asked.

Dutch thought a moment, then responded with a hand gesture towards the front door. "Today's weather is a good reminder. It seldom snows on the coast, and while we get great gales with rain so heavy that a man can fear drowning on high ground, it is not as miserable as here. Nay, I'll take the Pacific weather, any time."

Sandy slipped back into the booth with four fresh mugs of coffee. With this second round of libations, tongues got looser, and Dutch soon learned the true measure of their visit.

"Can we talk freely?" Eric asked.

"Aye," Dutch smiled. "I have no secrets from Sandy."

The Commodore looked Dutch straight in the eye. "What if we sent one of our ships full of trade goods, one year from this spring? You could open your own trading post, right there on the Columbia River, then trade your skins exclusively with us. And, for the first few seasons, you could teach the ship's Captain and his crew how to trade up and down the coast?"

Dutch was pleasantly surprised by the offer but he hesitated a moment, reminding himself that he was always too quick to trust.

"I'll write out your supply list and think on your scheme. What would be my share?"

Captain Jacobson answered firmly, "Twenty five percent of any profits we make on selling or trading the skins in China."

The table went silent for a moment. Then, with mug in hand, Sandy responded in his squeaky voice. "None of my affair, mates, but I reckon this venture will only succeed if everyone is treated equally."

Dutch picked up on Sandy's thoughts. "If I decide to be a part of your venture, I will require an equal share in gold," he said, looking directly at the Commodore.

The old man's face was stoic and hard to read, but then a grin slowly crossed his lips. "Fine, a full share it will be. Each year, when the supply ship comes, they will bring out your share in gold from the previous season. This amount will be less the cost of any personal needs, of course."

With thoughts of riches racing through his young head, Dutch replied, "Aye."

"Astor won't like this competition," Eric said in a firm voice.

"Aye," the Commodore echoed with a twinkle in his eyes, "But we know something Astor doesn't. There are rumors of war coming again soon, between England and America. And if that happens, the British will surely take over Astor's outpost. But the Netherlands is at peace with England, so if you fly a Dutch flag, your trading post should have no problems."

"How do you know this?" Sandy asked, concern written on his face.

The Commodore looked down at the mug in his hand, and then back up. "We have many friends in the British Admiralty. That is all I can say."

"Bloody hell! Another war with the Brits, I'll piss on their graves," Sandy said, with fire in his eyes.

As they finished their coffees, the table conversation turned to war and future relations between America and England. Eric and the Commodore were of the opinion that great profits could be made from the coming conflict, but it was a notion not held in high esteem by Sandy.

"All wars are foolish," Sandy said to the table. "In the end, only the devil wins."

As the men got up to leave, the Commodore invited Dutch and Sandy to the re-christening of his ship on the first day of March. In honor of his granddaughter, he had changed the name of the *Queen's Revenge* to the *Mary Rose*. "Come rain or shine, it will be a gala event. Bring us your supply list and, if you agree to our partnership, make a second list of any special needs you might have," he said while slipping on his heavy wool coat. At the door the four men shook hands, and then the Commodore and Captain stepped out into the grips of winter again.

While cleaning up the booth, Sandy asked, "What are you going to do about the Commodore's offer?"

"Don't rightly know. Reckon it may be a good endeavor," Dutch answered.

Sandy put a hand on Dutch's shoulder and looked him directly in the eye. "These Dutchman are not of your blood. They are rich men who would betray ya with a shift in the wind. I don't trust war profiteers. Think on it hard, lad."

For the rest of the day, Dutch worked around the pub, thinking brightly about owning a trading post on the Columbia River. The scheme was appealing...but Sandy's warning also rang true. He hardly knew these Dutchmen, and Captain Jacobson was such a standoffish fellow that he wasn't sure he liked him. This would be a big decision, one that he wouldn't make lightly.

The pub closed early that wintery night. With Sandy upstairs in his apartment, Dutch sat at the kitchen table, watching Kate make cheese. It was a fascinating process. She churned the milk for a good long time and then piled the curds on a fabric she called cheesecloth. Then, taking the four corners of the cloth, she twisted it to form a large ball of wet curds. She hung this ball from the rafters over the stove, with a pan underneath to catch the dripping whey. After hanging the curds for the next few days in the warm kitchen, she would have a two- or three-pound hard ball of cheese.

Dutch had learned much from watching Kate cook. Her meals were simple, tasty and much better than his normal trail-grub. Much of her secret was the spices she used to bring out the flavors of simple foods. Now, watching her make cheese, his head filled with ideas of doing the same, out in the Oregon Country. Knowing that he would have no cows, he wondered if goat's milk could be used.

"I have a question," he said to Kate as she stood by the stove.

"About the Dutchman's offer?" she replied.

Dutch cocked his head to one side. "No. How do you know of his offer?"

"Sandy's like an old woman," Kate answered, with a smile on her face. "He told me the whole scheme before your guests were scarcely out the door. Are you going to take up their offer?"

Dutch was surprised that she knew so much. "I'm not sure. It sounds like a good enterprise, and the Commodore has renamed his ship the *Mary Rose*. I can't seem to get her out of my mind."

"That young lassie again! You are smitten with her," Kate replied, wiping her hands on her apron.

"Do you believe in love at first glance?"

Moving to the table, Kate took a chair and looked at Dutch in the lamp light for the longest moment. "Love comes in many ways. Sometimes it's fast, sometimes it takes years and it comes in many forms. For instance, there's the love Sandy and I have for you. We worry about the dangers of the journey before you." Kate reached across the table and grabbed Dutch's hands. "Stay here with us. You are of our family now. Then, one day, the right lass will come along, and you will have a family of your own."

Dutch felt Kathleen's love in her touch and saw it in her tired eyes. He had thought many times of such an option, but the New England countryside was just too small. He had to roam, and he was determined to find riches to equal that of Mary's family.

"You two are indeed my white family," Dutch replied squeezing her hands. "For this, I will always rejoice. But my Indian family also awaits, and their land is my future."

That night, when Dutch crawled into bed, his head was still swirling with thoughts of family, friends and his future. He knew not what the long, crooked trail ahead held for him, but he did know that his trek to the Pacific would be the biggest challenge of his young life. *I will fear not,* he mused *my father will guide me.*

Sure enough, during the night, his father whispered in his ear, "This venture be your destiny, son."

The Christening ————

During February, Dutch worked diligently on the supply list for Commodore Clarke. He and Sandy spent hours standing behind the bar, recalling all of the different trade goods they had seen in their travels. In the end, Dutch wrote down over two hundred trade items in a gray ledger book, along with estimated values in both otter and beaver skins. The goods listed included simple trinkets such as colorful beads, hand mirrors, fish hooks and small glass bottles. Anything that glittered would be cherished by the Indians. Then there were iron tools of all sizes and types, and cooking pots and pans. Also included were blankets and cloths of all textures and colors. Finally, there was tobacco and weapons; arrowheads, knives, swords, axes and flintlock rifles. The most unusual items were different colored porcelain chamber pots, which the Indians admired for carrying water, and strands of dyed rope that the squaws would use for binding their legs. Dutch thought about including some Bibles and other books, but since the Natives were illiterate, those would be foolish goods. But he did plan to bring bright colored paint pigments for decorating their canoes and other artifacts.

Dutch made a second detailed list in the book for his own personal needs. For these goods, the cost would be deducted from his profits. At the top of the list were building tools, window glass, construction supplies, gardening implements, seeds, a woodstove to ease the damp winters, and two hundred pounds of books to read on gray days. He also specified dry goods such as coffee, tea, flour, spices and sugar. For his personal use, there would be twenty-five gallons of brandy and whiskey, and fifty gallons more of wine and vinegar. Then, with thoughts of wild bird eggs on his mind, Dutch added two dozen hens, three roosters and two lengths of chicken netting to his list. Climbing slippery rocks for wild eggs would be only a memory in his past.

When it was finished, his list held nearly a hundred different items, and he knew that they would more than likely wipe out any profits he might make during that first year. But Dutch paid that thought no heed, as he was determined to have as many Boston luxuries as a ship's hull could carry.

The last thing he did was to make a copy of the map of the mouth of the Columbia River that he had drawn a few months back. The new parchment was as detailed as his original, and he carefully folded it and inserted it into the ledger. At the end of a few weeks of work, he was ready and anxiously looking forward to the first day of March.

The door to Dutch's bedroom was quietly opened, and through it walked a shadowy figure carrying a turned-down lamp. From the corner of the room came the dim flicker of last night's coal fire, dancing a pale light across the planks. The room was cool, and the floor creaked softly as the figure reached the foot of Dutch's bed. Slowly, fingers grasped the stem of the oil lamp and turned it up.

As the brighter light washed across the bed, King raised his head and blinked his sleepy eyes at the light.

Reaching down, the figure shook one of Dutch's blanketed feet and said softly, "It's time."

At a second shake to his foot, Dutch mumbled something, then moved his leg away from the touch.

"It's time, Dutch," Kate said more loudly.

His eyes slowly opened, and he stared down the bed at the glow. "Time for what?" he finally asked in a drowsy voice.

"Time for you to learn how to make sourdough biscuits," she replied.

"What time is it?"

"Five," Kate answered.

"Five in the morning?" Dutch responded, his sleepy eyes now fully alive. "Why the hell are we getting up at this hour?"

"I get up every morning at this hour," Kate answered. "You say you love my biscuits, but I've never showed you how to make 'em. So this morning I will... and I'll give you some other tips on wilderness cooking, as well."

By now, Dutch had sat up in bed and was shaking his head in disbelief. "It's too damn early, Kate. We'll do it another time."

"Nay," she replied firmly. "Get your clothes on, lad, and join me in the kitchen. With the Lord's blessing, another day is upon us."

When Dutch and King came downstairs, they could see the faint light of a beckoning morning in the bar room. When Dutch opened the back door, the dog rushed out for the bushes while Dutch turned for the kitchen. "There's no coffee on," he said, surprised, as he entered the dark little room.

"Aye," Kate answered. "Getting the biscuits going comes first."

With a small fire burning in her stove and two lamps glowing, Kate explained how to use starter dough to mix up a new batch of biscuits.

"What's the starter dough for?" Dutch asked, while smelling a pungent bowl half covered with cheesecloth.

"It's the sour in the sourdough. This batch was originally my mother's, many years ago. I'll make up another starter from it for you to take west. See that dark liquid on top of the dough? It's called the hooch. It's alcohol produced from the fermenting dough. Taste it."

Dutch dabbed his finger in the liquid and tasted it. "Aye," he said with a smile. "Not as good as whiskey, but on a cold morning it could get you going."

Kate soon had all the ingredients mixed together, then rolled the dough into small balls the size of an egg. These she placed inside a deep skillet with an iron lid. Setting the pan aside on the stove to rise, she started making the coffee.

The making of Kate's sourdough biscuits was a fascinating process, and Dutch was soon asking a stream of questions about the different ingredients used. He had never heard of baking powder or baking soda, and was curious as to their use and purpose. Kate answered his questions and then explained at length about the importance of using lard, bacon grease and animal fats in preparing trail foods.

"If you make only one hardy meal a day, make it the morning meal. And, whenever possible, use your fat drippings. It be good for your system and it'll keep ye healthy."

Over the next few weeks, Kate offered Dutch many more such pointers on frontier cuisine. She taught him simple recipes for cooking with rice and beans, and for using wild plants such as onions, certain roots and seasonal fruits. Kate also promised to put together a small trail sack of the cooking spices and ingredients he would need on his trek across the continent.

During this time, they also seasoned and dried fifty pounds of venison for the first few weeks of his journey. After that point, Dutch hoped to be in buffalo country, where he could jerk bison meat.

These early morning culinary lessons were enjoyed by both teacher and pupil. Even Sandy and King loved them, as they got to sample the many meals that Kate and Dutch cooked together.

When the first of March finally came, Dutch stood looking at himself with displeasure in the bar mirror. He was dressed in his store-bought clothes, with his new trail boots and bowler hat, but his swarthy skin looked somewhat paler and his face was puffy from months of Kathleen's rich foods. He had bathed and shaved and pressed his clothes, but nothing could disguise his winter doldrums. He longed for spring and for the activity that would come with being on a trail again.

When Sandy came down from his apartment, he was dressed in a blue waistcoat, brown britches and a black tricorne hat. On his feet were his sea boots, and on his hip was Dutch's Christmas gift. He, too, looked pale and out of sorts from the long winter.

As the friends stood at the bar, Dutch poured two whiskeys.

Raising his glass Sandy said, "Here's to March, mate. She came in somewhat like a lamb, may she only improve."

"Aye," Dutch replied, "and may spring be on her heels."

From the kitchen, Kate joined them with a smile and slowly looked them over. "You be a dashing pair, but one more dashing than the other," she said, with a wink to Sandy.

"Aye." He smiled back. "Grab your book, lad. We better bustle or we'll be late."

As Dutch and Sandy walked out the door, Kate shouted across the room, "You boys play nice with the rich folks. I'll want to hear all the news."

The first day of March was cloudy and cool, with a threat of rain. As they walked down the street towards the docks, Dutch swore he could smell the first rich fragrances of Spring, but Sandy told him, with a smile, that the scent was just his bath oils.

It was only a short distance to the wharf. When they arrived they found a large crowd milling around Pier Five. There, rising up from the planks, was the newly refurbished brigantine. She was sleek and beautiful, freshly painted from the waterline to the crow's nest. Her rigging was full of colorful banners and the flags of both America and Holland. On her bow, scrolled in white lettering with gold relief, was her new name: *Mary Rose*.

As they walked the dock alongside the ship, Sandy compared her to the sloop *Lady Washington*.

"She be about 100 feet and 20 abeam. I'd put her at nearly 150 tons," he said, with a fondness in his voice. "She'll be fast, just like the *Lady*, and easy to maneuver in foul weather. This be a fine ship with a bright future."

In the crowd next to the gangway, they bumped into Miss Becky, who introduced them to her husband, Robert Hanson, the rich Boston merchant. He was a friendly, middle-aged bloke with a firm handshake and bright eyes. They talked for a few moments about the brigantine, and he pointed out several details of her construction. Then, from the bow a band started playing.

Dutch and Sandy strolled back through the hordes to witness the christening. From the wharf, they listened to Commodore Clarke give a short speech. He was an impressive looking gent, in his blue naval uniform with gold bars and stripes. The Commodore talked of trade, a shrinking youthful world, and the blessings of his new ship. Then they watched as the Commodore, Captain Jacobson and Mary Rose crashed a wine jug across the ship's bow. Seeing Mary again, Dutch's stomach turned to mush. Finally, as the visitors applauded, the Commodore invited everyone aboard for refreshments.

Once on deck, they found food and drink under a sail canopy. The food was lavish and the wine plentiful, all served by sailors in clean, bright uniforms. As Sandy and Dutch stood drinking the wine and watching a fiddler play, Mary Rose pushed through the crowd and joined them.

With a thick tongue and a racing heart, Dutch introduced her to Sandy. She was a beautiful sight, wearing a spring straw bonnet and a pale green dress with a black shawl around her creamy shoulders.

Shyly, she reached into her small purse and handed a coin to Dutch. "Papa had a few of these commemoratives struck, and I'd like you to have one."

The bronze coin showed the ship and date on one side and her image etched on the other. Dutch, initially speechless, recovered enough to say, "I will cherish it always."

They heard the sound of the Commodore's voice as he pushed through the visitors. Mary glanced toward him and then back to Dutch with an impish look on her face, "Quirky hat and all, you intrigue me, sir. I hope our paths cross again, someday."

Then, with Dutch still grasping the coin, and her sweet words swirling in his head, she turned and walked away.

Over the sounds of the music, Sandy quietly said, "She be a fine lady, Dutch. I now understand why she has beguiled you."

As the Commodore approached them, he said in a firm voice, "Shall we meet in the Captain's cabin? Was that Mary you were talking with, Dutch? What did she give you?"

Dutch showed him the coin in his palm.

With a sour look, the Commodore replied, "I saw how you looked at her at lunch, and now she gives you a gift. I remind you, sir, she is just fifteen."

Dutch was surprised by the rebuke, and wanted to tell him that, in the Indian culture, she would already be with child. But he didn't. Instead he said, "And I remind you, sir, I will be living on the other side of the world from Mary."

"Aye." He smiled. "Let's join the Captain in his cabin."

Just below the quarterdeck and down a dark passage, they found the Captain's sea cabin. It was a large stateroom for a brigantine, with freshly painted bulkheads and aft windows with a good view of the harbor. Unlike most ship's compartments, it smelled fresh, with many personal possessions scattered about. One such item, a small oval portrait of Mary, hung over his bunk. Dutch wanted to comment on it, but he didn't.

The Captain sat at his chart desk, with a Pacific coast map rolled out. Standing, he invited his three guests to chairs he had arranged in front of his desk. Then he poured out four small glasses of brandy and passed them around.

"Here's to the *Mary Rose*," he said with pride. "May she always find safe passage."

"Aye, aye," the men answered with glasses raised.

After finishing his drink, the Captain slumped back in his chair and turned to Dutch. "Well, lad, have ye thought about our offer?"

"Aye, and I've decided to join this venture. With your ships and trade goods and my knowledge of the Indians, this scheme can be profitable for all."

"Bloody good show," the Commodore responded, with an outstretched hand.

After shaking the old man's hand, Dutch did the same across the desk with the Captain. Then, after removing the map from the ledger, he laid the gray book on the desk.

"The first dozen pages are trade goods with estimated values in pelts. The next five pages are a list of my special needs."

The Captain opened the ledger and leafed through the entries. While he was doing this, Dutch turned to the Commodore and handed him the folded map.

"I drew this map of the mouth of the Columbia River from my personal memory and the charts of Captains Gray and Vancouver. I used both English and native names in my descriptions."

The Commodore unfolded the map and studied it for a few moments. Then he handed the map across to the Captain and took the ledger into his hands. The cabin went silent for a few more moments, except for the sounds of the topside soiree and the creaking of the ship's timbers.

"You need a blacksmith shop and a copper still?" the Commodore finally asked.

"Aye," Dutch replied.

Looking up from the map, Eric said, "Thought you were against trading whiskey with the Indians?"

"It's not for spirits," Dutch replied. "It's to distill sea water for sea salt."

"Sea salt?" Sandy asked with a curious look.

"Aye, only fools find salvation in animal hides, as they will soon be depleted. Long ago, a Tillamook told me his land had more trees than stars in the sky, and more fish in the rivers than grains of sand. That is the future. I have the notion of shipping back casts of salted salmon. If the fish can make that long journey without spoiling, and if you can find a market in Europe for Pacific Salmon, we will add to our profits."

The Commodore smiled. "I knew ye to be a lad of great enterprise."

With Captain Jacobson still studying the map, he asked many questions about bar conditions and entering the river, so Dutch got up from his chair and moved behind his desk to point out a few details.

"From what I have read, both Gray and Vancouver heaved to, a few miles off Point Adams. Then they sent out longboats to mark the channel before they crossed. The depths they found were from twelve to twenty fathoms. With winds from the west or southwest, they then came about, heading for the north-head, and crossed the Bar on a slack tide. Once they were a half mile from Cape Hancock, they bore to the southeast and followed the deep water of the river's southern shoreline. Hopefully, that is where I will be." Dutch pointed to a large bay some ten miles up-river. "Captain Vancouver named this inlet Young's Bay. This is the land I hope to buy from the Clatsops."

"You remember all these details from books?" a surprised Captain asked, looking up at Dutch.

"Aye," Sandy said quickly with pride on his face. "The lad has total recall from the books he reads."

"Nay, it's not quite total," Dutch added with humility in his voice.

The Captain was surprised by this savvy. "Is this some quirk of nature?"

"My father had the same ability. He told me it was God-given," Dutch replied.

"Aye," the Commodore said with a strange look on his face. "I have much the same talent, although my recall is for only maps and charts."

Dutch and the Commodore's eyes met for a moment, and they blinked their mutual respect.

For another hour, the four men talked of the expedition. Finally, Captain Jacobson filled the brandy glasses again and they made a final toast to their new venture.

When finished with the drink, Captain Jacobson extended his hand one final time and said, "One of our ships will find you on the Columbia River next spring, Dutch."

Dutch returned his hand clasp and replied, "If the Stony Mountains don't swallow me up, and if the Indians don't get my scalp, I'll be there. But aren't you forgetting something?"

"What's that?" the Commodore asked, wide-eyed.

"Twenty dollars and a Dutch flag," he answered with a grin on his lips.

IV
Virgin Country

—‹‹‹—

For thousands of years, the salmon had returned to the rivers to spawn, and the elk had multiplied in the endless forest of the Pacific coast. Here too, the Indians had flourished in perfect harmony with Mother Nature. Then the first European ship touched the wilderness shore, and began trading trinkets with the Natives. That first contact would change the history of this land forever. In the decades that followed, many other nations came and laid claim to portions of the Oregon Country, including early voyagers from Spain, Portugal, England and Holland. Then, the overland trappers and traders arrived from Canada and Russia. For a time, all of these nations believed they had dominion over the Pacific Northwest. Then the fledging Americans came.

On his first trip around Cape Horn, Captain Robert Gray discovered Tillamook Bay in 1788. On his second trip, in 1792, this black-eye-patched captain discovered and named Grays Harbor. A few days later, he found, named and charted part of the mighty Columbia River. Gray's early discoveries would later be used as proof that America had the only legitimate claim to the Oregon Country.

In 1804, the American President Thomas Jefferson, sent the Lewis & Clark Corps of Discovery across the continent. This band of brave men would winter at Fort Clatsop on the Pacific coast in 1806. When the expedition returned home in 1807 and published journals about their adventures, their words sparked the imagination of many American schemers and dreamers. Soon, the wilderness west of the Mississippi River filled with explorers and trappers, who prospered at the inland fur trade. Some of these mountain men climbed the Stony Mountains and walked all the way to the Pacific shore. Along the way they built log forts, homes and trading posts. But still, other nations challenged America's claim to the Pacific Northwest.

It would take another war, a few quirks of fate and a second expedition across the continent to finally resolve these disputes. This second enterprise would come to be called the Astor Overland Expedition or Overland Astorians. One would have to dig deep into American history to find another journey so fraught with drama, hardship and stubborn heroism.

Astor's original plan was to dispatch a thirty-man brigade of trappers and traders from St. Louis in the spring of 1810. These men would paddle up the Missouri River and cross the continent, following the Lewis & Clark trail. While these men trudged across the wilderness, Astor would send a ship, the *Tonquin,* around the Horn to meet up with the overland brigade on the Columbia River in the spring of 1811.

The expedition faced delays from the very beginning. First Astor had to form the Pacific Fur Company, of which his wholly owned American Fur Company held half of the shares. Ownership of the remaining half of the company was divided among working partners who made up the core of the expedition. Some of these partners, like Wilson Price Hunt, Donald Mackenzie and Ramsey Cook, would travel overland. Other partners, including Duncan McDougall and Alexander MacKay, traveled aboard the *Tonquin.* Astor and his partners spent many months selecting, purchasing and outfitting the *Tonquin,* and making preparations for the expedition. It wasn't until July of 1810 that the overland partners reached Montreal, Canada – which, at that time, was the center of the fur trade – to begin recruiting men for the journey.

Their competition, the Hudson Bay and the Northwest Fur Companies, stifled their efforts for weeks. Finally, near summer's end, they succeeded in forming a brigade of hunters, trappers, interpreters and Canadian *voyageurs*. After a change of leadership, this troop of men finally reached St. Louis in September, where a fateful decision was made to double the size of the brigade to sixty men. While some of the partners traveled off to secure the new men, other partners paddled and poled the original brigade up the Missouri River, four hundred and fifty miles to the confluence of the Nodaway River. There, away from the temptations of St. Louis, the men would winter, living off the land and awaiting reinforcements.

—\\\\\—

Horse Whisperer ————

With a head full of fantasies about his trading post and the bitter realities of an amorous future, Dutch returned to the Sea Witch after the christening of the *Mary Rose*. Once there, he drilled a small hole in the commemorative coin Mary had given him. Then, with a length of rawhide, he fastened the bronze plug around his neck and admired it in the bar room mirror. Her gift symbolized what could have been, and he pledged to wear the trinket as a fond reflection.

Early the next morning, he stood at the bar and wrote out a letter to Astor in New York City. The short message stated that he agreed to join the brigade crossing the continent, and that he would be in Saint Louis no later than the end of May to join up with the expedition. At the bottom of his note, he simply wrote, 'I await further instructions here in Boston.'

After posting the letter, Dutch waited patiently for the Spaniard to come into the pub for his noon meal. When he arrived, Dutch had a tankard of ale on his table before he found his way onto the chair.

"I'll need my mounts and trail supplies by the end of the month. I want to be in Saint Louis by May. Will this be a problem?" Dutch asked, with excitement in his voice.

As Tony came to rest, he looked up at the lad with a smile. "Ye seem awful jumpy, Dutch. Got cabin fever? April be a rainy month for travel."

"Aye, I've got the fever. My nose smells spring, and my feet want to beat it out of Boston. So, rain or shine, I'm going to leave." Dutch pulled out a chair and sat down across from the Spaniard. "I have a confession. I be not much of a horseman. In truth, the idea of riding horseback across the territory scares the hell out of me. Could ye give me some instruction?"

Tony took a long pull on his flagon, then wiped his mouth. "I be the wrong bloke to teach ya buckarooin'. I be skillful with teams, not single mounts. But I do have a young lad that works for me who's a real wrangler. His name is Henry and for a little money, I'm sure he'd teach ya some finer points of equitation."

"Where and when?" Dutch asked

"I'll select a couple of good horses for you, this week. Then I'll have Henry bring them and your trail gear around to the warehouse stables, early come Saturday morning. How will that be?"

"Just fine," Dutch replied while he retrieved a piece of parchment from his pocket. "Here's a list of other goods I'll be needing. Can ye provide these supplies?"

The Spaniard read the short list with one eyebrow raised. "Why twenty gallons of molasses? That be nearly eighty pounds for your packhorse."

"I want to make spruce beer to trade with the Indians, and my father always used molasses."

Tony shook his head slowly. "Way too much weight. Take twenty pounds of Jamaican sugar. It comes in five-pound watertight tins. Less burden on the trail and better sugar for your brew."

"Aye," Dutch conceded, and watched the Spaniard read farther down the list.

"Two bucksaws. What size?" Tony asked without glancing up.

"Four-foot rip and three-foot cross, without the frames."

"Four muskets? New ones cost near twenty-five dollars each," Tony said, looking up from the list. "I've got an uncle who's a gunsmith. He rebuilds used flintlocks and sells them for about twelve dollars each. Is that a problem?"

"Nay, not if they're trustworthy and well-mended."

"His muskets be better than new," Tony answered, folding the list into his pocket. "Take me a week or so to fill the order. Don't see no problems. Now, if you buy me another tankard, I'll tell ya how to get to Saint Louis from here."

The Spaniard's plan was clear enough. Dutch was to book passage on a livestock schooner to Philadelphia, then ride the Old Fort Pitt Road west for three hundred miles to the little village of Pittsburg. There he could buy passage on a flat-bottom keelboat and float down the Ohio River. About nine hundred miles down this flow, on the west side of the confluence of the Ohio and Mississippi Rivers, he would find the Missouri country. A hundred fifty miles north of this point was the frontier town of Saint Louis.

"I hear the place has grown since I was last there," Tony said, with a second draft of ale in his hand. "But it still ain't much. Full of breeds and scallywags, so watch your backside."

Early the next Saturday morning, Dutch and King walked down to the Spaniard's dockside freight company. Behind the red brick warehouse, they found a barn with a small outside corral. There, standing and talking in the morning sun, were Tony and a young lad. Tied to the rail next to them were two tall steeds. The larger one was light gray in color, while the smaller one was a chestnut.

"Good morning," Tony greeted Dutch warmly from within the corral.

Dutch opened a wooden gate, and he and King entered the arena and walked over to the two men.

"Like ya to meet Henry Adams. He be my top wrangler," Tony said.

As the two men clasped hands, Dutch apprised the lad's lanky string-bean body and youthful face. He looked to be just in his late teens, with his long legs already bowed.

"Fine-lookin' hat, Dutch. Sounds like you be off for quite an adventure," Henry said, with a firm grip and friendly face.

King didn't stop for a moment but went directly over to the horses and started to sniff around. Soon, the big gray shook its head and let out a loud whinny.

"Back off there," Dutch shouted to the dog.

King looked up at his master and then backed away.

The three men talked a few moments and then moved closer to the horses.

With pride on his face and a hand on the rump of the big gray, Tony said, "Both Henry and I think these mounts be perfect for your journey. The gray here is named Scout. He's a ten-year-old gelding, part Quarter Horse and part Appaloosa. That makes him fast and sure-footed. I bought him a few years back. He didn't take well to the harness, but he's perfect for you. Scout can easily carry twice your weight across the heartland."

"He can be a little stubborn," Henry added. "But if he trusts ya, he'll go the extra mile."

Scout was a fine-looking horse, standing almost seventeen hands tall. While his body was mostly light gray, he had midnight ears and mane, and a flowing tail. He also had small black spots on his rump.

Tony moved to the chestnut. "This be Willow. She's a twelve-year-old mare from a bloodline called Irish Draught. She be bred as a packhorse and is docile yet strong. And once you get to where you're goin', ye can slip a harness on her and she'll plow your fields for years to come. We used her for delivering mail out to the frontier, but we lost that contract, last year."

She was a beautiful animal with a chestnut coat that glistened in the sun. She had a white star and blaze on her face, and four white-stocking feet. Her flaxen mane and tail were of a lighter color, and she stood over fifteen hands tall.

"Willow can carry three hundred pounds all day long," Henry added.

Dutch was impressed with the horseflesh. He walked around both animals, checking their teeth and feet, and the clearness of their eyes.

"These be fine animals," he finally said. "I be pleased with your selection."

"Good," Tony answered. "I'm going to leave you two mates alone so Henry can give you some pointers. All your trail gear is inside the barn. By next Saturday, I should have all your trade goods. But I purchased no foodstuffs. That you'll have to do, yourself."

"No problem," Dutch answered. "How long do you reckon it will take me to get to Saint Louis?"

Tony thought for a moment. "A good four weeks, anyhow. I'd take six or eight weeks' worth of grub."

Dutch and Henry spent the rest of the day going over the many details of riding and caring for horses on a wilderness trail. Much of what he learned was new, while other pointers brought back memories of his father's horse, Amber. When he was a younker, he had ridden her many times, back on Skunk Creek. He remembered her being as gentle as spring rain. But that had been when he was just a boy. Now the horses at hand were big and strong, with notions of their own.

He had much to learn, and Henry proved to be the perfect teacher. With eyes as bright as his mind, he spoke slowly, as deliberate as his tall, lanky body. And Dutch absorbed his instruction like water to dry sand.

With a length of straw in his mouth, Henry walked around both mounts, pointing out their strengths and weakness. Then he looked Dutch straight in the eye and said, "Your horse be life itself, so care for it first in the morning and last at night."

Next, Henry tacked up both horses, using different kinds of bits, reins and harnesses. Then he showed Dutch how to saddle Scout, using a deep leather seat with a large horn on the front, quite different from the Spanish saddle Dutch had used as a boy. Willow got a pack saddle, and Henry talked at length about always balancing the weight of her burden.

Then Henry had Dutch mount Scout and ride him around the corral. It had been years since he was last in the saddle, and he felt awkward as hell. Finally, Henry shouted for him to stop.

"You're not riding a log. Your horse posture is frightful," he said, approaching Dutch and Scout. Standing next to them he began adjusting the saddle. "Your stirrups are too long. I'll shorten them up a few inches, until your legs are bent forward more. Hold the reins in front of the horn, not to the rear. When you want Scout to turn, use the reins and knee pressure to tell him which direction. And keep your back straight and your head up. Above all else, relax in the saddle. You're only along for the ride."

Dutch looked down at the kid adjusting the second stirrup. "It's been long time since I last sat in a saddle."

"I can tell," Henry replied, looking up with a good-natured smile. "Let your stirrups and legs do the work. At the end of the day, if your legs are sore, you rode with good posture. At the end of the day, if your butt or back is sore, you rode with crappy horse posture. Now try it again."

Henry stepped back, and Dutch rode again around the corral. This they did for the next three hours, with Henry shouting out pointers, tips and criticism. Eventually, Dutch had improved his posture and was feeling better about both himself and his mounts.

Finally, Henry waved his hand. "Enough!"

Dismounting, Dutch led Scout over to where Henry waited.

"You're getting the notion, Dutch, but learn to trust your horse."

"My worry," Dutch admitted, "is that Scout won't obey my commands."

Henry walked to the front of his horse and took his long nose into his gloved hands. Then, looking the animal straight in the eye, he answered, "That won't happen if he trusts ya. Take no whip to him. Be gentle but firm. And show no fear. He will see it in your eyes and hear it in your voice. When he does act up, whisper in his ears. He'll understand."

"Wish I had your confidence."

"You will," Henry answered with a broad smile, "by the time you reach trail's end."

The next week, Dutch and the dog went to the stables every day, and took each horse out for a short ride. With King watching from a bale of hay, he groomed them both, fed them and cleaned out their stalls. At first, Scout showed some aggression towards the dog, while Willow paid him no heed. After a few days, however, the two animals finally bonded, adopting a live-and-let-live attitude. By the end of the first week, some of Dutch's fears had waned, and he could finally envision himself riding across the continent.

At the stables, on the second Saturday, Henry gave Dutch a pair of rusty old spurs he had found in the tack room.

"These been collecting dust around here for years, so you take'em," he said in his good-natured way. "While I put little faith in the whip, I reckon a little heel prodding will get Scout's attention."

Then they loaded up both horses with all their gear and rode them out to the countryside, where Henry taught Dutch the finer points of horse commands and leading a packhorse on narrow switch-back trails. At noon, they stopped for lunch, and Dutch learned how to use a picket-line to secure his animals at night. Then, with the horses hobbled and grazing in a nearby field, Henry and Dutch went fishing in a small brook. Soon, they were seated around a campfire, cooking two fat trout Indian-style.

"A few years back," Henry said, with his fish on a stick over the flames, "I met an Irishman named Sullivan. He had come to Boston to train some horses. We became mates and I learned a lot from him."

Looking up from his fish, Dutch asked, "Like what?"

"Horse whispering," Henry replied in his hay-seed way. "It's a way of talking to your horse. Old Sullivan believed that horses aren't just one-trick ponies, that they have feelings, and can reason things out. He said the worst thing a fellow can do is take a whip to his horse, while the best thing is to stand real close and whisper in their ear."

Dutch pulled his fish from the flames and took a bite. "Sounds like old Sullivan was telling ya squaws' tales. What kind of words can a horse understand?"

"I know it sounds a little farfetched, since a horse's brain is only the size of a man's fist," Henry answered, eating his fish, "but its heart can weigh nine pounds, so keep it in mind, Dutch. Scout be a smart gelding with sensitive feels, so use his ears to build your trust."

Over the smoke and flames, Dutch watched Henry eat his fish, and he wondered at the young lad's words about horse whispering. Could old Sullivan be right? Well, he'd have over three thousand miles to figure that fable out.

On their ride back to the city, Henry continued to spout horse facts Dutch had never heard before, like a horse's ear is always pointing to where they were looking, and that, in a single day, a horse could drink up to ten gallons of water and shit up to fourteen times. But the most fascinating tidbit was that a horse only needed two hours of sleep a day, and most of the time they slept standing up!

"Where did you learn all this horse wisdom?" Dutch finally asked.

With a look of pride, Henry replied, "My pappy had me in the stirrups when I was just a younker. Guess the saddle has always been my home."

When they reached the city, they stopped off at John Cornwall's blacksmith shop and got both mounts freshly shod. The smithy also made a second pair of horseshoes for the trail. The cost was near ten dollars. Then they rode to the Sea Witch so Dutch could drop off his food trail pack and show off his steeds to Kathleen and Sandy. Standing in front of the tavern, they seemed impressed with the sheer size of his animals and the amount of gear he was taking on his journey.

"Ships be a better way of travel," Sandy said while inspecting Scout. "But I'll give them this – the wagon rests in winter, the sleigh in summer, but the horse never."

Henry gave Sandy a strange look. "I'll remember that line. You horse savvy?"

"Nay." Sandy smiled. "It's an old saying from China. I heard it many years ago. Come on inside, lads. I'll buy ya a drink."

Fond Farewells ————————

The following Monday, when the Spaniard came in for his noon meal, he brought along a detailed accounting for his services. Dutch had expected as much, and sat quietly at his table, reading the columns of items and numbers. The total cost at the bottom of the page glared up at him like a sunrise: $349.52, half of which was for the horses, saddles and all their tack. The other half of the expenses were for trail and trading supplies. This amount would wipe out all the remaining money he had earned from Astor, and most of his father's two hundred dollar legacy.

"My prices are fair and I provided only good horse flesh and a top line outfit," Tony said, watching Dutch read the list.

"How much do you figure it will cost to get to Philadelphia?" Dutch asked, looking up from the paper with numbers spinning in his head.

"This morning, I booked you passage on the livestock schooner *York*. She will sail with the morning tide on April first. It be a working ship, and berths were hard to come by, so I got ya three stalls. You and the dog will have to sleep in one. I've included the cost at the bottom of the page."

"How long is the passage?" Dutch asked.

"Two or three days. Sorry about sleeping in the stalls, but I couldn't even get ya a crew berth."

Dutch smiled at Tony, shaking his head. "Should be a robust trip, with a hull full of animals. Well, at least I'll be movin' in the right direction."

"Did ye see the muskets my uncle sent? They look like fine rifles to me."

"Aye, I fired them yesterday. Good action and fine workmanship."

Dutch returned his attention to the accounting and Tony watched again, slurping his brew.

Finally Dutch put the paper down and looked across to the Spaniard. "What do you figure it will cost to float down the Ohio?"

Tony noticed the concerned expression on Dutch's face. "A twenty-dollar gold piece should do it. You look worried, mate. Is it something I did?"

"Nay," Dutch quickly responded. "You did a fine job, Tony. Thank you. And while the costs are more than I thought, your wares and sound wisdom are worth every penny."

"If you're short on coin lad, I can lend you some until next we meet," the Spaniard said, with kindness in his voice.

"You're a good man Tony," Dutch replied, getting to his feet. "Thanks for the notion, but that won't be necessary. My money is upstairs. I'll be right back."

Once the Spaniard was paid and out the door, Dutch worked the remaining lunch crowd with his thoughts fixated on money. Finally, in the late afternoon, he stood behind the bar and counted out the remaining coins from his poke. He had two Spanish twenty-dollar gold pieces and three Continental dollars. His mind reeled at the meagerness of that forty-three dollars.

That's when he remembered his tip mug, under the bar. Often, when he played his flute for the late-night drinkers, they would leave him small coins in a chipped coffee mug. Now, taking the cup from under the bar, he poured out the contents. When he counted it up, it came to another $5.40.

He stared silently at the money on the counter top. Tony had said that it would cost twenty dollars to get downriver, and he would spend a similar amount on trial food. That meant that he would cross the continent with just nine dollars in his purse.

The sight of his shiny impoverishment on the bar top set him back on his heels. Quickly, his mind filled with worries over possible costs for the remaining trail supplies.

The sound of the kitchen door swinging open startled Dutch back to reality, and he looked over to find Sandy joining him behind the bar.

"Did you pay off the Spaniard?" Sandy asked, pouring himself a whiskey.

"Aye," Dutch answered, "Near three hundred and fifty dollars' worth."

Sandy stared down at the coins on the countertop, "That be a sizable sum," he replied while taking a sip of his dram. "Is that money on the bar what remains of your poke?"

With a sour face, Dutch answered, "Aye, just forty nine dollars separates me from poverty, but I reckon, where I'm goin', money's not worth spit."

Sandy put his arm around his friend's shoulder. "Money be like a good woman, lad. When ya have one, you don't appreciate her. When you're without, you long to have her sleeping next to you again."

Dutch looked at his mate with a grin and reminded himself that Sandy was the best damn barroom philosopher in Boston.

As Dutch scooped up the coins, Sandy added, "You've got a letter from New York City. I put it on your nightstand."

With his purse in hand, Dutch bolted upstairs and was soon reading the short note Astor had sent:

When you arrive at Saint Louis seek out the trader Wilson Price Hunt.

He is one of my partners and he will be leading the brigade west. Tell him you are my hire, and that the market for beaver remains strong. May this enterprise bring good luck for all.

John Astor

That evening, after the pub was closed, the three friends sat around the kitchen table, talking of the day's events. While Dutch drank a glass of milk and ate a freshly baked cookie, he showed them the accounting he had paid Tony.

"The horse flesh wasn't cheap, but I trust Scout and Willow to get me there," Dutch said in the glow of the oil lamp.

"They be fine horses," Sandy replied in his pitched voice, "but I still believe a good ship would be a better way of travel."

"It's not for us to say, Brother," Kate said, pouring herself a mug of coffee.

"My mistake was buying the four rifles," Dutch said, with the last of the sugar cake in his mouth. "They cost near fifty dollars, and burdened my packhorse by more than forty pounds."

"There's no wrong in it, lad. You told me the rifles would be worth many pelts out west?" Sandy said.

"Aye," Dutch replied, "I'd hoped to buy some Indian land with the flintlocks."

"Then don't look back, mate. What's done is done," Sandy replied.

"Your ship sails on Sunday?" Kate asked, with a sad face and a wrinkled nose.

"Aye," Dutch answered, finishing his glass of milk, "April first."

Kate reached across the table with the hem of her apron in hand. "Well, I've got your Bear Box packed, and I've cooked you up some trail food," she said, wiping the milk mustache from Dutch's upper lip. "You want to see it?"

"Sure."

Kate moved into the shadows of the storeroom and came back carrying a large, heavy canvas pack, which she lifted to the table top with a *thud*. Untying the strips, she pulled open the top of the pack. Inside was a wooden box, three feet long, two feet deep and two foot wide. Unlatching its lid, she opened the box and held the oil lamp high over the container.

Dutch stood to look inside, and found a treasure trove of tightly pack foodstuffs.

"You've got about ten pounds of venison jerky," Kate said, pointing to a muslin bag on one side of the box. "There are also small bags of flour, coffee, sugar, rice and beans. Underneath, you'll find a few jars of my chutney and jams and other cooking ingredients." Moving her finger to the other side of the box, she continued, "Over here is a bag of corn dodgers. My husband loved my corn biscuits.

There's also a tin of lard, a tin of sourdough, some cheese and a bag of apples, for both you and your horses. And I've even found room in one corner for my last bottle of good Spanish brandy. Drink it only on special occasions. Sunday morning, I'll add a slab of bacon, and some fresh biscuits." In the flickering lamp light, she finally closed the lid and turned to Dutch, her face glowing with pride. "The Bear Box weighs about forty-five pounds, but Willow can handle it. She be like me, strong and willing. This should get you to Saint Louis, lad. After that, you're on your own."

Dutch had stood with his mouth wide open while Kate rattled off all she had packed for his trail. He had not expected such gifts, or such caring.

Searching for the right words he finally stammered, "You overwhelm me with your generosity. I'm lost for words."

Standing, Sandy added, "Take some jugs of whisky from the barroom for your saddle bags, as well. They'll help pass the cold nights." Then he reached into his pocket and handed Dutch a small stack of gold coins. "And here's a hundred dollars, from the both of us. A man needs some jingle in his purse."

The room fell silent for the longest moment. Dutch stared at his friends, overcome with emotion. "You've done so much," he finally said in a choked voice. "You took me in for the winter, let me share your family and taught me things more valuable than life itself. No... you do too much. I can't take your hard-earned money."

"We ain't asking, Dutch," Kate said, with love written all over her face. "As Sandy once told you, I'm the kind of gal that gets my way."

With watery eyes, Dutch hugged both of his friends and held them tightly. Then he said in a soft, cracking voice, "If a man is measured by the friends he keeps, then I be the tallest man is Boston. God bless you both."

The next day, Dutch bought his remaining foodstuffs, along with ten pounds of tobacco and a bag of rock candy. When he returned to the Sea Witch, his poke still had hundred and twenty nine dollars in it.

He thought long and hard about this money. Along his journey, he might well run into highwaymen, Indians or other hooligans out to rob him. So he took a single Spanish twenty-dollar gold piece and concealed it inside his boot. Now, if needed, he'd have some security to fall back upon.

The Saturday night before Dutch's departure, many of his daytime customers stopped by to say their fare-thee wells. Vergil Hampton, the bee man and John Cornwall, the blacksmith, both came to the pub and raised their mug for Dutch to have a safe journey. Then there was the Spaniard and his wrangler, Henry, who came in and sat with Dutch for over an hour, raising their glasses and talking trail tips.

"Will you meet me tomorrow morning at the stable and help me get Scout and Willow aboard the schooner?" Dutch asked Henry.

"Aye," he replied, mug in hand. "I'll be there an hour after sunrise."

Dutch reached into his poke, brought out five Continental dollars, and gave Henry the coins. "This be for the time you spent teaching me buckarooin'. You're a good wrangler and I wish I had your horse-sense."

Henry's eyes got big as a full moon as he held a half-month's wages in the palm of his hand. "Thanks, Dutch. You're more than generous," he said, clutching the money. "Scout and Willow will get ya there. Along the way, just keep whispering in their ears."

Tony said, "I've got something for you, Dutch," and reached into his pouch. He then laid a ten-inch narrow wooden box on the table.

Dutch picked it up and opened the lid. Inside he found a small leather and brass spyglass.

"Bought that glass off a drunken sailor, right here in the Sea Witch, reckon he fleeced it from his ship. It's small enough for your saddle bags but powerful enough to see many miles ahead. It'll be handy on the trail."

Dutch was surprised and pleased with the gift. The spyglass had been made in England of the finest brass and optical glass. This was indeed a good addition to his journey, and he thanked the Spaniard with a second round of drinks.

The only regular customer, who didn't come in, that night, was old Doc Bates. John Cornwall had heard that he was doing poorly, and Dutch was saddened by that news. He liked the good doctor, and wished him well with a tip of his glass and a silent prayer.

Later that night, when only a few hard drinkers remained in the pub, the front door opened and in walked a lady, wearing a floppy straw bonnet and a winter coat with the collar raised. The pub went silent, all of the customers watching her walk across the room.

Sandy rushed from behind the bar for what Dutch expected would be a loud, profane rebuke and a hustle out the door. Instead, he quickly showed her to a shadowed booth at the back of the pub. With all the patrons staring, Sandy lit the candle on the table, and they talked for a few moments. Then, as he returned to the bar, he shouted to the room, "We'll be closing in ten minutes. Drink up mates!"

Dutch looked at the clock in surprise; it was just before ten. Sandy never closed that early on a Saturday night.

"The lady in the booth would like to see ya, Dutch," Sandy said, returning to his place behind the bar.

"Who is she?"

"Go find out. She won't bite."

As Dutch approached her booth, the lady removed her hat exposing her face and blond hair. It was Miss Becky.

"I've came to say farewell," she said to her surprised friend, "Will you join me for a glass of wine?"

"Aye," Dutch replied, smiling as he slid into the booth across from her. "You brighten this dingy establishment. Other than Kate, I believe you're the first real lady ever to walk through Sandy's front door. It is both a surprise and a pleasure."

Becky smiled coyly as she laid her hat on the seat next to her. "This is not my first time here, Dutch. Before Kathleen came to live with Sandy, I would visit him a few times each year, just like this. He would talk of your father and tell me of his recollections on the Pacific coast. We are dear friends."

In the flicking candlelight, Miss Becky looked twenty years younger, and Dutch could see the beauty his father had seen. "Sandy never told me of your visits."

"He wouldn't. He's a real gentleman."

"Aye, that be true..." He gathered his courage and asked, "Is Mary still staying with you?"

Becky's red lips turned up in a big smile. "She sailed home, last week, with her father and the Commodore. In her young way, she was quite smitten with you."

"She gave me this," Dutch replied, showing his necklace to her.

In the candlelight, she gazed upon the coin dangling from a strand of rawhide. "She gave me a coin, too, but I don't wear it around my neck. She is very young, Dutch."

The table went silent for a moment. Then Sandy appeared with a bottle of champagne and two glasses.

"Did you tell him our secret?" he asked, putting the glasses on the table.

"Yes," Becky replied with a smile. "He knows of our late-night rendezvous."

With bottle in hand, Sandy worked at removing the cork. "Kate and I will close up while you two talk awhile." *Pop* – the cork was out. While pouring the wine, he continued, "Listen to what Becky has to say, lad. It be important." Then, setting the bottle on the table, Sandy departed.

Becky's green eyes glowed as she raised her glass to Dutch. "Here's to a fine young man," she said as a toast, and they sipped the bubbly wine. "You see, Sandy has asked me to do the impossible."

"And what would that be?" Dutch asked.

"Convince you to stay here in Boston. We fear that your overland journey is too dangerous. Kathleen and Sandy consider you as part of their family now. And I would like to become your benefactor."

Dutch thought a moment. 'Benefactor' is not a word I know," he finally admitted.

Becky graced him with a serious look. "I would buy things that you need, see that you go to the finest schools, and introduce you to Boston society. A benefactor is a person who cares with lots of money."

Dutch stretched his neck and looked down at the table, baffled. Then he looked up again and met her gaze. "Never heard of such a thing. I can just imagine people saying. 'There goes Miss Becky's breed. He's a kept man.' No...I thank you but I will tuck my head for no man – or woman. My father taught me that."

"You misunderstand. It wouldn't be that way. In our culture, there are many benefactors for many people. And you're not a breed," Becky said forcefully.

Dutch smiled at her, "My mother was half Tolowa, and I'm proud of that. In the Indian culture, it wouldn't be right to be kept by a squaw. I'll make my own money and find my own way. But your offer is heartwarming, and I can see that is was kindly meant. Thank you for the notion."

Becky reached across the table, taking one of Dutch's hands in hers. "Your pride could be your ruin. But, in many ways, I understand it. Come what may, you'll always be welcome in my life."

"Thank you," Dutch replied, saluting her with a lift of his champagne glass. "May God bless both our trails."

After closing the pub, Kathleen and Sandy slipped into the booth with another bottle of champagne. They were disappointed, but not surprised, to learn that Becky had failed to dissuade Dutch from his adventure. For a short while, they tried to deter him from his journey, as well. But when that failed, the conversation turned lighter, and for the next few hours they simply enjoyed their fellowship.

Early the next morning, dressed in clean buckskins and with his bowler hat on, Dutch took one last, fond look at the empty pub, knowing that its drab walls and malodorous smells would not be soon forgotten. Then, lifting the Bear Box onto his shoulder, with King following at his heels, he walked to the waterfront stables.

With Henry's help, he loaded all of his equipment and supplies onto the backs of Scout and Willow. Then they walked both animals down to pier and secured them inside the hull of the schooner *York*. There were about thirty stalls in the forward hold, mostly filled with cattle and horses. Dutch and Henry found three empty stands near the hatch cover and unloaded the burdens of both horses. In the center stall, they stacked all the trail gear, making room for a sleeping area in one corner.

Once finished, they walked out of the ship on the livestock gangway and said their farewells below a cloudy sky. As they clasped hands for the last time, Henry asked Dutch, "Still got those rusty spurs?"

"Aye," Dutch replied.

"Use them wisely and gain the trust of your horses. They won't let you down."

As Henry walked away, Dutch heard the boatswain's whistle blow, signaling that the schooner was about to castoff. But just as he turned for the *York*, he saw Kate and Sandy walking his way.

"Thought we said our farewells last night," Dutch remarked as they approached.

"Aye," Sandy replied, "but I forgot to give you something."

"And what would that be, my friend? You've already given me too much."

Sandy reached into his pouch and pulled out a gold keyed pocket watch, which he handed to Dutch. "This be Captain Gray's," he said with watery eyes. "He gave it to me at the end of our second passage to the Northwest. You should have it now, and when you look at it, remember our time together."

"No tears mate," Dutch said, hugging Sandy. "I'll borrow your watch and return it the next time our trails cross." Pulling away from Sandy, he turned and hugged Kate. "No tears from you either, lady."

As they parted, she looked him straight in eye. "Don't you look just fine in that hat." Then she kissed him on the cheek. "If I was twenty years younger, I'd be joining you."

Dutch smiled back at her fondly. "If I was twenty years older, my boots would be under your bed."

The Trail Head —————

Under inky skies, the *York* sailed past Deer Island. Dutch stood at the stern rail, watching Boston slip away in her wake. He was filled with raw, conflicting emotions, both sad and happy to be leaving the city of his father. He had made many friends in Beantown, some of whom would remain in his heart forever, but the city was too big and dirty, filled with hordes of faceless people. He needed room to roam, with endless skies from sunrise to sunset.

With fresh drops of rain on his face, Dutch said a silent farewell to Boston and went below-deck to care for his animals.

Scout had been edgy when Henry put him in his stall. Now, with the ship moving and listing to one side, he stood wide-eyed and nervous. He looked like he could bolt at any moment. Carefully, Dutch picked up a brush and slowly moved into his dark stall. Then, with calm words and gentle movements, he curried his horse. His actions seemed to relax Scout, so he did the same for Willow.

After both horses had been groomed, Dutch removed his flute from his pouch and sat upon a tall rail. Facing his animals, he played them a few songs. They listened with curious faces and twitching ears as his music filled the dingy hold, and it seemed to soothe his animal's fears. Dutch repeated these musical brushing sessions two or three times each day. He also cleaned out their stalls, saw to their feed and brought them pails of fresh water. This constant care paid off with little trouble from his steeds.

Neither Dutch nor King could stomach sleeping in the hold, filled with the foul smells and loud noises of the lower-deck livestock.

Instead, after each brushing, they moved topside for fresh air and did their best not to be underfoot.

The Third Mate of the *York* was a seaman named Steve Miller. He had come into the Sea Witch many times and recognized Dutch right off. After talking with him, he made arrangements with his Captain to allow Dutch to take his meals with the crew and sleep in the corner of the sail-locker. There, for two long, cold, wet nights Dutch wrapped himself in a blanket and slept with King, upon a bed of sail canvas. With contrary winds and rough seas, the schooner slowly moved down the eastern seaboard, making an uneventful passage of 250 miles.

On the early morning of the third day, the *York* turned in at Delaware Bay and moved up the river, with ever-improving weather. A few hours later, the city of Philadelphia came into view. Its waterfront was a long series of warehouses and piers stretching for miles up and down the Delaware River. By mid-morning, the schooner docked at a wharf with a large dockside corral.

With a restless desire, Dutch and his skittish horses were the first down the livestock gangway. Once the steeds had been put inside the corral, both Scout and Willow stood shaking their bodies and whinnying loudly. They were delighted to be free of the ship.

Sharing a few apples with his mounts, Dutch was equally pleased to be on firm ground again. Over the next half hour, he transferred the heavy packs and saddles from the hold to the corral. Then he carefully tacked up both horses and put his trail bags in place.

When finished, he double-checked his work. Hanging from the saddle pommel on Scout were his two pistols in holsters, a canteen and a trail rope. On one side of the saddle, he slung his sheathed rifle. At the rear of the saddle, he secured his overstuffed saddle bags and bed roll. Willow was burdened with two large canvas saddlebags hanging on each side of her tall body. One poke carried trade goods, tools, log spikes, bags of seeds, six powder horns, a small barrel of extra gun powder and numerous pouches of balls and flints. The other poke carried containers of sugar, flower, coffee, beans and rice. Secured on top of the two side packs were the four extra scabbard rifles. On the very top of Willow's packsaddle, he had strapped down his Bear Box and a trail bag containing his tent and camp hardware. Standing back, admiring his shiny new outfit, Dutch guessed that Willow now carried over three hundred pounds, and Scout a third of that, not counting Dutch's own weight.

With a deep feeling of pride, he slipped on his riding gloves and started his arduous journey.

Moving across the cobbles of Philadelphia, Dutch wove in and around streets filled with commerce and clogged with traffic. The avenues were long and wide, the brick and stone buildings tall and impressive. Every corner seemed to have a pub, and all the streets were filled with faceless hordes scurrying about their business. Philadelphia was the biggest city in America, twice the size of Boston and four times the size of New York City. The Spaniard had warned him about the magnitude of the place, and had told him to keep moving west. Soon he would come to the Old Pit Road, which would take him 300 miles across the Commonwealth to the remote outpost of Pittsburg.

His horses were delighted to have stone underfoot, and they started to high-step their gait. Even King seemed to be prancing, as he lingered along in the rear. This movement, along with the sounds of the horses' hooves, turned a few heads from pedestrians on the sidewalks, and Dutch received a few tipped hats. He returned these gestures with a tip of his feathered bowler.

One passerby shouted out, "Hey, mountain man, where're ya heading?"

Dutch shouted back, with a broad smile, "The Oregon Country." He and his caravan were finally on the move, and their spirits were high.

Under brightening skies, he stopped a few times to ask for directions. One older gentleman he talked with gave him both directions and a copy of the local newspaper, while another bloke offered him a swig of rum from a walking-stick flask. These Philadelphians were friendly folks, and while their city sprawled out for miles, they demonstrated a kindness that Dutch would not soon forget.

Finally, in the early afternoon, he came upon the Old Pit Road. He turned there and followed the many wagons and carriages moving down the way. It wasn't until the late afternoon that the road turned from cobbles to gravel and dirt. With less traffic and fewer people, he picked up his gait and soon found himself riding across the rolling plains of the countryside.

Dutch had kept a keen eye on King as they moved through the city. In their time together they had mostly traveled by canoe, so the dog had at first seemed confused by the new scheme of things. But once they started moving across the countryside, his natural instincts kicked in; he bolted to the front of the pack and was soon sniffing out rabbits and squirrels.

Some ten miles outside of the city, Dutch came to a small farming town with a roadhouse called Sleepy Hollow. Here he found that he could stable his horses, enjoy a few libations, eat a hot meal and spend one last night sleeping on a feather bed. After spending two nights in a sail locker, the pub was indeed an oasis for a weary traveler.

Early the next morning, a light rain was falling. After a hardy breakfast, Dutch continued down the meandering Fort Pit Road. The way was wide and well-traveled, with many heavily timbered bridges crossing numerous creeks, rills and rivers. Some of the larger bridges were covered with gabled roofs, something Dutch had never seen before.

When the sky finally brightened and the rain diminished, Dutch picked up his pace. The rolling countryside over which he rode looked to be a rich land, with many farmhouses and homesteads dotting the fertile landscape.

That morning, he passed three slow-moving canvas-topped wagons, each pulled by a four-up team of oxen, with each buckboard manned by a lone driver, all heading west. Written across their tarps, in fading letters, was *Kingston Transfer Company, Philadelphia.* While riding alongside this heavily burdened caravan, Dutch struck up a conversation with a friendly teamster. As they talked, he learned that they were heading for Pittsburg, as well. The overland road appeared to be the only way to bring provisions to the western part of the Commonwealth. He learned that over a thousand wagons a year pass down the Pit Road. Dutch was surprised to find that much commerce moving west.

"What's your freight?" Dutch inquired from his saddle.

The smiling teamster yelled back, "You name it, we carry it. We do this route three times a month."

"Is your dog vicious?" the driver of the last wagon shouted.

"Nay," Dutch answered with a smile, "Only with Injuns."

Laughter rumbled from the wagons and the lead driver shouted, "Hey, Funny Hat, where you headin'?"

"Down the Ohio River," Dutch yelled back, and picked up his pace.

"Look out for pirates," the teamster replied as he passed by.

With the wave of his hand, Dutch shouted over his shoulder, "Good luck to ya, mates."

Did that fellow say 'pirates'? Dutch thought, perplexed, as he moved farther down the way. Along the road, that morning, he also passed other wagons heading east. Those buckboards looked to be carrying timber and farm goods back to Philadelphia. Dutch soon began to envision all that commerce, and its broad roads as a harbinger of what could happen on the Columbia River.

Every fifty or sixty miles, they rode through small farming villages, usually with a few corrals, stables, silos, a general store, a land office and a pub. For the most part, these sleepy little towns were only dusty havens next to the road.

At noon, beneath a bright sky full of colorful birds, Dutch rode over the crown of a steep hill and saw in the distance, for the first time, the blue, knobby peaks of the Alleghenies. The ruddy-faced innkeeper had told him about these mountains and had suggested he make camp before crossing over them. Stopping at the top of the hill, Dutch used his spyglass and estimated that the foothills were still forty or fifty miles off. If he rode hard and long, he could make it there before sunset.

In many ways, central Pennsylvania reminded Dutch of the Pacific coastal lands, filled with vivid wild flowers, lush vegetation and lazy, crystal-clear waterways. Around every bend in the road, God's fingerprint could be seen and his spirit could be felt. Dutch marveled at the beauty of the countryside, with its rolling hills and vast timber stands. While the local trees weren't as tall or as majestic as the Redwoods or the Pacific Firs, they stretched out over the land in an endless sea of green. With a warming sun in the sky, Dutch rode through the checkered sunshine and shadow of those woods.

Late in the afternoon, with the sun low, he came to the foothills of the Alleghenies. After searching out a proper campsite, he unloaded his animals and hobbled them in a green clearing to graze. Returning to camp, he noticed how sore his young legs were, which spoke to him of his improving posture on horseback.

Making a small fire for some coffee, he opened his trail bag and removed his coffee grinder. Then, for the first time, he opened his Bear Box, looking for his coffee beans. First, however, he untied the sack of venison jerky and reached in for a piece.

What he found on top of the strips was a folded parchment, which he promptly opened. In a delicate hand, it simply read;

With God's Word as your map and His Spirit as your compass, you're sure to stay on course. Love, Kathleen

Dutch would find half a dozen more such notes hidden in the nooks and crannies of his food box. Kate's loving words warmed his heart and lifted his sprits. It was as if she sat right next to him.

After a meal of bacon, cheese, biscuits and coffee, Dutch brought the horses in and picketed them in a grove of trees near his campsite. Brushing each animal, he talked to them in almost a whisper about their first full day on the trail.

Taking Scout's long snout into his gloved hands, he continued while looking him in the eye. "We be a team now. Trust me and I'll trust you."

Scout nickered loudly, while playfully nose-butting Dutch.

"Alright," Dutch responded with a smile. Taking an apple from his pouch, he cut it in half. "You both earned this today."

Then, returning to camp with the faint accompanying voices of the Whippoorwills, Dutch poured himself a tin cup of whiskey and sprawled his aching body out on his canvas bedroll, next to the fire. Gazing skyward, he watched the darkness creep in. Soon the black sky filled with stars, and the countryside came alive with the music of the night feral.

Those sounds and sights brought back a flood of memories. Some of his thoughts were warm and rich, when he remembered sweet Mary, Kathleen and Sandy. Other images were dark and tormenting, like killing that Kickapoo, or fighting off the Irish prick who had tried to have his way with Kate. But a few things were clear to Dutch: he had bonded with his animals, and he was one day closer to being home. Those musings, aided by the whiskey, warmed his inners and brightened his hopes for the future.

The next day was a remarkably fresh and beautiful April morning. Dutch had awakened at first light and departed a cold camp before the dew could dry. Now he rode up, and through, a rich and thriving forest lit with bright sunshine and enlivened by a multitude of vibrant birds. Climbing the Alleghenies had not been as arduous as he had feared, and he was making good time.

By mid-morning, he had crossed over the summit and was riding down into a vast plain that stretched west to more peaks of the mountain range. Once on the valley floor, the road wandered alongside many limpid lakes and crossed a number of streams and creeks. Gone were the farms and homesteads, replaced by a wilderness of luxuriant forests, rich green shrubbery and dark blue waterways.

That evening, to the distant growling of thunder, Dutch made camp at the foothills of the second row of mountains. Just after making a pot of coffee, his fire was drenched by a fast-moving rainsquall. He quickly set up his tent, and he and King were soon inside the canvas, watching the downpour. When the storm finally abated, he picketed his horses closer to his tent and ate a meal of hardtack, jerky and half-brewed coffee. With other storms rolling in, he soon closed his eyes and let the rain's tattoo drum him to sleep. The Spaniard, who had warned him that April was a wet month for travel, was being proven right.

They departed the cold camp at first light, the next morning. Under gray skies Dutch rode over the gentle hills and, by mid-morning, was traveling across a flat plain. Fort Pitt had been built fifty years before, during the French and Indian Wars, and had long since been abandoned. But around the forts bulwarks had sprung up the little village of Pittsburg. Here, the confluence of two rivers, the Allegany and Monongahela, flowed together to become the headwaters of the Ohio River. Some nine hundred miles downstream, he would find the Missouri Country.

Late in the afternoon of the third day, Dutch rode past the ruins of Fort Pitt and into the bustling village of Pittsburg. Here and there, on the muddy main street, he saw sober-looking frontiersmen wearing buckskins and dirty waistcoats. There were also buxom woman dressed in gingham, carrying colorful parasols and old umbrellas. And he heard an incessant hammering and banging from numerous blacksmith sheds, and saw them molding iron, fixing wagons and shoeing horses.

Stopping at one of the many general stores, Dutch inquired about buying passage down-river. The shopkeeper's wife, a rotund German lady named Helga, told him that over a half-dozen boats a day floated down the river. Remarking that it was the biggest industry in town, she directed him to the riverside docks where the flat-bottomed boats were built. "Those shipwrights can make ya any size or shape boat you might need. Cost you about five dollars a foot. But if ye float down the Ohio, lad, be mindful of the river pirates. They'll slit your gullet for a dime." Her final words rang in Dutch's ears as he walked out the front door.

The boatyards were on the shore of the Monongahela River, with the many shops of the different boat builders and the long floating docks with their finished barges. As Dutch rode up the waterfront, he kept a keen eye out for a boat large enough for livestock, and preferably one already in preparation for moving down the river.

At the third yard, he saw a large boat with piles of supplies, wagon wheels, harnesses and a multitude of nondescript articles resting dockside. The barge looked to be nearly sixty foot long and twenty wide. A short, flat roof covered two thirds of the length, and on top of this canopy was the long pole of the rudder and two rowing stations. Sitting on the dock next to the cargo, a little girl played with her doll while onboard, a man and a woman loaded the stacked goods onto the open bow of their boat.

Dismounting, he tied his animals to a fence post, then retrieved one of his pistols and placed it in his belt. Once he was armed, he and King walked down the gangway to the dock. As they moved past some smaller boats, the sun darted from behind a cloud, washing the moorage in bright, warming sunlight.

Approaching the larger boat, Dutch smiled at the little girl. "Hello, young lady. That's a fine-looking doll. Where are you taking her?"

With bright eyes, the cute girl looked up at him and replied, "Tennessee."

From within the boat, the stern voice of a woman shouted out, "Missy, don't go tellin' strangers where we're goin'."

Turning to the boat, Dutch found the girl's matronly mother standing in the open bow. She had chopped flaxen locks, hazel eyes and a sour angry look as she stood there, holding a pitch fork. Then from the shadows of the open cabin, her husband joined her, carrying an old Brown Bess musket.

"Sorry, folks," Dutch said, tipping his hat. "I meant no harm."

"What are you looking for, down here?" the surly-faced man asked, with a slight Irish accent and his finger on the hammer. He was a big bloke, with burly ape-like arms, a short weedy beard and glaring brown eyes.

"My name is Dutch Blackwell, recently from Boston. I'm lookin to buy my way downriver to the Missouri Country."

"Are you alone?" the woman asked firmly.

"Aye. Just me and my two horses…and, of course, my dog."

As he answered the question, the couple was joined from within the shadowy cabin by two teenaged boys, dressed in homespun clothes.

"Why are you going to Missouri? The husband asked.

"I'm on my way home to the Oregon Country."

"We've got no room for strangers. You best move on," the man answered.

"Aye." Dutch turned to leave, adding, "Thought you might need an extra hand and rifle for the long journey. Sorry if I intruded."

Before he had taken two steps, the lady asked, "How much were you thinkin' about paying?"

Turning back to the family, Dutch answered, "I'm real good with boats, and I can row or take the helm. And my dog and I are good hunters."

"What's your dog's name?" the older boy asked.

"King. He's got a good nose for Indians," Dutch replied with a smile.

"What about paying with money?" the woman demanded.

"I've got two ten-dollar gold pieces in my poke. Reckon I can give you one now and the other when I reach Missouri."

For the longest moment, the man and the woman looked at each other with surprised expressions. Finally, the woman asked, "You a Christian, Mr. Blackwell?"

"Aye," Dutch answered.

"Of what faith?"

Dutch thought for a moment and then replied, "I think of myself as a Jesuit of the forest. There's no stick-and-stone churches where I live. But I did go to a Methodist church a few times, while I was in Boston."

Resting the pitch fork against the boat's gunnels, she replied, "We're an Amish family. Would that be a problem?"

"Well, Ma'am, never heard of Amish before, so reckon it won't be a problem."

"We are pacifists," the woman added.

"I'm not familiar with that word," Dutch responded with curious look on his face.

"We don't fight or kill, it be against our creed."

"If that be so, why does your man there, carry that old musket?"

"Just for our protection... nothing more."

"Mother," the husband said, resting his weapon at his side, "we ain't got no room for two horses."

"The mule and cow can share a stall, Pa, and his horses use the other," the older boy inserted.

Shaking his head, the man said, "I don't know. He's a stranger. We don't need no trouble."

"You folks do seem a little edgy," Dutch replied.

"There's a lot of two-legged river rats on the docks. And everyone is warning us about river pirates. We have to be on guard," the husband answered.

"Benjamin, he be an extra rifle, so let's go look at his horses," the woman said, and slipped over the boat gunnels to the dock.

The entire family walked up the gangway and, along the way, pointed out their livestock, tied close to his horses. Once they were in front of Scout and Willow, they stood, gapping with their eyes wide and their mouths open, clearly amazed at their size and the amount of equipment each animal carried. The woman walked around Scout and then noticed Dutch's Kentucky long rifle hanging from his saddle. When she came to the four extra rifles lashed to Willow, she stopped and placed her hand on them.

"Why so many guns, Mr. Blackwell?" she asked.

"Once home, I'll trade them to the Indians for land," Dutch replied.

"Are you a farmer?" Benjamin asked.

"No, sir," Dutch replied. "Come next Spring, I'll be opening a trading post on the Columbia River."

Still touching the extra rifles, the lady asked, "Are you any good with a musket, Mr. Blackwell?"

"Aye, I was born to it."

"Good," she responded, and pulled her husband away from the group for a private talk. As they whispered to one another, Dutch overheard the lady saying, in a stern voice, "He's more than just one extra gun, and his tall horses can ride up in the open bow." Moments later they returned to the group. "We put our faith in the Lord, so we'll take you, Mr. Blackwell," the lady said in an amenable tone. "But there will be a few rules. We do not abide dancing, tobacco, coffee or spirits, so around our campfire there will be none. There will be no iniquitous language used around our children neither and I will not cook, clean or tend you in anyway. Is this agreeable?"

Dutch thought a long moment; he had never heard of such peculiarities. "I play a lively flute, so how about music? And each night I'll make my own camp. What say you?"

Husband and wife looked at each other, and then slowly nodded their agreement.

"Fine," Dutch replied. With a smile, he reached into his poke and handed the lady a ten-dollar coin. "When do we leave?"

"We'll shove off at first light tomorrow," a still reluctant Benjamin replied.

V
War Clouds

—◊—

*T*he dream of American expansion was an uncommon bond between common men. Prior to the nineteenth century, the lands west of the Mississippi River were occupied by scoundrels, savages and mountain men. The French, Canadian and American frontiersmen, who thrived on the inland fur trade, would blaze trails across the heartlands, over the Stony Mountains and touch upon the Pacific coast. Along the way, they befriended and traded with the Indians and made strong alliances with the tribes. They also marked their travels not on maps, but in their heads. The fearless men who survived this harsh life would become the guides, hunters and sentinels for the many pilgrims who would follow.

With the publication of the Lewis & Clark Journals, after the turn of the century, rumors abounded concerning the rich, primitive lands west of the Mississippi River. It was said that the Rocky Mountains were taller than the Himalayas. Gossip had it that there was a place in the west where dragons roamed the land, spouting fire and steam. That most of the rivers and streams had beds of gold and silver. That buffalo herds could blacken the landscape, as far as the eye could see. Another fable told of soil so rich that corn could be grown halfway to the heavens. These vast, abundant lands west of the Mississippi River were what dreams were made of.

Soon, other expeditions, explorers and voyagers headed west in search of an uncertain future from an uncertain land. The trappers and traders had blazed the way; now came the prospectors, miners, lumberjacks, merchants and a few hardy families that toiled the soil. What these newcomers found was a dangerous, lawless land with no protection from any government or army. The frontier had no roads, just trails and rivers, so the travelers moved by horseback or canoe. Ever so slowly, the shallow roots of civilization took hold in tiny settlements and dusty towns.

This expansion was only a trickle at first, but soon the flow of many rivers became the highways to the west. However, on the horizon behind this bright blue future were the dark clouds of war. James Madison, the fourth president of the United States, had been elected in 1809. This successor of Jefferson's stood just five-foot four-inches tall and had a diminutive stature much like Napoleon, but without the emperor's bellicose tendencies. Madison had inherited strained relations with England, but was reluctant to go to war. Ever since the American Revolution, the British had held nothing but contempt for American independence. After the turn of the century, England had ships patrolling the Atlantic lurking close to American ports and subjecting merchant vessels to search and seizure. They renewed the practice of impressment by seizing sailors judged to be either defectors from British naval service or simply British born. Mistakes were common, leading to American citizens being dragged into the miseries of the Crown's Navy. Seizing sailors from American merchant ships was bad enough, but this offense turned to outrage in 1807 when a British frigate opened fire on a merchant ship, killing three men before seizing four alleged Britons. On the Western frontier, the Indian tribes in the Northwest Territory, comprising the modern states of Ohio, Indiana, Illinois, Michigan and Wisconsin, had organized in opposition to American settlements, and were being armed by Redcoats and British traders from Canada.

These provocations stunned the American public and there were many full-throated calls for another war with England. But Madison, being the commander-and-chief of a standing army of less than seven thousand men, and with a navy of only a handful of warships, sought diplomatic ways of resolving these issues. He remained reluctant to go to war, but his Congress did not. They embraced the idea of saving the Republic before the British could recolonize the United States.

—⅏—

Down the Ohio ————

At dawn the next morning, Dutch awoke to find sticky dew across the canvas cover he slept under. The evening before, he had carried his heavy trail bags down to the barge and stacked them next to the animal stalls in the stern of the cabin. After that, he had moved his horses to a nearby grassy bluff and set up a camp for the evening. Now, under a scantly lit morning sky, he removed his animal's hobbles and slipped lead ropes over both their heads. After rolling up his bedroll, he saddled Scout and tied his sleeping sack onto the rear. Pausing a moment, he listened to the first faint songs of the river birds, then removed his pocket watch and checked the time in the dim light. It was just five AM.

Taking some jerky from his saddlebags, he placed the meat in his pouch and called out for the dog, then took the leads to his horses and moved slowly down the hill towards the waterfront. As he reached the wharf, the family's oldest boy rushed up the damp gangway. "Father sent me to help you with your steeds," he said in a near whisper.

Dutch stopped and let the lad approach. "What's your name?" he asked.

"Luke," the boy answered.

"Well, Luke, you can take Willow and follow me down the gangway," he said, handing the lead to the boy. "Watch her closely on the wet boards."

They moved carefully down the ramp and then turned onto the dock. After walking a few paces, Luke said from behind, "Your horses be too tall for the stalls. They will have to ride up front."

"Reckon that be true," Dutch responded. "They'd be a tight fit under that low cabin roof."

As they approached the boxy barge, Dutch noticed that three boards of the upper gunnel had been removed and were now being used as a gangway onto the open bow. In the dim light, he cautiously led Scout across and tied his lead to a cleat, then helped Luke do the same with Willow.

After hesitating dockside, the last to cross was King. Once aboard, he sniffed around the open cabin and then curled up on the deck, close to the horses. As Dutch and Luke finished securing the animals, Benjamin appeared from the darkened cabin and told Luke, sternly, to replace the gunnel boards and slip the lines from the dock.

In the pale light, he turned to Dutch and said in a surly voice, "Time to go. You take the oar on the right. We'll see if you're worth your salt."

With the boat slowly drifting away from the dock, Dutch stood on the cabin roof, using his long fifteen-foot paddle in its wooden yoke to turn the craft into the current. Luke was standing across the roof, working the portside oar, with Mr. Jameson manning the rudder at the stern rooftop.

The flat bottom boat moved down river and soon reached the confluence of the Monongahela and Allegany Rivers, which flowed together to become the headwaters of the Ohio River. From there, they could look back and see a spectacular sunrise over the distant Allegheny Mountains, with the dark outline of Pittsburg and old Fort Pitt underneath. The amber color in the eastern sky reflected off the river, producing a thousand flickers of golden light. It was a magnificent sight, reminiscent of sunsets Dutch had seen on the Pacific.

"And God gives us one more blessing," Benjamin said loudly, looking back from the helm. "May we do His work this day, and pray He gives us another."

The type of boat upon which they rowed was an ugly craft. The hull was built of rough-hewn planks caulked with black tar. The boards of the oblong framework were thick and wide, fastened to the superstructure with spikes and wooden plugs. The square prow of the open bow pushed hard against the water, making the helm difficult to manage. The stern of the boat was also square, with a heavy yoked timber that held the long rudder pole in place. Two-thirds of the boat's sixty-foot length was covered by a low, flat-roofed cabin that was open to the bow but closed in the stern. The inside of this deckhouse was packed tightly with all of the family's worldly goods. At the rear of the cabin were two small stalls for their cow and mule, with a short ladder that led up to a hatch just in front of the rooftop helm. The interior walls were stacked with dry goods, foodstuffs, tools, farming implements, wagon wheels, furniture and, where the family slept, inside the frame of a buckboard. Like the hull of the *York*, the quarters were cramped and poorly ventilated, with the bitter smells of their livestock. The boat had cost the family nearly their entire poke; when they finally arrived at their final destination, they would dismantle it and use the timbers for their new home.

With the spring runoff, the headwaters of the Ohio were wide and often lazy. But when the land narrowed, the current midstream was strong and fast. Up from the shoreline, the countryside was lush with thick groves of trees and an unbroken carpet of tall green grass that swayed in the morning breeze. Soon, a warming sun bathed the rooftop deck and lit the way downriver. At the helm, Benjamin kept steering for the quieter waters of the North shore, where Dutch's long paddle often hit the shallow bottom of the river.

"Move us to deeper water," he finally shouted out.

Benjamin glared back at him but continued on his course. He was a strange man, big in size and full of himself. At age fourteen, he and his brother, James Jameson, had emigrated from Ireland to Philadelphia during the Revolutionary War. They both promptly joined the Continental Army and went off to fight the Redcoats. Mr. Jameson became a drummer boy, while his brother, four years older, became a daring solider and war-time hero. After the conflict, the brothers returned home, and the commonwealth government gave James a war bonus consisting of a section of land in western Pennsylvania. The two brothers toiled on that farm for many years, first clearing the land, then plowing and planting the soil, building a cabin and a barn and watching their crops grow.

Once the farm was established, James took an Amish wife named Hannah. The newlyweds allowed Benjamin to stay on and had a great influence over his life. Soon, they had him converted to the Amish ways as well. He was a hard-working, quiet lad, with none of the social graces of the more educated folks in Lancaster County. He was twenty-five years old before he took a wife named Ruth. As a wedding gift, James gave the couple fifty acres of his farmland. Four years later, their first son Luke was born. Two years after, the second son, John was born, and eight years later their only daughter Missy was born.

During all those years, the countryside was changing as well. There had been a large influx of Mennonites, which distressed some of the local Amish. As a result, right after Missy's birth, James and his wife had sold their farm and moved to a new Amish community being established in Tennessee. Now, four years later, Benjamin and his family were doing the same.

Midmorning, Ruth and the little girl climbed up the stern ladder with a pail of drinking water. Benjamin was first to wet his lips, and Dutch was next.

"Well, Mr. Blackwell, what do you think about our boat?" Mrs. Jameson asked, wearing a plain black frock with a white bonnet covering her flaxen hair.

"She be a fine craft, ma'am," Dutch answered after drinking from the tin cup.

Ruth nodded her head with a smile and moved across the roof to Luke. But Missy stayed behind, still looking up at Dutch. Finally, her eyes wide with curiosity, she asked, "Are those tiger teeth around your neck?"

"Nay, they be cougar teeth."

"Why do you call this boat a she?"

Pushing his paddle with all his strength, Dutch looked down from his yoke with a smile. "Most all boats are named for she's."

"Why?"

Dutch paused for a moment. "Don't rightly know. I'll ponder it and tell you more later."

Missy's bright green eyes smiled back as she ran across the roof to join her mother, next to Luke. At sixteen, Luke was a fine-looking rascal with a young body as straight as a Redwood tree. He had short, sandy hair, blue eyes and muscles in his arms that glistened in the sunlight. He was a quiet fellow who only spoke when spoken to, but as Dutch watched him work his oar, he knew Luke would be able to hold his own if any trouble came their way.

The younger son John had been given the task of caring for the animals. He would see to their feed and water, and clean up their waste by using a pitch fork and pails of river water. Just below the main deck was a shallow bilge for any river leakage, rainwater or waste. After washing down the decks, John would use a hand pump at the stern of the boat to empty out the bilge. This was a demanding task for a young man with such a small frame, but he did it willingly, always with a smile on his face.

At noon, the boat slipped into a quiet inlet and was secured fore and aft with lines tied to large trees. With the gunnel planks forming a ramp, the animals were unloaded and allowed to graze nearby while the family went ashore for the noon meal. Dutch spent this time eating hardtack and jerky while hunting on foot with King. He saw many signs of Indians and game but none came under his barrel that day. An hour later, the boat was underway again.

That afternoon, they passed another barge as it poled its way up the river against the current. It was a large craft with an open pointed bow, a tapered stem, and a small cabin amidships. A crew of seven burly men rowed and poled the boat with long paddles.

They were on the same side of the river as the family's boat, so Dutch shouted, "Give them the way. They are against the current."

Benjamin snarled at Dutch but finally steered for deeper water, to pass them with the flow.

As they floated by, Dutch shouted across, "What's your cargo?"

The helmsman, a giant of a man, returned his call. "We have Tennessee whiskey, Kentucky tobacco and Missouri beaver skins."

"Any trouble with Indians or pirates?" Mr. Jameson shouted from his helm.

"Nay," the big fellow answered with a smile, "We have too many rifles, and we know what to do with river rats."

"Smooth sailing, mates," Dutch yelled with a wave of his hand as they slipped by. "Don't drink the cargo!"

Once past the barge, Benjamin turned again for the quieter waters closer to shore.

Dutch turned his way and said, "We make much better time in the deeper water."

Again, he glared at Dutch without saying a word. He was a hard man, as rigid as the pole he pulled.

The green Ohio River meandered under blue skies, presenting new vistas around each bend. Up from the water's shore stood a deep, tall forest with a canopy so thick it blocked the sun, rendering the jungle-like underbrush in shades of gray. Everywhere along the way the songs of Whippoorwills and other fowl could be heard echoing off the water. They passed many streams and small rivers that flowed into the Ohio, and paddled their way around numerous islands, limestone rocks and quiet eddies.

With the sun low in the sky they made their first camp in a little cove. After the boat was secured between large trees, the animals were led off and allowed to graze in a nearby clearing. King had bolted from the boat like a bullet and was off hunting, with his tail wagging. Dutch thought about joining him, but his arms felt like lead bricks from the hours of rowing. Instead, he walked into the woods, searching out any signs of Indians. After making a large sweep around their cove, he returned and cleared a camp site a few yards inside the forest, using the barge to block the sight of his fire. As he was unpacking his trail bag and food box from the boat, he noticed Benjamin and family setting up camp on a spit of sandy beach some thirty yards in front of the barge. The soft sand was a better campsite than the hard, lumpy ground of the forest, but their fire would be exposed to the river.

Walking over to their camp, Dutch watched the children gathering wood while Ruth unpacked her outfit and Mr. Jameson rolled log snags into place. Approaching Benjamin, he said, "Sir, this be a poor campsite selection. Your fire will be like a beacon upon the river, an open invitation for river rats and Indians."

Benjamin looked at him with anger in his face. "I need not your suggestions, Mr. Blackwell. I've been camping for many years."

In the early evening light, Dutch stared at him for the longest moment, then firmly replied, "Aye, suit yourself. But this be a pilgrim's mistake that could imperil your family." He then turned and moved back through the tall grass to his own campsite.

Some moments later, Dutch heard Luke and John clearing underbrush some twenty yards away in the woods. Soon they were joined by the rest of the family, and a fire was started. Dutch was pleased they had heeded his warning, as he knew they were new to the ways of the wilderness.

Their camp was close enough that he could overhear some of what was said. These were honest, hardworking folks with a rigid family structure, where faith and family always came first. As the mother and daughter prepared the evening meal, the father and sons read aloud from the bible. The words the family spoke to each other were neither joyful nor sad, but always respectful.

That evening, Dutch made a pot of coffee and then fried up a batch of bacon and beans. As always, as if by magic, King appeared with the first smells of food cooking. Resting his tired body against a large tree trunk, Dutch and the dog ate their food in silence, watching the darkness roll in like a tide. It was good to be on the trail again, and one day closer to home.

After cleaning up from the meal, Dutch retrieved his horses and picketed them close to his fire. Taking brush in hand, he groomed each animal, and then played them some flute music. When he looked up from his instrument, he found the three children standing in his campsite, watching and listening. After finishing his song, he wished his steeds a good night and returned to his fire.

With a sweet face and big eyes, Missy asked, "Will you play another song... please?"

"Aye," Dutch answered, sitting down on a snag.

The three children came to rest on the ground across from the flames as he played another tune. With his music filling the air, their young eyes turned bright with joyful smiles.

When the song finished, Luke asked, "Why do you play for your horses?"

"The music soothes their spirits."

"Who taught you to play the flute?" John asked.

"My father. He was a Boston man turned mountain man."

"And your mommy?" Missy asked.

"She was an Indian princess, and we lived deep in the Redwood forests of the Pacific Coast."

"Your mother's an Indian?" John asked, clearly curious.

Before Dutch could answer, Benjamin walked from the shadows into the firelight. "Enough questions, children," he said sternly, an oil lamp in hand. "It is time for bed."

As they walked away towards the boat, Dutch slipped his flute into his pouch and noticed, through the shadows of the forest, the slight glow of the family's fire, with Mrs. Jameson cleaning up.

Dutch threw out the cold remains of his coffee and replenished the tin cup with warm brew from the fireside pot. Then he added two fingers of whiskey to the cup. As he placed another log on the fire, he watched Mrs. Jameson go aboard the boat with her gear. Rolling out his bed, he sprawled on top of the canvas, resting his back against a tree trunk, thinking on the day's events. He was astounded by the hard work of rowing, the beauty of the countryside and the stubbornness of Benjamin, who seemed blind to life. Tonight, by contrast, the children had been full of questions and eager to learn. Dutch liked that. Looking up from his thoughts, he was surprised to see Mrs. Jameson leave the boat and walk his way.

"May I join you, Mr. Blackwell?" she asked approaching the fire.

"Aye," Dutch replied, with King sitting, bright eyed, next to him.

She came to rest on a snag, and stretched her hands toward the warmth of the fire. In the firelight, without a bonnet, she no longer looked matronly. She had high cheekbones, full lips and deep-set hazel eyes that flickered in the flames. In many ways, she reminded Dutch of Kate.

"Is your mother really an Indian princess?" she asked, staring at the flames and rubbing her hands together.

Dutch smiled across the fire to her. "Nay, she was a slave to a tribe of Tillamook Indians. My father bought her and then fell in love with her."

"Are they still alive?"

Dutch took a large drink from his cup, and wiped his fingers across his lips. This was a subject he did not relish. "My parents died three years ago," he answered, staring at his cup. "Mother was part Tolowa Indian and part Spanish. They accepted death as they accepted life, proudly. I miss them both deeply."

The campsite went quiet as a graveyard for the longest moment. The only sounds he heard were the crackling of the fire, the gurgle of the river and Benjamin snoring on the boat.

"I'm sorry for your loss," Mrs. Jameson said at last. "I lost my mother a few years back. What are you drinking?"

Dutch looked up at her, startled by the question. "Whisky and coffee," he answered sheepishly.

"Will you pour me the same?" she asked quickly.

Dutch was bewildered by her inquiry and blurted out, "But, Mrs. Jameson, what about your Amish peculiarities?"

She smiled at him, then answered calmly, "Ben be sleeping. Can't you hear him? And I was raised a Protestant. My mother always kept a jug of plum wine hidden behind her stove. As I got older, we would sit together each evening, listening to my father snore, drinking a glass of wine. I miss those times."

Smiling at her warm honesty, Dutch poured another cup of coffee and sweetened it from his jug.

When he handed the tin cup to her, she tipped it his way and said, "Much obliged, Mr. Blackwell." After taking a sip, she made a sour face and said, "This be much bolder than wine." Then, licking her lips she continued, "This be our secret. I'll put my trust in your goodwill."

"Aye," Dutch replied, reminding himself that nothing was ever quite what it seemed.

They spoke together around the campfire for another half hour. Mrs. Jameson was a rare woman for the times; she had strong convictions and high opinions. During their conversation, she apologized for her husband's stubborn ways, and promised to talk to him about traveling in deeper waters. She also talked about her fear of sleeping in Indian country. Dutch assured her that King, with his twitchy nose, would always be on guard. That seemed to ease her fears. Then they talked of her children and the family's new home in Tennessee.

"Ben's brother has too much sway over him," she said, drinking her whiskey. "He moves away, and now we must follow him to this new land of promise. We had a good life in Pennsylvania and that is now gone. What a shame."

She stood up, drained the last drops from her cup, and handed it to Dutch. Turning, she moved towards the shadows, then stopped and turned back to the fire. "May I call you Dutch?"

"Aye."

"You may call me Ruth. I hope we can do this again, Dutch. You've warmed my insides, and finally sleep is calling. Good night."

Early the next morning, as Dutch stood rowing on the rooftop, Missy approached carrying her doll. "Did you remember why boats are shes?"

"Aye." He smiled down at her. "All the early explorers like Columbus and Magellan named their ships for their mothers, wives or queens. It is a tradition of the sea."

Missy thought a moment before replying, "Then we should name this boat a she."

"Fine. We'll name her after your mommy."

"No," Missy said firmly, "after my doll."

"And what is her name?"

"Lulu," the little girl replied, with a big smile on her face.

"If your father and mother agree, then we will call this boat 'Lulu' forever."

At the noon stop, that day, with the family watching from the shore, Dutch took a piece of charcoal, waded into the river, and wrote *Lulu* across the square bow. As he finished, his audience, all but Benjamin, gave out a rousing 'Hip-hip-hooray!' Missy cheered the loudest of all; clearly proud that she had named the boat.

The next few days blended together like sea and sky. The boat moved ever so slowly in the quiet, slack waters, with Mr. Jameson heeding none of Dutch's suggestions to move to the faster waters midstream. Ruth's pleas for him to listen fell on deaf ears. Benjamin was determined to do things his own way, and he used his authority to bully his family into compliance. He had very few words for Dutch, other than loud and often angry commands.

At night, a chill swirled though the camps, not from a breeze but from his surly attitude. He built his fires close to the boat, and had Dutch and King move their camps farther into the woods. Gone, too, were times when the children could listen to Dutch's flute music and any late-night conversations with Ruth.

Troubled Waters ────────

Under cloudy skies on the fifth day, the drowsy river turned a bend and widened a few hundred yards. Downstream, in front of the boat, was a large tree-covered island with a sandy shoreline. To the left of this island was the mainstream; on the right was a narrow backwater channel with a slight flow. As the boat approached this land, Ruth ascended the aft ladder with her bucket of water.

As she stood next to Mr. Jameson with tin cup in hand, Dutch shouted, "Steer for the channel on the left. It be deeper and swifter."

From his rudder, Benjamin glared angrily at Dutch. "Your job, Mr. Blackwell, is to row and hunt, neither of which you do very well. I know what I'm doing," He asserted, and took a drink of water.

Dutch shrugged. "Suit yourself, sir."

As Ruth approached Dutch, Benjamin turned into the narrow channel. With paddle in hand, Dutch took a quick swig of water and then returned to rowing. Ruth turned and moved across the roof to Luke.

Working his pole, Dutch could feel the shallow bottom, and pondered shouting another warning. Across the roof, Luke pulled his long paddle from the water and took a drink from his mother's pail. By now the boat had drifted a few hundred yards into the channel. Just as Dutch drew breath to shout out another alarm, the slow-moving boat hit a submerged sandbar which stopped it instantly.

The force of the impact was so powerful that it jolted the men to the deck and catapulted Ruth off the rooftop and into the shallow water.

Dutch was the first to regain his footing. He rushed across to where Luke was just getting to his knees. Looking into the river, he spotted Ruth, face down in the murky green water. As he jumped from the roof, he shouted, "Mr. Jameson, you're a bastard!"

The backwater into which he jumped was only knee deep, and he was able to splash over to Ruth in two long strides. Reaching down, he grasped her from behind and jerked her body out of the water in one fluid move. As he did so, she began to spit out river water. He gave her another powerful pull with his arms around her stomach. She started gasping for air, coughing all the while, spitting up more water.

Dutch released his grip, to see if she could stand on her own. She was still dazed and groggy, with wobbly legs. They stood there in the water, dripping wet, for a long moment. Then he helped her to wade through the shallow water, back to the boat. Along the way, she quickly regained her wits and strength.

The entire mishap had lasted but a few heartbeats, but when they arrived at the boat, a relieved Benjamin and Luke had removed the gunnel boards so they could lift her gently aboard. With all the family crowded around, Luke placed a blanket around her shoulders. Ruth looked frightened, but seemed no worse for wear. After making sure everyone was all right, Dutch checked the animals' well-being. To his relief, all was fine. A few minutes later, the men waded into the water, to check the boat for any damage and to investigate the point where it went aground. They found the starboard bow stuck in the mud. Try as they might, using their long paddle poles as levers, they could not dislodge the craft from the muck.

"We will have to unload the animals and try again," Dutch suggested.

This time, there was no argument from Benjamin. Within the half-hour, all of the animals were safely secured on shore, with King standing guard. With that much weight off of the boat, they hoped it could be refloated. With all the family except Missy wading in the murky river, they tried again to leverage the boat from the mud.

At first, it would not budge, but with a second and third try, they made some progress, moving it to deeper waters. Finally, with one last pull of the poles, the boat was free and drifting with the current downstream. Luke, John and Dutch jumped onto the moving boat, leaving Ruth and Ben still knee-deep in the water.

Taking the helm, Dutch shouted back to them, "We'll put in at the end of the island and walk back for you and the animals."

"I have no rifle," a frustrated Benjamin shouted back.

"You have King. He be better than a rifle," Dutch yelled, working the helm.

With Luke and John paddling, they navigated the narrow shallows for about a mile. Then they turned the boat in at a quiet inlet at the end of the island. With some hard rowing, they maneuvered the *Lulu* close to shore and secured her in five feet of water.

After checking the mooring lines, they placed the ramp boards out, and Dutch retrieved a pistol and two rifles from the boat. He gave one of the rifles to Luke and the pistol to John. Then, with Missy in tow, they started walking back along the sandy shore.

Midway up the island, they found Benjamin and Ruth leading the animals down the shoreline. Mother and children were delighted to be reunited, rushing up to each other for a hug. Then, with a look of relief, Ruth handed the leads for the cow and mule to Luke and John.

Benjamin approached Dutch, leading his steeds, his deep-set brown eyes blazing and eyebrows twitching. As he handed the ropes to Dutch, he said in an angry voice, "You put us in danger by leaving us behind. You had no right to take my boat."

"Your daughter was aboard alone. Someone had to take control, and I was the closest," Dutch replied sharply.

Mr. Jameson stood fuming, his fists clinched. "Your vulgar ways have no place on my boat. If you defy me again, I'll slit your throat and plant you deep." With that, he turned and stomped off towards the end of the island.

Ruth glanced over to Dutch, her hazel eyes full of silent apologies. Luke and John stood, stunned by what they had just witnessed.

Finally, Missy looked up at her mother and asked, "Why is Daddy mad?"

No one saw fit to answer.

When they arrived back at the moorage area, they found Benjamin sitting on a log, reading his bible. As soon as everyone was within earshot, he looked up and said, "Tomorrow be the Sabbath. We will stay here until Monday morning. Luke and John, clear us a campsite."

With the sun still high in the sky, Dutch secured his camp and then saddled Scout. Soon they and the dog were wading across the shallow waters for a hunt.

What they found across the river was a deep band of trees and underbrush that opened up to rolling hills of tall, green, spring grass. With King in the lead, free of the dells, Dutch gave Scout his head, and they were soon galloping over the countryside. After a week of inactivity, Scout enjoyed the freedom of the open range, and they were soon jumping snags and leaping across shallow ravines. Horse and rider were one.

Three hours later, they returned to camp with a fat, dressed out three-point buck slung over the front of the saddle. The family was pleased with the fresh meat, and the boys hung the animal from a tree limb for butchering. To Dutch's surprise, even Benjamin seemed appreciative of the fresh game.

That night, both camps ate their fill of venison steaks. Even King gorged himself so badly that he turned up his nose at a meaty bone brought over to his camp by Missy. The little girl, full of questions and giggles, stayed awhile watching Dutch shaving himself in the firelight.

"Why do you use your knife as a razor? If your mommy is an Indian princess, are you a prince? Why is Daddy mad at you?"

Soon, her mother called her for bed. Once the family fire was out and everyone had retired, Dutch poured whiskey into his coffee and spread out his bedroll. Then, resting on the ground with his saddle as a pillow, he listened to the night critters and the songs of the frogs. In the distance, over the gurgle of the river, he heard the low murmur of thunder, as if God was clearing his throat. Staring at the fire, Dutch's thoughts drifted.

When Ruth quietly stepped from the shadows it startled him back to reality with a jolt. Even a surprised King bolted to his feet, with a snarl on his lips.

"Didn't mean to sneak up on you, Dutch. Please forgive me," she said, with the firelight dancing in her eyes. "You saved my life today, and I couldn't go to bed without thanking you."

"Would you like a drink?" he asked, holding his cup in the air.

"Aye," she replied, her eyelashes fluttering.

As Dutch poured her coffee and spiked it with one finger of whiskey, Ruth came to rest on a log close to the fire. He handed her the cup and said, "The fall just stunned you. Your husband and Luke were right behind me, ready to jump in, if you needed help."

She took a big drink from the cup and then licked her lips. "Ben treats you the way his brother treats him. He doesn't mean it. He just doesn't know any better. As for him jumping in the water to save me, I don't think so. He can't swim."

Dutch smiled broadly, his head slowly bobbing. "Now I understand why he seeks the shallow waters. He is fearful."

"He's not afraid of much. He's got more courage than most. But not when it comes to water," she replied, taking a second long drink.

"Most Indians don't know how to swim either. It's a funny thing. They just never seem to take the time to learn."

"Anyhow, Dutch, I wanted to thank you. Maybe you and Ben can find an understanding. It would make for a much more joyful trip." Ruth stood, drained her cup and handed it back. "Good night. Please feel free to join us tomorrow for our bible reads. The Sabbath be a day of fellowship." She smiled warmly, then turned and walked back into the shadows.

He did join the family the next day for their religious readings. Benjamin gave a short sermon on being faithful to God's Commandments. Then, to the delight of the children, Dutch played two gospel songs on his flute. It was a reminder for all that, even in the wilderness, God's words and music could be heard.

The boat departed early Monday morning under cloudy skies, with a cold, teeth-chattering wind swirling up from downriver. For the next few days, rain, sleet and hail storms blew in, one after the other. During this time, Ruth and Missy huddled under the cover of the cabin roof, while John worked the bilge pump almost constantly. On the exposed rooftop the men stood, weathering the many downpours while trying to keep control of the boat in the windswept waters. The fast-moving storms made it hard to see the way, and Benjamin continued steering the boat too close to the shore.

The horses got the worst of it. They stood in the open bow, with water rolling off their bodies, their heads hung low, making them look like drowned rats.

The night camps were cold and damp as well, with little dry tinder for campfires. The family slept under the roof of boat, but there were many leaks. Dutch and King found refuge in their tent, where they ate hardtack and jerky while trying to stay dry. It was a cold miserable time for all. Finally, some days later, the rains were swept away, replaced by a warming sun.

The Ohio River snaked its way along, with many narrow bends and turbulent curves. Early one morning, after the days of hellish weather, the boat floated into an unusually long, straight stretch of lazy green water. After they had paddled for about two hours down this unbowed length of the river, the land started rising up and narrowing, with many boulders protruding from the shoreline. From the rooftop, Dutch paused his rowing for a moment, to use his spyglass to peek downstream. What he found was an approaching sharp curve, leading into a tall, rocky gorge with a mainstream of fast-moving water. He feared the coming of rapids.

"There's a boat behind us!" Luke shouted from his paddle.

Dutch and Benjamin both turned from their stations and saw the distant speck of another boat in their wake.

Putting the glass again to his eye, Dutch responded, "It's a good-sized craft. Don't see any livestock. Four men are working the boat."

"Could they be pirates?" Benjamin asked from the helm.

"Don't rightly know. They're over a mile behind us," Dutch answered. He collapsed the spyglass and put it back in his pouch. "I'm more worried about what's in front of us."

"What did you see?" Benjamin asked with concern.

Dutch pointed his arm downstream. "Better warn everyone below. Rapids be coming." "Mr. Jameson, keep your helm mainstream and we'll be alright."

Within the half-hour, the boat was floating down an ever-narrowing river with a current of ever-increasing speed. Faced with a shore of rocky cliffs, Dutch yelled to Benjamin to keep the boat in the deeper water.

As usual, he was ignored. Mr. Jameson steered for the shallow waters of the north side of the river.

Using his paddle, Dutch tried to push the boat more towards the center flow.

With rocks now protruding from the shoreline, and the increasing roar of the current, the two men began to shout at each other. When the boat bounced around another sharp bend, they could see white water and boulders hindering their way. In the rush of the current, the boat picked up speed and became harder to steer. Dutch pulled his pole from the water and shouted for Luke to do the same. He then rushed to the helm to help.

Benjamin pushed him away just as the boat started twisting and shaking in the undertow of the white water. Dutch glanced downriver and realized that the boat was moving towards a narrow pass between two large boulders, but he feared the gap was too small.

"You're in the wrong damn channel. You'll get us all killed!" Dutch shouted over the roar of the river.

Seconds later, the boat bumped with a loud thud against one boulder, then recoiled across the fast-moving narrow gap to crash into a second tall boulder.

Everyone aboard was thrown to the deck as the long helm pole broke in half like a twig, leaving the boat without a rudder. The helpless craft turned one hundred and eighty degrees in the violent water, hit a few more rocks, and then started moving backwards in the flow. With a fearful Benjamin standing frozen in place, still holding the broken tiller, Dutch grabbed his rowing paddle and yelled for Luke to do the same. The two men jumped down to the open bow, which was now the stern. As they did so, they were drenched with white water as the boat came crashing down another rapid. Regaining their footing, they moved between the two frightened horses and used their long paddles as rudders. Finally, they managed to stop the boat from twisting, and maneuvered her into deeper waters.

With the cabin blocking their view, they had a hard time seeing ahead. When they yelled for help, a frightened, white-faced Benjamin appeared on the rooftop to give them hand signals. They maneuvered the boat around a few more boulders, and then looked at their wake to find the worst of the rapids slipping away.

With the river widening and currents slackening, the vigorous waters soon turned lazy again. Returning to their rowing stations Luke and Dutch paddled the damaged craft into the quiet waters of a small cove, where they secured the boat.

While a somber Benjamin inspected the inside of the boat for damage, the boys and Dutch moved the agitated livestock to a nearby patch of grass. When they returned, they found Benjamin waist-deep in the water, looking over the hull's planks. On shore stood his wife, reliving her ride down the rapids in a loud, furious voice. From the water, Mr. Jameson nodded a few times at her rant and looked her way sheepishly, without saying a word.

When he waded ashore, he looked relieved, and told everyone that while a few of the boat planks were scraped and gouged, the boat still seemed watertight. He then called for building a new rudder. Finally, he said, with a long face, "I misjudged the rapids and my stubbornness put my family at risk. For this, I'm deeply sorry."

His candid atonement surprised them all. It took courage for this big, strong man to speak of his weaknesses, and everyone's eyes filled with an unspoken forgiveness.

As the family prepared to climb aboard to fetch the proper tools to craft a new rudder, they looked upriver and spotted the other boat shooting the rapids. It was a somewhat smaller craft than the *Lulu*, with an open bow and stern, and a small cabin amidships. It looked as though four men were working the paddles and rudder. After completing the bumpy ride down the white water, the little boat turned directly for where the *Lulu* was moored.

As the boat approached, Dutch and Luke stood in the open bow with rifles in hand, while Ruth, John and Missy took shelter in the shadows of the cabin. Standing on the rooftop, Benjamin greeted the boat with a shout. "We are the Jameson family, on our way to Tennessee."

"We be the Wilkins family, on our way to Kentucky," the middle-aged helmsman shouted back. "My name is Henry. Upriver we saw a rudder smashed against some boulders and were wondering if you folks needed any help."

Mr. Wilkins was an unusual-looking fellow, dressed in blue canvas overalls, with a full head of straggly, salt-and-pepper hair and a midnight goatee that was perfectly trimmed. From the continued conversation, they learned that Henry was a carpenter; and he offered to help build a new rudder. He was joined on deck by his wife, Helen, who wore a white bonnet and homespun dark-blue dress.

Henry introduced his three paddlers. As each of their names was spoken, they removed their hats. To the surprise of everyone, they were all girls.

Benjamin called his wife and children up from the cabin below and introduced his family, as well. Soon, both boats were gleefully chattering across the water with each other. Dutch and the boys helped the Wilkins family secure their boat alongside the *Lulu*, and both families came ashore.

With the two men working on building a new rudder, the women got busy preparing the noon meal. It was a happy time for both Helen and Ruth, and over the cooking pots they gossiped about all things family. With the children pressed into fetching firewood and supplies from the boats, Luke slipped away strolling by the river with the oldest daughter, while Dutch saddled Scout so that he and King could go out for a hunt.

Two hours later, Dutch returned to camp with a deer slung over his saddle. Dismounting, he found both families eating a stew of beans, bacon and potato. He also noticed that the men had completed the new rudder but that it was not yet installed.

Helen Wilkins handed him a plate of food and poured him a cup of coffee from her pot. Dutch came to rest on a log snag and ate his meal, watching the two families enjoy their fellowship. After he finished with his food, he and Henry Wilkins, with his malicious looking Scottish knife, butchered the deer, sharing the meat between the two families.

The Wilkins were a fine family with a neighborly spirit of sharing and helping. After the camp was cleaned up, they were the first to leave the cove. While Benjamin and Luke installed the new rudder, Dutch and John loaded the animals. The Jameson's paddled out of the cove two hours later. But as Dutch prepared to take up his rowing position, Benjamin asked him, with a broad smile, to take the helm.

Both Dutch and Luke were surprised by his offer, and soon the boat was in the mainstream, making good time with a stiff current.

That night, after the family had retired, Benjamin stopped by Dutch's camp and apologized for his earlier behavior. "We made good time this afternoon. I should have been listening to you, all along." He took a seat on a snag next to the fire. "God cursed me with stubborn pride, and now I must pray for His forgiveness and for yours, as well," he continued with a somber expression.

As Dutch listened to Benjamin's atonement, he took his pipe from his pouch and filled it with tobacco. Then, with Ben still mumbling about his faults, Dutch lit the pipe, using a punk from the fire. Soon, the aroma of pipe smoke filled the campsite.

Mr. Jameson promptly stopped his rambling and sniffed the air. "The smell of tobacco reminds me of the war," he finally commented in a reflective voice. "May I have a puff?"

For the next half hour, the two men sat together, passing the pipe as if attending an Indian powwow. Benjamin fondly told stories of his days as a drummer boy in the Great War, and how he had smoked a pipe or chewed tobacco during his many battles.

For the first time on the trip, Dutch found Mr. Jameson friendly, warm and talkative. At one point, he considered offering him a whiskey, but then thought better of it. No point in pouring salt on an open wound. After all, Amish folks had strange beliefs.

Clarksville ————

Under a brilliant blue sky, on the afternoon of the second Saturday of the journey, Dutch turned the boat into a small, fast-flowing tributary of the Ohio River. With hard paddling and poling, the craft was soon maneuvered inside a small still-water cove and secured next to a sandy beach. There the family could take their weekly baths in the fresh cold river water while preparing for the Sabbath.

First off the boat was Dutch and Benjamin, rifles in hand, to search the area for any sign of Indians. Once they were confident that the inlet was safe, Luke and John went to work clearing a camp site close to the sandy shore. Soon, the livestock were removed to a grassy knoll just outside of a grove of trees. Then the family set about fetching food and supplies from the boat. After setting up his own camp, Dutch saddled Scout, and he and King set off for their usual evening hunt.

With a warm breeze at their back, they moved quietly up the small river, looking for any animals that might be seeking fresh water. Dutch found many game trails and followed them as best he could, always with King on point. About three miles up the shore, part of the river backed up into a marshy inlet thick with tall scrub trees and with a bottom of soft black mud. Not sure of his footing, Dutch dismounted Scout and proceeded on foot down a soggy trail.

He hadn't taken a dozen steps before King reappeared in front of him, with his nose twitching and his back-hair bristling.

Just then Dutch heard strange grunting sounds from deep within the dark marsh. Fearful that Indians were about, he checked his rifle and led his horse around a clump of trees to the narrow, soft shoreline of the swamp. Tying Scout to a tree, while giving King hand signals to stay, he moved to the water's edge and peered into the dark misty bog.

Hearing a squeal, he removed his boots and socks, rolled up his leggings and waded into the shallow black water.

With every step he feared quicksand, as he slowly moved in the direction of the sound. The swamp was dank and smelt of rotting foliage. When he rounded another clump of trees, the water turned deeper, and the suction of the mud pulled harder with every foothold. He finally stopped in his tracks and pondered his next move. Then, out of the corner of his eye, he spotted something move, not thirty feet away. Turning in that direction, to his surprise, he saw a hog belly-deep in the mud, busily feeding on the long green stems of wild plants.

The fat, dirty pig was no wild boar, just an escapee from some farmer's paddock. Overjoyed, Dutch didn't think twice about killing the animal, as fresh pork would be a pleasant addition to their venison diet.

Bang!

The pig went down with one shot to the head. The last sound it made was a loud squeal that echoed around the swamp like a clap of thunder.

Retrieving his saddle rope, Dutch waded over to the dead hog and tied the end around the animal's back legs. Before returning to his horse, he pulled from the mud a few of the green stems the pig had been eating. To his amazement, he found that the plants roots were thumb thick wild onions. He pulled a few handfuls and then splashed ashore to place the onions in his saddle bags. Using Scout, he then dragged the dead hog to dry land.

With King standing guard, he gutted the animal, leaving its stinky and steaming entrails for other forest scavengers. It was a slimy, smelly job that left his arms and buckskins stained and soiled with blood and guts. Once the pig was dressed out, he washed the carcass with muddy swamp water and cleaned the animal as best he could. Then he lifted the hog across his horse's shoulders, in front of his saddle, just as he had done with numerous other kills. But this time, for some reason, Scout bolted, bucking off the carcass while crying out with a loud, angry whinny.

Dutch was astounded with Scouts actions. He stood furious, shouting curse words at his wild-eyed steed. Finally, he walked over to the tall grass where the hog had landed, and gazed down on the limp animal. Would *he* now have to carry this eighty-pound pig on his shoulders and lead his horse back to camp? That was something he didn't want to do, as the hog smelled as rotten as the swamp.

That was when it dawned on him the reason for his horse's behavior. Scout didn't want the noxious animal draped across his shoulders, any more than Dutch did.

Moving back, Dutch took the horse's long nose into his hands and whispered softly in his ear, "I got it, mate. No dead hog on your shoulders. I'll sling it on your rump and keep your nose to the wind. When we come to the river, I'll wash it again in fresh water."

Scout's eyes looked into his. Then he whinnied and shook his head. They had come to terms.

With the shadows lengthening, he led his horse slowly out of the bog, nostrils to the breeze, dead pig slung across his rump. As Dutch walked along, he recalled Kate talking about a German stew made of pork. He would celebrate this kill by inviting the family to his camp, the next evening, for just such a meal. Once on the shore of the river, he stopped and carried the carcass to the fresh water, where he cleaned it again. Then, placing it back on Scout's backside, he remounted. As they rode off down the river, Dutch took pride that his 'horse whispering' had worked.

When he arrived back in camp, the family was just finishing their evening meal. As he rode in, they looked his way and gazed with great excitement upon his kill.

"We haven't had fresh pork in months," Ruth said with a broad smile.

"Is that a wild hog?" Benjamin asked.

From the saddle Dutch replied, "Nay, he was some farmer's escapee. I found him eating wild onions, up in a swamp. Should make for a pleasant change in our diet."

"What is that awful smell?" Ruth asked as she approached Dutch and his horse.

"That would be me," he answered. "Between a week's work, the swamp and cleaning the pig, I've become quite rancid."

"Stay downwind from us, lad," Benjamin said, with his fingers pinching his nose. "The boys can do the butcherin' while you jump in the river to clean up."

"Aye," Dutch answered. Dismounting, he handed Scout's reins to Luke. "I'd like the hog's legs, half the belly and a few chops for my Bear Box."

Under a red and pink sky, Dutch slipped into the river with soap in hand. An hour later, by moonlight, he returned to his camp, carrying his wet laundry and dressed only in his damp small clothes. There in the firelight, Luke was waiting. He had built Dutch's fire up and had run a rope line close to the flames. He had also placed his saddle and bedroll on the ground, with a warm blanket waiting on top. As Dutch wrapped the dry blanket around his cold shoulders, Luke carried his wet buckskins to the line.

"Scout is hobbled and grazing with Willow," the boy said, hanging up the garments. "I'll bring them in when you're ready. And I put your meat in your box."

Dutch poured himself a cup of whiskey from the jug in his saddle bags and stepped close to the fire to drink it. "Much obliged, Luke. Any trouble butchering the hog?"

"Nay," he answered. "I've done them before. But I ain't ever killed one with a rifle. Will you tell me about your hunt?"

For the next hour, they huddled around the fire and talked hunting, tracking and the finer points of slaughtering game. It was the longest conversation Dutch had yet shared with Luke, who was a fine lad with a bright mind and sharp wits.

The next morning, after the bible readings and a sermon, Dutch played his flute and then invited the family to his camp for a special meal to celebrate the killing of the pig. "I have but one problem," he said to the family. "I only have place settings for myself and the dog. So please bring your own."

Ruth was pleased with his invitation and sat, curious faced, on the milking stool. "Your offer is indeed surprising. What will your menu be?"

"A German dish told to me by a lady friend who is a cook at a public house."

"Will you need any help?" Ruth offered.

"Just bring your own outfits and come two hours before sunset."

That afternoon, Dutch got busy preparing his meal. His first task was burning the hair off the four pig legs and cleaning the skin thoroughly. Then, using his hatchet, he cut off the hog hoofs and cut each leg in half. Those eight pieces of pork he dredged in flour and set aside. His next task was to make a batch of Katie's sourdough biscuits, a task which took the better part of an hour. Once they were cooling on a tin plate, he melted more lard in his deep iron skillet and browned all the leg parts. Then he added ten cups of water to the pot and brought it to a boil. As this liquid brewed, he added some of his wild onions and a few of the special spices Kate had packed away. Watching the pot, he waited until half the broth had boiled away before he added four cups of rice. To that mixture, he stirred in more onions and spices, then covered the pot and took the heavy skillet off the flames.

An hour later, just as the family arrived, each carrying their own tableware, his meal was ready.

"It smells delicious," Ruth said, coming to rest on a long log that Dutch had rolled into camp.

"Would you like to say the prayers?" Benjamin asked of Dutch.

"Aye," Dutch responded, standing in front of the family. "Let us all join hands."

Dutch continued, with his head bowed. "The Tillamook Indians believe that the salmon that come to their bays twice each year are the spirits of their departed relatives. The meat the fish provides is sent from their Gods. If this be so, then the Lord has sent us this pig. May we find sustenance from its flesh and faith from its deliverance. Amen."

Dutch first served hot water boiled with cinnamon sticks to his guests. Then he passed around the plate of sourdough biscuits, followed by servings of the pork legs and rice. Once all the plates were filled, everyone ate.

"Your biscuits are outstanding and your food is wonderful," Ruth said, after her third spoonful. "There are flavors here I've long forgotten. What spices did you use?"

"Paprika, thyme, crushed dried garlic, fresh wild onions, salt and red pepper. My lady friend Kate also talked of mushrooms, but I couldn't find any."

"Is this mysterious lady Kate your girlfriend, Dutch?" Ruth asked.

"She could have been," Dutch replied biscuit in hand, "had not twenty years separated us."

"Years are only numbers, lad," Ruth murmured, and took another spoonful.

With specks of rice stuck to his beard, Benjamin was as quiet as death, as were the boys as they savored every mouthful of the food. Finally, little Missy looked up from her empty plate and asked, "What do you call this meal?"

Dutch thought for a long moment and then replied, "Pig Knuckle Stew."

It was a delightful evening. In the end, there wasn't a crumb of a biscuit or a grain of rice remaining. Even the knuckles were eaten to the bone and then dragged off by the dog. The evening finished off with flute music and laughter floating across the calm cove.

With warm days and cool nights, the boat continued down the wide, green, lazy river. Along the way, they passed a few tiny towns with dirt roads and log huts, but they never pulled ashore. The family's boat builder had told them that the only town worth stopping at was Clarksville. There they could replenish provisions and find out the condition of the river falls, which was a two-mile stretch of rapids. He had also said that this tiny hamlet would mark the halfway point for the family's journey, and had directed them to look for it on the north shore, alongside a large river island.

With eyes as sharp as a hawk, Luke was the first to call out "Clarksville," the following Saturday afternoon. From the river, it didn't look like much of a town, with only a few buildings high on a bluff above the river, and a small floating log-wharf on the shoreline.

Dutch turned ashore. Soon the boat was secured to the dock, and the entire family walked up a steep ramp to the frontier town. Once on high ground, they passed a few log houses and a stable with a large corral, then turned down a dirt street and discovered a large number of shops. Above the wide boardwalks, the town had a dry goods store, a general store, a blacksmith's shop, a land office, and numerous other establishments. To their surprise, there was even a two-story public house, named The Grand Hotel. Clarksville, with its tree-lined streets and wood-frame buildings, was a little oasis in the middle of a wilderness.

The family walked the length of the main street and then turned back for the general store. Inside the shop, they found all of the things necessary to live on the frontier hanging from the ceiling, stuffed into bins and arrayed on shelves. As they strolled around the store, they met the proprietor, a Mr. Wheeler and his wife, Hazel. He was gray haired, short and skinny, with a pair of spectacles hanging off his bony nose. She was as big as a horse, middle aged with midnight hair. They made an odd couple but were full of valuable information.

"If you folks are going down the rapids, you should walk the river road first," Mr. Wheeler said. "That way, you can get a good look at the best way to navigate the rapids."

"Are they dangerous?" Benjamin asked, looking at some ropes.

"With this spring runoff, not so bad, but the current is strong and there are plenty of limestone boulders protruding from the waters. Most boats unload their livestock and women folks here, and walk them down the two miles to a safe landing."

"Can boats move upriver, as well?"

"Aye, there is a local farmer with a team of oxen. He helps pull the boats upstream, using ropes from the road. It's a long, thorny pull against the current."

"Is there any place to camp around here?" Ruth asked, examining a bolt of cloth.

"Most folks stay across the river, on the island," Hazel replied, placing a gray ledger book on the countertop. "Will you sign our river book, please? We like to keep track of the families going up and down the river."

As Ruth crossed the shop to sign the book, Dutch asked, "Is Clarksville named for William Clark of Lewis and Clark?"

"Nay," Mr. Wheeler answered, "for General George Clark. He was the older brother to William. After the Great War, the government gave him 150,000 acres of land for his services, and he set aside a thousand acres for our town. But Meriwether Lewis and William Clark planned their 1804 expedition from right here at Clarksville."

Dutch was impressed to be standing where such heroes had once stood.

"Well lookee here," Ruth said with glee, pointing a finger to the ledger page. "The Wilkins family signed the book, three days ago."

"Aye," Hazel replied. "We get three or four families a week passing through. Most travelers stock up on what they need. It's a long stretch between stores, out here."

And that's what they did. They purchased fresh eggs, butter, flour and sugar, as well as burlap sacks of oats for the animals. Dutch also bought five pounds of coffee, three strands of tobacco for his pipe and two jugs of whiskey that Mr. Wheeler distilled behind his store. Dutch's final purchase was a bag of hard candy, which he shared with Missy, John and Luke. It was a delightful afternoon, talking with the town folks and learning more about the historic little hamlet of Clarksville.

After loading their supplies aboard the boat, the family and Dutch walked the two miles down the river, keeping a keen eye on the fast-moving waters. What they found were some stretches of treacherous white water, with many boulders protruding from the flow. As they walked along, Dutch noticed that Benjamin had fear written across his face. With each bend of the river, the men talked at length about how they would navigate the rapids, and how they would have to work together as a team. Luke and John seemed eager to go, while Mr. Jameson held his tongue, not saying a dozen words during the entire walk downstream. Finally, they came to a well-used safe area where they could put ashore to retrieve the livestock and women.

On the walk back up the river, Benjamin broke his silence, "Tomorrow be the Sabbath, our usual day of reflection. But I fear I'll fuss all day, worrying about this rivers flow. So let us not put it off. We will ride the rapids tomorrow."

With the shadows long, they returned to the boat and paddled across the river to the large island. There they set up camp and ate a savory meal of bacon, eggs and freshly churned butter for their biscuits.

Early the next morning, they returned to the dock and unloaded the livestock and females. The plan was to have John join his mother and sister for the walk downstream while leading the animals.

With all the family and livestock on the dock, Dutch said to them, "Mr. Jameson, I think your wife and daughter will need your protection on the road. We have no idea what trouble might be lurking in the weeds. Take your rifle and both of my pistols. John can take your spot on the roof."

Both Luke and John were eager for the scheme, but Benjamin was hesitant. Finally, it was Ruth and Missy who convinced him to agree. Mr. Wheeler had warned the family that the local Indians were hostile, and told them to stay alert. There was a hint of relief in Benjamin's face as he led Dutch's steeds up the ramp and down the river road. His fear of the water would not be tested on this day.

The family had agreed to give the walking party an hour's head start, so the boys hung around the dock, while Dutch kept checking his pocket watch. As they waited, they talked again about their approach to the rapids. Time drew out like a long sword, and soon Dutch was chewing some of his tobacco. The boys watched him and then asked for a pinch. At first he said no, but then passed the tobacco around.

"This be our secret," he said, with a pinch between his lips and gum. "Don't go getting me in trouble."

Both boys looked at him with innocent faces. "This isn't our first chew, Dutch," Luke admitted. "We've been stealing chews from Father's stash for years."

As they paddled the boat away from the dock, Dutch stood at the helm, thinking out his navigation for every bend in the river and every protruding rock. As they approached the end of the island they had camped on, the current got stronger and started to pull them downriver with ever-increasing speed. Passing the end of the island, they could see a limestone shelf with a short waterfall between the island and the opposite shore. They paddled clear of this white water.

Around the next bend, large boulders grew tall out of the water, offering only narrow passages in and around the rocks. Steering and paddling in this long stretch of turbulent water took all the strength the lads could muster. The boat rode the strong currents like a cork in the surf; it twisted and pitched and bobbed up and down. The square bow pushed against the flow, raising the prow up only to have it come crashing down again, spraying cold water as high as the rooftop.

At the next bend, they found only a narrow passage between two tall monoliths. In the roar of the river, the boys struggled to keep the boat on course. Then the churning white waters took hold and shot the craft like a bullet through the narrow gap, where it missed crashing against the boulders by only a few feet.

They dodged half a dozen more boulders, but that was the last of it. Around the final bend, the river widened, and the current became manageable. The entire ride had lasted just under thirty minutes. Turning for the north shore, the lads were jubilant with their white-water journey.

Wow! That was something," Luke shouted from his oar.

"Quickest two miles I've ever traveled," John added with a broad smile. "I'd do it again."

"Well, it sure got our hearts going. You men did a great job." Dutch said from the helm.

The lads puffed up with pride upon hearing Dutch call them men. But then, youth seldom recognizes danger and often feels no fear in precarious situations.

Moments later, they arrived at the safe harbor area and secured the boat between two trees. As they waited, they relived their white-water ride with loud boasting, full of high-spirited delight.

Within the half-hour, Ruth, Missy and Ben arrived with the livestock. They had watched from the shore in frightened disbelief as the current had hurled the boat between the two large monoliths. Now everyone was pleased to be reunited. The family rejoiced at the knowledge that they were halfway to their new home. With the last of the river obstacles behind them, they would have smooth sailing all the way to Tennessee.

VI
Mountain Men

—ᴍ—

There would be no mountain men without the fur trade. This enterprise was driven by the fashions of the time. Euro-Americans demanded hats made of beaver skins and coats made of buffalo hides. In China and Europe, there was a great clamor for otter pelts and other skins. To answer these calls, powerful fur companies were formed. The British controlled the Hudson Bay Company, the French dominated the North West Company and John Astor monopolized the American Fur Company and later the Pacific Fur Company. These companies, and the many other smaller regional fur outfits, would flourish economically for the first half of the nineteenth century.

There were essentially three realms of business: the Maritime trade, the Rocky Mountain trade and the Upper Missouri fur trade. All these regions had particular circumstances and hence very different methods of operating. The Maritime trade operated primarily on the Pacific coast, and required shiploads of goods, as well as fearless sailors to trade with the many different Indian Nations. In this realm, the most desired pelts were otter and beaver, which were killed and cured by the local Indians.

The Upper Missouri trade relied on the Indian tribes to bring their buffalo skins to trading posts and forts. There, the robes were sold and then sent to St. Louis, via river.

The Rocky Mountain realm was quite different, and beaver was the fur of choice. The beaver were trapped mainly by Canadian and American mountain men traveling in large troops. The hides were sold at a yearly rendezvous, with the buyers traveling overland to the designated site and then hauling out the furs via mule train or wagon train to be sold in the cities. This system allowed the mountain men to stay in the wilderness year-round, as they did not have to travel to a trading post to sell their pelts.

The mountain man was a slave to the fur market created by the competing fur companies. In a good year, a beaver pelt could be worth ten dollars; in a bad year, it brought only half that amount. The control a company had over a trapper depended on his contract. 'Engages' were men who were supplied and salaried by the company. The furs they collected were the property of the company. 'Skin Trappers' were outfitted by the company in exchange for a set share of their pelts at the end of the season. The 'Free-Trapper' was at the top of this social pyramid, and was beholden to no company. He outfitted himself and trapped wherever and with whomever he pleased.

Contrary to the common belief of lone trappers plying the waters for beaver, the mountain men usually traveled in brigades of forty to sixty men, including camp tenders, meat hunters, scouts and interpreters. From base camps, they would fan out and trap in parties of two or three. It was then that the trappers were most vulnerable to Indian attack. Indians were a constant threat, and confrontation was common. Once the beaver were trapped, they were skinned immediately; the pelts were allowed to dry, and then were folded in half, fur to the inside. Unlike buffalo skins, beaver pelts were compact, light and portable.

The mountain man's life was not ruled by the calendar or clock, but by the climate and seasons. The legends and feats of famous mountain men such as Jedediah Smith, Jim Bridger and Christopher (Kit) Carson, to name but a few, have survived the test of time because there was truth to the tales they told. The life of the mountain man was rough, and brought him face to face with death on a regular basis; sometimes through the slow agony of starvation, dehydration, burning heat, or freezing cold and sometimes by the surprise attack of animal or Indian.

But the rewards for these hardships could also be bright. Jedediah Smith came out of the wilderness in eleven years with a half-million-dollar fortune, in today's money. The lucrative earnings of the fur trade helped propel John Astor to his status as America's richest man.

Joe Meek, a famous trapper and early pioneer in the Oregon Country, once wrote of the mountain men: "...They prided themselves on their hardihood and courage, even on their recklessness and profligacy. Each claimed to own the best horse; to have had the wildest adventure; to have made the narrowest escapes; to have killed the greatest number of bears and Indians; to be the greatest favorite with the Indian belles, the greatest consumer of alcohol, and to have the most money to spend..."

It is estimated that over one thousand mountain men roamed the American West from 1820 to 1840, the heyday of the fur trade.

—ɯ—

Cave-in-the-Rock ———

The rolling green hills of the Ohio River basin rose up like ocean swells, with thickly sprinkled groves of trees under a dark blue sky with wispy cotton-like clouds. This valley was a jewel with rich, fertile lands and an endless, clear-blue river that stretched out to meet the horizon. God's fingerprints were everywhere.

With the last of the river obstacles behind them, and good harmony aboard, the *Lulu* continued down the river. Early on, Dutch had learned how to navigate the keelboat in the different river winds. On the rare occasions when the wind was coming from upstream, the boxy boat was easy to maneuver, with little effort needed from the tiller or paddles. During these times, with the helm secured, the boat would ride the currents while the crew relaxed and marveled at the countryside. If the breeze was coming from downstream, or from the port or starboard quarters, then the rudder and paddles were needed to keep the four-square craft from drifting off course.

Three days out of Clarksville, under a blue sky with a warm stern breeze, Ruth ascended the aft ladder with her pail of water. What she found topside were the oars lying across the roof, and her husband and son Luke sprawled out on their backs basking in the sun. At the helm, Dutch had tied off the rudder with a length of rope and was sitting upon the milk stool, with his spyglass in hand.

Ruth pulled herself through the hatch and stood gazing at the crew's inactivity with a smile. "You boys aren't breaking a sweat, this day. Maybe pillows would be better than water."

Benjamin pushed himself up from the roof and came to rest with his knees crossed. "Mother, this be a fine day for doing nothin'."

"Look at the wing span of that falcon," Luke shouted, still on his backside, and pointing to the sky.

Everyone twisted to his gesture. High above the boat, soaring in the warm wind currents was a monster of a bird, plying the river for prey.

From his stool, Dutch put the glass to his eye. "That be a red-tailed hawk."

"Look at his size," Luke answered. "He be one mean hombre."

Ruth, dressed in her plain black frock and white bonnet, stood with one hand shading her eyes, watching the bird. Soon, the hawk's wings came alive, and the bird flew off towards the north shore.

Still with the glass to his eye, Dutch commented, "He be worth two prime beaver pelts from some Indian medicine man."

"How could anyone kill such a magnificent brute?" Benjamin asked, watching the bird fly off.

Ruth removed her hand from her eyes and turned Dutch's way. "Mr. Blackwell, have you ever killed such creatures?"

"Aye," Dutch replied, folding up his telescope, "Reckon I've killed most every kind of critter in the forest."

"That be sinful," Benjamin said sharply, turning his gaze to Dutch. "Your parents should have taught you better."

"They taught me how to survive. Animals are worth only food or fur."

"You are shameless," Benjamin replied with a frown.

"Have you ever killed a man?" Luke asked, his earnest face twisting Dutch's way.

Dutch stood, moved to Ruth's pail, took the ladle in hand and drank some water.

"Well, Mr. Blackwell, have you?" Benjamin asked.

Wiping the drops from his lips, Dutch replied with sadness in his eyes. "Aye... two or three, don't rightly know. It be something I'm not proud of."

Ruth witnesses his remorse. "Were they white men?"

"White or red, it makes no difference. They are still dead."

"That's why we be Amish," Benjamin said with a determined look. "Our creed forbids killing for any reason."

Dutch turned back to the stool and took his seat. With the warm breeze on the back of his neck, he thought a moment and then responded. "Your faith be yours, full of many man-made peculiarities. The Indians have many funny wonts, as well. But then, quirky religions are common among most men. I believe in the Lord's Commandments and my God-given common sense. My Lord loves people of all faiths – Christians or infidels, white or red."

Benjamin shook his head with a sad face. "That be blasphemy Mr. Blackwell. The red man's religion cannot be compared to our faith. No man can be saved unless he changes his ways. We all must pay the price of our faith by living by the Lord's decrees."

"Aye," Dutch answered, "but not man's decrees. The only person on this boat who is free from the sins of your man-made edicts is Missy. But she too will fall from grace; after all, she is only human."

"What do you mean by that?" Benjamin demanded.

"You know all too well about your religious oddities," Dutch said, looking him straight in eye. "But it is not my place to judge others, and I don't expect others to judge me."

"You are right, Mr. Blackwell. None of us is without sin," Ruth answered with a serious face. "But all good Christians must convert the heathen to the Lord's ways."

"The bible says He loves us just the way we are," Dutch retorted.

"Aye, but He never leaves us the same, once we know His words. We are the shepherds of His flock."

Dutch smiled at Ruth fondly. "I'll leave the redemptions up to the preachers. In the meantime, you can pray for my sins. Killing those Indians weighs heavy on my mind."

"I am pleased you feel that way," Benjamin answered, standing and moving to the water bucket. "There is still hope for your soul."

"The breeze is shifting to port. Let us man our stations," Dutch replied, standing and untying the rudder. But as he watched the family move to their tasks, he couldn't help wondering about their Amish religion and its demand for total faith and allegiance.

On the morning of their sixth day out of Clarksville, they awoke to a river covered by a dense, low-hanging fog. As they paddled and poled their way slowly onto the river, they found themselves in a gray haze void of any sounds other than the gurgle of the river and the swishing of their oars. From the rooftop, the crew could see only a few yards in front of the boat, so they called for John to stand with the horses in the open bow and shout out the way.

"This be like swamp fog," Luke said in a near whisper, slowly pulling on his paddle.

"What makes this so eerie is the quiet," Benjamin added from his station.

Dutch looked at his pocket watch. It was just a few minutes past six A.M. They had departed earlier than usual. "This will burn off soon," he said from the helm.

Suddenly there came the sound of a dreadful scream rolling across the water like an ocean wave. It was faint and far off, but distinct to all. Then another scream echoed off the water, fainter than the first.

"What the devil was that?" Luke asked.

"It sounded like a woman screaming, and it came from downstream," Benjamin replied.

"Quiet," Dutch said in a whisper, with one hand raised.

They stopped rowing and waited to hear more, but they were greeted only by the sounds of the water lapping against the boat.

After a few long moments, Benjamin asked, "What do you think it was?"

"Could have been the call of a bird," Luke answered.

"Nay," Dutch said from the tiller, "That was the cry of death. I've heard it before. There may be Indians downstream. Let's heave too until this fog lifts, and get some rifles up here."

Benjamin looked at Dutch through the gray haze and responded, with one eyebrow raised, "We want no trouble."

Helped by a slight breeze from downstream, the fog slowly lifted. During this time, Dutch brought his rifle to the helm, and stacked his extra muskets, powder horns and a pouch of balls just below the hatch cover. Then he had Luke and John carry two large burlap sacks of oats to the roof. Even Benjamin reluctantly brought his old Brown Bess musket to his rowing station.

Before proceeding downriver, Dutch gathered the family on the roof and offered them words of caution. "I know the Indian ways, and I speak many of their words. If they think us frightened of them, we will be easy prey. Keep a straight face and let me do the talking."

"I refuse to do any killing," Benjamin said in a determined voice.

"I want no killing, either. Let's keep Ruth and Missy out of sight, but us four men very visible. If they see us to be many and armed, maybe they will be dissuaded," Dutch replied.

For the next few hours, the boat moved with the current down the calm, wide river. From the rooftop, everyone kept a keen eye on both shorelines and the downstream approaches.

The landscape slowly changed from a thin line of trees to tall, rocky cliffs that rose up from both shores. Soon the boat was moving in a shallow hollow, with many boulders protruding from the water's edge. They came to a bend in the river and, after making the turn, saw a canoe paddling out from the shore, directly towards them. Quickly, Dutch put his telescope to his eye.

What he saw was three white men rowing the boat. The man in the center of the canoe wore a funny-looking felt top hat and was dressed in a red waistcoat. The other two men looked to be ruffians, with feathered wide-brimmed hats, and dressed in soiled buckskins. They all had rifles at their sides. The small birch Indian canoe had a slight curved prow, fore and aft, and glided quickly across the water.

"They're white," Dutch said, with the glass to his eye. "Let's see what they want."

The crew stopped rowing, and Luke disappeared down the hatch, while Benjamin and Dutch grabbed their muskets. A few moments later, the canoe came alongside but stood off a few yards from the keelboat.

The man with the funny hat was the first to speak. "Welcome to Hardin County, Illinois. I be Bully Wilson, the proprietor of a public cave just around the next bend. I would like to invite you folks to stop in and partake of some good Kentucky whiskey, meet a few of our wenches and eat some fine vittles. We've even got a patch of grass for your horses there."

On the rooftop, Dutch and Ben stood shoulder to shoulder. Bully Wilson seemed friendly enough, and he spoke with a bright inviting voice. But the other two men in the canoe had long, sour faces, and were grasping tightly to their muskets.

"Thank you, Mr. Wilson, for the invite," Dutch answered. "We be Amish men and don't partake in drinking spirits."

"Never heard of such a thing," Bully Wilson said, slowly shaking his head. He had a dirty bacon-face, with a black handle-bar mustache. The red waistcoat he wore was too tight for his chubby body. He was a ridiculous figure of a man for the middle of the wilderness. "Still, you gotta eat, don't ya? We've got ourselves a real good cook at the cave. You boys pull in and we'll fill your bellies," he said with a kindly smile.

"Thanks again, Mr. Wilson. Very neighborly of you," Dutch answered. "But we have to keep moving on."

Bully's smile quickly turned to a smirk. "You don't keep a very friendly boat."

Dutch tapped the rooftop with his toe, a prearranged signal for John and Luke to step from the shadows of the cabin, carrying rifles.

When the lads came into view, Bully asked in a stern voice, "How many of you are there?"

"We've got a boat load," Dutch replied with a benevolent smile.

By now, both boats had drifted around the river bend. On shore, behind Bully's canoe, Dutch could see a granite monolith with a tall, dark cave opening that faced the river. Across the entrance was a painted canvas banner that read: 'Wilson's Liquor Vault and House for Entertainment.' On the shoreline in front of the cave were two empty canoes, with a number of men milling around the opening.

"Here's your last chance, boys. Come ashore and have some fun," Bully said, with a half-hearted smile.

"Sorry, Mr. Wilson. We've got urgent business downriver," Dutch answered, keeping a keen eye on Bully's boat.

The men in the canoe gave Dutch an angry glare and mumbled something to each other. Then they paddled off.

As the canoe departed for the north shore, Luke returned to the rooftop and, with all good haste, the boat got underway.

"Let's put some water between us and those men," Dutch said from the helm.

"Mr. Wilson seemed friendly enough," Luke answered, pulling his paddle.

Dutch smiled at the lad. "Mr. Wilson is a spider, weaving a web for unsuspecting pilgrims. I reckon that cave be an emporium of river pirates."

A few minutes later, they turned the next bend in the river and saw in the distance what looked to be another keelboat resting in a calm cove on the north shore. Quickly, Dutch put his glass to his eye and searched the waters and shoreline around the boat for any trouble. All he saw looked quiet. Then the look of the boat struck him. "That's the Wilkins boat!" he shouted, with his glass still raised. Soon he noticed a lady coming onto the open deck, wearing a dark dress with a white apron and bonnet. Spotting him, she began waving a white cloth over her head.

"Is that Mrs. Wilkins waving?" Benjamin asked.

"Don't rightly know. We're still a good half mile away," Dutch answered.

"Let's pick up our speed, Luke. They might need our help," Benjamin added.

After closing the distance to a quarter mile, Dutch scanned the boat again with his glass, trying to get a better view of the woman waving the cloth. When he looked closely, he spotted the faint darkness of whiskers under the white bonnet. Then he looked beyond the boat, into a grove of trees. There in the shadows, caught in a small shaft of sunlight, he saw the horrifying sight of two naked figures hanging by ropes from a tree. In that frozen instant, he recognized Mr. Wilkins's trimmed goatee.

"Well, Mr. Blackwell, is that them?" Benjamin demanded.

Dutch removed the glass from his eye and firmly said, "Stop rowing." Then he moved to Benjamin and handed him the glass. "Take a close look at her face, and then in the trees just behind the boat. That's the screams we heard, this morning."

"What is it?" Luke asked, but no one responded.

Benjamin stood with the telescope to his eye, and his mouth gaped open. He looked for a long moment, then returned the glass to Dutch with a frightened face.

No one said a thing, and no one moved.

Finally the silence was shattered by Luke demanding, "What's going on?"

Dutch turned to the lad and said, with a sad face, "The Wilkins family is dead, and their boat taken by pirates. We need to get moving."

Luke's mouth dropped open, and he snatched the glass from Dutch's hand. He put it to his eye and twisted his body toward the north shore.

"Look at the woman's face," Dutch repeated. "Then in the trees just beyond the boat."

It only took a few seconds for Luke to see the ruse and the evidence of death. When he removed the glass from his eye, he handed it back to Dutch with a trembling hand.

"What of the daughters? I only saw the husband and wife," he said in a quivering voice.

"More than likely they'll be sold, fresh white girls will bring many pelts," Dutch said, putting the glass back into his pouch."

"Now what?" Luke asked with panic in his voice.

"We get the hell out of these waters," Dutch replied.

"We have to go rescue the girls!" Luke blurted angrily.

"We want no trouble," Benjamin said firmly. "Let's man our oars and get back to the mainstream."

"We can't just leave them here," Luke pleaded.

"It is my family at risk now," Benjamin added, taking his oar in hand.

With the men rowing, Dutch turned the boat for the center flow. As he did so, a rifle shot rang out from the north shore. The distance was over two hundred yards, and the lead ball fell harmlessly in the boat's wake. Dutch thought about returning their fire, but the distance was too great. Then came two more puffs of smoke from the shore, and the crackle of rifle fire.

Those bullets also fell well short of the boat. Dutch turned the boat again into the main flow.

Ruth's head popped up from the hatch. "What's going on? Was that rifle fire?" she asked with an alarmed voice.

"Aye," Dutch answered from the tiller. "Do you know how to load rifles?"

"My wife will have no part of killing," Benjamin shouted.

"What killing? What's going on?" Ruth asked, with only her head above the hatch.

"Henry and Helen Wilkins are dead. We saw their boat and their bodies back there on the shore," Dutch answered.

"Good God!" Ruth yelled. "What of their children?"

"We don't know," Luke answered, while pulling his paddle as fast as he could.

"If the pirates come after us, can you load my rifles?" Dutch asked again in a firm voice.

"Pirates! Yes, yes, I know how to load rifles," Ruth answered.

Moments later, Luke's keen eyes spotted a large canoe turning the cave-in-the-rock bend of the river. It found the mainstream current, making good speed.

Dutch tied off the helm and put the glass to his eye.

Aboard the canoe were five men, all paddling with the savvy and rhythm of Indian warriors. From the north shore, another canoe with three men paddled out from behind the Wilkins's boat. "Our square bow be like an anchor," Dutch said, removing the glass from his eye. "We need more speed," he shouted to Luke and Ben, while stacking the bags of oats on each side of the tiller yoke.

Soon the canoes came within a quarter mile and opened fire. Their bullets splashed in the boat's watery wake, some twenty yards off. Dutch took a kneeling position behind a sack of oats, with his Kentucky long rifle primed and the hammer back.

"They be out of range," Benjamin shouted.

Taking careful aim at the big canoe, Dutch yelled back, "Shot many an elk from this distance."

Fizz-Bang!

When the smoked cleared, the lead rower had a bloody tunic, with Dutch's ball in his right shoulder. Dutch quickly lowered his big rifle down the hatch to Ruth and took from her one of the refurbished muskets. This time, he took aim at the smaller boat, with full knowledge that the rifle wouldn't have the range.

Fizz-Bang!

The shot was short by only a few yards. Grabbing another rifle from Ruth, he took aim on the big boat again. This time, his ball ripped through the bark of the canoe.

Just then, both dugouts answered his fire with rifle volleys of their own. One bullet hit his sack of oats, another ripped into the tiller yoke, and still another ball whistled by his ear.

"Everyone down," he shouted, retrieving another rifle.

Luke dropped to the rooftop and crawled behind another sack. "Give me a rifle."

"No killing!" Benjamin yelled, his body prone to the rooftop.

Dutch handed the lad a rifle. "Aim for the water line of the canoe."

"Why?" Luke asked, with anger in his eyes.

Dutch reached down the hatch and Ruth held up the next musket. "Our bullets can rip apart their brittle canoes. We need not kill these blokes."

Taking up a position behind the other bag of oats, Dutch took aim. Then they both shot.

Fizz-Bang!

As the smoke cleared, they could see that Luke had missed badly and that Dutch had wounded one of the paddlers of the second boat. Both canoes were still moving quickly, closing the gap to their keelboat.

Lowering the spent rifles down to Ruth, Dutch yelled for Benjamin to give Luke his Brown Bess musket.

Reluctantly, Benjamin handed his son the musket, while Ruth handed up the primed and loaded long-rifle.

As Luke and Dutch took up their position behind the bags of oats, another rifle volley rang out from the canoes. The balls sang across the rooftop, one hitting the helm yoke and exploding the wood.

Dutch felt the sting of a splinter slicing into the flesh of his neck. But his adrenalin was pumping, and he shook off the pain. Preparing to return fire, he shouted to Luke. "It's all about breathing, lad. After you exhale, hold your breath for a count and then drop the hammer."

Fizz-Bang!

His aim was true, and Dutch watched his bullet rip open the bark of the small canoe.

Fizz-Bang!

Luke fired, and his ball hit the large canoe, just above the waterline.

Ruth handed up two more rifles. They fired again, and this time Dutch hit the second canoe, again just at the waterline, while Luke's ball fell just short of the big boat.

Both dugouts slowed in the water. With both crafts damaged, and two pirates wounded, the battle was over.

Spent rifles in hand, Dutch and Luke watched as the canoes slipped away.

Benjamin crawled to the two men and asked, "Are we out of range?"

Dutch turned his way, with sweat running down his face. "Aye."

Ben looked at Dutch with a stunned expression. "You're hit!" he exclaimed, and Dutch felt the warm blood trickling down his neck. "Mother!" Benjamin yelled towards the hatch, "The battle is over, and Dutch is wounded. Grab your kit and send John up to help row."

With Benjamin at the helm and his two sons rowing, the *Lulu* returned to the mainstream and continued down the river. Ruth came to the rooftop with her medical kit and Dutch's jug of whisky from his saddle bags. She had Dutch lay prone, with his head in her lap. She removed two large wood splinters from his neck, one of which had missed his main artery by less than a half-inch. She also removed a half dozen smaller slivers, and cleaned the wounds with alcohol. Then she wrapped his neck with a cloth bandage and tied it off.

"You be fine," Ruth said, finishing up with Dutch, "but your tunic is covered with blood. Take it off and I'll wash it for you."

Dutch pulled his buckskin shirt off and handed it to her with a smile. "Thought you said you wouldn't care for me in any way."

"Shush. This be our secret," she answered with a grin, and placed a finger on her lips.

The boys and Ben let out a chuckle.

"Well, at least we didn't kill anyone," Benjamin said, with the rudder pole in hand.

"But they did," Luke said angrily. "The Wilkins are dead, and their girls kidnapped."

"We haven't killed *yet*," Dutch answered, sitting Indian-style on the roof. "We won that battle because their canoe bark was brittle, while our heavy planks swallowed up their bullets. Once repaired though, their canoes are twice as fast as our boat. Come nightfall, those same river rats could come searching for us."

"So what do we do?" Luke asked.

"We stay on the river until sunset," Dutch said. "Then we'll hide the boat in a cove while making a cold camp. The family will remain aboard the boat, armed and ready to go."

"Tomorrow be the Sabbath," Benjamin said firmly.

"With those river rats roaming, we can't risk an extra day," Dutch said.

"What of the livestock?" Ruth asked.

"King and I will watch over them on the shore," Dutch answered. "But if we get attacked again, we might have to leave them behind."

"We can't afford to leave them behind," Benjamin said, looking appalled.

Dutch stared at Benjamin for a long moment. "We can buy more animals, but not a new life."

Eight hours later with the sun low in the sky, Dutch stood in his clean buckskins, scanning the waters behind the boat for any sign of canoes. When he was confident that no one was following them, he had Benjamin turn for the south shore. Half a mile farther down the flow, they came to a shallow river tributary. They turned and slowly poled the keelboat upstream to a small grassy island with a tiny grove of trees. Concealing the boat at the far end of the island, they unloaded the livestock and allowed them graze in the tall grass. Everyone was exhausted but, with darkness beckoning, Dutch had the boys chop down tree limbs to camouflage the boat even further. Once that task was complete, he reminded the family of the need for total darkness, then removed himself and King to the other end of the island, where the livestock were feeding. After double checking their hobbles, he stumbled through the darkness and took up a position on a shallow, sandy beach that overlooked the tributary all the way to the Ohio River. There he unrolled his bedroll and perched his rifle and two pistols on a nearby snag.

Sitting quietly on the canvas, he and King ate jerky and hardtack from his pouch. Under a starlit sky with a slight breeze from the north, Dutch spent the night listening for trouble. Once, he thought he saw a light on the river, but when he looked again, he saw nothing. In the darkness, his mind could have been playing tricks on him.

His thoughts were of the Wilkins family and their demise. The harsh frontier could gobble up good folks and spit them out, in the blink of an eye. It was no place for tenderfoots and pacifists.

Dutch dozed off a number of times, only to be startled awake by dark and violent reveries throughout the long night.

Under a cloudy sky, at first light the next morning, the livestock was loaded aboard and the *Lulu* sailed back down the tributary and out onto the river. With Dutch back at the helm, the men worked their stations with rifles at their sides. As they rounded bends in the river and drifted past the rocky shoreline, everyone kept a keen eye out for any trouble.

Working the boat with fears of pirates soon became a tedious task. Midmorning it started to rain, soft and gentle at first, then with gusto. Ruth brought hats and canvas tarps up to the roof, and passed the protection around to the men. "Do you think we can stop for lunch?" she asked Dutch in the downpour.

"Nay," he answered, wrapping the tarp around his shoulders. "We'll only be safe once we get to the Missouri Country."

She nodded sadly and returned below to the dryness of the cabin.

The rain danced on the river's surface and on the rooftop with a rhythm all its own. At times, the men lost sight of shore in the sheets of pouring rain. The weather made for a miserable and frightful passage.

The storm ceased in the early afternoon, and the dark clouds parted to reveal a warming sun that bathed the rooftop and lifted the men's spirits. Ruth soon reappeared, collecting the tarps and passing out jerky and hardtack. "Everyone is exhausted, Dutch. Let's put in early for a hot meal."

With steam rising from the rooftop, he answered, "Just a few more bends in the river. Then we'll see."

Late in the afternoon, they came to the confluence of the Ohio River and Mississippi River. The men stopped rowing, and Dutch stood with his long glass, surveying the turbulent merging of the two flows. The Ohio was clean and blue, while the Mississippi muddy and brown. In the distance, beyond the conflux, he could make out the thin outline of the Missouri Country.

"We're here, boys," he said, smiling, the glass still pressed to his eye. "Let's cross this confluence now and find a safe harbor in Missouri."

"We're all weary," Benjamin said, resting against the yoke of his station. "Let's put in to the north shore and get a hot meal and a good night's sleep."

"Nay," Dutch answered firmly. "We'll not spend another night in Bully Wilson's Illinois. A hot meal and safety are only a few miles away."

There was some grumbling about continuing on, but the mention of Bully Wilson's name motivated the family more than their fatigue. With the entire family on the rooftop, and the sun low in the sky, the *Lulu* drifted the final few hundred yards of the Ohio River and then, with a strong current, bounced out and onto the murky flow of the Mississippi. They had been thirty-one days on the Ohio River, and Dutch's next destination was at hand.

Mountain Jack ————

With great relief, they paddled and poled the *Lulu* into a calm cove just across the Mississippi River. First off the boat was Dutch and King, who searched the area for any signs of trouble. When they found none, the boat was secured and the camps made.

That night, Dutch joined the family for a farewell dinner. Ruth cooked a marvelous venison stew, complete with potatoes and carrots. The mood was festive and friendly, but everyone was exhausted from the past few days, and bed beckoned with the last mouthful of food.

As the family shuffled their tired bodies to the boat, Dutch unrolled his bedroll and put another log on the fire. Once everyone was gone, he cracked open the jug from his saddle bags and poured three fingers of whisky into his tin cup. Soon, King returned from the weeds and curled up next him by the fire. Sleep would come easy, this night, but he feared more dark dreams about the Wilkins family.

Turning his gaze from the flames, he saw Ruth leave the boat with the oil lantern in hand. She walked his way and stepped into the fire light.

"May I join you, Dutch?" she asked in a quiet voice.

"Aye. Would you like a drink?"

"Nay, my drinking days are over," she answered, turning down the lantern. "I'm afraid you think us hypocrites with our beliefs."

"It is not for me to say," Dutch answered, and raised the cup to his lips.

Coming to rest on a snag, Ruth continued, "I'd hoped by now you would see things our way. It takes a strong person, like you, to have a strong faith like ours."

"Faith comes from the heart, not the head," Dutch answered.

"Yes, I've come to realize that. You be like that red-tailed hawk. No one could clip his wings or tell him where to fly. You, too, are a free spirit. Your strong personality for fighting evil would never conform to the Amish ways."

Dutch smiled at Ruth. "You give me too much credit. I'm no saint."

Around the campfire, they talked of faith and God for the next half hour. Ruth had come to respect Dutch's faith, and he hers. The evening ended with the tin cup empty and fond words of goodwill.

Early the next morning, Dutch removed his trail bags and personal gear from the boat. Then he helped Luke load the livestock. Standing next to the ramp, he said his farewells to each member of the family as they loaded the boat. Luke and John were fine lads, the backbone of the family. Missy had a wonderful way about her, and he wished her and her doll much happiness. He shook Benjamin's hand with a firm grip. Dutch had come to respect him, even with his bizarre ways. Then there was Ruth, a tower of strength and the smartest of the bunch.

"You could come with us, Dutch. We could find you a nice Amish girl."

"And teach you how to be a farmer," Benjamin added with a smile.

"Sounds very exciting," Dutch answered with a grin. "But I reckon I'll stay on the trail and see what's around the next bend."

"Aren't you forgetting something?" Ruth asked with a sly look on her face.

"Nay," Dutch answered. He reached into his poke, then handed Ruth a ten-dollar gold piece, adding, "You folks have only a few more days before you reach Tennessee. Don't stop for anything and don't trust anyone. This wilderness can swallow up good folks like you. God speed."

Dutch stood on the shore of the cove and watched the boat paddle onto the Mississippi River. From their place on the rooftop, he received one final wave from the family, which he answered smartly. Even King sang out with a farewell bark. The Jameson's were a fine family and he would miss their fellowship. But he worried about their safety and their pacifist ways. *The meek will not inherit this wilderness*, Dutch reflected, *not with men like Bully Wilson roaming the land. May God have mercy on his murdering soul.*

Returning to the empty camp, Dutch made a pot of coffee and fried his last two eggs. As he sat quietly, eating his food, he realized how lonely the journey would be. He had grown used to the family's chatter and the daily activities of the boat. The realization surprised him, as he had always considered himself a loner.

Finishing his meal, he fed King a couple pieces of bacon. "It be just us now. We'll find a trail and head north."

King gobbled up the meat and stood, bright-eyed, with tail wagging, ready to go.

After loading up his horses, Dutch broke camp and rode out of the little cove and onto the western shore of the Mississippi River. A hundred and fifty miles upstream, he knew he would find the little outpost of St. Louis. His plan was to ride the river shoreline all the way north.

The first few miles were easy going, with flat sandy beaches and few obstacles. But then the way turned, broken with steep hills, and large boulders protruding into the rivers flow. Dutch turned inland and rode to the high ground, a half-mile away. Then he turned north again, keeping the river in sight.

The emerald green prairie he rode was open, with rolling hills of buffalo grass, thickly sprinkled with groves of scab trees. On his right was the broad and turbid Mississippi, with its eddies, sand-bars, rugged islands and thinly forested shores, stretching for as far as the eye could see. The northern sky was blue, with puffy white clouds stacked up like so much cordwood.

A strong, warm breeze from the west filled the air with pollen and dust. Dutch stopped for a moment, tightened his hat's chin strap, and fastened a red bandana across his face, then moved on. King roamed a few hundred yards ahead, with his nose twitching and tail wagging, apparently delighted to be off the boat and on a trail again.

They made good time that morning, and rested at noon in a shallow hollow with a spring creek, out of the wind. While the animals drank and grazed, Dutch filled the canteens and took a short snooze.

That afternoon, the hills became taller and the ravines deeper. At the bottom of the gullies, they forded streams and crossed rills, all flowing out to the river. During the entire day, Dutch did not see or hear another living thing. The Missouri country seemed filled with only rocks, buffalo grass, water and scrub.

With the sun low in the sky, he made camp in a shallow gulch with a clear-water stream and a thick grove of aspen trees. The only way in was a rocky trail from the west that snaked its way down to a gorge that was protected from the tedious winds.

Dutch unpacked his trail bags and hobbled his animals to feed on the grass that grew at the water's edge. Then he chopped some wood, built a fire and set up his camp. Soon, coffee was brewing and he knelt at his Bear Box, planning his meal.

As Dutch was preparing to soak beans in water, King returned from up the rocky trail, clearly agitated. From the dog's excitement, Dutch knew something was wrong, but that it wasn't Indians.

"Somebody coming?" he asked the dog.

King made a tight circle and then headed back up the trail. Dutch put his pot of water and beans aside, then rested his rifle against a tree, away from the fire but in plain view. With that accomplished, he brought his two pistols close to the fire and concealed them behind the log snag upon which he sat. He waited for several minutes, tin cup in hand, before he heard hooves against stone. Looking to the top of the trail, he spotted a lone rider and two horses silhouetted against the setting sun.

The rider stopped for a moment and then slowly moved down the rocky trail. Once on the gulley floor, he moved his steeds directly towards Dutch.

As he approached the fire, he reined in his horse. "Whoa Buck… You must be a goddam pilgrim to let some stranger ride into your camp," the man said with a southern twang. "I could have been an Indian, and you'd be without a scalp."

The rider wore a red blanket-coat, a broad hat of felt, dusty boots, and fringed buckskins. His knife was stuck in his belt, his bullet pouch and powder horn hung at his side, and his double-barreled smooth-bore lay before him, resting against the high pommel of his saddle. All of his outfit had seen hard service and was much the worse for wear, with the exception of an Indian-decorated pouch which hung from his shoulder. He was mounted on a large sorrel horse, and leading a smaller packhorse. The rider sat a good six feet high in the saddle and was powerfully and gracefully molded. In the last rays of the sunset, Dutch noted the strong features and bone-white teeth of his weathered Anglo face.

"Not much chance of you being an Indian," Dutch replied without getting up from his stump.

"Why's that?" the man asked.

"King would have told me, long before you got here."

"Who the hell is King, and where is he?"

"Look behind you."

The man twisted in his creaking saddle and spotted the dog high atop a boulder, not twenty feet away, ready to pounce.

The stranger turned back to Dutch with a grin on his seasoned face.

"And you don't sit your horse like an Indian," Dutch continued, retrieving his two pistols. "Of course, if I was wrong about all that, I was ready to greet you with these two hand-cannons."

"Don't go getting puffed up, lad. I can see you're no pilgrim," the mountain man answered. "I just smelt your coffee and wondered if you'd share."

"What's your name?"

"James Claybo, out of Franklin County, Kentucky. My friends call me Jack. What's yours?"

Dutch got up from the fire and approached the man, offering him an outstretched hand, "I'm Dutch Blackwell, recently from Boston, and the mutt there is King."

They shook hands.

Dutch smiled broadly up at the stranger, then invited him to step down and have a cup of coffee.

There was something about this mountain man that Dutch liked right away. In some ways, he reminded him of his father. The two men sat and talked awhile over their tin cups. As they did, Jack got up and retrieved a jug from his saddle backs. Returning to the fire, he sweetened both coffees with whisky.

"You going in or coming out?" Dutch asked, after tasting the spiked brew.

Jack looked down at his cup and swirled it. "Came out about two years ago, after nearly twenty years of trapping up on the Bitterroot. Had a vision that my folks had died, so I came out to see if it was true." Jack's pale blue eyes twinkled in the firelight as he took a drink from his cup.

"Never heard of the Bitterroot. Was your vision true?"

"Aye, they had gone under from the pox, the year before. The Bitterroots are a mountain range in what's now being called the Oregon Country."

Dutch was surprised by this information. "Are you returning there?"

Jack took another drink from his cup. "Aye, that be my home. Where you heading?"

"The Oregon Country, as well," Dutch answered with a grin. "Joining a brigade of men in St. Louis. Our destination is the mouth of the Columbia River."

Jack smiled. "I paddled that flow, four or five years back. Never made it to the ocean, though. Which way are you going in?"

"Same as Clark, up the Missouri."

Jack shook his head with a frown. "That's the way we went in '89. I was just a younker then, and didn't know any better. It's a miserable trail. We lost a dozen men before we got to the Snake River. No, when I get to St. Louis, I'm going in the way I came out, on the Sweetwater Trail."

"I've read all the Lewis and Clark journals, and I don't recall any mention of such a trail," Dutch replied, his curiosity sparked.

"Free trappers have been using the trail for years. It's the easiest, fastest way over the Stony Mountains. I'll be home before the leaves turn color."

Dutch was astounded by the news. Astor had told him that the Missouri route would take a full year, and here Jack sat, talking of only a few months! He was the real thing, a mountain man who had survived this wilderness.

Over a second cup of whisky, Dutch invited him to make camp, and he cooked up a pan of bacon and beans. After the meal, they spread their bedrolls and sat around the fire, talking some more. That was when Dutch remembered the bottle of Spanish Brandy in his Bear Box. Kate had said to keep it for a special occasion, such as fate delivering this mountain man to his campfire?

Cracking open the bottle they shared the sweet brandy. The men talked more of family, the wilderness and the Indians they had encountered. Dutch learned that Jack's packhorse was named Gray and that he had traveled the Sweetwater Trial three times before. With great hesitation, Dutch finally told Jack of his childhood on the Pacific Coast, and of his father and Indian mother.

At the end of his childhood story, Jack looked at him with a smile and said, "I figured you for a breed, the moment I saw ya. Your swarthy look and thick lips are a dead giveaway."

"My mother was only half Indian, the other half Spanish," Dutch replied, facing Jack down with a proud look.

Before the evening was over, they were old friends, and the brandy bottle was half empty.

The last thing Jack asked that night was, "If I get up in the middle of the night, will your dog come after me?"

"Nay." Dutch smiled from across the fire. "Just don't piss on him by mistake."

As the camp fell quiet, they were serenaded by a far-off lone coyote.

At first light the next morning, the men made coffee and ate some jerky before loading up their animals. As the two of them finally approached their mounts, Dutch paused a moment, then slipped on his bowler hat and tightened the chin strap.

Mountain Jack did a double take from his saddle and then asked, with a wide grin on his face, "You're wearing that funny hat?"

"Aye," Dutch answered, pulling himself onto the saddle. "A lady friend gave it to me, and I promised to wear it across the continent."

Jack chuckled. "You've got more courage than me, mate."

The two riders rode up the rocky trail and turned north once again. It was a remarkably fresh and beautiful May morning. The green, ocean-like expanse of the prairie stretched, swell after swell, to the horizon. Gone was the horrible westerly wind, replaced by the humming of numerous insects.

It was good to have a partner on the trail and Dutch let Jack ramble on from his saddle. When he had arrived home to Kentucky, Jack explained, he not only found his parents dead, but discovered that his younger sister had married a scoundrel named Hector who had taken over the family tobacco farm. "He was as dumb as a post and as slow as a snail. I stayed on for over a year, but when my sister had her first brat and the boy looked just like his father, I lit out. I'd rather live alone in the Bitterroots than on a farm full of Hectors." Jack was quite a talker, and his stories went on for hours, which helped the trail-time pass.

That afternoon, they came upon a windswept forest of scrub trees. The well-traveled trail they rode twisted through summits of trees, some living and some dead, some erect, while others windfallen. While in the forest, they saw and heard a few birds, but found no tracks of animals.

Early that afternoon, the hot and dusty westerly breeze showed its ugly self again. Stopping along the trail, both men covered their faces with bandanas and tightened their chin straps before proceeding down the dusty way.

Hours later, with the sun low in the sky, they came to a cluster of aspens, where they made camp. The trees gave them protection from the ceaseless wind and provided fuel for their fire. Close to the grove was a marshy area with a small, shallow pond surrounded with buffalo grass for the animals to graze upon. Unpacking the horses, the men led them to the grassy pool. Once there, Jack knelt by the water and gazed into it with his keen blue eyes.

"This be a fool's pond. We will take what we need, but boil it all before we use it," Jack said after holding a wet palm to his nose.

"Why?" Dutch asked.

"See those white specks floating on top of the water? Hear the hum of the bugs? Pools of still water like this will twist your gut for days to come."

"What of the horses?"

Looking up, Jack gave a toothy smile. "Not to worry. They have iron bellies. You and I will drink brandy while the water is curing."

"I've never heard of curing water. Where did you learn this?"

Jack stood and turned his lanky body to Dutch, with the sun setting over his shoulder. "A wise old trapper told me of this remedy, years ago, and my gut has never twisted since."

Mountain Jack was like that, full of trail tricks and wisdom from his years on the frontier. Dutch knew that providence had provided him with good fortune when Jack rode into his camp.

That night, the two travelers enjoyed the last of the rice and pork from Dutch's Bear Box, and drank what remained of the bottle of brandy.

"Walked all around this clump of trees, this evening, and didn't see any sign of a living creature," Jack said, tin cup in hand. "Not even a coon or squirrel. This land is hard."

"Reckon that's why we haven't seen any Indians," Dutch replied.

At the mention of Indians, Jack started talking about the tribes of the Bitterroot Mountains. "We got the Nez Perce to the west, a fine culture of people. They live peacefully on the shores of the rivers. Their men are tall and strong, and their woman curvy and friendly. Then to the south is the Snake Indians, great hunters and fierce warriors. Their culture is given to the hardships of life. But if they respect you and you respect their lands, you will have no trouble. I have traded fairly with these two tribes for twenty years, and call them my friends."

Dutch sat quietly on a log snag close to the fire, listening to Jack ramble on about the Indians, finding his words fascinating, colorful and intriguing. Pouring himself another cup of brandy, Dutch asked, "Of which tribe is your Indian pouch from?"

Jack pulled the small pouch from his hip and held it up in the firelight. The bag was made of rawhide, the front flap decorated with brightly colored beads and the claw of a bear. "Riding across the prairie, two years ago, we came upon a band of Sioux in the midst of a buffalo hunt. From the crest of a hill, we saw an old brave get bucked off his horse. Then the bull he been chasing stopped, in a cloud of dust, and turned back to the Indian, mad as hell. The Indian had lost his weapons, but he stood his ground as the buffalo charged him. I shot and killed that bison right from my saddle. It was a lucky shot, damn near a hundred and fifty yards. That bull hit the ground dead, not ten feet from that Indian. Turns out that old redskin was a Lakota medicine man, and he gave me the buffalo hide and this pouch in gratitude for me saving his life." Jack paused a moment and took another swig from his cup. "Of course, I had to dump out all the snake skins, animal claws and roots he had inside.

Now my pouch is filled with my bag of bullets, some jerky and my tobacco."

Jack rambled on for another half-hour about the Sioux Indians and the praise they gave him. Dutch enjoyed the story and was impressed with his wisdom and judgment. Listening to Jack talk was like listening to himself.

For the next two days, they rode together and camped each night in protective hollows of the prairie. As for food, they made do with biscuits and jerky, as the land strangely produced little game. There was not even a prairie hen to be had.

St. Louis —————

On the afternoon of the fourth day, they arrived at the outpost of St. Louis. Dutch found the river town larger than he had expected, near five thousand souls.

Jack had been to the settlement many times before and talked of the town with a fancy. As they rode the main street, they passed two churches, two general stores, the land office, bakery, tavern, two blacksmiths sheds, numerous trading posts, and then found a stable across the street from the Gateway Hotel. The town's wide boardwalks were filled with long-haired men, dressed in buckskins and canvas overalls, as well as busty woman wearing ruffled dresses and holding parasols over their painted faces. Just like Clarksville, St. Louis was an oasis in the middle of a wilderness.

Jack and Dutch stopped at the livery and were greeted by its snake-eyed owner, a man named Axel.

"What's the overnight cost?" Dutch asked with a friendly face.

The owner looked over their four steeds with his beady eyes. "Four bits each, includes a pail of oats for each horse."

"Four bits?" Dutch answered back. "That's outrageous!"

"Welcome to St. Louis, boys," Axel replied soberly. "Out here, there ain't nothin' cheap."

They finally agreed to the extortion, but with the condition that King would stay with the animals and keep an eye on their outfits.

Then they carried their trail bags into the horses' stalls and unsaddled the mounts, turning them loose in the corral.

In the barn, Dutch knelt to the dog and told him to stay, directions King was disappointed to hear.

Walking across the dusty street, carrying only their saddle bags and rifles, Jack said brightly, "I taste a thick beef steak, a few drams of whiskey and maybe a twist with a wench. But it be one last night in a feather bed that I seek the most."

"Sounds like expensive desires, given the prices around here," Dutch replied, tucking his single pistol into his belt.

"Aye," Jack answered fondly. "Don't rightly care. Where I'm going, money ain't worth spit."

The Gateway Hotel was a two-story wood-framed building that had rooms on the top floor and a restaurant and bar on the lower floor. Dutch was outraged to learn from the proprietor, a Frenchman named Louie, that a room with two beds cost three dollars for the night.

"That's more than twice what I paid for a room in New York City," he said angrily.

Louie didn't blink an eye or raise an eyebrow. He simply explained that most of *their type* camped out on the outskirts of town.

"And what *type* are we?" Jack asked, his face reddening.

"You mountain men are all the same," Louie answered, looking down his long, bony nose. "You come to town in your dirty clothes, drink our whiskey, chase our woman and then complain about the cost of civilized society."

"I be here on business," Dutch answered indignantly. "Can you tell me where I might find Mr. Wilson Price Hunt?"

Louie looked at Dutch for a long moment, then gave him directions to one of the trading posts, five doors down.

After a little more grumbling, they paid the man, since neither Dutch nor Jack had the stomach to sleep another night on the hard ground. After cleaning up and storing away their saddle bags in the room, Jack and Dutch walked down to the trading post. The sign above the door read 'Missouri Fur Company.' Inside, they found an older, gray-haired woman working behind a long counter stacked with blankets and trading trinkets.

As Jack looked at some rain gear, Dutch approached the lady. "I be looking for Mr. Wilson Price Hunt."

The lady looked up from her work with a surprised expression. "He's not here, lad."

"John Astor gave me instructions to look up Mr. Hunt when I arrived here in St. Louis. He's leading a brigade across the country to the Pacific Northwest."

A strange smile raced across the lady's wrinkled lips. "John Astor, huh? Well, lad, Mr. Hunt is up in Montreal. He should be back in town come September or October."

"I was told to come in May. I can't wait all summer for him."

"Well," the lady replied, "you could paddle up to Montreal. I'm sure he's recruiting men for the brigade as we speak."

Dutch was astounded by the news. Montreal was a long canoe ride away, and he'd lose the entire traveling season. With his mind spinning, he helped Jack pick out a seal-skin slicker, and they paid the lady.

When Dutch walked out of the Missouri trading post, that afternoon, all of his plans and schemes had faded away like a sunset.

That evening, Jack and Dutch sat in the crowded, smoky barroom of the Gateway Hotel, drinking whiskey and eating beefsteaks. The room was long and narrow, with an ornate mahogany bar on one side and dozens of small, round, wooden tables and chairs on the other side. At the back of the room, next to the tiny cribs that the whores used, was a piano player banging on the ivories. The Frenchman, Louie, worked the back bar, dressed in a clean, white apron, with his black hair slicked back. The food cost two dollars a plate and the drinks two bits each. St. Louis was no place for a miser like Dutch.

Jack chewed on the last of his near raw steak. Then, speaking over the piercing twang of the music, he said, "It be simple enough. You can ride with me."

"Two lone men crossing Indian country sounds a little crazy to me," Dutch replied, whiskey in hand.

"That's the way I came out, just me and Jeddah Smith. We found the Lakota Sioux quite friendly and had no trouble."

"My destination ain't the Bitterroots."

"I know," Jack answered, picking up his drink. "We go up the Platte River, then up the Sweetwater." He paused a moment, and took a large swallow. "Then it's an easy cross of the Stony Mountains and down the other side to the Snake River. We follow that flow and, when it turns north, I go with it. You, on the other hand, will head northwest. After a few hundred miles you'll come to the Columbia. From there, you can float all the way down to the ocean. You should be there by September."

"You make it sound so easy, like it be just a Sunday outing."

Jack beamed at Dutch, his bone-white teeth flashing in the faint light of the bar.

Just then, a high-pitched female voice shouted out over the incessant piano music, "Mountain Jack, is that you?"

When Dutch looked up, he found a woman in a red, revealing dress with fishnet stockings and heels coming their way.

Jack stood with a smile as she approached, and he hugged her. Then, pulling back from the embrace, he said, "Rose, you still working the trade? Thought you retired."

The lady pulled up an extra chair and sat down. "Girls like me just have too much to give," she chuckled. "Are you going to buy me a drink?"

Jack shouted to Louie for another round of drinks. In the dim light, Dutch noticed the many wrinkles of the lady's painted face, and the dark circles beneath her blood-shot eyes. Rose reeked of lilac water, which cloaked the stench of the room. She had to be near fifty years old!

"Who's this handsome lad in the funny hat?" Rose asked, looking Dutch's way.

"Dutch Blackwell from Boston. He and I are going into the frontier together," Jack replied.

"We're not sure of that," Dutch added.

Rose shook her head with a frown. "That be a rough life, only fit for squaw-lovers. Two years ago, you told me you were giving up the frontier life."

"Aye, I did. It just didn't work out. Life on the flatlands isn't for me."

As the piano man finally stopped playing his music, a sandy-haired waiter with a dirty apron approached with the drinks and placed them on the table. While he cleaned away the dinner plates, Rose looked up at him and said, "Thanks, Freddie."

Dutch glanced around the dim room, and saw other painted ladies talking to the customers.

Over the whiskeys, they talked of life in the wilderness and what Rose had seen in her many years of living in St. Louis. Her spirited stories were as tall as Jack's, and her dirty jokes as funny as a jester. Rose was indeed a party wench.

When she finished her drink, she turned to Jack and asked, in a matter-of-fact way, "You want a poke, honey?"

"What's your price?" Jack asked.

Rose didn't blink an eye. "Been gettin' two dollars, these days, but because you're such an old-time customer," she laughed and slapped his arm, "I'll give ya my preacher's rate of only a dollar."

Jack got up from the table with a fond look on his face. "Sounds fine to me."

As Rose got to her feet, she asked, "What about Dutch? Should I get him a tart?"

Dutch felt his face flush. "No... not me," he finally heard himself stammer.

Jack chuckled with a big smile and grabbed onto Rose's arm, "Don't worry about him. He be a breed that only favors squaws." As they turned and walked towards the cribs, Jack stopped and turned back to Dutch. "Watch my rifle, mate. I'll be right back."

Dutch got up and switched to Jack's chair, so that his back was against the wall. With the double-barreled musket at his side, he sipped his whiskey and watched the crowd in the smoky dim light of the barroom. As he did so, he thought about his change in plans. If he rode with Jack, he could be home by September, which would be an amazing passage. But there were lots of Indians between here and there. Without the safety of a brigade, he wondered about the wisdom of it.

Two hooligans sat at a table to his left, drinking and swearing like sailors. Their loud, offensive language broke Dutch's concentration, and he looked their way. Both men were dressed in soiled buckskin and wore ragged moccasins. One man was large, with a pot belly, a weedy brown beard and a pistol in his belt. The other man was tall and skinny, with a ruddy face. They were arguing about money for another jug. Finally, the skinny fellow jumped to his feet and moved to the bar. From his belt, he removed his sheath knife. He banged the blunt end of it on top of bar and shouted, with a drunken stutter, "My name is Bully Wilson. I be from up the Ohio, and I have a fine foreign knife to sell for only ten dollars. Come and take a look at it, gents. It be a special type of blade." The man removed the knife from its sheath and held it up for the hushed room to see. Even in the dim light, Dutch knew instantly, from the shape of the blade, that the knife had belonged to Henry Wilkins. Revenge swelled up in his gut, something had to be done.

A few men stepped forward to look at the knife, but none bought. Where the hell was Jack? Finally, Dutch got to his feet and walked across the room to the bar. Standing next to the pretender, he took a quick glance at the blade. It had Gaelic words etched in the Scottish steel, including the family name of Wilkins.

"I know this knife," Dutch said loudly, looking directly at the skinny fellow. "I helped butcher a deer with it, not two weeks back. At the time, it belonged to one Henry Wilkins. If you look there on the blade, you can see his name etched into it."

Louie moved down the bar, took the knife, and looked carefully at the blade. "The lad's telling the truth," he shouted to the room.

"What's more, I've met Bully Wilson, and you're not him. Where did you get the knife?"

Anger raced across the man's ruddy face. "Are you calling me a liar?"

Slowly removing his pistol, Dutch put it on the bar, with his thumb on the hammer. "I'm calling you worse than that. Six days ago, Bully Wilson killed Henry Wilkins and his wife, and sold their children into Indian slavery. That was after he and his men had pirated their keelboat. I know this because I witnessed their bodies hanging from a tree when we rowed by. So I ask again, where did you get the knife?"

The room had gone quiet as a graveyard. The imposter's eyes bulged, and sweat ran down his forehead.

Dutch picked up the pistol, pulled back the hammer, and then pointed the barrel at his face. "Well?"

From across the room, someone shouted, "Hey, funny hat, leave my mate alone."

Dutch twisted to the voice and saw in the shadows, his jelly-bellied friend with pistol in hand.

Everyone between them moved away.

Dutch twisted back to the now-quivering pretender. "He might get me," he said in a firm, fearless voice, "but you'll be without a head."

Right then, the skinny fellow pissed himself.

From across the room, Jack's strong voice rang out. "Mr. Blackwell, I've got your back."

Dutch glanced his way, and saw Jack standing next to Rose, with his musket in hand.

"And, mister piano man," Jack continued," keep your hands where I can see 'em. I've got two barrels here, primed and loaded."

Dutch grinned at his friend and turned back to the skinny guy. "Well? Are you an ark ruffian, did you take a hand in the killings?"

The imposter looked down at the bar and shook his head, saying softly, "I ain't no river pirate. I bought the knife from Bully at his liquor emporium, two days ago. Honest to God, we know nothing of any murders!"

Dutch thought a long moment, with his pistol still trained on the man's face. "What did you pay?"

"One dollar," he whispered back.

Dutch reached for his purse with his right hand and dumped it on the bar top. Finding one of the blood stained dollar coins, he slid it to the skinny fellow. "Here's your blood money. Take it and your friend, and get the hell out of my sight. If I see you again, I'll blow your head off."

The man's eyes filled with relief as he dropped the knife and scooped up the coin. He and his mate were out the door as fast as a prairie storm.

The room exhaled, and the piano man started playing again. Louie looked at Dutch from behind the bar and said, "One gutsy mountain man."

Dutch smiled, closed the hammer on his pistol, and returned it to his belt. He then gathered up his coins, placing them back in his purse before grabbing the knife. Turning from the bar, he walked back to the table and joined Jack and Rose.

As Dutch came to rest in his chair, Jack said, wide-eyed, "You've got more brass than a monkey! I go for a poke and come back to a brawl."

Just then, the sandy-haired waiter approached again, with more drinks. "Is your name really Blackwell?" he asked, looking at Dutch with a puzzled expression.

VII
The Fur Trade

—ɯ—

From his offices in New York City, John Astor kept a keen eye on the news of the fur trade. He knew the London market for beaver skins, and what a buffalo hide would fetch in Boston, and even the China market for sea otter pelts. When he read of the mysterious, untimely death of Meriwether Lewis, he saw opportunity where others saw tragedy.

After his return from the expedition of the Corp of Discovery, Lewis had been rewarded with 1,600 acres of land and a contract from a publisher for his journals, but writing those memoirs had proven to be a difficult task. Additionally, in 1807, President Jefferson appointed him as the governor of the Louisiana Territory. Meriwether promptly moved to St. Louis.

His record as governor was mixed. Lewis established some frontier roads and was a strong proponent of a regulated fur trade. He also protected the western lands from encroachment by settlers. But he often quarreled with local politicians about his policies of approving trading licenses and land grants. He also was a heavy drinker and a poor administrator.

On September 3, 1809, Meriwether set out for Washington D.C., with his journals finally completed. He had planned to travel to Washington by ship from New Orleans, but he changed his plans while in route, deciding instead to make an overland journey on the old pioneer road near Nashville, Tennessee. On the evening of October tenth, Lewis stopped at a public house called Grinders Stand.

After dinner and the consumption of much liquor, Meriwether went to his bedroom. In the small hours of the morning, the inn-keeper's wife heard gunshots. The next morning, servants found Lewis badly injured from multiple gunshot wounds, including one to the head. He died shortly after sunrise, with his journals missing.

Most believe Meriwether Lewis's death was suicide, while others believed it was murder. The inn-keeper's wife claimed Lewis had acted strangely at dinner. She said he stood and paced the room, while talking to himself like a lawyer, his face flushed and his words rambling. After he retired for the evening, she continued to hear him talking to himself. At some point that night, she heard multiple gunshots. She never explained why she did not investigate the source of the gunshots. It was said, her testimony proved suicide. Others believed that her husband, the inn-keeper, killed and robbed Captain Lewis in his room. His death is a mystery that will never be resolved.

With Lewis and his fur licenses out of the way, Astor saw the opportunity to send his planned Overland Astorians to the Columbia River. By October of 1810, he had a thirty-man brigade moving up the Missouri River to a winter camp on the Nodaway River. That same month, he received a message from his ship, the *Tonquin,* which had departed New York harbor a few months earlier. The message stated that there was treachery aboard the ship. The note warned Astor that not all of his partners in the newly formed Pacific Fur Company were loyal to him or to the enterprise.

This intrigue with the men should not have come as a surprise. For reasons known only to himself, Astor had mostly recruited foreigners for his overland expedition. He had Canadians, Scotsmen and Frenchmen, with only a few colonists within the ranks. Immediately upon receiving the message from the ship, Astor sent instructions to his overland partners, promoting the American, Wilson Price Hunt, to sole commander and making Donald Mackenzie, a Canadian, his second in command. Hunt wasn't a leader of men and had not traveled much farther west than St. Louis, but he knew the fur trade. Mackenzie, by contrast, was an excellent leader of men and a seasoned trapper who knew the upper reaches of the Missouri River. This change in leadership would complicate matters, fueling the disaffection of the men even further.

—ɷ—

Freddie ——————

The wide-eyed waiter with the dirty apron stood, holding the tray of drinks, while he stared down at the men seated at the table. "Is your name really Blackwell?" he asked, looking at Dutch with apparent puzzlement.

Dutch looked up at the sandy-haired waiter. "Aye, that be my name."

"That's my name, as well. Fred Blackwell," he replied.

At first, with Dutch's mind foggy from whiskey, and his veins still pumping adrenalin from the brawl, he barely took in what the waiter had said. But, as the man placed their drinks on the table, the meaning of his words struck Dutch like a lightning bolt.

"Let me see your right forearm," Dutch demanded.

"What?" The waiter drew back, with a surprised look on his face.

"I want to see your right forearm," Dutch repeated firmly.

The waiter looked at him for the longest moment, then pulled up his right sleeve.

Dutch moved the table candle close to his arm. There in the shadows, he found what he had hoped to see: a long, ruby-red scar. Looking up at the waiter with a grin, he said, "Your given name is Fredrick, your father is Samuel, and your brother is Joseph."

Freddie's mouth dropped open, and his eyes bugged out. "How do you know these things?"

"From your scar. John Cornwall, the man who bought your blacksmith shop, told me of your forge accident."

"Who the hell are you?" Freddie asked in confusion.

"I'm Dutch, your nephew. Joseph is my father, Samuel my grandfather."

A look of wonderment lit Freddie's face. "So my brother Joseph lives!"

"Nay," Dutch corrected. "He was killed by Indians on the Columbia River, three years ago. My mother died shortly after that."

Jack and Rose were silent as the two men talked, clearly enthralled by the melodrama. As Freddie pulled up a chair and slumped down onto it, Dutch looked closely at his uncle in the dim light. He was middle-aged, with straggly amber hair, a smudged face, deep-set hazel eyes and a thin, dark pencil mustache under a bony nose. He bore little family resemblance to his brother or to Dutch.

"I'm on my way back to the Pacific," Dutch told Freddie. "You could join me, if you wish."

Freddie shook his head, "Wow, what news! I wish I could…but I can't leave here for another six months."

"Why not?" Jack asked from across the table.

Freddie turned to Dutch with a face full of sorrow. "I be in servitude to the Frenchman, Louie. He holds papers on me. I can't go anywhere for another half year."

"What the hell, you're no colored man," Jack said indignantly.

"It ain't like that," Freddie replied. "It be forced labor, imposed by the law."

"I don't understand," Dutch replied.

"A judge gave me two years for killing a pig, and fined me twenty dollars. I had no money to pay, so Louie paid the fine and got the papers on me for the two years."

"Two years for a killing pig? That's barbaric!" Jack said loudly.

"Not when the pig belonged to the governor," Rose added, with a smirk on her face.

From across the room Louie shouted, "Freddie, get off your ass or I'll come over there and thump your head."

In a heartbeat, Freddie grabbed his tray and jumped from the chair, with fear on his face. As he turned to walk away, Dutch stood and asked, "Do you truly want to come with us?"

Looking at Dutch, his uncle answered, "Where are you going again?"

"The Columbia River...where your brother is buried."

Freddie looked confused for a moment, then said, "Reckon I'll come along. You're the only family I have."

"I'll talk to the Frenchman."

With a sour face, his uncle whispered, "He's a black-hearted bastard. Watch yourself."

As Freddie left, Jack said, "I can't believe that prick Louie gets two years of slave labor for twenty dollars."

Rose stood and looked down on Jack. "It's the way of the land around here, sweetie. I better get moving or the Frenchman will thump *my* head." She glanced across the table to Dutch. "Sure you don't want a poke, honey? I'm better than an Injun squaw."

With a red face, Dutch stammered, "No thank you, ma'am."

As Rose turned to leave, Jack reached up and grabbed her arm. "You're not in that prick's servitude, are you?"

She smiled at him. "Nay, but he takes twenty-five percent of my trade. If I don't give him two dollars a night, he'll throw me to the weather."

Jack let go of her arm, and she looked down on the table with an honest smile and said, "Much luck, mates. Stay safe." Then she turned and slipped back into the murmuring crowd.

Once she was gone, Jack turned to Dutch with a serious face. "Rose told me something you should know. Last week, a barge full of trappers started up the Missouri. She thinks they work for Astor."

"Could we catch up with them?" Dutch asked.

Jack sipped his drink and then answered, "Aye, if we ride hard. We could beat them to St. Joe. That's a hell of a lot closer than Montreal!"

Dutch thought a moment and replied, "Fine. We will ride together as far as St. Joe."

With that decided, the two men talked awhile of Freddie's problems. The only solutions they came up with were for Dutch to buy his uncle's papers, or hijack him from town and quickly cross the country before anyone was the wiser. Jack liked the thought of having an extra man, and continued to try and convince Dutch that the Sweetwater Trail was the best way.

An hour later, with the crowd thinning, Jack excused himself for his last night in a feather bed. Dutch finished his drink, and with his mind still spinning with thoughts of his newly found uncle, he got up from the table and moved to the end of the bar.

Louie moved down his way. "Want another drink, lad?"

"Nay," Dutch replied. "I'd like to speak to you about Freddie."

"What did he do?" Louie asked, with anger in his voice.

"I understand you have papers on him."

"Aye. What's it to you?"

"As it turns out, he's my long-lost uncle. I'd like to buy his papers."

A grin raced across the Frenchman's lips. "He ain't much of a bargain, family or not. I'd leave him lost, if I were you."

"He's the only blood relative I have. So I'd pay you five dollars."

Louie's grin turned to a broad smile, his greasy black hair glistening in the dim light. "I paid twenty dollars for them papers and wouldn't take anything less than thirty for them today."

"That's outrageous!" Dutch replied. "You got a year and half of slave labor out of him. I'll pay ya ten." As he talked, he slowly moved one of his hands to the butt of the pistol tucked into his belt.

"I know you have grit, lad. You proved that tonight. But you don't scare me. I've got the law on my side. If you try to snatch him away, the sheriff will find you both and bring you back to face the judge. But… because he ain't worth piss as a worker, I'll take twenty dollars. That's my final offer." Just then, two customers called out for more drinks. As Louie turned away for the other end of the bar, he simply asked, "Is your uncle worth twenty dollars?"

Dutch stood there for a long moment, mulling over the question. Of course Freddie was worth the money, and the last thing Dutch needed was trouble with a hayseed sheriff. But it just wasn't fair. Five dollars was fair!

Dutch finally paid the Frenchman, who signed over Freddie's papers to him. "Your uncle be a whiner and a slacker. He ain't no prize," Louie said with a sour face.

After reading the document, Dutch waved the signed paper in the air to dry the fresh ink. "Good or bad, he be of my blood," Dutch said. "We leave in the morning. If you go thumping on my uncle tonight, I'll come back and put this paper up your ass. Do you understand?" The Frenchman slowly shook his head in agreement, while Dutch folded the paper and put it in his pouch. "Have him meet us at the livery two hours after sunrise. Tell him to bring his traps."

Louie extended his hand to Dutch and replied, "Aye." The two men shook hands and then Dutch departed the barroom. He felt mad as hell over having to buy human flesh. It just wasn't right.

The next morning, Jack and Dutch were at the stable on time and started tacking up their animals. King was pleased with their arrival and promptly lit out for a hunt behind the barn. Within the half hour, Dutch was loading the last of his trail bags onto Willow's back. Time had ticked away, with no uncle in sight.

"Where's Freddie?" Jack asked while paying Axel his overnight fee.

"Don't know. He should have been here long ago," Dutch replied, tightening the last pack strap.

Axel smirked. "If you're talking about Freddie from the hotel, he be about as dependable as the weather."

Dutch walked Willow outside and tied her in the sunlight next to Scout at the corral. Moving back inside the barn, he paid Axel his fee. As they were finishing up, Freddie strolled through the barn doors with a bright smile on his face. He wore a soiled black rag of a waistcoat with a dirty linen shirt and tattered trousers. He carried nothing, and had no hat, and on his feet were a pair of well-worn moccasins.

"Where's your outfit, uncle?" Dutch asked, startled by his appearance.

"Don't have no outfit. The sheriff took it all," Freddie replied nonchalantly.

"You don't have a horse?" Jack asked loudly.

"Nay," Axel inserted quickly, "I sold his horse and outfit and give the money to the Judge to pay for the governor's pig."

Everyone in town seemed to know of Freddie's crime. "That's the most expense pig I've ever heard of!" Dutch replied. "How the hell were you planning on crossing the country? Walking?"

Freddie looked at Dutch with a blank stare. "You've got my papers now, nephew. Figured you'd also have an extra horse."

Axel moved to one of the barn walls and removed a cobweb-covered canvas bag from a wooden peg. "I've got his old trail kit here," he said. "It's full of dirty clothes and some personal effects. Two dollars should cover the cost for storing the bag."

Freddie dumped out the contents on the dirt floor and searched through the pile of rags.

"Any boots in there?" Dutch asked.

His uncle shook his head no.

Dutch chuckled to himself and turned to Axel. "Do you have a horse for sale?"

The men moved outside to the corral, where Axel pointed out the two animals he had for sale. One was an old gray Indian mare with a swayed back. She had seen her better days and, from the look of her teeth, was near thirty years old. Her cost was sixty dollars. The other animal was a mule named Dolly, small in size, brown in color and stubborn by nature, at a cost of thirty dollars, including an old saddle.

"I ain't riding no mule cross-country. It ain't dignified," Freddie said in protest.

Turning to his uncle Dutch replied firmly, "Then you'll be afoot."

Dutch bargained Axel out of the two extra dollars for the bag storage and even convinced him to throw in a used saddle blanket for Dolly. Then he paid the man, and told Freddie to tack up the mule.

He did a lousy job of cinching down the saddle, all the while complaining about riding a 'squaw horse.' When finally he went to get on Dolly, she promptly bucked him off in a cloud of dust. Everyone watching roared with laughter.

"Uncle, get off your backside," Dutch shouted with a smile. "Try that again, but this time cinch up her saddle properly."

On the second try, Freddie stayed aboard the mule. Dolly was a spirited animal. Dutch liked that.

On their way out of town, they stopped at one of the general stores. Jack and Dutch bought all the needed trail provisions, including more tobacco and whiskey. Dutch bought his uncle a pair of boots, a set of buckskins and a leather belt. He also bought him a canvas tarp, two blankets, a canteen and a tin food kit. By the time they were done, Dutch had used up most of his poke. Having an uncle was an expensive proposition.

Once outside, Dutch gave his uncle the sheath knife that had belonged to Henry Wilkins, and one of his pistols.

"I'll need a hat," Freddie demanded.

Dutch searched through his trail bag and pulled out his winter hat. Then he asked Jack to give Freddie his old raincoat.

Jack rolled his blue eyes. "Guess I'll do anything to get the hell out of town."

Dutch handed the articles to Freddie, who looked at the hat with a sour face. "Never seen a skunk hat before, but I reckon it will be better than that chamber pot on your head, nephew." After putting the hat on, he held up the raincoat to the sunlight. "There be some holes in this coat!"

"Aye," Jack said. "Foolish me, that's why I bought a new one. Can we please get the hell on the trail?"

After strapping everything into place, the three men mounted their animals, and Dutch started calling out for the dog. As they rode past the livery stable again, King reappeared from behind the barn, taking the point lead.

In the morning light, Dutch turned to his uncle and noticed how much of a frontiersman he now looked. Sure, his uncle had some warts, but didn't most all relatives have flaws? The real question now was whether he had any grit inside.

"Who belongs to the mutt?" Freddie asked from his mule.

"His name is King, Uncle. He's been with me two years," Dutch replied.

"Don't much like dogs," Freddie said.

Dutch smiled, "He don't much like people. Give him a wide berth until he gets used to you."

Under a warming sky, the men rode at a trot down a well-traveled dirt road, heading due west. A short time later, the way came to the banks of the Missouri River. Here the road turned into a wide trail with many wagons ruts that followed the river upstream. With the spring runoff, the waters of the Big Muddy were deep and swift. A few miles farther downstream was the confluence of the Missouri and Mississippi Rivers. The countryside through which they now rode, was an open prairie of gentle hills with an unbroken carpet of grass gracefully rising up in ocean-like swells on each side of the broad brown river. Casting shadows on the water's flow was a fringed shoreline of cottonwood and willow trees. The colorful basin was a beautiful sight, primitive and violent, yet peaceful and calming.

Stopping at the trailhead, Jack and Dutch waited for Freddie and Dolly to catch up. "You should have taken a poke at Rose," Jack said with a wistful grin. "That mare knows how to buck. She can take the kinks out of man."

Dutch returned his grin and changed the subject. "How far to St. Joe?"

"About three hundred miles," Jack replied. "It be the last spot of humanity between here and the Pacific."

"How long to get there?" Dutch asked.

"Well, you and I could make it in three days of hard riding," Jack answered, taking a drink from his canteen. "But with Freddie and that damn mule, it will likely take us six."

When Freddie finally rejoined the group, he started grousing right off, about his mule, the weather and everything else. Jack and Dutch glanced at each other, shaking their heads, and then turned their animals upstream.

Dutch had thought Jack was a talker, but along this trail, Freddie's voice was like the wind, constant and annoying. He chattered about a liaison with a young wench in Nashville and his daring keelboat crossing of the Mississippi. Among his many stories, he did explain how he came upon the governor's pig. He said he hadn't eaten for days, and found the fat hog grazing in a field, just off the road leading into St. Louis.

"Was he fenced in?" Jack asked from his saddle.

"Don't rightly remember," Freddie answered. "I was too hungry at the time."

Stopping on the road, Freddie had shot the pig from horseback. Then he went into the pasture and butchered it. When he finally looked up, he found two riders watching him. One was Meriwether Lewis, the Governor, and the other was the sheriff. End of story. But to hear Uncle Freddie tell it, he had done nothing wrong. He placed the fault on the sheriff and the local judge.

"They were in cahoots against me."

Twisting in his saddle, Dutch said, "Mr. Cornwall told me he paid you handsomely for the blacksmith shop. Why were you broke?"

"I was set upon by highwaymen, just outside of Nashville. They took all my money," Freddie replied.

Jack turned in his saddle with a surprised look. "You said you rode into St. Louis. The road rogues didn't take your horse?"

"Nay, just my money."

Jack grinned at Freddie. "Most highwaymen take everything, right down to your boots. For them not to take your horse or rifle doesn't make any sense."

"Well, that's the way it was," Freddie answered with lips shading to gray.

Jack rolled his eyes, spurred his horse and galloped up the trail. Dutch had listened to enough of his uncle's stories to know full well he had not heard the truth of it.

The well-marked trail crossed many creeks and rills, heading due west with the Missouri River always on the caravan's right shoulder. The unending vastness of the prairie reminded Dutch of a sea of grass-covered anthills rolling across the horizon for as far as the eye could see. It was a monotonous view but an easy ride.

Early in the afternoon, Jack reined in his steed and put his nose to the air. "Storm be a-coming," he said to no one in particular.

Dutch and Freddie twisted in their saddles but saw only a few clouds in the sky. An hour later, however, a tremendous thunder storm rolled across the plain. The incessant flashes of lighting and the continuous roar of thunder were of such fury that the caravan searched out a gorge and took shelter behind some large rocks. There they held tightly to their mounts and packhorses. The clouds turned the day black as night, and then came the rain, followed by hail the size of musket balls.

Within the half-hour, the gale had passed and the warming sun had returned. Such afternoon thunder storms would become a common occurrence as they crossed the prairie.

With the sun low in the sky, they made camp in a small cluster of aspen trees with a lazy stream nearby. Freddie was the last to straggle into camp. Sliding off the mule, he fell to the ground, nearly landing on King, who jumped backed with a snarl on his lips. Freddie lay on the grass, protesting his soreness, his hunger and his thirst.

Jack stood over the prone complainer and kicked him gently with his boot. "On your feet. We need wood for the fire and water from the stream. There will be no slackers in my camp."

Ever so slowly, Freddie got to his feet and started gathering wood, while Jack and Dutch unpacked the animals and moved them out to graze.

That evening, with a stunning sunset backdrop, Dutch cooked up bacon and beans. Once the meal was finished, Jack pulled a jug from his saddle bags. Opening the earthen bottle, he poured himself and Dutch a half cup of whiskey.

Freddie threw away the remains of his coffee and held his empty cup out to Jack, "What about me?"

Jack looked at him with disdain. "After ya clean up from the meal and picket the animals in the trees, there may be a taste of whiskey for you."

"Why me?" Freddie asked, with an empty cup and indignant voice.

Jack moved to the fire and came to rest on his bedroll, with his saddle as a backrest. "It's my whiskey, and in my camp everyone pulls their own weight."

Moments later, in the last of the amber light, Freddie was at the stream, cleaning up the iron skillet and tin plates.

With Freddie out of earshot, Jack turned to Dutch and said, "Your uncle is a no-account and very annoying."

Dutch took a sip from his cup. "He's a hard man to figure."

"Did you hear him at supper? He said the beans weren't cooked to his liking. I damn near threw my plate in his face. That man's got brass balls!"

"King don't much like him, either. I'll have a talk with him."

Jack squatted over the fire, adding more fuel. "He be like a magpie, always squawking." Warming his hands he continued, "I was thinkin' he reminds of Hector, back on the farm. Now that's a black-hearted thought."

Dutch took another sip of whiskey. "I'll talk to him."

"Aye, and tell him to take a bath! I can't stand the stench."

Discord ———————

Late that night, Dutch awoke to a darkened camp, with the fire only embers. As he sat up on his bedroll, he saw Jack in the shadows, asleep on his left, and his uncle the same to his right. Curled up next to him was King, also dead to the world. But next to the red glow of the fire he spotted the faint, ghostly image of his father sitting on a log snag.

Drowsy and surprised, Dutch rubbed his eyes, trying to focus more clearly.

His father spoke. "My brother Fredrick has had a woeful life. He was only twelve, the day our mother died. Full of grief and anger, Papa got drunk and came after him with a hammer and crushed his little finger before I took an iron poker to his head. He dropped to the floor with such a thud that I feared I had killed him. I tried to set my brother's finger, but it didn't take well. That was the night when our lives changed forever. I tell you these things so you might know how cruel life has been for Fredrick. He is a good soul. Give him patience and understanding." With those words, Joseph's image started melting away. "Mary Rose thinks of you often."

For the longest time, Dutch just sat on his blankets, reflecting on the visitation. Then he slowly slipped his boots on and got to his feet. With an owl hooting in the distance, he walked behind the camp and relieved himself. As he stood there, he looked up at the wonderment of a canopy of bright stars. He would heed his father's words about his uncle, but was perplexed by his mention of Mary Rose. She was an impossible dream, a name he had shoved far from his mind many months ago.

The next morning, the men awoke to a cool breeze and light rain. After a meal of hardtack and jerky, they mounted up and rode out of camp. As usual, Jack and King were the first to leave, followed by Dutch and his uncle. On his tall horse, riding abreast with Fredrick, Dutch towered over him by a good six inches. The dreary morning air was damp and crisp. On the trail of unbroken hills, they could watch Jack and his horses some fifty yards ahead of them. King was in front of him, just a fast-moving dark speck against a hazy carpet of green.

Fredrick had started the morning by carping about no coffee, no hat brim to keep the rain off his face and the bleakness of the weather. Dutch listened to his grumbling and waited for the right moment.

"Uncle," he finally said from his saddle, "you see Jack up there and the dog? They don't much like you because you're such a gloomy bloke."

"I bloody well don't give a shit what they think," Freddie replied with a vinegar face.

"I do. They are our blade against trouble. King can smell Indians half mile out, and Jack has been down this trail many times. Our fate rests with them."

Freddie thought for a moment and then twisted to Dutch. "Well then, tell Jack to stop bossing me around, and have your dog stay clear of me. I'm better than them."

"You are not better," Dutch answered in a firm voice. "I know the story of your mother's death and your mangled little finger. How your older brother protected you. Now I'll protect you, *but* you must stop the bellyaching and make friends with King. If you don't, you'll be cast out like dish water."

"How do you know of my finger?" Freddie asked, holding his bent finger out.

From his saddle, Dutch turned to his uncle with a wolfish look. "Father visits me sometimes. Last night, he asked me to have patience with you."

Fredrick scoffed, with a trickle of rain running down his cheek, "Nephew, you've been with the Indians too long. If my brother *is* dead, he ain't making no visits. He must have told you this tale when you were a young'un."

Dutch smiled back. "Have it your way, Uncle, but please stop the grumbling. And make peace with the dog."

For the next few hours, the two men rode alongside each other without another word passing their lips, both unwilling to say any more. With the skies finally clearing, the trail monotony was suddenly broken when the dog came running over the crest of a hill and straight for Dutch. Rushing to the front of Scout, King made a tight circle with his head high and his eyes bright. Then, without pausing, he moved back towards the hill he had just crossed.

"The dog has found something. Let's get a move on," Dutch shouted to Jack.

"Is it Indians?" Freddie asked with a concerned face.

"Nay, he had no snarl."

Dutch spurred his horses up the trail at a gallop and then turned for the crest of the hill. Jack did the same and was close behind. Once on the ridge, they came to halt. What King had found was a shallow valley with a river that flowed into the Missouri. The stream looked to be fifty yards wide, with a fringed shoreline of scrub brush, grass and aspen trees. The dog was at the bottom of the hill, next to some tall grass, making more tight circles.

Once Fredrick had joined them on the hill, the trio moved down to the valley floor. With rifles in hand, Jack and Dutch quickly dismounted and handed their reins to Freddie. Crouched down, both men moved slowly with the dog through the tall grass. Once at the shoreline, King came to a stop and stood frozen, pointing his nose across the river. Peering through the grass in the direction of the point, the men spotted three antelope drinking water on the opposite shore. They were a skittish bunch, moving one at a time from behind cover to the river's edge and back to cover again. The largest antelope in the group was a young male, brown and white in color, with small horns that curved inward. He looked to weigh over a hundred pounds.

Dutch dropped to a knee, with his long rifle on his shoulder. Only his barrel protruded from the shore grass.

"That be a long shot," Jack whispered.

"I make it a hundred and sixty yards," Dutch answered, adjusting the rifle's rear sight. Then he waited and watched. The antelope were slowly moving farther upstream, and he knew he would have to take the shot or lose them to the bush. Finally, the larger male returned to the water. Dutch took a deep breath and exhaled.

Fizz-Bang!

The distance was great, and the antelope skittish. Dutch nicked him in the shoulder but he didn't go down. In an instant, all three of the animals broke for cover.

Jack moved quickly for his horse. "I'll chase him down. You mates get across the river and I'll catch up." Jack was atop his mount and galloping across the river in just a few heartbeats. King was right behind him.

As they splashed through the water, Dutch noticed how shallow the riverbed was. The middle of the stream was only a few feet deep. After reloading his rifle, Dutch took his reins from Freddie and mounted Scout. "You lead Gray across and I'll follow from behind."

Freddie didn't say a word or move an inch. He seemed frozen in his saddle gazing at the river with a fearful face. Finally, he mumbled, "I don't swim."

"You saw Jack go across. The stream is shallow."

"Nay, you go first and take Jack's packhorse. I ain't doing for him."

Dutch looked carefully at his uncle's weasel eyes, disappointed again with his grit. "I'll take Willow across first and come back for Gray. All you have to do is hold his reins for a few more minutes. Can you do that for me, Uncle?"

With Freddie watching, Dutch moved Scout and Willow across the shallow river. Halfway over, he heard a rifle shot from upstream. Jack must have finished off the antelope. Once on the other side, Dutch tied Willow to a tree limb. Just then, the sounds of a second shot filled the valley. Had Jack downed another animal? Returning to the river, Dutch spurred Scout across the water again.

As he took the packhorse's reins from Fredrick, he asked, "Do you want to go next? I'll be right behind you."

"Nay, I want to watch you once more before I cross."

"Uncle, on our journey we will cross many rivers to get to the Pacific. Always trust your mount."

Within a few minutes, Dutch was on the opposite side of the river with the packhorse. He paused on the shore, shouting encouragement back across to Freddie.

Ever so slowly, Freddie and Dolly moved to the water's edge and started to cross. Holding his legs out high above the water, he looked every bit like an Eastern greenhorn, but the mule soon found her footing, and they started walking across the rocky riverbed. As they moved through the water, he started his bellyaching again. "I can't swim. It's cold. There may be snakes in the water." Just then, Jack and the dog reappeared and came up alongside Dutch. "Antelope got away, but your dog flushed out these hens for the cook pot," Jack said with a toothy smile, pointing at two prairie hens tied to his pommel. "Your uncle looks to be having a hard time. I'll go give him a hand."

Before Dutch could say a word, Jack spurred his horse and went splashing across the water. He held up at midstream and waited for Freddie and his mule. "You're in bad way. I'll give ya a hand." As Freddie came next to Jack, he pulled his knees high up to the saddle and reached out for Jack's hand. Instead of a hand, he got a boot. Jack kicked him off the saddle, and he splashed into the cold river. "You need a bath, ass hole. I could smell you upstream."

Freddie flailed in the water for a few seconds, screaming for help. But once his feet touched the bottom of the river, his composure returned. Finally, standing up in knee-deep water, he screamed at Jack, "Why did you do that?"

Staring down at a dripping wet Freddie, Jack frowned and replied, "I've had it with your smell and your squawking." He then turned Buck in the water and rejoined Dutch on the shore.

"Get your uncle dried off," he said to Dutch. "Then take him back to St. Louis. His bellyaching is no longer welcome in my camp. Do you understand?"

"Aye," Dutch replied, shaking his head.

Jack took the reins for Gray and said, "Hope to see ya, up-trail. I'll wait for you two days at St. Joe."

The two men shook hands and, Jack rode off for the trail west.

With King watching from the riverbank, Dutch rode out into the water and searched his saddle bag. "Here's a bar of soap. Clean yourself and your clothes." He took the mule's reins from Freddie and turned for shore. "I'll start a fire."

Half an hour later, beside a drying blaze, uncle and nephew had words. Fredrick stood in his small clothes before the fire while his other clothes hung from ropes close to the flames. Dutch sat on a log snag, with coffee cup in hand. Fed up with the whining and camp drama, he told Freddie in firm terms that they were returning to town. "Uncle, you be like an old owl who only hoots but one gloomy song. I will leave you in St. Louis and catch up with Jack on the trail."

Freddie protested loudly that he had no wish to return to St. Louis and that he wanted to stay with his only blood kin.

Dutch shook his head regretfully. "I have watched you closely, Uncle, and I cannot find the shadow of my father in your face. We are as different as fire and ice. I was raised in the wilderness, while you grew up in Boston. A city is where you belong."

With a long face, Freddie talked at length about his brother Joseph and how close they had been. For the first time, Dutch heard some passion in his voice, but it didn't change the facts.

"Jack has heard your constant grousing and listened to your untruthful tales, and believes you a fool."

Fredrick stared at the flames, shaking his head.

"Life is harsh out here. It takes courage to live on the frontier, a disposition you don't have. That be your true tragedy."

Freddie pleaded that he had such courage and that, given another chance, he would make Jack see his worth. Then, with tears in his eyes, he sobbed, "The money Mr. Cornwall paid for the shop, I lost gambling in Nashville. There was no wench there, and crossing the Mississippi was uneventful. Other than this trail and you, I have nothing! Please don't forsake me now."

His words seemed heartfelt, but old horses have bad habits. Again, Dutch shook his head.

Fredrick then reminded Dutch that Joseph had asked him for patience. Dutch could see a pleading hope in his uncle's eyes, and he felt himself weakening.

"Jack knows how to keep a wilderness camp," he said at last. "Learn from him. Don't squabble with him."

Freddie promised he would do just that and would show Jack his grit with deeds, not words.

"If I vouch for you again, you can't let me down. Do you understand?"

Fredrick looked up from the flames with a sincere expression and said, "Aye, Nephew, trust me."

Dutch gazed at him for a long moment and then told him to get dressed and saddle up. "You must prove you're worth. As we ride, I'll teach you the rules of camp."

After six hours of hard riding, the rutted trail came to an abrupt halt on the rocky shores of another river. This stream was wider than the last, with a lazy curve as it flowed into the Missouri. The shoreline on both sides was thick with scrub and cottonwood trees. Dutch could see where the trail picked up again on the other side of the river. Dismounting his horse, he handed the reins to Freddie. Then, with rifle in hand, he walked out onto the riverbank. Across the river, hidden by tall trees, he could just make out the faint wisps of white smoke from a campfire. He looked upstream, but found nothing but the thread of the green water and trees. This could be Jack's camp, or that of other trappers…or maybe an Indian camp.

He shouted across the flow, "Hello in the camp!" Then he waited. After a few moments, he shouted again. Finally, from the bushes Jack's lanky body appeared.

"Is that you, Dutch?" Jack shouted from the opposite shore.

"Aye. Can I come across?"

"Come ahead. The water's only horse-belly deep."

Returning to Freddie, Dutch mounted up and walked his animals to the shoreline. Then Scout and Willow slowly moved across the wide riverbed. At the deepest point, their stomachs were washed by the rushing waters. King followed, swimming across with his powerful paws keeping his head high above the water. Once on shore, Dutch dismounted and lead his animals to where Jack stood.

"Did you leave your uncle behind, lad?" Jack asked with a curious face.

"Nay, he is beyond the river. He asks for another chance. I think he's come to Jesus, but if you're not keen on it, just tell me."

Jack put a plug of tobacco in his mouth and stared across the river. "He is just a silly pilgrim, but forgiveness is divine. Think he can cross this flow without a gripe?"

"I reckon he can."

Jack cupped his hands to his mouth and called out across the flow, "Okay, Freddie, come across."

He and his mule moved from behind some underbrush and approached the river. Ever so slowly, Dolly found her footing on the slippery rocks and started crossing the river. By midstream, the water was up to Freddie's knees and he hadn't said a word.

Flash...Crack!

Thunder roared from up-river. Seconds later, another flash of blue-white light lit up the river like a cannon blast, followed by another deafening clap of thunder that echoed over the basin.

Jack and Dutch quickly retreated with the animals to under some trees. As they did so, Jack yelled out, "Get off that river now!"

Freddie's eyes were as big as the moon. He spurred Dolly hard, but she hesitated, frozen in place. Another bolt of lightning and crack of thunder roared overhead. The mule finally came alive and bolted across the water like a bullet.

Once on dry land, a clammy skinned, wholly unnerved, Freddie slipped off his mule and rushed her under the safety of the same tree. The three men stood silently, holding their animals and watching the storm. Finally, Jack turned to Freddie and yelled, over the sounds of rain, "Fastest I've ever seen you move."

Freddie thought a moment and then replied, "On a trail, there are doers and talkers. I'm a doer."

Dutch smiled to himself, as those had been his very words to Freddie, less than an hour before.

Once the downpour had passed, and without saying a word, Freddie took the reins of all the animals and led them to the nearby camp. With Jack and Dutch searching for dry tinder for the fire, Freddie unsaddled and unpacked all the animals. He then tied them to a picket line and hobbled their legs. Returning to camp with a few heavy trail bags, Freddie found Jack and Dutch feeding dry fuel to the restarted fire. Stacking the bags close to the flames, he turned for more. As he walked by, Jack asked, "Do you need a hand?"

Without stopping Freddie replied with a bright voice, "If I need a hand, I'll look to the end of my arm."

With a smile, Jack turned to Dutch and said, "Guess Jesus *has* come into his life."

Harmony had returned to camp.

The next morning, without a complaint to be heard, they broke a cold camp and rode further down the trail. As the miles slipped by, the landscape slowly changed. The gentle green rolling hills gave way to taller peaks with golden and flaxen grass and fewer groves of trees. The weather also warmed, with a breeze from the west, and puffball clouds stacked up in an azure sky.

Late that morning, the caravan came to a halt after Jack killed an antelope. When they had finished butchering the animal, alongside the trail, it dressed out to almost sixty pounds of meat. To celebrate the kill, they started a fire and fried up several antelope steaks.

As the three men gorged themselves on the meat, King sat on his rump, patiently awaiting his share. Freddie was the first to cut off a few pieces of his steak and put the meat in the dog's tin. With a curious look, King stared at the food for a long moment, then turned to Dutch. He grinned and shook his head yes. With that assurance, the dog snapped up the meat. Freddie had broken the ice with King.

Early that afternoon, they crossed another small river that flowed into the Missouri. A few miles later, the main river twisted to the north. Riding the crest of a tall ridge, Jack stopped and pointed down to the Missouri River basin.

"Here the river changes direction and so do we." He moved his arm and pointed westward. "We will travel northwest in open country. Within a couple of days, we will come upon the Missouri again." He lowered his arm and reached for his canteen. "This shortcut will save us a half day." He took a swig of water. "But the open land we cross belongs to the Osage Indians."

"Are they friendly?" Freddie asked with concern.

Jack grinned and winked at Dutch, "As friendly as scorpions. Let's make camp down by the river and do some practice shooting. I want to watch Freddie handle a rifle."

That afternoon, they learned a few things: Dutch's Kentucky long rifle was far superior to Jack's smooth-bore rifle for targets over a hundred yards, and Freddie was a horrible rifleman. Dutch gave his uncle instructions, under the watchful eye of Jack, but in the end there was little improvement. He flinched too often, and had the bad habit of closing his eyes while squeezing the rifle trigger. In addition, he was slow on the reload. The only weapon he was proficient with was the pistol, which was only accurate at close range. In the future, Freddie would tend the animals while Jack and Dutch did the rifle shooting.

The next morning, after filling their canteens and canvas water bags from the river, the trio changed direction and started the trek across the desolate unbroken prairie. Jack used no compass to find his way. Like Dutch, he had a God-given sense for direction. The wagon-rutted trail had stayed with the river, so Jack now navigated his own way.

The landscape was only blonde grass that grew upon high, rolling mounds that could swallow a rider from view. The men rode in silence, keeping a keen eye on the many grassy hills that surrounded them. It was a remarkably remote area, with nary a tree or bush for shade. The trail they traveled was littered with bison bones, bleached white in the blazing sun. Dutch mused from his saddle about the stark contrast between this bleak plain and the fertile lands of the Pacific. The Indians who survived here must differ greatly from the tribes of the lakes and ocean shores. He wondered about their manner of life.

That afternoon, the troop experienced another thunder storm of such violence that the men took cover under their animals. On the open prairie, it was the only half-safe place they could find. For nearly a half-hour, they held tight to their frightened mounts as thunder roared across the sky like cannon fire, and lightning bolts rocked the land like doomsday. Then rain and hail came, ricocheting off their animals' flanks. Mother Nature's misery would be repeated in the days to come, but she only made their determination stronger.

That night, the men slept on the open plain, using dry bison dung to fuel their fire, and drinking whiskey to wash down the antelope meat. They talked about one person staying awake and standing guard, but after a third cup of whiskey they were too tired to care.

In the early afternoon of the next day, the troop came upon the meandering Missouri River. Here they turned onto the rutted trail again. They traveled but a few hours more before they came to a bend in the road around which they stopped in their tracks. A mile in front of them was a long, dark speck on high ground, blocking the way.

Removing the telescope from his pouch, Dutch put the glass to his eye. "Be some kind of stockade, I can make out blockhouses, log walls and an American flag." Dutch handed the glass to Jack so that he could see.

"I'll be damned," Jack said with glee. "When I came out two years ago, that fort was just a pile of stone rubble and raw logs. Now look at her." He handed the glass to Freddie.

"Does this place have a name?" Freddie asked, with the lens to his eye.

"Don't rightly recollect," Jack replied.

St. Joe ————

As the caravan approached the palisade, they noticed how the fort commanded the high ground overlooking the bends and currents of the Missouri River. The vertical log walls were built at different angles to the river and were anchored with timber blockhouses on the corners. Just outside the eastern wall was a large vegetable garden. And in a meadow, next to the south wall, they could see a large Indian camp with dozens of tented lodges. The cone-shaped tepees were made with long wooden poles covered with buffalo hides stretched tightly. Each lodge had an oblong opening, with smoke flaps on top. These dwellings were quite different from the wigwams of the Pacific.

Riding through an unguarded log gate, they noticed the name of the fort carved on a freshly honed cross-timber: *Fort Osage*. Once inside the walls, they found a fort within a fort. The large field they

entered upon was surrounded with a log bulwarks with a trio of
two-story timber bastions. On the right was another stockade with
more blockhouses, rows of army tents, and a parade ground with a
tall, white-washed flag pole. The gate to this fort was also open and
unguarded.

As they rode across the field, they noticed soldiers working in the
different parts of the fort. At the far end of the field was a stable, a
corral and a large log building with a sign that read 'Trading Post.'
There they came to a stop and dismounted. As they were tying their
animals to the hitching post, they were greeted by a short bulldog of
a man in a blue uniform and tricorne hat.

"Good afternoon, men. I'm Captain Clemson, commander of
Fort Osage. Are you men coming out or going in?"

"Going in," Jack answered.

"Do you have your licenses?" the Captain asked.

"License for what?" Jack snapped back.

"You men look like trappers," the Captain answered while eyeing
them more closely. "If you're trapping anywhere in the Louisiana
Territory, you're required to have a license signed by the Governor."

Jack gave the officer one of his toothy smiles. "We be heading
for the Oregon Country. I live up on the Bitterroots, and these two
blokes are going to the mouth of the Columbia River. Reckon we
don't need no license."

"Aye, no license required," the officer replied, with a friendly
nod.

After introductions and handshakes, the Captain took the men
inside the trading post, where he and another man, George Sibley,
told them of the news and rules. They were welcome to stay the night
in a special bivouac area set up for travelers.

"There be two civilians from the War Department in one of the
tents. The others are vacant, so just take your pick," the Captain said.

Their horses could be joined in with the army steeds in the
corral. The camp gates closed at sunset and reopened at sunrise.
Sentries were posted while the gates were closed. Fort Osage was
the most distant outpost in the American system of stockades. It had

been built in 1808, its location and construction supervised by the famous Captain William Clark, who had only recently departed for Washington. Captain Clemson had eighty officers and enlisted men under his command. Their duty was to protect the territory from foreign intrusion, regulate the fur trade and keep the peace with the tribes.

"What of the Indians outside your walls?" Jack asked.

"They are a band of Osage who wintered here. They are friendly enough, and will be leaving in a few days for their spring hunt in the west," Mr. Sibley answered.

"Have you seen a barge poling up the river in the last few days?" Dutch asked.

"Aye, three or four days ago," Clemson replied.

"Did they stop here?" Dutch asked.

"Nay, they were the Missouri Fur Company boys, and consider us their competitor. They just poled right by us, without even a tip of a hat," Captain Clemson answered with a frown.

"Oh," Dutch replied, surprised. "I'm looking for a group of John Astor's men. They are crossing the continent some time this season."

The Captain shook his head. "If that be so, lad, then don't trust those Missouri boys. They don't much like John Astor."

"Do you know a bloke in St. Louis named Wilson Price Hunt?" Dutch asked.

"Aye," the Captain answered, and went on to explain that his office was right across the street from the Missouri Fur Company. "He passed through here three months ago, on his way to Montreal. He should be retuning soon."

Dutch scowled. "When I inquired about him at the hotel in St. Louis, they sent me to the Missouri Fur Company. An older lady there told me that Mr. Hunt would be gone all summer."

"Was that Louie who sent you?" the Captain asked. "He is one of the partners of the Missouri Company."

"Why would they deceive me?"

Clemson stroked his bushy black mustache and grinned. "They hate Astor and want to dissuade his men. It's all about money."

Dutch had been tricked. He should have stayed in St. Louis. Now what? "If I leave Mr. Hunt a letter, will you see that he gets it?" Dutch asked.

"Aye," the Captain replied.

The men purchased a few supplies from Mr. Sibley, and then walked their animals towards the bivouac area next to the stables.

"What do you think, Jack?" Dutch asked as they strolled along.

"Three bits for a plug of tobacco? That just ain't right."

"I mean about Louie and that old lady. Why did they betray me, and what do I do now?"

Jack had a sly look on his face. "Out here, trust only in yourself. Now I reckon you'll ride with me. I'll have ye floating the Columbia before the first snow."

"Aye," Freddie added. "We can't go back to St. Louis. There ain't nothing there for us."

The campground had half a dozen white Army canvas tents, with cooking fire-pits out front. Inside the shelters, they found wooden floors, canvas cots, chairs, tables and a small cast-iron stove for heat. After days on the rutted trail, these accommodations looked agreeable.

As Freddie unloaded the animals, Dutch and Jack built a fire and set up their camp. Then the three men walked their animals to the nearby corral, where their stock was folded in with a herd of fifty Army horses. Dutch and the others lingered awhile, talking with the fort's wrangler and two soldiers. From this conversation, they learned that the fort had three squadrons of troops, one of which was out on patrol. Soldiers enlisted in the Army for a minimum of five years and were paid up to five dollars a month, depending on service and rank. They were also paid for extra duty: ten cents a day for common labor or sixteen cents a day for skilled labor. Also, all officers and enlisted men received one gill of rum per day. Most of the men lived in canvas shelters, slept on hard cots and worked twelve hours a day. Being a soldier at Fort Osage was a grueling, lonely life.

When the men walked back to camp, they found a frontiersman, with long hair and buckskins, crouched next to their fire with his rifle across his knees and a basket resting next to him. He stood and greeted them with a French accent.

"Good day. I be Marcel, one of the post hunters. Got some vittles for trade."

"What flavor?" Jack asked with a smile.

"Four plump rabbits, skinned and gutted, and some Indian greens."

"What do you need in trade?" Dutch asked, looking down at the basket of food.

"Someone has run off with my tinderbox. Mr. Sibley wants half a dollar for a new one, but that seems a little steep to me."

"Aye," Dutch answered, "I've got an extra box in my trail bags. We'll do the trade."

Marcel turned out to be a fine fellow and, stayed for supper. He was one of six hunters who worked at the fort. The hunters worked in two-man teams, stalking everything from prairie hens to buffalo. He and Jack talked about hunting, over a half a jug of whiskey, while the rabbits stewed.

Later that evening, the two civilians from the War Department came by with another jug and a fiddle. Once the bowing started, Dutch joined in with his flute. Even King added a few yelps and howls, to the delight of all around the fire. As the gates closed that night, Fort Osage sang out with an old-fashioned hootenanny. Soon, other soldiers joined the bonfire with their gills of rum, and enjoyed the merriment. Even Captain Clemson stopped by to tip his hat and make a toast to President Madison. It was a fine shindig with total strangers sharing fellowship and revelry.

Some hours later, Dutch staggered to his tent and plopped himself down on the hard cot. The room seemed to be spinning, and he had to keep one foot on the floorboards. *A man must know his limitations,* he thought, while cursing himself for over imbibing. Soon, Jack and Freddie stumbled into the tent and found their cots, as well.

The last thing Dutch remembered was Jack asking, "You riding with me tomorrow?"

With droopy eyes and a spinning head, Dutch replied, "Aye, we'll give the Sweetwater Trail a try."

The next morning started slowly, with little chatter, as the three comrades were all nursing hangovers. Ever so slowly, the animals were saddled, and the trail bags lashed into place. When finished, the three men stood around the fire pit, drinking the last drags of the coffee. Then, still wobbly on their feet, they mounted up and headed for the main gate, with King at the point.

As they passed the trading post Dutch, stopped and handed Captain Clemson a letter he had penned the previous night for Mr. Hunt. He then tipped his hat and thanked the Captain for the hospitality. Fort Osage had been an unexpected oasis.

Out the main gate, the troop turned south. The night before, they had been given the lowdown on the Osage Indians, and now they would see their village firsthand. The Osage were semi-nomadic people with a lifeway based on hunting, foraging and gardening. The tribe had three principal hunts each year, in the spring, summer and fall. The men hunted bison, deer, elk, bear and smaller game, while the women butchered the animals and dried or smoked the meat. Osage villages were laid out with lodges on either side of a main road that always ran due east to west. On one side of the road lived the Sky People; on the other side of the road lived the Earth People, traditionally two different clans of Indians.

As the caravan turned down this road, King retreated from the point and walked close to Scout, with a snarl on his lips. Riding the way, the men found a remarkably clean and well-organized camp, with children playing and dogs yapping. The tepees were well maintained, with many colorful designs painted on the pale, stretched buffalo hides. They could also see many war shields and spears, and a few rifles.

From within the camp, the Indians paid the caravan little heed as Dutch and the others rode down their dusty road. The Osage men were tall and brawny, with copper skin that glistened in the sun. Their heads were shaved, leaving only a scalp-lock from the forehead to the back of the neck. They wore deerskin loincloths, leggings and moccasins. Many of the warriors also had beaded armbands, and tattoos across their chests. The bronze women had long black hair and wore deerskin dresses, woven belts, leggings and moccasins. The squaws also decorated their bodies with earrings, pendants and tattoos. The Osage People were a handsome tribe.

Dutch would have liked to stop and talk awhile, but Jack would have none of it. Once beyond the village, the caravan turned for the river trail. When the Missouri River was in sight again, Jack picked up the pace. It was one day's hard ride to St. Joe.

The bleak prairie they now crossed had come alive with spring flowers. The blanket of grass was sprinkled with hues of red, yellow and white. There was a scent in the air, the sweet smell of renewal. This newness lifted the men's spirits and brightened their outlook.

At midday, the troop crossed a ridge and came upon a lone buffalo grazing on the other side. The men stopped and stayed in their saddles, watching the bison. He was an old bull, waiting for death. His hide was matted and caked with mud. On one flank, dried blood and open wounds made by wolves were visible. He was a pathetic-looking animal.

"Let's kill that old bull," Jack said, with a glint in his eye.

"Why? His meat be too tough to eat," Dutch replied, astounded by the wretched idea.

"That old hide will fetch two jugs at St. Joe."

Jack dismounted Buck and handed Dutch his leads. Then with rifle in hand, he slowly walked down the hill, keeping the breeze in his face. Taking aim, he shot the old bull.

Once the animal was down, Dutch and Freddie joined him and skinned the buffalo. The only meat they kept was the tongue and liver. Jack claimed that, if they were boiled long enough, they would be tender enough to eat. After scraping and washing the hide in a nearby creek, the troop moved on, leaving the remains for other scavengers.

Under a rich early evening light, the caravan arrived at St. Joe. They had been six days on the trail. Both Dutch and Freddie were surprised to find that the only building, the trading post, was on the other side of the deep and fast-flowing Missouri. Jack, unconcerned, pointed out a bull-boat roped to a tree on their side of the river. But Freddie wanted no part in crossing the river in such a flimsy craft.

The men made camp by a tall willow tree and unloaded the animals, then picketed and hobbled their horses at the edge of the prairie. Returning to the river, Dutch and Jack prepared to float across in the boat, leaving Freddie in charge.

"Keep a keen eye on the animals. There's Injuns about." Jack told Freddie.

The bull-boat was round and small, made from a skeletal wood frame and stretched buffalo hides. It proved difficult to steer in the fast-moving waters. Jack and Dutch paddled as best they could, but by the time they reached the other shore, they were a quarter mile downstream. The men wasted no time walking the boat back upstream and taking care of business at the trading post.

Because of the poor condition of the gnarled bison hide, Jack was only able to secure one jug of whiskey. Dutch had barely enough money to buy another five pounds of coffee. He figured he could go without whiskey, but not his morning brew.

With sunset approaching, the men put their trade goods into the boat and walked it another quarter mile upstream. Launching the boat again, they made another daring passage back across the river. St. Joe had hardly been worth the effort.

When the men arrived back in camp, they found Freddie gone. They called out his name but received no response. When they rushed to where the picketed animals grazed, they found Scout and Dolly missing, as well. After searching the area for tracks, Jack saddled Buck.

"Get a fire started. I'll go after him," Jack said angrily.

"What do you think happened?"

"The mule slipped her hobbles and wandered off. Your damn fool uncle then saddled up Scout and went after her."

"With darkness coming, he be lost to the prairie."

"Aye," Jack replied pulling himself onto his mount. With the warm glow of the late sun on his face, he continued, "I've taken a liking to your uncle, Dutch, but he be like a loose shoe on a lame horse. I won't trust him with your life or mine!"

VIII
Indians of the Plains

—ɯɯ—

$\mathcal{T}$he prairie Indians were as diverse and unpredictable as the weather. There were common threads amongst the tribes, but with uncommon cultures. An artist would have to paint with broad brush strokes and vivid colors to depict the life and times of these Indians. Their hardy nations, sometimes referred to as the Buffalo Culture, roamed the great prairies from the Mississippi River in the east to the Rocky Mountains in the west, and from the Texas plains to the Canadian Rockies. These indigenous people were a civilization like no other on Earth.

Some of these people were completely nomadic, moving across the land with the vast buffalo herds, but a few of these roving tribes also engaged in agriculture by growing tobacco and corn. These were the Blackfoot, Cheyenne, Crow and Lakota Sioux, to name a few. The others, in addition to hunting the bison, lived in permanent villages, raised crops, and traded freely with other tribes. These were nations like the Pawnee, Osage, Wichita and Mandan.

Much of the culture of the plains Indians revolved around the land, the buffalo and the horse. Before the horse, the Indians found that their weapons were not powerful enough to down the great bison, so they developed different methods for hunting. One way was for a brave to cover his body with wolf skins and mingle closely enough with the herd to kill with his bow. Another was for the tribe members to work as a team to stampede the animals off tall cliffs.

The Indians began acquiring horses in the 17th Century, through trading or by stealing them from Spanish colonists in New Mexico. The Comanche were among the first to commit to a fully mounted society. This equestrian culture spread rapidly though the nations of the prairie. Now the Indians could hunt the bison from horseback, getting close enough to use their spears and arrows.

No part of the buffalo went to waste. The meat was cooked, dried, boiled and the offal made into sausage. The hides were cured and used as clothing and coverings for their tipis. The bull horns were used as spoons, cups and toys. Tools and weapons were made from the bones. The tail was used as a fly brush or whip, and the stomach and intestines were used to carry water. The Indians even made a type of glue from ground-up buffalo hooves.

The plains Indians followed no single culture, but the bison, the horse and Mother Nature were the common threads that bonded the tribes together.

—᙭—

Buffalo Hunt ————

Dutch moved Willow and Gray to a picket line near camp and then made a fire and put the coffee on. He paced around the flames nervously, watching the last traces of sunlight dance off the horizon. With the night crowding in, he mused that he was totally alone, in a strange land, with no help at hand.

A lone wolf cried out in the distance.

Why hadn't Jack returned? And where the hell was Freddie? He should cook something, but he wasn't hungry, he was worried. King also paced the empty camp, working his nose, curious about the solitude. Long moments passed as the coffee brewed. Dutch poured himself a cup and sweetened it with a splash of whiskey. Putting the drink to his lips, he heard from the shadows, "Hope you've saved some rotgut for me."

Jack had returned! As he rode through the veil of darkness, Dutch was pleased to see he had found the mule.

Reining in Buck by the fire, Jack sat in his saddle, grinning broadly. "Damn, it's hard to track at night."

Dutch handed up his cup, and Jack took a drink. "Got a quick view of Dolly, three hills over. By the time I got to her, night had dropped. But we used the stars and made our way back. What of Freddie?"

"No sign. Hope he's holed up somewhere," Dutch said, taking back his cup. "Riding the prairie at night is a damn fool idea."

That evening, the men sat quietly around the campfire, half expecting Freddie to ride in at any moment. But he didn't. Instead, the night air filled with the distant calls of wolves.

The next morning, just as the coffee finished brewing, Dutch looked up from the campfire to see Freddie and Scout moving down the river trail from upstream. Dutch smiled. "The prodigal returns," he shouted out to Jack, who was taking care of business in some nearby bushes.

Jack stepped out from behind the underbrush, pulling up his trousers, and looked up-trail. "Good. We don't have to waste time looking for the fool."

Over the morning brew, Freddie told the story of his lonely night on the prairie. The day before, he had dozed off when Jack and Dutch had gone to the trading post. When he awoke, he found Dolly gone. Fearing that some Indians had stolen her, he saddled up Scout and lit out to steal her back. But once the sun went down, he got lost. He rode around for a few hours, calling out for help, but only the wind and wolves answered back. Finally, with the help of starlight, he found a thicket and tried to start a fire, but he had no tinderbox. He spent the sleepless night sitting on the ground, holding Scout's reins in one hand and his pistol in the other. At first light, he rode towards the sun and soon came to the Missouri River. Once on the trail again, he rode downstream, with the scent of coffee in his nostrils.

When Freddie finished with his story, Jack gave him a bitter look. "We left you in charge of the animals, and you snoozed. No Indian worth his feathers would steal a mule, with four horses standing by. And why didn't ye use the flint from the pistol to light your fire?"

Freddie shook his head with a long face. "Sorry Jack. I just don't think like you."

"That be your problem, Freddie," he replied. "A fool wanders the prairie, while a wise man travels it. Let's get packed up and get on the trail. It be a hundred miles to the Platte."

Freddie protested loudly that he was tired and hungry and wanted to stay the day. Jack would have none of it, and told him to eat some hardtack and sleep in the saddle. "We ain't burning daylight for a fool like you."

As they rode farther up the Missouri, the river trail became more obscured. Long gone were the wagon ruts, replaced by a few burnt-out fire pits and chopped-down trees. The caravan kept moving north, crossing without difficulty, the many rivers and streams flowing from the west. Around the bends and curves of the trail, Dutch expected to find other mountain men coming out or going in, but they were alone on the desolate sea of the prairie.

On the second day out of St. Joe, the trio came to a stop on the shores of a wide, turbulent river that drained into the Missouri.

"This be the North Platte River, boys," Jack said from his saddle. "Here we turn west and follow this flow all the way to the Sweetwater."

"We don't have to cross this monster, do we?" Freddie asked, wide-eyed.

"Not here and not now. But we will cross to the north in a few days."

"How far to the Sweetwater?" Dutch asked.

Jack wiped his face with his bandanna. "Reckon it be just over 700 miles. Take us a couple weeks, if we don't have any Injun problems."

"If we be crossing Indian lands, I should have a rifle," Freddie said.

"I agree," Jack answered, with his toothy smile. "Know you can't do no damage with it, but the Indians will think we are three armed men."

"What tribes are we facing?" Dutch asked.

Jacked pointed. "Cheyenne to the south, Pawnee to the north, and in front of us the Lakota Sioux. We be riding into the belly of the beast, from here on out."

"Why do you call the Sioux, Lakota Sioux?" Freddie asked.

"Lakota be their language. Other Sioux speak different tongues."

With a few hours of sunlight remaining, the troop turned west and started riding up the Platte. It was a hot afternoon, with no signs of a cooling breeze or thunder shower. Dutch contemplated from his creaking saddle that the day was the end of May. He had been on his odyssey for two months, and now he was facing the most arduous part of his journey. Sandy might have been right; a ship would have been a better way.

On the prairie, the days were devilish hot, while the nights were beastly cold, but comfort could be found for a few hours each day, around sunset and sunrise. That evening, the men washed off the dust of the day and cooled themselves in the river. Afterward, Dutch outfitted his uncle with one of the extra rifles and gave him more pointers on using the weapon. With the fear of Indians fresh in his mind, Freddie seemed more alert to his instruction and made some good inquires.

After the evening meal, the men sat around the fire talking of Indians and plans of action.

"Show no fear," Jack said, looking directly at Freddie in the firelight. "Injuns only respect strength. And keep your mouth shut. Don't go trying to talk with them or sign with them. You might say something that will piss them off. And don't go pointing that rifle at anything," Jack continued, putting another log on the fire. "We want to pass through their lands, not start a war."

Freddie sat quietly during the talk of Indians, and Dutch wondered about his uncle's grit, if they found any trouble.

Soon, Jack started to ramble about the Snake Indians and Nez Perce. He talked of their culture and ways. He even retold the story of saving the old Sioux medicine man on the buffalo hunt. Jack held his medicine pouch up to the fire light. "Pokes like this have great power with the Indians. They believe special spirits live inside." So enthralled was Freddie with his tales, hardly a word passed his lips.

Two hot days later, the trio crossed a small stream that drained into the river. Once on the other side, the troop came to a halt, and

Jack said, "This be Salt Creek." Then he pointed to the river and continued, "The Platte bends north here, and we will take another shortcut west. Fill your canteens and water bags. The dry prairie crossing will take three or four days."

"In this sun, with the needs of our horses, we can't carry but two days' worth of water," Dutch said, wiping the sweat off his brow.

"Aye," replied Jack. "But there are a few 'fool's pools' along the way for the horses. And we can cure the water at night."

After packing away as much water as possible, the men splashed themselves cool on the creek's shore and then mounted up, with wet bandannas on their heads. Turning to the west, the troop said farewell to the refreshing waters of the Platte and navigated a trail across an unbroken open range of scrub brush and buffalo grass.

Some hours later, while riding the ridge of one high hill, the trio came upon the prodigious view of the vast plains, with the distant barrier of the Stony Mountains in the background. The tall, snow-clad peaks seemed to grow out of a blue-gray haze that shimmered in the sun. Above the mountains was a dark blue sky with puffy white clouds like a cotton field. This was an endless land, with God's hand apparent everywhere.

At night, the temperature dropped to near freezing, and the men huddled around a bison-dung fire, drinking whiskey and trying to keep warm. During the day, the prairie was like a desert, with no shade and temperatures hovering near the century mark. This land was as hard as the rock it grew from and as desolate as the moon.

Early on the morning of the third day, the troop reached the crest of a tall hill and came to a stop. Before them was a sight few white men had ever seen. Grazing across the plains was a herd of buffalo the size of which they guessed was near ten-thousand strong. The herd looked like ants, slowly moving from one hill to the next, in no particular direction. There were calves and cows, young bulls and old bulls, as well. The animals had shaggy brown coats with large, round heads of midnight fur. Some of the males stood almost six feet tall, with curved horns two feet long. The vista was a spectacular reminder of the size and dominance of the American bison.

The men sat silently in their saddles, watching the herd for the longest time. Finally, Jack said, "A buffalo hide makes for a soft bed on the trail and a warm robe at night. I think we should kill a few."

"And fresh meat for the Bear Box," Freddie added.

"How do we hunt them?" Dutch asked, with canteen in hand.

"Most white men sneak up on the herd and kill them one at a time."

"Don't they run off?" Freddie asked.

"Nay, if you don't spook'em, they will just stand in place until the hunter is without powder or ball. It's the damndest thing I've ever seen."

"How do the Indians hunt them?" Dutch asked.

Jack grinned. "They ride with the herd. It is the most exciting way of killing I have ever watched. It's the way we should hunt today."

Jack explained the details of riding with the herd. It was a dangerous way of killing the bison, but the Indians hunted this way because their weapons weren't powerful enough to down the animals from a distance. "A wounded or dying bull can gore hunter and horse with one angry charge, so go for a cow."

"Where is the kill spot?" Dutch asked.

"Behind the ear or in the heart. They're a hard animal to bring down," Jack replied.

Their plan was simple enough: Freddie would remain with the packhorses and King, while Jack and Dutch slowly moved downhill and blended into the herd. Once each man had selected a target, they would spur their horses and give chase. As the hunter came alongside the chosen animal, he would fire his rifle and hope for a kill. When the bison's were down, Freddie would join them and help skin the animals.

It was a fine morning for a buffalo hunt. With dew still on the grass, and a cool breeze from the south, the two men slowly walked their steeds down the hill. Scout sensed the approaching sport and let out a nervous whinny, and Dutch felt his muscles tighten.

Once on the valley floor, Dutch pulled his rifle from the leather sheath and checked that the weapon was primed and loaded. With rifles in hand, they slowly moved closer to the herd, while turning south to keep the breeze on their faces. Finally approaching a group of grazing bison, Jack whispered, "Make no quick moves or sounds until we are in position. They will think us just more buffalo." Slumped low in the saddle, the two men ever so slowly merged into the herd. Some of the bulls turned their heads and glanced at the intruders, but didn't move away. Dutch turned towards a young cow, fifty feet away. Just as he did, Jack's horse rose up on its haunches and let out a loud whinny that startled the herd.

Shit!

Ears went up and heads turned. Then the buffalo mob stampeded.

Dutch lost sight of the cow as Scout bolted, propelling them with the herd. In a heartbeat, horse and rider were surrounded by thousands of buffalo, all running in the same direction. With the herd pounding the hard ground like an earthquake, their hooves kicked up thousands of turf torpedoes.

With his heart in his mouth, Dutch struggled to stay in his saddle. He was surprised by the speed of the bison, but his powerful horse stayed with them, stride for stride. Dutch tried to maneuver Scout from the middle of the group to an outside edge, but it was difficult to do with all the stampeding animals so tightly packed. The herd thundered over a hill and down into a mile-long valley, then turned and came running back the way they had come.

Globs of sweat rolled off Dutch's mount and blew onto his face, mixing with the dust to form a mask of mud. Many times during the chase, the animals ran so close to Dutch that he used his rifle barrel to push them away. Then, with dust flying and hooves thundering, the herd changed direction again.

This time, Dutch found himself running on the outside of the pack. In front of him was a young bull with only spikes for horns. He wasn't a cow, but Dutch didn't care; he wanted this hunt over. Spurring his horse, he rode up next to the animal. With Scout's mane dripping with sweat, they ran hoof to hoof for a few moments. Then Dutch let go of his reins, pointed his heavy rifle at the back of the animal's head, and pulled the trigger.

Fizz Bang!

The bull fell in a cloud of dust almost instantly. At that same time, however, Scout tripped, throwing Dutch high into the air. He did an unexpected double somersault, which flung his rifle to the ground before, fortuitously, Dutch landed on both feet, not twenty feet in front of the downed bull. Stunned and disoriented for a second, Dutch tried to recall what had just happened. Then his father's voice called out, *What of your horse?*

Twisting down-prairie, Dutch watched as Scout come to a stop, favoring a rear leg. Quickly turning around, he saw the last of the stampeding mob pass him by. With an unsteady hand, he wiped the mud and sweat from his eyes. When his view cleared, he found the downed bull thrashing about and trying to get to its feet. Rushing up to the wounded bison, he pulled his pistol from his belt, and fired a ball directly into one of the animal's brown eyes.

Fizz Bang!

The animal fell dead, while Dutch stood with his smoking pistol in hand, shaking like a fish on a line. Never before had so much adrenalin pumped through his body for so long. He slumped to his knees, caked in mud and staring at the buffalo. If running with the great shaggy bison was some manly notion, it was stupid! And for what? A buffalo hide and a few scraps of meat? Dutch had almost broken his neck and now, if Scout was lame, he'd be afoot. He was an idiot!

Moments later, Dutch found King at his side, growling and snarling at the dead bison. Looking up, he saw his uncle and the packhorses riding down the hill. The kill had happened not a hundred yards in front of where they waited.

"Wow! Was that something to watch!" Freddie said in tones of disbelief. "Never seen no stampede before."

"Damn fool idea," Dutch answered, getting to his feet. "What of Jack?"

"He went over the hill with the herd, just behind you. A few moments later, I heard the faint sound of a shot, but he didn't return."

Walking over to where Scout had come to rest, Dutch knelt down and made a close examination of the horse's right rear foot. He found the hock swollen, bruised and tender to the touch, but nothing seemed broken, thank God. He would wrap Scout's ankle tightly with cloth strips and give it some time to heal. "Sorry, boy," he said to his horse, face to face. "What a stupid thing for me to ask you to do."

Scout whinnied, shaking his head.

Freddie rode over to the next ridge and saw Jack in the distance working on his kill. Returning to Dutch, the men worked for the next few hours in the hot sun, skinning the bull and taking only the choicest cuts of meat. By the time they finished, what remained of the animal was a swollen carcass. After loading up the hide and meat, they walked their animals in Jack's direction.

On the valley ridge, Dutch stopped and turned back to look at the bloated, bloody mess they had left on the prairie. *What a crying shame*, were the only words that came to mind.

Half a mile down the valley, they found Jack just finishing up with a young cow he had shot. He was elated with the hunt, and while the men loaded the hide on his packhorse, he told them every detail of his kill. "Sorry Buck spooked, Dutch. He started the damn stampede. But it was one hell of a ride!"

Dutch turned and looked at Buck, then noticed a gut bag hanging from his saddle horn. "What's in the belly bag?" he asked Jack.

"Bison brains. We'll use them to tan the hides." Jack paused a moment and looked to the sky. "Midday is coming. Let's find a fool's pool where we can wash up and get our hides stretched out to dry."

Before leaving, Jack made up a buffalo blood and clay poultice and helped Dutch bind up Scout's lame leg. He and Freddie then mounted up and rode west, searching for water. Dutch and King headed the same way, leading both horses. Scout began the walk with a limp, but after a few miles his gait improved. Dutch considered himself lucky that his horse wasn't permanently hobbled.

The hot sun hung in the sky like a fire ball, with heat rolling off the land in waves. Dutch was still caked with mud from the hunt, and this condition added to his misery. With each step of his walk, he dizzily daydreamed of cool water for a bath, and shade for comfort. Crossing the prairie on foot was a dreadful way to travel.

Finally, Jack and his horse appeared atop the next ridge. "There be a fool's pool just over yonder," he yelled out, pointing to the next valley. "I'll see you there."

They made camp in a marshy area with grass for their mounts and water for their needs. The only shade to be found came from the tall rocks that surrounded the little gorge. After washing up in the cool water, Jack and Dutch went to work on the skins. The hides were scraped and washed, rubbed thoroughly with the bloody bison brains, and stretched out with ropes to dry in the hot sun. While this was happening, Freddie made a small dung fire and collected two coffee pots full of water for curing.

It was late afternoon before the men found some relief in the rock shade. As they sat with their knees up and their backs against the boulder, Jack said "We should come upon the Platte tomorrow. We can wash and rub our hides again at the river."

"Why the stinky bison brains?" Freddie asked, canteen in hand.

"It's the Indian way," Jack replied. "It will make our hides soft and supple."

"I don't have a hide," Freddie answered. "I should have shot my own buffalo."

"You can have my skin," Dutch said, eyes closed and head back.

"What!" Jack exclaimed. "After all this work, you'd give up your robe?"

Dutch opened his eyes and turned his head towards Jack. "It would only remind me of my stupidity. I damn near killed my mount today. That's a pilgrim's mistake."

Iron Belly ———

The next day's trek was long and hard. With Scout's lame leg, Dutch straggled behind, walking both horses for miles at a time, then riding a few miles before walking again. Late in the afternoon, the troop came upon the Platte and made camp near the river. They were delighted to find a small grove of cottonwoods that would provide shade and fuel.

After washing off the day's dust, Dutch set up camp and cooked buffalo flanks and beans while Jack and Freddie worked on their hides. The fresh bison meat was a good addition to the Bear Box, but with the hot weather it would quickly turn rancid.

After dinner, the chill night air crept in, and the comrades sat around the campfire drinking whiskey, mending their wares and talking.

"I had me a buffalo robe once," Jack said. "I traded for it with some Snake Indians. But it burned up in the fire."

"What fire?" Dutch asked.

Jack swirled the whiskey in his cup. "Guess I've never told ya. I had me an Injun wife once. She was a Nez Perce squaw named Morning Glory," Jack answered with a wistful expression. "She was a good woman. We built a cabin up in the mountains and lived together for near five years. She bore me a son. I named the little tyke Virgil, after my father. We all slept on that buffalo skin." Jack took a drink from his cup. "Those were the good old days."

Dutch was astounded by his story. "What happened?"

Jack's upper lip tightened and his face soured. "Buck and I went out to check my trap lines, one spring day. When I returned the next morning, I found my wife dead and my son missing. From the signs, I knew it to be the work of a Crow war party. Those black-hearted bastards had hung Morning Glory from a tree and skinned her alive, then run off with my son. He was only three at the time. Well, I cut my wife's bloody body down and took her inside and wrapped her in that buffalo skin. Then I burnt the cabin down."

"Did you go after your son and the Indians?" Freddie asked.

"Yep. Never found the boy, but I had me a lodge pole with nine Crow scalps within the year. Then I grew tired. Killing is easy. It's living that's hard." He raised his cup in the air. "Life goes on."

"What of the scalp pole?" Freddie asked.

"Burnt it up, as well. It was just a stick of shame."

Jack was a man of many parts, and his tragic tale reminded Dutch of the harsh realities of living in the wilderness. The frontier was as unforgiving as a mother bear.

The next day, with Scout's leg much improved, the troop moved up the river. The men were pleased to be off the open prairie and moving amongst a few trees that offered some shade. At midday, the troop rode around a river bend and came upon a large treed island in the middle of the water's flow. Reining in their animals, the men stopped at the river's shore. There was a channel of fast-flowing water on each side of the island. The conduit they now confronted was only thirty feet wide.

"This is where we cross to the north shore," Jack said from his saddle.

Freddie face turned flush. "That's a deep, fast flow. I don't like the looks of it."

"I'll take the lead. You ride behind me, and Dutch will take the rear. Trust your mule Freddie, Dolly won't let you down."

From the south shore, they slowly moved across the first channel to the island. The flow was fast, but the water was only knee-deep. Then, cutting through the trees and underbrush, they crossed the island and came to the main flow on the other side. This channel was fifty yards across, with a strong cold current of what looked to be deep water. With fear on his face, Freddie started grousing again.

"Don't slip back to your old ways, Uncle," Dutch said, dismounting his horse. "You ride Scout across. He's the tallest of the steeds, and I'll ride Dolly."

Ever so slowly, Jack and Buck led the way across the rocky riverbed. At the deepest point, the water was just above the rider's knees, with a swift flow that pushed and curled against their mounts. The men stayed in a straight line, walking hoof for hoof. With Dutch riding the shortest animal, he found the water depth nearly saddle-high, but Dolly proved to be sure-footed and as calm as a morning breeze. The troop finally made the north shore, with wet butts and cool heads.

After trading mounts again, the caravan moved upstream, with the Platte now on their left shoulder.

Three days later, the troop came to the conflux of the North and South Platte Rivers. The area where the waters merged was sparsely timbered with many marshy pools and tall buffalo grass. The travelers finally came to rest under an elm tree, and set up their camp. Half an hour later, just as Dutch was putting the coffee on, King raced into the encampment from downstream and made a tight circle, with a snarl on his lips.

Dutch whistled out loudly for his comrades and then called, "Indians are coming."

Jack and Freddie quickly joined him, with rifles in hand.

"Let's not confront our guests with weapons," Dutch said, resting his rifle next to the fire. "Keep them close at hand, but not in a threatening way."

The men rolled log snags in around the fire and took seats, with their rifles nearby and tin cups in hand. With King on his rump, and a snarl still on his lips, the men waited and watched the downstream trail. The coffee brewed and Dutch poured each friend a cup. When finished, he looked up and found five Indians riding towards his fire.

Jack whispered, "They look like Sioux."

The mounts they rode were three palominos and two appaloosas all without saddles. The Indians themselves were all bare-chested, wearing only rawhide loincloths, leggings and moccasins. None of the braves were wearing war paint. All of the Indians had feathers stuck in their midnight hair, and they carried weapons of spears or sheaths with bow and arrows on their backs. Dangling from their belts were iron knifes and tomahawks. In a cloud of dust, they reined in their steeds, twenty yards from the fire.

Everyone glared at each other for the longest while. These copper-skinned Indians were a fine-looking band, with high cheekbones, deep-set brown eyes, wide noses and small mouths with full lips. Finally, a brave with three feathers in his hair started yelling out Lakota words while flapping his arms about. Dutch slowly rose from his log seat and approached the Indians, all the while working his hands with sign. The dog moved with his master and heeled at his side, with his fur bristling. Dutch moved his hands in a quick, abrupt fashion, and the three-feathered brave answered his signs.

Dutch spoke to his companions. "I told them we were trappers crossing the land. He told me this was Sioux land and, like the wind, we should blow away."

Dutch worked his hands again, and the brave's face turned angry as he answered with a quick palm-down sign.

"I told him we would leave tomorrow. He said now."

Jack stood, working his hands, and walked over next to Dutch. Then he slipped the medicine pouch off his shoulder and held it out for the Indians to see. All their faces turned curious, and they quickly started talking amongst themselves.

Jack said, "I told them the pouch was given to me by a Lakota medicine man for saving his life, and that we are friends of the Sioux."

The three-feathered brave spoke with Lakota words as he moved his hands with a rapid sign.

"Did you catch all of that?" Jack asked.

"Something about an iron stomach," Dutch replied.

The brave repeated his sign more slowly.

"It's a man's name. Iron Belly," Dutch said.

"Aye," Jack answered, working his hands and smiling broadly. "The medicine man I saved was Iron Belly. We are friends."

The Indian faces turned somber and, from their signs, Jack and Dutch learned that Iron Belly was near death. 'Three feathers' wanted Jack and his medicine pouch to come with him, back to the village, to save Iron Belly again. "That be a foolish idea. If he dies, I will be blamed," Jack said out loud in English. With sign, he resisted their invitation. But the Indians made it clear it was not a request. Out of desperation, Jack signed that Dutch was a Shaman with special healing powers and that he should come, as well. They agreed.

"Thanks," Dutch whispered to Jack. "Why am I being put upon? He is your friend."

"What the hell do I know about doctoring? You have the medical kit."

"Aye, and now we both will be at risk."

After a few more signs, Dutch and Jack started saddling up their horses, with the Indians watching their every move.

"What of me?" Freddie asked.

"You will stay in camp with King," Dutch replied. "I told them you were my slave and not to be trusted. Two of the Indians will stay here to keep an eye on you."

"Why did you do that?" his uncle said angrily.

"Sioux don't kill slaves, they trade them away," Jack replied cinching up his saddle. "If things go badly at the village, your life will be spared."

Dutch rummaged through one of his trail bags for old Doc Bates' kit and a jug of brandy. After depositing these items in his saddle bags, he strapped his rifle on his back, then walked over to the dog and knelt. "You will stay here with Freddie," he said to King, face to face. Then, standing, he turned for his horse.

The three-feathered Indian signed something as he walked by, and Dutch quickly answered.

"What did he say?" Freddie asked as Dutch mounted.

"He said dogs are only good in cook pots. I told him, he wasn't really a dog, but a hawk who could fly away from any pot."

"Did he believe you?"

"We'll see," Dutch replied. "Stay alert and make no trouble. We will return… I hope."

"Do you want your hat?" Freddie asked.

Dutch looked at his uncle with a sly grin. "No. I want respect, not ridicule."

With the sun low in the sky, the riders rode out of camp at a gallop, heading north. With 'three feathers' in the lead, the band crossed a hilly, grassy plain. The Indian ponies were small but proved to be fleet of foot. An hour later, they crested a high hill that looked down upon a prairie valley, with the blue shadows of mountains in the distance. Here, sprawled on the grassy plain, was an Indian village of over a hundred tipis. Next to this settlement, in a shallow depression, was the channel of a creek with a large herd of Indian ponies on its shore.

As they rode over the ridge and toward the village, the three-feathered Indian let out a loud whooping call to alert the sentries. Once on the valley floor, they splashed across the water and up into the settlement.

Slowly, throughout the village, people began to come out of their lodges and gather around with curious eyes. Many of the tipis they passed bore brightly colored designs of different animals and nature scenes. The Indians themselves were quite impressive, and looked to be healthy and well-fed.

Not far from the creek, they came to a tipi with a painted red fireball above the entry. Here they stopped. An older man came out from the lodge and looked upon the band with a bitter face, then said a few angry words.

'Three feathers' slid off his horse, walked over to Jack and took the medicine pouch from his shoulder. He showed the bag to the older man, and they talked with great animation. Then he pointed at Dutch, and they talked some more.

With each word they spoke, Dutch's keen ears began to sort out the meanings. Given time, he knew he could master their language.

Dutch and Jack were finally told to come inside the lodge, without any weapons. Under the watchful eye of the gathered crowd, they dismounted, hung their guns from their pommels, loosened their saddle girths, and gave their reins to an Indian boy. The tipi they entered was tall and smelt of sweat and rancid food. The top of the cone had scorched buffalo hides around the smoke hole. The earthen floor was over twenty feet across and, in the twilight, the buffalo-skin walls were almost translucent, glowing with a golden light.

Littered around the perimeter of a small fire, were blankets, animal hides, cooking utensils and clothing. Hanging from the lodge poles were an assortment of weapons and battle shields. Stuck in the ground, next to the entry, was a spear with many scalps. Across from this entry, laid upon a white buffalo hide and covered with a red wool blanket, was the mound of a sleeping, big-chested man.

Once inside, Dutch and Jack learned that the three-feathered brave was called White Bear and that the older man was Yellow Hawk, the son of Iron Belly. He was middle aged, with a few strands of gray in his tightly pulled-back midnight hair. The son wore deerskins that were decorated with colorful beads and a chest plate made of small buffalo bones. Using signs, he told Jack and Dutch that his father has been sick for two moons. "The old man eats, but grows weaker each day, and talks often of a death spirit inside his body." With other Indians coming into the lodge and squatting by the fire, he signed that he was skeptical that white men would have any healing powers, but he believed the old medicine pouch would have such spirits.

Yellow Hawk knelt by his father, with the pouch in hand, and called out for him to awaken. Ever so slowly there was movement under the blanket, then some mumbling. Yellow Hawk held out the pouch and said in Lakota, "Your medicine pouch has returned."

The old man stirred and, with the help of his son, sat up on the white buffalo robe. As he did so, the blanket fell away, revealing the old man dressed in a chest plate of Spanish armor. It was rusty and dented, and the figure that protruded from the iron neck-hole was a skinny, gaunt faced Indian with deep-set eyes and hair as white as snow.

"Do you remember him in armor?" Dutch whispered to Jack.

"Nay," he answered quietly.

With bright eyes, the old man placed his hands on the pouch and chanted softly. Then he looked inside the bag, and his face turned to stone. He whispered something to his son, and Yellow Hawk motioned for Jack to join them.

Jack took up a kneeling position on the other side of the old man and signed, "Pleased to see my old friend sitting up."

Iron Belly forced a smile and with his skinny arms signed back, "Where is my medicine?" The old man dumped out the contents of the pouch, which was only tobacco and lead shot.

There was a loud murmur from the Indians watching.

Jack was clearly startled by the question. Tension filled the tent, with all the Indians glaring at Jack. He signed back, with an earnest face, "I lost your medicine."

The Indians gasped, and the murmur grew louder.

White Bear stood from the fire and shouted, "He is not worthy of life. Our healer is dying, and he loses his medicine."

Quickly, other Indians stood, fingering their hip knifes and tomahawks.

Dutch raised his hand for quiet and then signed to Yellow Hawk, "I have medicine. It be an Indian cure from the Tillamook Tribe."

"Yes," Jack quickly signed, "he is a Shaman of the Tillamook People. He has great powers."

"What do we know of the Tillamooks?" White Bear yelled. "And why care?"

Dutch moved to squat in front of Iron Belly and signed, "My people live on the Big Waters, and know much about the death spirits. Will you trust me?"

The old man gazed at Dutch and then shifted his gaze to Jack. He thought for a moment and then signed, "I will trust the Tillamook ways. This evil spirit must be driven from my body."

Dutch smiled at the old man, stood and signed to the Indians, "My medicine is with my horse. I will return."

Dutch moved outside, with Jack on his heels. The day was fading and a chill filled the air. Scout and Buck were still being held by the same Indian lad. Dutch moved to his steed's cantle and retrieved the medical kit and the jug of brandy from the saddle bags.

"What the hell are we doing?" Jack asked. "Should we try to run?"

"We wouldn't get far, and I have no idea about what I'm doing."

"If he dies, we die," Jack replied with a sober face.

They returned to the tipi with the last rays of the sun in sky. Dutch opened his medical kit and showed the contents to the assembled Indians. They touched the glass bottles, bandages and instruments with wide eyes, and chattered with each other.

Dutch knelt next to Iron Belly, with Jack on the other side. Using a few Lakota words and signs, he asked the old man if they could remove his armor.

"Why?" he answered.

"My powers won't work through steel," Dutch replied.

Slowly, the old man nodded in agreement.

Jack and Dutch helped Iron Belly sit up straight, and slipped the heavy breast plate off. The gathered Indians gasped, for what they saw underneath the iron was an emaciated body that couldn't have weighed any more then seventy five pounds. The old man was now naked from the waist up, and wore only a loincloth. His ribs showed through his wrinkled skin, and his arms and legs were only skinny sticks. But upon his stomach grew an ugly, fleshy mound the size of two fists. Jack helped Iron Belly lay back down, using the armor as a headrest. As he was doing this, Dutch reached out and touched the stomach lump, and found it firm.

"What the bloody hell is that?" Jack whispered.

"Don't rightly know," Dutch replied. "Something be growing in his gut."

Next to the bed, Dutch found a hollowed buffalo horn that the Indians used as a cup. Taking the jug, he poured the horn half full of brandy. Placing the cup close to the old man's lips, he said in a mixture of English and Lakota, "Drink this, Iron Belly. It will make you warm inside."

In the dim light, the old man took a sip. Then his eyes brightened and he said loudly in English, "White man's whiskey. I love whiskey!" His voice was strident and raspy. Quickly, his scrawny hands grabbed onto the horn and he drank more.

As he did, Dutch spoke again. "Your white buffalo skin is a good omen for removing the death spirit. The Tillamooks know these things, and taught me their secrets."

The old man handed Dutch his empty cup, "The spirit moves inside when I do not. I feel it. More whiskey…Tillamook Man."

Dutch poured more brandy into the horn, then reached inside his kit for the bottle of cod liver oil. A few drops of this liquid he added to the liquor, and gave the horn back to Iron Belly. He then did this twice more; the next with a mixture of brandy and calomel, and finally a half-horn of laudanum. As the old man drank, Dutch placed his hands on his forehead and sang out with the rhythmic drone of Tillamook chants.

With the last few drops of the laudanum, the old man's eyes grew droopy and his breathing turned heavy. "You will sleep now," Dutch said in Lakota. "Tomorrow you will be free of the death spirit." Jack covered the old man gently with the blanket. With Iron Belly asleep, Jack and Dutch gathered up their things and stood turning to Yellow Hawk.

"He be better in the morning," Dutch signed. "We have to get back to our camp."

With a scowl, Yellow Hawk shook his head no and told them to sit by the fire. With the village now fully engulfed in darkness, bonfires were lit outside, and drums began to sound. Soon, many Indians began to dance around the flames, chanting their spirit prayers for Iron Belly.

With the chill in the air the lodge fire was built up, casting long, dark shadows across the walls. Dutch and Jack sat nervously watching the old man sleep, as most of the other Indians departed the lodge. Only Yellow Hawk and White Bear remained to continue the vigil.

"What's going to happen?" Jack asked, filling the horn with brandy.

"I don't rightly know," Dutch replied. "The brandy should help him sleep. The cod liver oil and calomel cure any ills, and the laudanum will relieve any pain."

Jack took a drink from the horn. "Or he just might die."

In the flickering firelight, Dutch shifted his eyes to the bed of Iron Belly and replied, "Aye."

A few minutes later, an old squaw came through the entry with wooden bowls of food for all of the man. It was some kind of stew. Dutch tasted it and found it to his liking.

"What kind of stew is this?" he asked of Jack.

In the firelight, Jack smiled broadly and replied, "Dog."

The waiting and watching went on for hours as the outside bonfires grew bigger and brighter, casting longer shadows about the lodge. Jack and Dutch sat next to the fire, knees up and heads down, trying to catch some uneasy sleep.

Just before midnight, the old man stirred, opened his eyes and yelled in Lakota, "The spirit moves." He rolled over onto his side and slumped back asleep. His loud words had startled all the men from their slumber. With all eyes now fixed on Iron Belly, they waited to see if he would speak again.

In the deep shadows, the old man's lips seemed to part, and what looked like the tip of his tongue came out. But it slowly grew in size. It wasn't his tongue; it was some kind of serpent slowly slithering from his mouth. All the men let out a loud gasp and jumped to their feet. Yellow Hawk pulled his knife and rushed to his father's bed.

Dutch reached for a spear and rushed to his bedside, as well. "No kill snake," Dutch commanded in Lakota. "Let it come out." The slimy pink creature had no eyes, and its head was the size of a thumb. All the men stood dumbfounded around the bed, not believing what they were seeing. As the scaly viper slithered further into the firelight, its girth grew. With almost three feet of the serpent out of his mouth, the old man started gagging. By now, its girth was near the size of a child's wrist. Fearing that Iron Belly might choke to death, Dutch speared the snake's fat body and jerked it the rest of the way out of the old man's mouth. It was nearly three feet long as it curled its wounded body around the spear point.

With the snake removed, Iron Belly started coughing.

"Give him water," Dutch yelled, holding the spear.

Yellow Hawk quickly knelt to his father and gave him a horn of water. The old man opened his eyes and, while he took a drink, Dutch held the spear-end out, so he could see.

"This be your death spirit. You are free of it!" Dutch yelled with a triumphal look.

White Bear let out a loud Indian yell and rushed outside to tell the others.

Dutch gave the spear to Yellow Hawk. "Let no man or beast devour this evil spirit. Burn it in your bonfire and cast the ashes to the wind."

Wide-eyed, Yellow Hawk took the spear and rushed outside, whooping while carrying the serpent high above his head. There was a great cry of joy from the Indians.

"More whiskey, Tillamook Man," Iron Belly shouted from his bed.

Kneeling by the old man, Dutch looked at Jack and said, "Look at his belly, the mound is gone."

"What the hell just happened?" Jack asked.

Dutch poured a small amount of brandy into the horn and, with shaking hands, gave Iron Belly a mouthful. "Old Doc Bates once told me of a scrawny sailor that died aboard his ship. As the sail-maker was sewing up his shroud, a large worm slithered from the dead man's mouth. He called it a tapered worm, just like what we saw here tonight."

"I don't understand. How do you get such a worm? What do they do?"

Dutch rose from the old man's bedside and took a drink from the jug. "The Doc thought from wormy spoiled meats. The worm lives inside the stomach and robs all the food that the man eats. When the man dies from starvation, the serpent crawls out of the body, looking for food."

Jack followed Dutch to the fire. "Why did it come out tonight?"

Dutch took another drink and shrugged his shoulders, "Not sure. Reckon we got it drunk and it crawled out."

Jack rolled his eyes with a smirk.

"More whiskey, Tillamook Man," Iron Belly yelled again.

The men spent the rest of the night inside the tipi, watching a cadre of old squaws tending Iron Belly. He was fed stew, washed with water and oils, and dressed in buckskins. Finally, he fell into a deep sleep. With the celebration still roaring outside, Jack and Dutch wrapped themselves with blankets and slumbered upon some soft animal hides. It had been a night of fear and fate, and Dutch praised the Lord that he was still alive.

When Dutch awoke, the next morning, he found Iron Belly sitting crossed legged by the burnt-out fire. Next to him was the white buffalo skin and the medicine pouch. Dutch poked Jack awake, and they gathered up the medical kit and what remained of the jug of brandy. "We must return to our camp," Dutch signed to the old man, standing up.

He nodded his head in agreement and then said, in his raspy voice, "My head is on fire, but once again I can crap like a bear. Tillamook Man has great powers. My death spirit gone. I have gifts." Iron Belly handed Jack the medicine pouch. "You keep this. It remind you of me." He then handed Dutch the rolled-up buffalo skin. "Tillamook Man take this white hide. It will bring you much good fortune," he said, his face full of honesty.

The men were surprised by his gratitude. Jack remarked quietly to Dutch how rare a white buffalo skin was, and they both thanked Iron Belly for the gifts.

Just then, Yellow Hawk entered the tipi, with a young girl in hand. His face was long, and he looked away from Jack and Dutch.

Iron Belly looked up fondly at the girl and then twisted back to Dutch. "This is my youngest granddaughter, Song Bird. She just became woman. You leave your seed with her. I want your powers with my clan."

Dutch was astounded by his request. Jack quickly whispered in his ear, "If you value our scalps, you will agree."

The pretty young maiden was no older than Mary Rose. With that thought, Dutch felt desire in his groin. Annoyed with these feelings, he turned his eyes away from the girl and finally said, "Shamans of the Tillamooks are not allowed pleasures of the flesh. If I violate this oath, my powers will be lost."

The old man gazed up at Dutch for a long moment with a face of stone. Finally he replied, "Your ways are different than ours, but I understand." Twisting to his son, he continued, "Help me to my feet and put my armor on. I wish to say farewell to these men outside."

Outside the lodge, they found White Bear and his two other braves sitting on their mounts. Next to them was the same Indian boy, still holding the reins for their horses. When the crowd of Indians saw Iron Belly, faces turned to joy, and the air filled with whoops, while the faces of Yellow Hawk and Song Bird were lit with relief.

"White Bear will guide you as far as Finger Rock," the old man told Dutch. "You will have no troubles crossing our land."

"That is not needed," he replied.

"It is my wish," the old man answered with a determined face.

Dutch tied down his new robe and slipped his rifle onto his back. After cinching up their saddles, Jack and Dutch said their farewells.

As they mounted up, Iron Belly shouted, "Your visit will be spoken of for many seasons to come." He waved goodbye and then yelled, in friendly jest, "More whiskey, Tillamook Man."

Strange Strangers ───────

They were back to the river camp within the hour. The dog was relieved and excited by their return. Over a cup of coffee and some hardtack, they told Freddie of Iron Belly's gut worm. It was a tale the uncle found repulsive, but he wanted every detail. They also talked of White Bear and his braves. Having an escort was not to their liking, but there was nothing they could do about it. Packing up the animals, they were soon moving up-river again.

Once on the trail, the Indians took up positions. One brave was sent to the rear, while another scouted a mile ahead, and a third rode the troop's northern flank. Two Indians remained with the caravan, riding point. The consort knew what they were doing, as they had protected many columns of their people before.

A few miles out of camp, Dutch spurred Scout and rode abreast of Jack. "Have you heard of this Finger Rock before?"

"Aye," Jack answered, wiping the sweat from his face. "Think it be a rocky mound with a tall steeple, although it didn't look like a finger to me."

"How many days ride from here?" Dutch asked.

"Three or four," Jack replied, then abruptly pointed to the trail. "There it is again!"

Dutch followed the line of his finger but couldn't see anything remarkable. "What?"

"Wagon ruts. I first saw them near our camp, this morning. What fool brings a wagon out here?"

Dutch's eyes searched the trail for any ruts, but found none, "How many wheels?"

"Two."

"Might just be trappers pulling a cart of winter pelts back to St. Louis."

"Nay," Jack replied, looking for more signs. "They be going in, not out. And the wagon is being pulled by a mule, with a horse and rider alongside. From their faint tracks, I guess they be a week or more ahead of us."

Jack was like a bird dog; he could learn more from a scent in the air or from tracks on the ground than most men could learn from books. Being an expert scout was one of the many traits that made Mountain Jack a seasoned frontiersman.

The river trail soon moved away from shore and rose up among granite mounds that looked down upon the waters. Some of the rocky cliffs were three or four hundred feet above the river's flow. The few trees that grew between the rocks were scrawny, and the open trail exposed them to unbearable heat. After a few miles however, the hills would flatten and the way would again meander by the cool river's shore.

They made camp that night in a cottonwood grove close to the river. The Indians were called in, and they made camp a few hundred yards away. The brave that rode the northern flank had killed an antelope during the day, and he rode into camp with it slung upon his horse. After talking with White Bear, the Indians cut up the animal and gave a hindquarter to the white-man's camp. It was an unexpected gesture, and that night the men enjoyed the fresh kill.

As Freddie cleaned up from the meal and Jack chopped more fire wood, Dutch lit his pipe and walked to the river. With the sun low in the sky, and a slight cool breeze off the water, it was a near-perfect evening. As he walked along the shore, smoking and admiring the view, White Bear approached him with a friendly expression on his face.

Dutch greeted the Indian in Lakota. "It is a fine night for a walk."

White Bear asked, "How do you know our words so fast?"

The two men walked side by side, slowly up the river. "It is a gift I have for most Indian words." He handed his pipe to White Bear. "Have a pull. It's good tobacco."

The Indian puffed on the corncob stem and then said, "It is good that you not violate Song Bird. She would have been shunned by all the Sioux braves."

"Because I am white?"

"Yes," White Bear answered, handing the pipe back to Dutch. "Whites are not trusted and full of sickness."

"That be a foolish notion," Dutch replied, puffing on the pipe. "In the coming seasons, many whites will cross this land. We live in a time that moves faster than our thoughts."

White Bear stopped and turned to Dutch with curiosity. "How many whites are there?"

Dutch pointed to the sky. "More than there are stars at night."

A frown chased across the brave's face as they started walking again. "Will all these people cross our lands?"

"No," Dutch replied, tapping out the fire from his pipe. "This land is too hard for most. Only a few like us will travel your way."

"Good," White Bear replied. "Then our rivers won't run red with white blood."

This was the first walk the two men would have, but it would be repeated each night, as both were curious about the other.

That night around the campfire, the men finished what remained of the brandy jug, after which, Dutch spread out his white buffalo hide and slept on it for the first time. It was soft like fresh grass and an unexpected luxury. The robe would forever remind him of Iron Belly.

For the next three days, the troop pressed west without incident. As they rode the river ridges, the view was constantly changing. One day, on the south shore of the Platte, they found a range of small, sharp-pointed hills that ran in an almost straight line for miles. The shape of the hills reminded Dutch of an animal with sharp bristles, so he named them the Porcupine Hills. Often from the high ridges, they could see the snow-clad peaks of the Stony Mountains, which seemed to get bigger and taller with each passing day. The trail itself changed, as well, with more vegetation growing from the granite cracks. There were also more groves of trees, and slowly their types changed to evergreens and cedars. Dutch was surprised to find cedar on such an arid plain, as it grew with abundance on the rainy shores of the Pacific. But when he cut into this wood, he found the core fiber almost blood red, while the outside pulp was near white. Blood cedar was softwood that could easily be cut and used; it had a wonderful scent and made for fast, hot fires.

In the afternoon of the fourth day, the trail moved down some high bluffs and into a large river valley. As the caravan moved down this rocky way, they could see in the distance an enormous mound of rocks rising to a tall, narrow spiral. This was Finger Rock, although Dutch mused from his saddle that the steeple looked more like a chimney than a finger.

Once on the valley floor, White Bear rode up to Dutch, pointing to the tall rock. "Our land ends here." With a few hours of sun still remaining, the Indians were anxious to start for home. Dutch agreed, but asked White Bear to walk with him one final time, down by the river.

The troop found some shade in a grove of cedar trees and dismounted for a few moments of rest. Dutch rummaged through one of his trail bags, then joined White Bear, and they walked to the river.

"Thank Iron Belly for the escort," Dutch said to the Indian. "You and your band did a skillful job, and I have a gift for you." Reaching into his pouch, Dutch pulled out a sheathed knife and handed it to White Bear. "It is made of British steel, with a whale-bone handle. Steel is stronger than the iron knife you have on your belt."

The Indian removed the blade from the rawhide sheath and admired the knife with a surprised look on his face. "Impressive," he said. "I am pleased to have had words with a white man who understands Indian ways."

"More of us are coming. Get to know our ways. Then our people will have peace."

They talked a few moments more about war and peace. Then Dutch ended the conversation with Jack's words. "Killing is easy. It's living that's hard."

"I must ask you…is your dog really a hawk?"

Dutch smiled and replied, "He thinks he is."

As the men walked back to the cedar grove, White Bear was quiet, holding the knife and thinking of the words just spoken.

A few minutes later, all the men remounted, and White Bear nudged his horse alongside of Dutch. He pushed his spear deep into the soil next to Scout. "You take my lance, Tillamook Man. You will always be welcome on Sioux land." Abruptly, he turned his horse and rode off with the other Indians.

Dutch pulled the spear from the ground and found the shaft covered in hand-carved symbols of animals. He would treasure the lance as a symbol of hope for a peaceful future.

"I'm glad they're gone," Jack said from his saddle.

"Let's ride out to that tall rock and give it a look-see," Dutch replied.

"Nay," Jack answered firmly. "We ain't on holiday."

The days blended together like ocean swells. The men hunted in the morning and evening, rode hard during the day, and tended their animals and maintained their equipment at night. Twice from the tall ridges, they saw large herds of buffalo, and once a band of twenty Indians. But these sightings were always many miles away. Then the land flattened again, and they found themselves riding across a level, arid plain with few trees for shade. Thunderstorms visited them almost daily, leaving the hot days dripping with humidity. Crossing the continent was a long, hazardous journey without glory.

On a day like any other, a mound of tall rocks came into the distant view. Jack said the place was called Rocky Bluffs by the traveling trappers. It marked the halfway point from the Missouri River to the South Pass. From the trail, these rocks looked like a gigantic granite fortress, but the bluffs were a few miles north of the Platte, and the troop just kept moving up-river. A few miles later, Jack rode the crest of a hill and came to a stop, where he waited in the hot sun for Dutch and Freddie to catch up.

As the men joined him, he pointed down into a shallow valley below and asked, "What the hell is that?"

With the heat rolling off the land in shimmering waves, what could be seen was only a black smudge in the far distance. Dutch took out his spyglass and put it to his eye. At first, he couldn't believe his view. Then he said, "It's a broken-down buggy. There is someone on a horse and another fixing the wheel."

Dutch handed the glass to Jack. With an angry face, Jack put it to his eye and grumbled, "Who the bloody hell are these strange strangers?"

IX
The Oregon Country

—∿—

he *Oregon Country* was an American term referring to the dis-
puted lands of the Pacific Northwest. Early explorers referred to
this region by several names: New Albion, Oregan or Ouragon. The
Columbia River appeared on early Spanish maps as River Oregon
and was later revised to the River of the West. Before 1810, this land
was mainly occupied by British and French Canadian fur traders.
Therefore, the British called these lands the *Columbia District* and,
later, *British Columbia.*

The fate of the Oregon Country was one of the major issues of
the early 19th century. The Oregon Territory stretched from the
Pacific Coast to the Rocky Mountains, encompassing an area which
included present-day Oregon, Washington and Idaho, as well as
parts of Wyoming, Montana, and most of British Columbia. Spain,
Great Britain, Russia and the United States all claimed the territory.

After the War of 1812, many Americans believed that the United
States had won the right of *Manifest Destiny* to extend its rule and
liberties across the entire North American continent. The U.S. claim
of ownership was based on the explorations of Captain Robert Gray,
Lewis and Clark, and the establishment of John Jacob Astor's trading
post at the mouth of the Columbia River. Great Britain based its claim,

in part, on Captain Cooks and Captain Vancouver's exploration of the region and on the many Hudson Bay trading posts found within the Territory.

After nearly thirty years of haggling, the Oregon Treaty of 1846 ended the dispute and established a British-American boundary at the 49th Parallel. The U.S. Senate ratified the treaty by a vote of 41-14 on June 18, 1846, and President James Polk signed the Oregon Territory into law.

—⚋—

The Devil's Face ————

Jack handed back the telescope with a frown. "We should just ride on."

"Those folks might need help," Dutch replied, putting the glass into his pouch.

"We can't just turn a blind eye," Freddie added from his saddle.

Jack shook his head with a scowl. "Alright, but it's just a waste of bloody time."

As the trio moved down the gentle ridge, Dutch whistled for King. The damaged cart was at the bottom of a shallow ravine, half a mile away. Soon, the dog appeared and walked with the troop down the hill. From a distance, they saw a man with a broad-brimmed hat atop a white horse and another, also in a pale fedora, squatting next to one of the buggy wheels. The cart rested at a steep angle, as if it were stuck, and was hitched to a single mule.

As they approached, the man on the horse came into better view. He was a big-barreled fellow wearing a black waistcoat, white linen shirt and brown riding knickers. His boots were knee-high, and his straw hat had a feather in the band. Beneath the brim was a face colored either by much sun or the result of being native born.

Reining in close to the buggy, Dutch said, "Hello. Do you folks need some help?"

The man on the horse smiled. "I told you, Cora, the Lord would provide." His English sounded Southern, but his look was Indian.

Dutch's dog sat on his rump, with a snarl on his lips.

When the other person stood up from the wagon and turned to the troop, it turned out to be a young Negro girl dressed in a dark blue frock and a straw hat. Her complexion was a light chocolate brown.

"Are you an Indian?" Freddie asked. "And is she a Negro?"

"Aye, on both accounts," the horseman replied. "I'm Reverend Onaconah. In Cherokee, that means White Owl, and she is my slave. I call her Cora."

"Never heard of a Cherokee before," Jack said, scowling from his creaking saddle.

The Reverend glared back. "We are a civilized nation. We attend the white man's schools and have come to their faith, as well."

The men were bewildered. Christian Indians with Negro slaves? Impossible! "Well, Preacher," Jack finally said, "what seems to be your problem?"

"I am told we have a broken wheel. Cora can't seem to fix it."

"I ain't never fixed no wagon wheel," Cora said in high-pitched voice. "The menfolk worked on the wagons."

Freddie dismounted and walked over to the buggy. As he looked at the damaged wheel, Cora continued to ramble about all of the things she could do. Her voice filled the air like fingernails on a blackboard.

Freddie finally looked up from hub and said, "The wheel is stuck in a rut and has a broken spoke. If you have a spare, and some tools, I can fix it."

"There should be more wheels under the cargo bed, and there's a tool box on the other side of the buggy," the Reverend answered with a tone of contempt.

Freddie looked under the back of the wagon and saw two spare wheels. Walking to the other side of the carriage, he found a hanging wooden tool box. There was even a can of axle grease inside the chest. The two-wheeled buggy was six feet wide and ten feet long, with a bench seat and a dark cloth canopy up front. The cargo area behind the seat was made of wood planks fastened to the iron frame. On one side of the cargo box was the tool chest; on the other side was a small wooden water cast.

The men went to work. The mule was unharnessed and given to the Reverend. The buggy was unloaded while Freddie removed the extra wheels from beneath the cargo area. Then all the men and Cora lifted the buggy from the rocky rut. With the broken wheel on firm ground, Freddie worked on the hub with an iron wrench. Once the wheel was loosened, Dutch, Jack and Cora lifted the wagon up. Freddie slipped the broken wheel off, and greased up the axle.

As the buggy dangled in the air, Dutch asked Cora, "What in damnation are you doing out here?"

She looked at him, with beads of sweat on her chocolate cheeks. "The Reverend be doing the Lord's work, showing the Indians a virtuous life."

"That's a fool's errand," Jack chided, holding the buggy.

Freddie rolled the spare into position and then lifted it to the axel. Quickly, he placed the lug nut into position and spun the nut tight to the axle. The others lowered the buggy to the ground, and Freddie tightened the nut again with the wrench. With sweat rolling off his face, he said to Dutch, "The other wheel needs replacing, as well, but it's too goddamn hot out here."

"No blaspheme," the Reverend shouted from his mount.

Over loud protests from Jack, they decided to load up the wagon and move it to the river trail to search out some shade. Then Freddie would replace the other wheel.

It was early afternoon by the time they found a grove of trees and made camp. Jack and the Reverend remained on their horses while Freddie slid from Dolly. Dutch and Cora dismounted and emptied the buggy again. One of the items they removed was a heavy wooden box.

Jack asked from his saddle, "What's in the box, preacher?"

"My bibles," the Reverend replied from his saddle. White Owl was a big-shouldered man, superbly mounted on a tall horse. His face was thin-lipped, square-jawed and so bronzed that the dark hair at his temples looked almost white. His manners were rude and superior.

Jack scoffed. "Indians can't read, and they have their own religion. You are on a fool's quest if you think your red brother will turn Christian."

"It is my mission. The Indians *will* come to salvation."

Jack glared at the Reverend with disbelief, and then turned to Dutch. "King and I'll ride upstream and scout the trail. Be back before supper."

When Jack and the dog had ridden out of camp and headed west, White Owl turned his steed east and rode down the river trail.

"Where the blazes is he going?" Dutch asked Cora.

"He wanders off each day, looking for Indians," she replied in her pitchy voice.

When Freddie returned from tending the animals, they all went to work, replacing the other wheel. While they toiled in the warm shade, Cora answered their questions, in her frivolous, rambling way. They learned that it was not uncommon for Cherokee Indians to have Negro slaves. White Owl's family had owned a large cotton plantation in Tennessee that was worked by fifty such slaves. As a young boy, White Owl had been sent off to white missionary schools, where he was taught the white man's ways. He returned home and worked the family farm for many years. After both of his parents died, he had a religious awakening and offered the plantation to his church, in exchange for being made an ordained minister. The white elders quickly agreed, and sent him north for training. When he returned, a few years later, the church sent him out into the western wilderness to convert the heathens. White Owl had wanted only his own Cherokee church; instead, he was sent on a mission fraught with danger. The elders had taken with one hand but had not given with the other. This greedy treatment toward red men and black men was sadly common.

After the buggy was fixed, Dutch, Freddie and Cora cooled themselves at the river's edge. The two men took off their boots, waded into the water with their clothes on, and sat down in cool pools. "How old are you?" Dutch asked of Cora.

"Don't rightly know," she replied from the shore while splashing water on her face. "Don't know my numbers or letters. The Reverend said I ain't ready yet." She fanned herself with her hand. "So blasted hot today," she said, gazing out at the water.

Without another word, she proceeded to remove her hat, then unbuttoned her blue frock and let it slip to the shore. Under her dress, she wore only white pantaloons and sandals. Dutch and Freddie gasped at her actions and then watched her walk out into the water.

She had a sweet, slender face, with high cheekbones and full lips. Her shapely figure was petite, with perky breasts, smooth chocolate skin and long black curly hair that glistened in the sunlight. Cora splashed around in the shallow water with a coy smile on her lips, knowing full well that they were watching. Then she dove and swam into the deeper flow.

The men couldn't turn away.

Freddie whispered, "There's a body meant for pleasure."

With a glare fixed on Cora, Dutch replied, "Aye, but with a mind like a butterfly."

They watched for a few more moments. Then Dutch stood and told his uncle to gather some firewood. With sunset approaching and temperatures moderating, Dutch walked back to camp to start his cook fire.

Cora had no modesty. He knew watching her had been improper, but he had enjoyed it, as she had reminded him that there was more to life than a dusty trail.

Just before sundown, Jack and King returned to camp. After taking care of his mount, Jack strolled to the fire to see what was cooking. "What's for dinner?" he asked Dutch, with Cora at his side.

With pots and kettle steaming, Dutch replied, "Beans and the last of our antelope meat."

"Thought we were out of beans."

"Aye, but Cora gave us some of her supply."

"Why the two coffee pots?" he asked.

"The Reverend prefers tea," Cora answered.

"Where is the preacher?" Jack asked, pouring some coffee.

"He's wandered off, looking for Indians," Dutch replied.

Jack frowned. "Tomorrow, we leave at first light. I reckon we're only a few days from the Sweetwater."

"Can we ride with you?" Cora asked.

"No!" Jack replied quickly. "We can't waste any more time on a fool preacher."

At twilight, the Reverend rode into camp and found everyone already eating. Cora jumped from her place to take care of his mount. Without saying a word, the preacher dismounted, sauntered to the fire and dished up a plate of food. Sitting cross-legged on the ground, he removed his hat, said a short prayer aloud and started to eat.

"Find any Injuns?" Jack asked sarcastically, spoon in hand.

In the fading light, White Owl replied, "Nay, not today."

"Do you have a gun, Reverend?" Dutch asked respectfully.

"Nay, my bible is my weapon."

The girl returned to the fire and poured a cup of tea for her master.

"Without a gun, how do you hunt?" Freddie asked.

"Cora is good with her slingshot. She gets a few squirrels, prairie hens and other birds. The Lord provides."

Jack stood from his snag and put his empty plate in the dirty cook pot. He then placed another log on the fire. "So you wander this land without even a pistol in your belt?" Jack turned to the preacher. "You are a damn fool, Reverend! God will not protect you from this violent land."

After dinner, White Owl began talking about the Cherokee Nation and how civilized a people they were. He told of how the elder Chiefs had met with the American Chief George Washington during the Great War, and how he had granted land to the Cherokee people in Tennessee. "He sent us missionaries who built schools and churches, and showed us how to grow cotton and cultivate the soil, using black slaves." Over and over again, he kept repeating, "We are a civilized people."

The continuing drone of his voice hung in the cold air like smoke from the fire. Finally, the men spread out their buffalo hides and bedrolls and were soon dozing off. The dog curled up close to Dutch, and put both of his paws to his ears.

From his blanket, Jack looked down at King with a grin on his face. "That man loves the sound of his own voice," he whispered to Dutch.

"Aye, but then a fool always likes to hear from another fool."

Soon, only Cora remained awake, listening to the preacher ramble on like the river.

At first light the next morning, Jack quietly roused Dutch and Freddie, and they saddled and loaded their animals. As they were about to turn upstream, Cora awoke from alongside the burnt-out campfire and asked sleepily, "Can't we ride along with you?"

"No," Jack said sharply. "Maybe we will see you up-trail."

Dutch and Freddie tipped their hats to the young girl, and the trio rode out of camp.

Jack pushed them hard, that day, wanting as many miles as possible between him and the preacher's buggy. The trail hugged the river shore and crossed many sandbars and streams. Before long, they found themselves riding on the floor of a deep river gorge with tall granite mountains on either side. The sound of their horse's hooves echoed off the canyon walls, making an eerie clumping sound that ricocheted around the ravine.

Early in the afternoon, the trail gave way to a large grassy valley surrounded by treed hills to the north. The gentle, mounded land made for easy travel. With the sun low in the sky, Jack found a suitable campsite in a grove of trees, near a stream that drained into the Platte River.

The next day, the trio started out in the valley and ended the day in the shadows of the foothills of the Stony Mountains. Here, the landscape changed to high, rocky bluffs and sandstone ridges with numerous dells of pine and cedar trees. The weather had changed, as well. It was still hot during the day, but not the sweltering heat they had faced only a few days before.

Early that evening, the troop stopped at a pine grove. Leaving Freddie to tend the animals and set up camp, Jack and Dutch set out for a hunt.

With rifle in hand and King at his side, Dutch backtracked down the river, while Jack headed upstream. Keeping a keen eye on the flow, both men looked for any animals seeking water. Not long out of camp, Dutch heard the report of Jack's smooth-bore and knew he had had some luck. Just around the next corner of the trail Dutch heard the crack of a twig and saw a wild turkey scampering for cover.

Before he could level his rifle, King was off at full speed. The bird clucked, turned and raced for a thicket. The dog leapt in just behind him. Dutch caught a few glimpses of the bird's flapping wings, and heard its loud clucking, with the dog in hot pursuit. The turkey was fast, but King was determined. When the snarling ball of dust cleared, the dog walked back onto the trail and sat on his rump, with the dead bird in his mouth. Dutch dismounted, walked over to the dog and knelt to him. He praised King and scratched him behind his ears. The dog dropped the turkey and looked at his master with pride on his face.

Just then, a high-pitched voice yelled, "Mr. Dutch, is that you?"

Standing, he looked down the trail. Through the distant tree limbs, he saw the buggy heading towards him in a cloud of dust. "What the bloody hell?" he said dumbfounded.

Dutch and Cora made it back to camp just as Jack arrived with a small mule deer slung across his saddle. At the sight of the cart, Jack's expression was one of wonderment. How could the preacher have caught up with the troop?

Dutch dismounted, leaving the turkey hanging from his pommel, and walked over to the wagon. "Where's the Reverend? How did ya get here so fast?"

Cora stepped down from the buggy, shook some dust off and walked over to her mule. "This old stubborn jenny was bent on catching up. She thinks she's safe with you boys. The master will be along soon."

With a look as hard as ice, Jack carried the deer to the campfire and dropped it to the ground. Turning to Cora he said, in a truculent voice, "You're not welcome here. No Injuns or niggers allowed."

"Wait a minute," Freddie said angrily from the fire. "I ain't got no problem with this Negro girl or the Cherokee, so don't go talkin' for me."

Dutch walked over to the fire and rejoined, "Good for you, uncle. I don't have any problems, either. Being part Indian your aspersions insult me Jack, and I ain't no slaver."

Jack clenched his fists tightly, his eyes narrowing and his face contorted with anger. "I'm the leader of this bunch, and you sons-of-bitches shouldn't forget it!"

Cora, her dark face sad, rushed up to the men to dispel the dispute. "I can butcher that deer and have it ready for the cook fire in no time," she said in a desperate voice.

An uneasy hush fell over the camp, with none of the men backing down. They had come a long way together. Was this the end?

Just then, Jack's stomach made a loud growling noise. His frown slowly turned to a wry grin. "I'm hungry," he finally said. "Let's get some food cooking."

Within the hour, Dutch was frying up fresh venison steaks and rice. The Reverend rode into camp just before sunset and joined everyone around the fire. As he drank his tea and ate his food, he talked of Cora and her determination to catch up with the troop. "She would have my breakfast ready before sunrise. Then she harnessed the wagon, loaded it up and rode off to look for your tracks. Don't think she slept more than a few hours each night. She thinks you boys were God-sent."

After the meal, Freddie and Cora cleaned up at the river, while White Owl and Dutch walked the shore, talking. When finished, Cora returned to camp with the clean utensils and put them back in the Bear Box. Taking a tin cup, she walked to the water barrel hanging from the buggy and scooped it half full. She then walked over to the fire where Jack was mending his tunic. "You drink this, Mr. Jack," she said, handing the cup to Jack with a friendly expression. "I'll finish your shirt."

Taking the cup, he asked, "Water?"

Cora smiled at him. "Smell it."

Jack put his nose to it and a smile chased across his lips. He took a taste. "Back home, we call this moonshine," Cora whispered. "This be our secret. Don't go telling the Reverend or I'll get a whippin'."

"Wow." Jack licked his lips. "This hooch has a kick. Why does the preacher have a cast of whiskey?"

"It is his Holy Water. He gives it to the Indians. Then they listen better."

Jack savored another mouthful and then blew through his lips. "This is jolly good, but it needs to be watered down some."

His cup was empty by the time everyone returned to camp, and Cora's secret was safe. Even Dutch noticed Jack's improved attitude about having the strangers around the campfire, and he wondered whether maybe Cora had softened his edge by mending his shirt.

Late that evening, a cold breeze blew off the snowcapped mountains and stirred the treetops. To help ward off the bite, Jack removed his last whiskey jug from his saddle bags and poured two fingers for each man.

"How about you, preacher? Would you like a taste?" he asked.

Shaking his head, the man replied, "Cherokees no drink whiskey."

Knowing the truth of it, Jack flashed a grin at Cora.

"How many jugs did you bring in?" Freddie asked.

"Four," Jack answered with his cup to his lips. "But Dutch had three jugs. How much remains?"

"Half a jug of whiskey. That's it," Dutch replied.

Jack poured himself another two fingers and passed the jug to Dutch. "We'll be dry by the time we reach the Sweetwater," he said, then raised his head, working his nose in the breeze. "Storm's coming. And there's something else..." Jack jumped to his feet, motioning for quiet. He walked across the camp to the shadows and put his ear to the breeze. For a long moment, only the crackling of the fire filled the air. "Do you hear that?" he asked no one in particular.

"Nay," Dutch said, pouring out more whiskey.

Jack turned and slowly walked back into the flickering light. "Indian drums. I reckon three or four miles away. Don't like it." Jack turned and looked directly at the Reverend. "Don't go wandering off, tomorrow morning. It ain't safe," he said, and walked back to his bedroll, where he sat down and took a drink from his cup.

"Should we post a guard?" Freddie asked.

"Nay," Jack answered. "They're somewhere up in the foothills. But we will move out at first light."

Dutch reached down to King, who was curled up next to him, and patted his head. "The dog will be on guard. If any Indian comes within a half-mile, he'll wake me up."

From across camp, the Reverend's face popped above the flames. "I'm an Indian."

Dutch smiled at him. "Aye, but he knows your scent."

Jack looked down at the dog, sprawled out on the buffalo skin. "I swear, you two are inseparable."

Dutch pulled up his blankets and placed his head on his saddle. Turning to Jack with an earnest face, he replied, "He ain't no trouble."

Just before dawn, Dutch awoke and stumbled behind the camp to relieve himself. When he returned, he noticed that the Reverend's white horse was missing. Turning to look beyond the coals of the fire, he found the preacher gone, as well. Shit! He poked Jack with his boot. "The Reverend's gone."

Jack sat up quickly in his bedroll, rubbing his eyes. "How long?" he asked.

"I have no idea."

Jack slipped on his boots and walked over to the horses. In the first dim hint of sunrise, he looked for tracks. With Freddie and Cora awake now, he returned and said, "That scoundrel rode off towards the Indians I heard last night. I say we leave him behind and get the hell out of here."

"We can't just ride off," Dutch replied.

"He be alright," Cora said. "He's done this before."

Dutch moved towards the horses. "The dog and I'll go look for him. You get packed up and ready to go."

With a gusty sigh, Jack joined him at the picket line. "I'll track for you. He's a fool, but it be the right thing to do."

The sun was just beckoning as they galloped out of the camp, heading northwest. The morning was crisp, with the same cold breeze off the mountains, and in the east, a cloudy sunrise with wispy shafts of golden light. With the dog in the lead, and Jack's eyes on the hoof prints, they rode hard for almost an hour. After crossing some gentle hills, they found themselves facing the high slopes of the foothills of the Stony Mountains.

After approaching one tall, rocky ridge, the dog came racing back down-trail with a snarl on his lips, and made a tight circle.

The men stopped and listened to the wind. Gone were the drums, replaced by faint war cries and whooping. Dismounting, they tied their horses to a tree, and quickly moved up the ridge, rifles in hand. Then, from the cover of some boulders, they peered down the other side of the rim.

With snow-clad mountain peaks as a backdrop, they saw a shallow valley with a creek running through it. Next to the shore was a grove of pine trees, where fate delivered one more bitter surprise: the seeds of death had been planted, the preacher was hanging from a tall tree limb. He was naked from the waist up, with his hands bound high over his head. A dozen Indians danced around him, taunting, jeering and poking him with their spears. His body was covered with dark spots of blood, and he screamed out with each jab of the lance.

Dutch reached for his telescope and watched more closely. Just inside the tree line, he could see two Indians inspecting the Reverend's white horse. The preacher screamed out again, and Dutch quickly moved the lens to his face. He was only half conscious, and one of the Indians kept throwing water onto his face, after which the torment would continue.

Dutch handed the spyglass to Jack, who put it to his eye.

"They be Cheyenne," Jack announced grimly, "black-hearted bastards. This taunting will go on for hours. They will keep him awake, just to skin him in the end."

"Do you think we could trade for his life?"

"You dream, my friend! Look at what they are doing to their own kind. What do you think they would do to us?"

Dutch looked up from the valley and noticed that the azure sky, above the mountains, was filling with dark thunder clouds. "We can't turn away," he said, shaking his head.

"The fool got himself into this, after I warned him not to, and there ain't nothin' we can do about it."

The faint sounds of thunder rolled across the ridge. "Yes, there is," Dutch answered. Moving into a prone position, he brought his rifle to his shoulder. "I make it 200 yards," he said, adjusting the rear sight.

"Dutch, you start shooting up them Indians and we'll all die."

Dutch rested his cheek against his rifle and watched the thunder clouds move with the breeze. He waited for a flash of light, then counted silently until he heard the thunder. Pulling the trigger hammer all the way back, he took aim and waited again, all the while worrying about the wind, the distance…and his grit. But he reasoned that the thunder would conceal the rifle report, and the breeze would hopefully blow away the gun's smoke.

"If I miss, tell me by how much."

"You poke that hive, lad, and them bees are going to sting us," Jack said with the lens positioned against his eye.

Dutch waited, sweat rolling down his face. Seconds turned into minutes, and all the while the preacher was screaming in agony. Suddenly, from the densest fold of the clouds, a flash leaped out, quivering across the valley floor.

Dutch counted to two and pulled the trigger.

Thunder rolled across the ridge.

Fizz – Bang!

Dutch watched with sad eyes as his lead ball raced across the valley, over the stream and into the chest of the Reverend. Blood spouted, his body shook and his head slumped dead to his chest.

It was a lucky shot. The Indians stopped their torture and looked at one another with surprised faces, clearly wondering what the hell had just happened.

"Jesus, Dutch, you killed the preacher!" Jack removed the lens from his eye.

Rolling over onto his back, with his breathing husky and the rifle clutched in his hands, Dutch replied, "May God forgive me… the notion of it was better than the doing… no one deserves that slow death."

It started to rain, and Jack handed the spyglass back, with a sad grimace. "There's no God out here lad… sometimes, I think you're too soft for this hard country. Then you do the right thing, like this. Let's get the hell out of here before the Indians figure it out."

As the men moved quickly downhill towards their mounts, Dutch's eyes welled up with tears. He had killed a man of God, and now he would have to live with that truth.

With the fear that the Cheyenne might be just behind them, Jack and Dutch raced across the land in a downpour of rain. Once at the camp, they alerted Freddie and Cora about the Indians, and had their little troop ready to move within minutes.

"What of the Reverend?" Cora asked, pulling herself into the wet buggy seat.

Dutch sat silent in his saddle, with rain bouncing off his hat and rawhides.

"Not now, woman," Jack answered. "We have to get moving."

The gully-washer had been God-sent, as it would help wash away any signs of their campsite. Quickly, they splashed across the Platte River to the south shore and then moved inland, heading west.

Once across the river, Jack dismounted and swept the soft shore sand with a bush to remove any tracks. With the rain letting up and the sky brightening, Jack mounted up again and took the point.

There wasn't much of a trail on the south shore, so they stayed close to the river's flow. The troop crossed a few sandbars and streams before the Platte entered into a deep river gorge. Often, their way was blocked by boulders and high ridges, so they waded through the shallow river waters. On the rocky riverbed, the buggy bounced, quivered and shook, but Cora kept up with the men.

Some hours later, the gorge gave way to a small valley, and Jack called a halt.

South Pass ————

The three men stayed in their creaking saddles and gathered around Cora at the buggy. With a warming sun now in the sky, Dutch took off his hat and wiped his brow. "The Reverend is dead," he finally said. "The Cheyenne had him in a bad way. I killed him to end his suffering."

"It was the right thing to do," Jack added. "He was dying today, one way or the other."

Freddie looked saddened by the news, while Cora's face didn't react at all. She finally looked directly at Dutch and said, in her squeaky voice, "What of me? Am I *your* slave now?"

"Nay, you're nobody's slave," he answered. "You're free to come and go as you please."

Cora pulled up the hem of her blue dress and wiped her face. "Well then, I be pleased to return to Tennessee, if one of you fine gentlemen will ride with me."

"Sorry, lady," Jack answered firmly. "I'm too close to home."

Dutch dismounted and tied his reins to the wagon wheel. Looking at Cora, he said, "Sorry, my uncle and I have urgent business on the Columbia River."

"That don't seem right," she replied. "You kill my master and forsake me?"

"You can come with us or return on your own," Dutch said, and walked to the rear of the buggy.

"Wait a minute," Jack said. "We ain't takin' no nigrous with us. She and her damn buggy will just slow us down."

"I can keep up with you, sir, and I'm a good worker," Cora answered, twisting to face Jack.

"We ain't takin' this wagon any further," Jack stated.

"Hold on, Jack," Dutch answered. "We can lighten the load on our animals by putting some gear and the Bear Box in the back of the wagon."

"Cora is a good horseman, and handy around camp," Freddie inserted, dismounting from Dolly.

Jack sat in his saddle, fuming for a moment, then nodded his reluctant agreement. "Fine. She and her buggy can come along, but I ain't riskin' my life for no darkie."

They all pitched in, unloading the cargo. The heavy box of bibles was the first thing to be discarded. They kept Cora's bedroll, the sacks of beans, rice, tea, and other camp utensils. When Cora emptied out the preacher's duffel bag, she found an extra blanket, while Freddie took a shirt and heavy coat. Dutch went through what remained and found a straight razor and a crumpled-up straw hat, which he promptly put on.

"What of your bowler?" Freddie asked, looking at his nephew.

Dutch looked fondly at his old hat. "It ain't practical, out here. I'll keep it for better times."

Jack wanted none of the Reverend's belongings.

In all, Dutch estimated that they discarded nearly seventy pounds of cargo. After reloading the buggy, he and Jack were able to add one saddle bag and the Bear Box to the back of the wagon.

The final thing they did was tie down a canvas tarp over the cargo. "The only thing we didn't find was a good jug of whiskey," Dutch said with a grin while pulling on the tarpaulin.

Jack smiled at him, finished his loop, and tossed the rope back to Dutch. "You just didn't look in the right place. Put your nose to the water barrel."

Dutch unlatched the wooden lid and put his nostrils close. Abruptly, he pulled his head back and flashed Jack a toothy smile. "What the hell!"

"Holy water. We've got near three gallons of it," Jack said, making the final knot. "It's hooch with a kick. We be drinking all the way home."

Jack and Dutch tied their packhorses to the back of the buggy and told Freddie to stay close to the wagon. Then they moved out, with Dutch and the dog on point and Jack on drag.

Slowly, the troop moved farther west, up the river's flow. As they did, the fear of Indians faded with the day. But the travel was slow, with many obstacles blocking the way, and so early the next morning they crossed back over to the north shore.

Late that afternoon, the river curved to the southwest and sank into a deep ravine. The troop moved inland, riding a high plateau with tall mountains all around. Soon, they came to a huge, rocky ledge that looked like an egg half buried in the ground. Jack recognized the landmark, and they made camp in the shadows of the rocks. That day marked the first of July. They had been on the Platte River trail for one solid month.

Around the campfire, that evening, Jack and the 'holy water' became good friends, to the point that he slurred his words and began making lewd and lustful comments to Cora. She finally moved away from the fire and asked if she could place her bedroll between Dutch and Freddie. They agreed, and soon King curled up next to Cora. As this was happening, Jack became louder and more belligerent, cursing his campmates and bragging on himself.

Finally, Dutch had had enough. "The Devil's got your tongue tonight, Jack. Cora isn't one of your whores, and we aren't no slackers. So button your lip or move to your own fire."

Jacks glassy eyes stared at Dutch in the firelight. He slurred, "How dare... you..." and passed out.

Dutch apologized to Cora for Jack's behavior. "He's not normally like this."

She pulled a blanket over herself. "It's the moonshine talking. The Reverend told me it was the Devil's brew, but it was the only way to get the Indians to listen."

Early the next morning, before the rest of the camp had awakened, Dutch dumped out the 'holy water' and filled the cast with fresh water. Never again did he want to hear such hateful words from a man he had come to respect.

Jack was furious when he learned the moonshine was gone, but his hangover reminded him that those who drink whiskey with the owls at night cannot soar with the eagles the next day.

They changed course with the river that morning and traveled southwest. The high grass range the troop rode was mostly level, with a few swells and rocky ravines. They continued riding this plateau until the land flattened again to the river shore. A few miles later, they came to the confluence of the Sweetwater and the Platte Rivers. Here they turned west, up the Sweetwater. This river drained from the tall mountains in the west. Its green-blue water was shallow, cold and crystal clear.

Late in the afternoon, they rode across a valley floor surrounded on all sides by tall, rocky ridges that seemed to block their way. As they rode, Jack pointed out a small, distant defile in one mountain that he called the Devil's Hall.

"Over the ages, like a saw blade, the Sweetwater River cut through these mountains, leaving a hallway to the South Pass. The Spanish explorers found this slit a long time ago and kept it secret. Then the trappers found it, and we have been going in and coming out this way for years."

"How far to the South Pass?" Dutch asked.

"Three or four days," Jack answered. "We'll make camp at the Hall's entrance. If I remember right, there are some fine fish in this river."

With reins in hand, Cora asked, "Is this hall wide enough for my buggy?"

Jack twisted to her with a smile. "Reckon so, but it be a bumpy ride."

Devil's Hall was a long, narrow gully filled with the Sweetwater. In the early spring, the flow was deep and fast, but in the summer the water was shallow and slow-moving. The sandstone walls of the cut rose straight up four-hundred feet on each side, leaving a narrow gap that was engulfed in shade most of the day. This dark, rocky hallway snaked through the tall mountains for as far as the eye could see.

The troop started out early the next morning and found the gorge a breathtaking sight, with trees and underbrush growing out of small granite cracks, and the tall walls of rocks seemed to be perched in the sky. Not far inside the gully, the buggy started having a difficult time moving up the stream. The riverbed was full of smooth underwater sandstone boulders that sometimes dropped off into large, dark pools of water. The cart had no brake, and these sharp drop-offs were damaging the buggy wheels. Soon, a remedy was found: Jack took both packhorses and led the way up the slit, while Dutch and Freddie tied their mounts to the back of the buggy and waded alongside the wheels, acting as human brakes. Three times that day, the wagon was unloaded and unharnessed, then carried over and around tall boulders that blocked the way. The hard granite trail gave forth the sounds of their passing hoofs echoing off the tall cliff walls.

Soon, the gully turned into an oven, with the only saving grace being the knee-deep cold water in which they waded. It was a long, laborious trudge up the flow, with the men cursing the buggy, the heat and the riverbed.

Late that day, they exited Devil's Hall onto a narrow, treed plain that gently sloped up towards the west. In open country again, the buggy returned to dry land and made its way up a game trail next to the river. They soon made camp, and while Cora started a cook fire and prepared a meal, the men worked on fixing the two bent wheels.

The next day, with the repairs completed, Jack picked up the pace again. The plateau trail they traveled sloped always upward, twisting around large boulders that protruded from the land. Soon, the party moved above the tree line and onto open ground. Over the next two days, they watched the Sweetwater slowly turn from river to creek, and then to but a trickle.

Jack stopped next to one dribbling brook and pointed to the water. "This be the Continental Divide, boys. This creek is the last flow heading east to the Atlantic. Over the next hill is the South Pass, where all the water flows west to the Pacific."

Dutch twisted in his saddle and looked back down the plain. In the far, hazy distance, he could see the tiny defile they had traveled. Nature had built the Sweetwater Trail to be both marvelous and mysterious. He now understood why Jack called it the Devil's Hall. Looking back up the plain, he mused from his saddle that he now rode on the very spine of the American continent. Unbelievable!

Early the next morning, the caravan crossed the final hill and turned into the South Pass. Dutch was surprised to find a smooth prairie, filled with sagebrush and buffalo grass. The scenery was graceful and pleasing, and he quickly rode ahead and climbed a slight hill for a better view.

Reining in Scout, Dutch lifted one leg around his pommel and looked upon the view with his telescope. The vast plain was many miles wide, with clusters of tall snow-crested mountains to the north and south. The land between these ridges had a gentle slope, promising an easy passage for many miles to come. The sky was big and filled with small wispy white clouds that drifted with the wind. Dutch turned his lens to the approaching buggy, and watched the little caravan travel effortlessly across the wide-open plain. As he took the telescope from his eye, a broad smile chased his lips. This South Pass was heaven-sent and offered an easy way.

With creaking leather, Jack joined him on the hillside and pointed west. "Those blue mountains in the far distance are the Oregon Country. Thirty more miles and we'll be there. Once over those peaks, we'll drop down to the Snake River."

Dutch removed his hat and wiped his brow. "Look at how easy the buggy travels this country. Someday, this land will be filled with wagons and families moving west."

Jack shook his head. "You be a dreamer, lad. This country is too hard for pilgrims. It's only fit for rabbits, Indians and trappers."

Dutch put his hat back on and moved his resting leg to the stirrup. "You may be right for now, but we live in an ever-changing time. Someday, this pass will be like a highway." Dutch turned Scout toward the buggy. "I'll take the drag and see ya up-trail."

As he rode past the wagon, Cora pointed at the sky and called from her seat, "Mr. Dutch, what kind of bird is that?"

He twisted his head upward and shouted back, "That be a Red Tailed Hawk. They are fine hunters."

With a head full of visions of immigrants, Dutch took up his position behind the buggy. He gave thanks for the land and wondered about Cora. She knew little of the world and couldn't even read or write. Now, somehow, he felt responsible for her well-being. He mused that life was like a book, with each day a new page.

With a pleasant jog-trot trail under hoof, Dutch soon found himself in a deep reverie. He dreamed of his future and worried about his past. But then, a man in a saddle has much time to think.

That night, the troop camped for the first time in the Oregon Country, next to a stream that Jack called Pacific Creek. With the Bear Box near empty, they celebrated the crossing of the South Pass with a meager meal of beans and hot coffee. With blankets on their shoulders, they sat around the fire, and Jack talked about what would come next.

"We will cross these next few peaks and then drop down to the Snake River Valley. It will be a hard passage. The mountains are tall and the trails hard to find. With the damn buggy, I reckon it will take us the better part of two weeks."

"Are there Indians about?" Freddie asked.

"Nay, I don't think so. We're too high up. But we should see lots of Bighorn Sheep. Their pelts and horns are highly valued, and their meat is sweet."

"How do we hunt them?" Dutch asked.

"They live on the sides of the rocky slopes and graze on the scrub. They are easily spooked, so your long rifle be our best weapon. The problem with a Bighorn is getting it out, once you have killed it. They can weigh near three hundred pounds, and live in the high crevices where no man has ever walked."

Dutch took a sip of his coffee and then wrapped his cold hands around the warm cup. With a doleful face, he said, "Well, I'm lucky with long shots. Just ask the good Reverend."

The next two weeks proved to be the most arduous of the journey. The days were long and hot, and the trails steep, narrow and unforgiving. The buggy was almost lost twice over the cliffs of switchback trails filled with loose rock. Each time, Cora and Freddie saved the wagon from tumbling down the mountainside. Using ropes and working as human brakes, the men pushed, pulled and dragged the buggy across the tall peaks.

Along the way, Dutch was able to kill two Bighorn Sheep. They also killed a few rabbits and a mule deer from the trail. Jack cured the hides and the horns, while Cora packed the Bear Box full of the meat. With their larder filled, and dead tired from the journey, the troop finally reached their destination in the third week of July.

The Snake River flowed through a large valley that was surrounded on three sides by tall granite pinnacles, some of which still showed late-season snow. Being below the tree line again, the shores of the river had dells of evergreen, with a sprinkling of deciduous hardwoods and tall golden grass. The narrow river flow was dark blue, crystal clear and only horse-belly deep at the point of their arrival on the south shore.

Here, for the first time, they rested and repaired their equipment for one full day. During this respite, Jack and the dog went downriver for a hunt, while Dutch and Freddie worked on the buggy. Cora mended some clothes and filled the wagon cast, bags, and canteens with fresh water. After that, she went fishing with a willow stick.

It was a day of relaxation, reflection and giving the body time to heal after months in the saddle. In the early afternoon, with repairs completed and Jack still away from camp, Dutch and Freddie walked to the river shore to bathe, and found Cora still fishing. She showed them her catch of fat trout, and told them she only needed one more for King. Not wanting to scare off other fish, she sent the men farther downstream.

At a small, rocky cove, they removed their boots and shirts. Then, with soap in hand, they waded out into the cool water. As they washed away weeks of grime, Cora appeared, her catch-line filled with trout. After placing the dead fish in the water, she slipped off all her clothes and waded out to join the men.

"Them blood-gilled fish are big, and good fighters," she said, splashing her body with cool water.

"Why do you undress in front of men? Do you have no shame?" Dutch asked with gruff amazement.

Cora had a coy look on her face. "When the white elders from the church came to visit, they always watched me bathing behind the barn. They seemed to enjoy it."

Freddie smiled. "I can see why…but it's just not proper."

Cora proudly exposed her breasts. "Am I to be ashamed of my body?"

Dutch handed her the soap. "You should save that pleasure for your husband."

Jack, having just arrived at the shoreline, cleared his throat.

All three swimmers twisted his way.

With a stare as cold as glass, he said, "When I spoke about the darkie, you said the Devil had my tongue, and now you boys are naked with her. Where's the Devil now?"

Dutch stood, with his trousers still on. "It ain't like that, Jack. Cora came to bathe and took off all her clothes. Reckon she don't know any better."

Jack flashed a suspicious glare at her, then turned and walked away without another word.

After a fine fish-fry that night, Dutch opened his trail bag, and removed a stealthily saved bottle of Spanish brandy. The other men were surprised by his offer to sweeten their coffee. "Let us celebrate arriving on the Snake River safely. This is the last of my stash. Enough brandy for a few drinks tonight, and a few more when we part company with Jack." Only Cora refused his offer.

"When will that be?" Freddie asked, sipping his coffee.

Jack replied, "Another week or so in the saddle, I'll turn for the Bitterroot Mountains, while you'll turn for the Columbia River."

Dutch put another log on the fire. "Can we build a raft and float down this river?"

"Many have tried," Jack answered, with his cup to his lips. "But this river has always had the better of it. No, we will ride the south shore for a few hundred miles and then say our farewells."

Bittersweet ————

Accompanied by the voices of the Whippoorwills, the troop packed up and rode west with the river's flow. The fine morning was warm, tranquil and bright, with a slight breeze from the west. The shimmering river soaked along the forested shores and rippled through tall clumps of grass.

The troop was a somber and silent bunch, each occupied with their own thoughts as they traveled a land that few men had ever seen. They were an oddly assorted group to be the vanguards of this wilderness trail: an aging Mountain Man with more grit than sense, a courageous young slave girl, a man who had squandered his family fortune, and a breed born to an Indian squaw in a Tillamook village.

As Dutch approached the buggy, Cora pointed skyward to three birds soaring high above the blue ribbon of water. "Mr. Dutch, what kind of birds is these?"

Dutch looked upward. "Those be Bald Eagles, the most majestic of them all. When it rains, most birds seek shelter, while these eagles fly high above the clouds."

Cora sat on her hard bench seat, with the reins in hand, and her head tilted skyward in curiosity. Then she twisted back to Dutch. "Why do they call them bald? They have white feathers on their head."

Cora was a different stamp of a woman. She had an easy temper, with the fortitude of a man, and she was pleasing to the eye. But God had made her slow-minded and had given her a voice as shrill as a gull. Surely, the Lord worked in mysterious ways.

For the first few days, the troop rode with the songs of crickets and frogs, enjoying an easy passage alongside the blue river. But then the land started rising up on either side of the flow, and the water soon turned to green. The troop was forced to move inland, away from water, and soon rode atop a high, rocky plateau. Only a few clumps of trees relieved the monotony of the high, arid wasteland. The trail became a repetition of yesterday, and the days went from hot to sweltering, as the river sank ever deeper into a rocky gorge. Soon the river was out of reach, although not out of sight. The hunting went from good to bad, and the oppressive heat caused their water supply to dwindle and their food to turn rancid.

Early one afternoon, with heat radiating off the hardscape, Jack and the dog broke from the point and returned to the troop. "We've got three riders coming. They be Injuns."

Jack, Dutch and Freddie rode alongside the buggy, their rifles in hand. Across the flat plateau, the riders seemed to materialize from the shimmering heat. Jack used the telescope to get a closer view. "They be Snake Indians," he said, handing the glass back to Dutch. "Let me do the talking."

Dutch turned to Cora and firmly said, "Pull your hat brim down low so they don't know ya to be a woman."

The Indians approached slowly, and it seemed at one point that they planned to pass the buggy by. But then they turned and headed straight for the troop. Reining in their horses twenty feet from the stopped wagon, they gazed upon it with curious eyes.

The begrimed, unkempt riders looked more like ghosts than Indians. One pug-faced brave had a head that was shaven, except for a ridge of hair reaching over his crown from his forehead to his nape. The other two had matted, tangled hair that was shoulder length. They were all bare-chested, wearing only loincloths, leggings and moccasins. They carried knives, war clubs and spears, but they were a pitiful-looking horde.

From his saddle, Jack signed to the intruders. At first, they were two busy talking amongst themselves to answer. Finally, the Indian with the shaved head answered Jack's signs.

"They have never seen a wheeled cart before. I told them it was our land canoe. They are astounded by such a boat."

The pug-faced Indian continued signing with much vigor. His face was somber and his quick signs were threatening.

"He says they demand food and water, or they will kill us and steal our canoe," Jack said, working his hands. "I told them of my alliance with the Snake Indians up in the Bitterroots. They don't care. They are valley Shoshone, not mountain Indians."

Dutch dismounted and tied Scout to the wagon wheel. He handed Jack his rifle and, with King on his heels, walked to the back of the buggy and removed one sheep hide. Moving to the side of the cart, he lifted the barrel lid and dipped a cup into what remained of their water. Returning to the Indians, he handed the hide and the cup to the pug-faced Indian. He then signed, "I give you this hide in tribute and one cup of water in friendship. There is no more."

Slowly walking back to Jack, he retrieved his rifle and stood glaring at the Indians while making new signs. "Our rifles only talk of death, while our hearts only speak of life. Which shall it be today:

Life or death?" The dog sat next to Dutch, with his fur bristling and a snarl on his lips.

The bald native handed the cup to his friends, who each took a drink and handed the cup back. He drank what remained and then signed just one word: life. He threw the cup to the ground in front of Dutch, said something in Shoshone and gave out a loud war cry, then the trio turned and rode away.

As the Indians moved east, Cora lifted her head with frightened eyes and squeaked, "Mr. Dutch, I thought we were dead for sure."

"They were just travelers, hungry and thirsty, with more fear of us than we of them," Dutch replied, remounting Scout.

From his saddle, Jack wiped the sweat from his brow. "Why the hell did you give away one of our sheep skins?"

With a creaking saddle, Dutch nudged Scout next to Jack. "If you pay some tribute, you'll buy some respect."

Jack grinned at his young friend. "Don't tell me, I know, that's something your father taught you. Let's move out."

Whipping the reins, Cora clucked to her mule and started out again.

Soon, in the sultriness of the day, black clouds stacked up in the western sky, and thunder growled in the distance. But rain never came. Instead, the troop was attacked by the ceaseless hum and chirp of myriads of insects. This high Snake River plain was a wasteland, offering nary a drop of water or morsel of meat.

That evening, the party camped on a grassy flat overlooking the deep canyon. Here they built their campfire, drank the last of their water, and ate dried sheep meat. Like a slow Indian torture, their view from the ridge was of the broad emerald green river with its fresh water and forested shores, stretching on for as far as the eye could see. The men talked of climbing down the sheer walls to the riverbed, but the drop-off was taller than all of their ropes combined, and only a foolish thought.

The next day was a repeat of day before, and the misery of the trail slowed the caravan to a snail's pace. The horses and mules foamed at the mouth from lack of water, and stumbled across the barren rocks, with their riders now afoot. With tongues swollen, the men cursed the dry desert heat and staggered forward trying to breath. They kept keen eyes out for any fool's pools, but none were found. Their clothes were stained white from sweat, and their mouths were as dry as stone. At times, it felt as if the sun was burning through the tops of their hats. Still, they trudged on.

Early in the afternoon, the western sky once again stacked up with thunderheads, and everyone prayed for rain. Soon, they noticed that the humming of unnumbered mosquitoes had been replaced by a warm breeze that helped to cool their sweaty bodies. Then a few big drops of rain splashed upon their faces. With nose bags and tongues at the ready, they continued to stagger west, watching the ever-changing sky. Slowly, ever so slowly, it started to rain.

Everyone stopped and lifted their mouths to the sky to savor a few trickles of water. Nothing had ever tasted so good! Soon, the first few sprinkles turned into an earnest rain, and the troop danced around in the downpour, collecting water in the feedbags. "Don't let the animals drink too fast or too much," Jack shouted with relief. "They could bloat up and die."

After giving short drinks to the animals, Dutch and Freddie held a canvas tarp around the top of the water cast, while Jack and Cora caught rainwater in canteens, pots and kettles. Within the hour, their water supply was replenished.

The next day, the high plateau gradually gave way to the river once again. Dutch rode to the last ridge and put his telescope to his eye. What he saw ahead was a basin filled with tall, golden grass stretching out to the horizon, and the Snake River bending gently to the northwest. Gone were the high mountains and tall ridges. Thank God!

Jack joined Dutch on the ridge and looked down at the river view. "I know this bend in the river. Within the week, I'll be turning north," Jack said from his saddle.

Dutch smiled at his friend. "I reckon today is my birthday."

"Really? What day is this, and how old are you?" Jack asked with a surprised look.

"I think twenty-two, and it's the middle of August."

"You don't know?"

Dutch removed his straw hat and wiped his brow. "Nay, we had no calendars where I was born, only seasons. My mother told me it was the hottest day of the season, so I've always guessed it was the middle of August."

Jack looked at his friend. "I'm not sure of my birthday, neither. Ain't that something? Two grown men that don't even know when they were born. Well, lad, I got ya close to home. That be my birthday present to you."

That night, they once again bathed and washed their clothes in the cool waters of the Snake River. By the last rays of the setting sun, the comrades sat around the campfire, talking of birthdays past. Only Freddie knew the exact date of his birth.

Four days later, after much good hunting, the way again turned to a high rocky plateau, but the very next day it flattened out again at a series of waterfalls and fast flowing rapids. Along these shores the troop made their last camp together. After a fine meal of fresh venison and river greens, the friends sat around the fire, talking of their odyssey and future.

While Dutch was sweetening the coffee with his Spanish brandy, Jack told them of their next move. "Tomorrow, you will ride northwest with the river. Soon, the Snake will turn north and you should continue traveling northwest. Within a few days you should see in the far distance a range of purple mountains. Once over those peaks, you'll find the Columbia River."

"What about you?" Dutch retorted.

"I'll cross the river in the morning and head north. Within the week, I will be home." Jack took a drink from his cup. "Why don't you all come with me? The Bitterroots are a good place to be."

Dutch poured Jack another splash of brandy. "It's a tempting offer, my friend. But I have important business on the coast. Why don't you join us?"

Jack smiled broadly. "I've enjoyed our time on the trail. I've even come to respect you all, so I'll think on it, tonight. Now let's finish your bottle."

A wet nose poked his cheek, not once, but twice.

Dutch slowly opened his eyes, still lost in his dreams. With the dog standing over him, he blinked a few times, and then pulled his mind back to reality. Quickly, he sat up on his bedroll and looked at King.

There was a snarl on the dog's lips. Indians were about.

Sliding on his boots, Dutch stood and looked around camp. The fire was but a bed of glowing coals, and Jack was missing from his buffalo skin. Under a half-moon, Dutch quickly moved to the picket line and counted the animals. They were all there. The dog moved to the edge of camp and made a tight circle, whimpering softly.

Just then, the still night air was pierced by the faint sounds of Jack's double-barreled smooth-bore: *Bang...bang!*

Dutch raced back to his bedroll, reached for his rifle and pistol, and ran out of camp, with the dog in the lead.

With the moon high in the sky, King ran east without hesitation. The rifle shots had come from far off, maybe a mile or more. Dutch ran like a deer down the trail, through dells of elms and prickly brambles, with his heart racing and adrenalin pumping. His friend was in danger, and he was determined to help.

They passed clumps of underbrush with the river in the background, shimmering in the moonlight, then crossed two shallow gullies. As the trail approached a large boulder King slowed his pace and came to a stop. Dutch stopped as well, and caught his breath for a moment. Then he and dog walked stealthily around the corner and farther down the trail.

In a grove of trees, next to the river, he heard some soft chanting. Dutch and the dog moved silently through the thin line of the dell to the edge of a moon-lit clearing, where fate delivered another bitter surprise.

Jack sat on his rump, in the middle of the expanse, scalping an Indian. Next to him was his rifle, and around the perimeter of the clearing were three other dead bodies.

Dutch waited and watched wondering the meaning of it. Why was Jack chanting and scalping an Indian? It made no sense. Finally, from his hiding place, he softly said, "Jack, this is Dutch. Don't go shooting me. I'm coming in."

Jack looked up as he approached, his pallid face flecked with spots of blood. "What the hell are you doing here?"

"I reckon that's my question," Dutch replied, looking around the clearing. He espied a canoe down on the shore, and the glowing coals of a campfire next to where two bodies lay. All of the dead Indians were without their scalps.

"Got me all four of them black-hearted bastards," Jack said with a sinister smile. "Killed the guard first. He had fallen asleep. Then I shot two more while they slept. This one," he added, looking down at the bloodied body on his lap, "tried to run, but my knife found its way between his shoulder blades."

"Why?"

"King smelt them out and came to wake you. I stopped him and told him I'd take care of this. He led me here and watched me slit the throat of the guard, then lit out up the trail. Your damn dog betrayed me!"

"Jack, you're making no sense. Why did you kill these Indians?"

Jack seemed stunned by the question. "They're Crows, mate, just like the Indians that killed my wife."

"Thought you grew tired of killin'."

"Aye, I did…but I needed me a scalp pole for my new lodge."

Dutch shook his head slowly in the moonlight; his friend had clearly lost his senses. "The Devil's got you, Jack. This is barbaric.

These braves didn't kill your wife. Your actions are dreadful, so I'll be leaving you to your wretchedness."

Jack gave Dutch a surly look. "Aren't you the righteous one! You killed the preacher without a blink, and now you call *me* a devil! Well, lad, I got me a fine canoe. Why don't you leave your uncle and that girl behind, and come with me?"

"Nay. I'm no thief, dead Indians or not, and I don't go killing people in their sleep. You scare the hell out of me, Jack. May God have mercy on your soul!"

Dutch turned and walked away, with King on his heels. As they moved through the trees, Jack screamed, "You're too soft for this hard land. You be just a goddamn breed, with flatland dreams and old squaw words. See ya in hell!"

The walk back to camp was slow and troubled. Dutch couldn't shake the image of Jack scalping that Indian in the moonlight. He had respected Jack, looked up to him, had even wanted to be like him. What the hell had gone wrong?

Once back in camp, he lay for hours on his bedroll, with dark thoughts swirling in his head. King seemed to sense his master's bitter anguish, and curled up next to him.

Dutch was angry, but he was also sad. He felt betrayed, and he cursed his own trusting stupidity. Finally, he fell into an uneasy sleep.

Sometime later, his father's voice roared through his head, *Wake up! There is trouble afoot!*

From behind the camp, he heard a loud, piercing yelp and an agonizing whine. Dutch sat straight up on his bedroll, blinking his eyes. The eastern sky showed the first light of day, and the dog was gone! Grabbing his rifle, he jumped to his feet and raced for the back of the camp.

There in the dim light, he saw King sprawled out on the ground, with the Lakota spear through his body. With a gasp and a lump in his throat, he rushed to his dog and stood looking down on King's motionless body.

Jack's yell split the morning stillness. "Now you know how I feel!"

Dutch twisted east, looking toward a grassy hill some hundred yards away, and spotted Jack and his horses silhouetted against the amber sunrise. His rifle was on his back, and in his right hand he carried his scalp pole.

With a face flushed with anguish, Dutch yelled back, "Why the dog?"

"Because you loved him, and he betrayed me. Now you can taste my anger and understand my hatred for the Crows."

Dutch raised his rifle to his shoulder and pulled the hammer back one click. "I should drop you where you stand."

Jack answered with a maniacal laugh. "Reckon I ain't foolish enough to leave a loaded rifle next to you. If you want my scalp, lad, come on after me." Jack paused a moment, then raised his scalp pole high in the air and let out an Indian whoop. "If you've got grit, I'll look for ya up-trail."

With that, Jack twisted Buck's head with a pull on the reins, and rode off towards obscurity.

While Jack was still in view, Freddie ran from the camp, rifle in hand, with Cora right behind. "What the hell is going on?" he yelled.

Dutch still held the rifle to his shoulder. He hadn't pulled the hammer all the way back or squeezed the trigger. He was sure Jack was lying about it being unloaded, but he didn't have the heart to kill him. With tears running down his cheeks, Dutch turned to face his uncle and said bleakly, "King is dead."

X
Northwest Indians

—ɯ—

*T*he Northwest Tribes were considered rich by their neighbors on the prairie, not because they were truly wealthy, but because they had an abundance of food and safe, sturdy shelter from the weather. If land, buffalo and horses were the cornerstones to the Plains Indians, than cedar trees, canoes and salmon were the keystones of the Northwest Indian. These indigenous people lived in two distinct areas of the Oregon Territory: the interior, or woodland tribes, and the coastal tribes. The cultures of these regions were as diverse as the mountains that separated them.

The interior tribes had few horses and often followed the movement of the big herds of elk and deer. They lived in tipis, mostly along the shores of rivers and lakes, built canoes and fished for the majestic salmon. Only a few of these tribes cultivated the land, mostly for Indian tobacco, corn and a few other staples. These were the nations like the Spokane, Yakima, Umatilla, and Nez Perce.

The Costal Indians lived in permanent villages along the shores, bays and rivers of the Pacific Ocean. Just before contact with the Euro-Americans, these people were the most densely populated areas of all indigenous people. These Indians made longhouses built of thick cedar planks, and crafted huge canoes that could hold twenty warriors and thousands of pounds of cargo. They ate the bounty of the sea, hunted the plentiful forest and feasted on fresh fowl. These were the nations like the Chinooks, Siuslaw, Tillamooks and Coos.

The Northwest Tribes occasionally gathered together for a potlatch. The brave hosting the festival gave away as many gifts to his guests as he could. This showed that he was wealthy. Such ceremonies could last for days, with singing, dancing and story-telling, all part of the celebration.

In the late 18th Century, the maritime fur trade gave rise to a tremendous accumulation of wealth among the coastal Indians, and much of that wealth was spent on lavish ceremonial feasts, frequently accompanied by the construction and erection of totem poles. Poles were commissioned by many wealthy leaders to represent their social status and the importance of their families and clans.

The inland tribes often raided the costal tribes, stealing canoes, food, and taking prisoners that would become slaves. The costal Indians retaliated with wars that could last for years. When necessary, the Northwest Indians were a brutal people.

The Pacific Indians followed no single culture, but the cedar tree, canoe and salmon were the common thread that bound the tribes together.

—ɯ—

The Blues ————

With a *click*, Dutch pulled the hammer all the way back, his finger resting on the trigger. Jack was two hundred yards away, about to disappear. Could he kill his friend? He blinked, with tears stinging his eyes, then twisted his body, took aim at a nearby tree, and pulled the trigger.

Fizz – Bang!

The rifle was loaded! Twisting back to Jack, he yelled, "You lying son of a bitch, you should be dead!"

With one last wave of his scalp pole, Jack turned into some trees and disappeared.

"Do you want me to saddle Scout?" Freddie asked.

"Nay, killing him ain't the answer," Dutch replied, removing the rifle from his shoulder.

"Mr. Dutch," Cora exclaimed, kneeling next to King, "your dog be breathin' some."

Dutch hurled his rifle to his uncle and raced to Cora's side. Sure enough, there was a shallow breath. The lance had struck the dog in the left shoulder and had pierced through his body to just behind his left leg. Dutch carefully rolled King over to his right side and looked at the exit wound. There was blood everywhere. "Boil some water and get me some clean cloths," he said to Cora. Looking up at Freddie, he continued, "Grab the medical kit and my razor...quickly."

As they searched out his needs, Dutch took his knife and cut the iron point away from the tip of the spear. The dog whimpered and snarled a few times, barely conscious. Dutch stroked his head and spoke softly to him. "You'll be all right boy."

When Freddie finally returned with the kit and razor, Dutch used scissors and the razor to carefully cut the fur away from around the lance at the entry and exit points. Then, using a few dabs of rubbing alcohol, he cleaned the wounds even further.

Reaching inside the kit, he removed the bottle of laudanum and handed it to Freddie. "I'm going to pull the lance out. If he snarls, dribble some laudanum into his mouth. Cora? Where are you, girl?"

She came running, with hot water and cloths.

With everyone in position, Dutch took hold of the lance. "Uncle, hold his head down. He won't know if we are friend or foe, so don't let him bite you. Cora, use the wet clothes over his holes, so he don't bleed out. I'll pull the lance out and then stich up the wounds."

Dutch knelt by his dog and drew the lance out with one firm pull.

King let out a yelp and tried to snap at them, but Freddie held his snout, and got a few drops of laudanum into the dog's mouth. With Cora holding a cloth on the exit wound, Dutch sutured six stiches into the shoulder wound. Then Cora moved aside, and Dutch placed four more stitches in the lower leg wound. King growled a few times before losing consciousness again.

Dutch worried; he had expected more of a fight. Wrapping each wound with cloth, he prayed that he had done the right thing.

"Will he live?" Cora whispered.

"Don't know." Dutch frowned. "He may be bleeding inside. We don't know what damage that damn spear did."

"Why did Jack do this?" Freddie asked angrily.

"Don't rightly know. Last night, down by the river, he killed four sleeping Indians and took their scalps. The dog woke me up and showed me to the place. Jack was crazed. The Devil had him, for sure. He said King had betrayed him, which makes no sense."

"What now?" Freddie asked.

"We'll spend the day here and see if the dog gets any better."

"What happens if he doesn't?" Freddie retorted.

Dutch met his uncle's gaze with sad eyes. "Then we bury him here."

They moved King back to camp on the white buffalo skin and laid him close to the fire. All that day, an intense solitude lay over the camp like a blanket. Dutch sat on a stump, drinking coffee and staring at his dog. His mind was filled with dark thoughts of Jack's actions and with dread of losing King.

Hours later, the dog finally opened his eyes. Dutch dribbled some water down his throat, but King went right back to sleep.

In the early afternoon, he awoke again, this time with brighter eyes and a slight wag of his tail. He drank more water. When Dutch checked his wounds for any fresh blood, he found none. Carefully, he lifted King from the robe and stood him, three-legged, on some grass. King promptly peed, then panted softly as Dutch laid him down again.

It was a heartening sign. Dutch softened up a little dried meat in his mouth and offered it to his dog. King ate some, although not much, and went back to sleep.

The long hours of waiting and watching had taken a toll on Dutch. He started pacing around the campsite and soon found himself at the river's edge. Jack had told him to stay two more days on this trail and then, when the river turned north, the troop should continue traveling northwest. But why should he trust anything Jack had said? The river looked peaceful. Why not build a raft and float down to the Columbia? It would be easy…wouldn't it?

But Jack had called it a deathtrap.

Looking out at the river, with the late sun on his face, Dutch shouted, "Jack, you son-of-a-bitch!" Then he walked back to camp.

Cora and Freddie had been melancholy all day and hadn't said a dozen words. Finally, while adding a log to the fire, Core asked, "Why Mr. Jack kill those Indians?"

"I don't know," Dutch replied, pouring more coffee. "Reckon something snapped like a twig inside of him, and the demons took hold. He wasn't the mate I figured him to be."

Freddie jumped from his bedroll. "I'm going to saddle up Dolly and scout out tomorrow's trail. This waiting has me on edge, and I'm still mad as hell."

With a sad face, Cora watched Freddie stomp out of camp. Then she twisted back to Dutch. "King can ride with me tomorrow. We can put him on the sheep skin, right under my seat, where I can keep an eye on him."

Cora was a good person, and her wrinkled brow showed Dutch that she was genuinely worried about his dog.

That evening, he kept the fire going all night, and slept on the ground next to King. In the flickering light, he watched the dog's every move and heard his labored breathing. Twice during the night, King woke, drank more water and, with some help, peed again. He even ate a few more bites of softened meat. Dutch was encouraged, and thanked the Lord for the blessing of this dog. He finally fell asleep, just a few hours before dawn.

The next morning, as the animals were made ready, Dutch loaded King onto the sheep skin and placed him underneath Cora's seat. Just before the trio moved out, he checked the dog's wounds again.

"You keep a keen eye on him," he said to Cora as he mounted Scout. "If he starts moving about or whimpering, you call out and we'll stop."

She put one hand down on King's head and gently stroked him. "Not to worry, Mr. Dutch," she replied with a bright smile. "I keep a hawk eye on him, all day." Then, taking the reins in her hand, she clucked to her mule and started on the trail again.

With the Snake River flowing northwest, they rode over a rocky prairie that rose in swells and undulations, expanding into a wide basin. At midday, Dutch stopped at a small creek and checked on his dog. Cora said that King had been awake for a few hours but hadn't been any trouble.

Under the hot sun, Dutch lifted him from the buggy and took him creek-side. There, standing three-legged, King peed and drank a good amount of the cool, fresh water. He even chewed a few morsels of meat. Then Dutch placed him back under the shade of the seat.

"He be doing just fine, Mr. Dutch," Cora assured him from her seat as they moved out again.

That evening, they camped in a dell of pines overlooking the green waters of the river. While Freddie tended the animals and Cora cooked a meal, Dutch carried his dog to a nearby grassy bluff to watch the sunset. King was much improved and could hobble around, favoring his left leg.

With a slight breeze in his face, Dutch lit his pipe and watched his dog sniff around the ridge and finally pee.

"You're on the mend, boy. You will soon be walking normal again. Reckon you got more grit than Jack."

Under a pink and amber sky, King sat next to his master as the sun slowly sank behind the broad brim of the horizon. It was a spectacular view, with golden shafts of light racing across the sky and sparkling off the water. Soon, with a serenade of crickets and frogs, King curled up and placed his head in Dutch's lap, and together they watched the sky fill with a million stars. Man and dog, the very essence of love and trust.

Late the next day, when the river bent north, the troop stopped and took their fill of water. Then they said farewell to the Snake River and rode on, heading northwest over land that was a waste of rock and sage in a wide, dry basin.

The following day, the landscape gave way to mounds of tall, blonde grass that blew in waves with the gentle breeze. Such open, smooth country made for a fast passage. Soon, in the distance, they could make out the long, thin line of a mountain range.

"Those mountains look more blue than purple to me," Freddie said, riding next to Dutch.

"Aye," he replied. "The mountains get taller towards the north, so we'll ride a little south and see if we can get around them."

Without Jack as a beacon, Dutch became the navigator. All the trail decisions now fell on his shoulders. With his keen eyes and good sense of direction, he was confident about this new job, but worried over his troops mood. Ever since Jack's hasty departure, the trio had been gloomy, devoid of any merriment. He was determined to change those doldrums and make it a hopeful journey again.

That night, they camped on the foothills of the final barrier to the Columbia River. After a meal of rice and the last of their dried meat, the trio sat around the fire with long faces and few words.

Watching Freddie pour another cup of coffee, Dutch finally said, "Uncle, I reckon it's time we teach Cora to read and write. What say you?"

"And how would we do that?" Freddie answered with a surprised look.

"Each night around the fire, I'll work with her on writing, while you'll work with her on reading."

"Reading what?"

Dutch opened his pouch, removed his Bible, and handed it to his uncle. "She can learn the way I learned, from the Good Book."

Freddie took the book and opened it with a shy look. "Not sure I've ever read the Bible."

"And I'm not sure I'm ready for any learnin'," Cora squalled.

Dutch smiled at them. "The book is a great story, about life and death, greed and good, and how Christ came to be our Savior. Cora come sit next to me. I'll show you how to write out your name."

For the next half hour, they worked together with pencil and paper, while Freddie sat quietly reading the Bible. Finally, Cora had a small parchment with her name written out by her own hand. She was thrilled, and proudly showed the paper to Freddie.

"I be Cora. **C-O-R-A**," she kept repeating with a smile.

With Cora seated next him, Freddie started reading aloud from the Bible, but he only got as far as Adam and Eve before the many questions began.

"Mr. Dutch, what does 'begat' mean?"

"Nephew, why was the apple forbidden?"

With much excitement, Dutch spent the rest of the evening explaining the Garden of Eden. Time flew by, with smiles all around. The biblical stories of tribulation gave the trio hope for their present journey. Their evening sessions would go on for months, and would deeply change the lives of Cora and Freddie. Praise be the Lord, as His stories always lift the burdened heart.

With King still hobbling, the troop spent the next two days ascending the east slope of the mountains. They blazed a trail over grassy hills, as the summits stretched out in front of them like ripples on a pond. Along the way, they found a few groves of pines, crossed many creeks, and forded many streams. At times, they were forced to push, pull and carry the buggy around the many obstacles that blocked their path. The weather remained hot, but not the sweltering heat of the flatlands.

On the morning of the third day, they came to a shallow stream that flowed north towards the Columbia. This flow would mark their path.

With the larder near empty, the trio kept keen eyes out for any game. Cora killed a few squirrels with her slingshot, and Dutch shot a rabbit, but only a few pounds of beans and handfuls of rice remained in the Bear Box, so food was an issue on everyone's mind.

On the fourth night they camped in a ravine alongside the stream they had followed all day. With Cora setting up and Freddie tending the animals, Dutch and King walked out of camp for an evening hunt. The dog was walking on all four legs again, with only a slight limp. His spirits were high, and he pushed himself hard, each day on the trail.

A few hundred yards downstream, the ravine started narrowing, with high, rocky walls and many crags protruding from the water flow. Dutch stopped and carefully studied the gully. Many obstacles blocked the trail; they would have to backtrack and cross over the mountain away from the stream. But as Dutch turned for camp, King came racing from upstream and made a tight circle, bright-eyed. There was no snarl on his lips, so Dutch knew he had found some game.

Around the next bend, with the help of the dog's point, Dutch spotted a young mule deer drinking water on the other side of the creek. His rifle report echoed off the rocky walls, as he took an easy shot of only fifty yards. As the echoes died away, he waded across the water, lifted the carcass onto his shoulders, and turned again for camp.

Cora and Dutch gutted and skinned the deer close to the stream. The animal was young and thin, but its hindquarters would make a few meals, while the front quarters would yield a few stews. For now, their larder had been replenished, and all was right with the world.

That night, they feasted on venison steaks as they planned the next day's journey. After the meal, Freddie read from the Bible while Cora struggled with her alphabet. Then, after much chatter about the evening lessons, the trio found their bedrolls. With an owl hooting in the distance, Dutch added more logs to the fire and turned in. Soon he was asleep, with his dog curled up next him.

A few hours later, from a deep slumber, Dutch heard a loud, angry roar and a snarling bark. Were they real noises or a dream? He heard the sounds again, and this time his eyes popped open, and he sat straight up in his bedroll.

In the dim of the firelight he saw King standing with bristling fur, growling at a bear who stood tall next to the buggy.

Dutch jumped to his feet and reached for his rifle. The brown bear was the size of a man, and it was pawing and clawing at the Bear Box.

"No, King," he yelled at the dog.

In the blink of an eye, Freddie was on his feet, pistol in hand. Cora stood up next, and a fearful scream escaped her as she saw the dog moving ever closer to the bear.

"No, King!" Dutch yelled again.

Fizz – Bang!

Freddie pulled his trigger, and the bullet raced across the camp, hitting the bear in the chest. With gun smoke and confusion swirling around, the lead ball of the pistol bounced right off the thick hide of the bear. But now the brute was mad, and it turned away from the box towards the camp.

King leapt at the snarling bear.

With one quick wave of the bear's powerful paw, the dog was tossed into the air and came crashing down to the ground with a loud yelp.

Dutch glanced at King, then back up to the bear. Shouldering his rifle, he drew the hammer all the way back and pulled the trigger.

Fizz –

Misfire!

"Shoot him again," Dutch yelled to his uncle, while dropping the rifle and rushing to the fire. The bear, now on all fours, started to charge Dutch, who quickly reached down to grab a burning fire log, which he threw at the raging animal. With sparks flying, the burning branch hit the bear in the face.

The beast stopped and began to back away. Dutch grasped another burning log and held it out in front of his body. A quick glance showed him that his uncle was just priming his reloaded pistol. Turning back to the bear, Dutch watched as the burly brute rose onto his two hind legs again and let out a deafening roar.

"Shoot him!" Dutch yelled.

As Freddie raised the gun in his shaking hand and pulled the hammer back, Dutch saw that the ramrod was still in the barrel. Before he could call out a warning, his uncle pulled the trigger.

Fizz – Bang!

The ten-inch iron rod sailed across the camp like an arrow and pierced the bear's thick fur.

With the rod driven deep into his chest, the brute dropped back onto all four legs and let out a wounded cry. Dutch rushed him with the burning log and tossed it at his face, then backed off for more fire logs.

For a moment, the bear was frozen in place. Then, quickly, it turned and shambled off into the night shadows.

With the danger over, everyone stood for a moment, shaken by the fear they had just felt. Finally, Dutch turned and headed toward his dog, calling, "Put more logs on the fire, Uncle."

Fortunately, the only real damage to King was his pride. None of his healing wounds had reopened, nor had any new ones been inflicted. With just the wind knocked out him, he was walking around the campsite again in just a few minutes.

The trio spent their next few hours reliving Freddie's ramrod shot, and building a tall fire to protect against the bear's return. Bears and Bear Boxes were never a good mix.

The next morning, as they back-tracked up stream, they paused a moment where the deer had been gutted, the night before. Almost nothing remained of the carcass. It had been picked clean, apparently by the bear. Dutch knew he had committed a pilgrim's mistake. No game should ever have been cleaned and gutted so close to camp. The blood scent had served as an open invitation that they were lucky to have survived.

Two days later, the troop came to the last tall ridge on the north side of the mountains. From there, in the distance, they could see the thin, blue line of the Columbia River bisecting a broad basin of grassy, rolling hills. They were within sight of their destination.

The next day, they came to the confluence of the Columbia River and the small river they had been following for days. They paused, looking out upon a slow-moving, wide, green river. Both shores were a treeless wasteland, with tall blonde grass and boulders almost black in color.

"Not what I expected, Nephew," Freddie said from his crackling saddle. "How do we build a raft with no trees?"

"Don't judge this mighty river by this lazy current. We will ride downstream until we pass the long narrows, and there we will find many trees," Dutch replied.

"How do you know this?" Freddie asked.

Dutch removed his straw hat and wiped his brow. "In Captain Clark's journals, he noted a portage of over two miles around a great falls where the Indians fished. We will find that same way."

The troop turned west and rode a well-beaten river trail. It was the last day of August, five months to the day since Dutch had begun his odyssey to the Pacific.

River Song

Late in the afternoon, they came to another small river that drained from the purple mountains and flowed into the Columbia. Dutch was first to cross, and found the water only horse-belly deep.

Freddie and Dolly soon joined him. Leaving Willow with his uncle, Dutch returned across the river to help Cora and the buggy. After they had tied Scout to the rear of the cart, Cora moved across, with Dutch wading alongside one of the wheels to act as the brake. This had become their method of crossing rivers ever since Devil's Hall, and they'd had no problems. But this day was different. For some reason, halfway across, Cora's mule spooked and reared high into the air. The cart jerked sideways, almost overturning. With a thud, one wheel slipped deep into an underwater rut.

It took almost an hour to unload and free the buggy from the trench. When it was finally removed and carried to the other shore, the wheel no longer spun. They placed the cart on its side so Freddie could assess the damage. He removed the wheel and inspected the axle, to find it bent.

"Can it be fixed?" Dutch asked, standing next to the underside of the buggy.

"Aye," Freddie answered, "if I had a proper forge. But out here? Impossible."

They camped that night on the small river's edge. With great reluctance, the decision was made to abandon the buggy. They had carried, pushed and pulled the damn cart halfway across the continent, but now it was nothing more than a worthless pile of memories. Still, Dutch held out hope of fixing the 'land canoe' someday, so they dismantled the buggy and hid all of the parts in a thicket of sagebrush, far off the trail.

The next morning, the Bear Box was once again strapped on Willow's pack saddle, and the balance of the cargo was distributed on the backs of the troop. Cora rode her mule, but without a saddle, and with only a makeshift bit and reins. As the troop moved out, Freddie joked to Cora that riding a mule was still better than walking.

Some hours later, the trio noticed that the arid river basin was narrowing, and the current was picking up speed. Soon, the waters were churned by rugged rocks protruding from the riverbed. Around the next bend, the troop heard a roar, and soon came to a place like no other on Earth. Captain Clark had called it the long narrows. It was without a doubt an amazing sight to behold. Over the millennia, the powerful Columbia River had cut a swath of rapids through giant, jagged, perpendicular rocks. These flumes of whitewater were two or three hundred feet wide, with the whole of the river rushing violently down.

In the foaming white current, countless salmon struggled to swim upstream to spawn. On the shore of the rapids, attached to the tall vertical rocks, they saw small wooden platforms, with Indians fishing in the river's mist. Some of these Natives used long, sharp rods to spear the fish, while others used poles with hooped nets. All of the Indians were balanced precariously on rickety, slippery wooden scaffolding. Once a fish was snatched from the turbulent flow, the fisherman would pole it down to another Indian on the shore.

The long series of rapids blocked any navigation from the upper to the lower river. Never before had Dutch experienced such a powerful river, or witnessed such unyielding determination of both fish and fisherman.

With the river roar, mist and tiny rainbows hanging in the air, the troop kept moving slowly down the rocky trail.

"Keep a keen eye out. These Indians can be thieves," Dutch yelled.

When they came to a few shabby huts, where squaws were cleaning and drying the fish, they stopped and dismounted. By then, the Indians fishing the rapids were quite aware of the three strangers, and some of the fishermen began moving their way. The troop stood in the hot sun, watching the squaws work. The women all used iron knives and had trade beads around their necks; they had seen white traders before.

Dutch and his troop were soon approached by three men, one of whom had falcon-eyes and black, scruffy hair; he appeared to be the fishing Chief. These Indians were quite different from Plains Indians. Their facial features were bolder, their bodies more stoutly built and their dress more primitive. Dutch greeted the men with the sign of peace and asked if he could trade for some fish. The Indians stood frozen in place, gaping at Cora. Using his hands, Dutch asked again about trading for food. One of the squaws yelled something over the roar of the river. The falcon-eyed Chief moved towards Cora and quickly lifted up the hem of her dress and touched her bare leg. She squealed and pulled away, with a stark look of fear on her face.

"They have never seen a Negro before," Dutch shouted. "Hold up your dress so everyone can see your legs. You are in no danger."

Cora flashed Dutch a look of disbelief, but slowly lifted her dress, turning around for all to see. The wide-eyed Indians pointed and chattered with each other. The Chief signed a few questions and watched carefully as Dutch signed back the answers.

"They ask if your skin is always dirty, and if you were my slave. I told them you were from a faraway land and that I was your slave."

The squaws snickered at his answer; a man being a slave to a woman was unbelievable. The Chief placed his copper arm next to Cora's and rubbed her skin, then showed his palm to the other Indians. Nothing had rubbed off. Finally with his curiosity satisfied, the Chief signed that a trade for food could be made. Dutch promptly reached into his pouch and showed the Chief a twist of tobacco. For this sum, the troop received a large, fat fish and a basket of greens.

It was a good trade, for Dutch also learned that the local Indians called this place "The Dalles," and that many more Indians would come here to fish within the next moon. Dutch asked where they might find a campsite with many trees, and was directed to a down-river cove with tall pines. Dutch thanked the Indians with a smile, and handed out a few colorful beads. After hanging the salmon from his pommel, the troop saddled up and moved further downstream.

A few miles later, with the river roar gone, they found the cove and set up camp. The inlet was surrounded with a dell of tall, straight pines, a few stands of oak and a grassy shoreline where their animals could graze. The water of the cove was only a few feet deep and opened to the Columbia currents. It was the perfect place to build their raft.

Freddie and Dutch unloaded the iron implements from the saddle bags and went to work, crafting handles. They had picks, axes, bucksaws, hammers, board knifes and chisels, all needing handgrips.

Dutch was sitting by the fire, finishing his first axe handle, when Cora asked, "Mr. Dutch, I ain't never cooked with no Indians greens before. Can you show me how?"

Dutch got up, walked to the fire and inspected the basket. The Wapato plant had about twenty thick roots, which he cut away and placed in a bucket. "These tubers are like small potatoes," he said to Cora. "Clean them good and then boil them in your kettle." He picked up one of the green sprouts with an onion root larger than his fist. "Never seen an Indian onion this big before." Taking his knife, he cut away a chunk and put it in his mouth. A curious smile chased his face. "This be the sweetest onion I have ever tasted. Clean the onions and the green tops, and boil them with the Wapato. We should have a fine meal tonight."

With Cora at the water's edge, Dutch returned to his stump to craft another handle.

"Never seen such big fish before," Freddie commented.

"The Pacific salmon is a giant of a fish. The fish is the treasure of the West."

"What kind of raft will we build?"

Dutch took a stick and started drawing on the dirt. "The bow will be pointed and the stern square. This will require a frame of five thick pine log stringers. The center one will be twenty-four feet long, while the two outside stringers are twenty feet in length. The width of the craft will be fifteen feet, with split pine logs running across the five stringers. There will be a rowing yoke on each side and a rudder yoke at the stern. We will use oak for our sailing mast, rudder and oars. The raft will carry our animals, so a railing will have to be built so we can tether them securely. We will row when we have to, and sail when we can."

"Why do you know this design so well?"

"It's been in my head since the Ohio River. When we arrive on the Pacific, we can disassemble the raft and use the timbers for our cabin."

"How will we fasten the split logs to the frame?" Freddie asked.

"I packed in sixty iron log spikes. We'll notch all the split timbers and use a spike at each lap, and then oak plugs to reinforce the joinery. From what I've read, we still face a few rapids downstream, so our raft must be stout."

That night, the troop gorged themselves on the tasty pink meat of the salmon and ate their fill of boiled onions and potatoes. Even the dog came back for seconds.

The next few days were filled with toil and sweat. Trees were chopped down and cut to length. Large-girth timbers were used as the stringers, while smaller straight pines were split and notched. As the split logs were fastened across the stringers, Dutch showed Cora how to bore holes and hammer oak plugs in place. She also worked with the draw knife to smooth out the oak plugs and remove deck splinters. Slowly, in the quiet waters of the cove, their raft took shape. Twice during this time, Dutch returned to The Dalles to trade tobacco for more food. On those trips, he found the falcon-eyed Chief friendly and willing to make fair trades.

With the raft nearing completion, Dutch decided he was not willing to leave the buggy behind. Once the troop reached the Pacific, a proper forge could be built, and the cart repaired. Dutch explained his plans to Freddie and Cora, and they wanted to come along. But with so many Indians nearby, he couldn't leave anyone alone, even with the dog. So the others would stay in camp to protect the raft and supplies.

"I'll be gone but a day. King will alert you if any Indians approach. Do not trust these Dalles Indians."

Early the next morning, while Cora sewed two canvas tarps together for a sail and Freddie built a railing for the raft, Dutch rode Willow out of the cove, dragging an empty travois. He had made the sled from two long oak poles attached to the packsaddle, with a few oak sticks lashed to the bottom of the spars. This Indian device was sturdily built, and Willow was strong enough to drag the damaged buggy back.

Dutch made good time and rode through the long narrows with the sun still low in the sky, highlighting the river mist that hung over the many rapids like a veil. He found only a few Indians fishing and rode quickly past the river roar. Back tracking alongside the Columbia, many miles later he came to the small river they had crossed the week before. Off the trail and behind some sagebrush, he found the buggy undisturbed. Working in the hot sun, he lashed the cart frame to his travois, and then tied all four rickety wheels on top. The last items were the harness poles, which he fastened to the side of the cargo bed. With the skid spars bending from the heavy load, it was midday by the time he walked Willow back to the river trail.

Dutch felt a warm breeze on the nape of his neck as they started dragging the travois downstream. But as they moved along, Willow started whinnying loudly and jerking on Dutch's lead rope. This was surprising behavior for his normally docile packhorse, and he had to stop a few time to whisper in her ear.

A few hours later, when he approached The Dalles again, he found many new faces watching his slow march down the rocky way. Dutch looked for the falcon-eyed Chief, but he was nowhere to be seen. Soon, Dutch came to the shanties where the squaws sat cleaning and drying the fish. There he stopped. Reaching into his pouch, he removed another twist of tobacco and approached the women.

With a wave of their hands, however, they refused his offer of trade.

Returning the twist to his pouch, he retrieved his tinderbox and showed it to the squaws. A few held the brass case with curious looks, and they talked amongst themselves. Dutch knelt and heaped some dried grass in front of them. Then, with the flint of the tinderbox, he started a small fire. Their eyes grew wide, and with much excitement, they talked to each other again. Soon, a large basket appeared, filled with greens and two fat fish. Dutch nodded his agreement with the trade, and smiled at the woman. The trade made good sense, since the squaws made all the fires. After passing out a few more trade beads, Dutch fastened the basket to his travois and continued down the rocky path.

Walking his packhorse into camp, he was greeted by his happy dog. When Dutch took the food basket over to Cora, she told him all had gone well in his absence. Returning to Willow, he unloaded the buggy and removed the poles from her packsaddle. He wondered if the travois had caused her discomfort, but even after it was removed she was still troublesome. Kneeling down, Dutch checked her legs for burrs but found none. Her shoes were well worn, but nothing seemed wrong with her hooves. While finishing with the last hind leg, Dutch noticed the size of her belly. Putting a hand on it, he thumped it with his knuckles. A firm, hollow sound bounced back. Dutch stood, scratching his head and wearing a puzzled look.

"What's the matter?" Cora asked from the campfire.

Dutch turned to her with a grin and chortled, "I think Willow is pregnant!"

Cora rushed to his side and checked the horse herself. "Aye," she said, feeling Willows underside, "she's with foal. I'd guess a couple months. I've seen this many times, back on the farm."

Dutch smiled broadly. "Jack's sorrel had his way with her. Damn, we just can't shake Mountain Jack's grasp."

That night, after dinner, the conversation was all about Willow and her pregnancy. Luckily, the hardest part of her journey was nearly complete, and she likely wouldn't give birth until June. That gave the troop time to build a proper barn and prepare for a foal.

At dawn the next morning, the trio loaded their supplies and livestock onto the raft. Then, using the long oak poles from the travois, they pushed and pulled the craft through a narrow lagoon channel and onto the Columbia River.

Once on the open water, the troop rowed around an island and were soon drifting with the strong river current. At each corner of the crowded craft, a tethered animal faced forward. Freddie rowed from the portside while Cora rowed from the starboard station. The middle of the raft was filled with the dismantled buggy, saddle bags and all of their other equipment. King found his place on the bow and barked at the water as the scenery slipped by. Dutch stood at the stern, working a large oak rudder that was secured in a strong wooden yoke. He was pleased with the raft's stout construction and how it answered the helm.

The weather was pleasant, with the sun low in the eastern sky and a slight breeze from upstream. The craft drifted northwest in a wide basin with a rocky shoreline. Above the riverbanks stood tall, arid mountains with brown granite ridges and a few clumps of trees.

With the strong current, very little rowing was needed as Dutch kept the craft in the main flow. Soon, as the river bent west, the mountains grew taller and the trees more plentiful. The raft navigated a few narrow rocky gaps with turbulent waters and passed a few islands. At times, in the far distance, Dutch and the others could see a few Indian villages, high up on the river shore. This was an effortless way of travel, and they were making good time.

"We should name this boat," Freddie said, oar in hand.

"Aye," Cora answered with a smile in her voice. "Let's name the raft, Columbia."

Dutch moved the rudder slightly and guided the craft around the next bend. "That name has already been used. Captain Gray discovered this river and named it for his ship, the *Columbia*. I think we should call her the *Cora*."

Cora twisted her head to give Dutch a curious look. "Why me?"

Dutch thought for a moment. "Well, most boats are named for women and this raft is just like you: strong, with fine lines."

"Reckon that be a grand idea," Freddie answered, gazing across the deck.

A shy smile chased across Cora's lips as she turned away and murmured, "Never had no boat named after me before."

Around a few more river bends, they saw in the far distance the top of a snow-capped mountain standing like a god in the sky. This monolith towered over the many other peaks.

Curve by curve, Dutch kept a keen eye on the river basin. Soon he noticed it narrowing, and the current increasing. Turning the raft from the main flow, he guided it into some quiet waters alongside an island. From the helm he said, "We are coming to what Clark called the Cascade Rapids. It's going to be a rough ride. Let's turn the animals with their asses to the bow, so they can't see what's coming. Make sure they are tethered tightly. We don't want to lose any of them now."

With the animals newly secured and the cargo tied down, they rowed the raft back out into the main channel. Soon, they passed a few rocky islands where the river basin narrowed to only a few hundred yards. As the current flung the raft ever faster down the gap, Dutch shouted commands. "Cora, pull harder! Uncle, back off... that's enough."

The troop navigated around a few rocks and found before them a series of rapids that dropped off sharply. Dutch steered for the main channel of the first falls.

"Pull in your oars, and hold on," he yelled over the roar. The raft twisted, bounced off a few boulders, and came crashing down in white water, drenching the deck. Before Dutch could react, another rapid had them in its grip. The raft bounced over some rocks with the current swirling over the stern, as they turned sharply in the white water. With all his strength, Dutch pulled the rudder, correcting their course.

With the first few giant rapids behind them, they bobbed down the fast current toward the next few falls. The raft twisted, quivered and bucked, but these new rapids proved to be more yielding and within a few moments, they were in open water again. Finally, with the basin widening, they drifted past a large island and turned through another bend. It had been a few miles of hell, and the troop was wet and scared, but no one was hurt. The *Cora* had proved her worth.

"The worst is over," Dutch said from the helm, drying his face. "From here to the Pacific, we will have open water."

When the troop finally looked up from the wet deck, their fears vanished as quickly as the rapids. Before them was a strange sight: on the shore, protruding from the water, were dozens of ragged petrified stumps. Dutch steered next to these trees of stone so that everyone could touch a few as the raft drifted by. These fossilized timbers were as mysterious as the river itself.

Around the next bend, they came upon some Indians who were fishing from dugouts. On the north shore, they could see a dozen or more tipis, with more pirogues on the beach. As they approached the village, one of the shore dugouts headed their way. Dutch turned the raft into some quiet water and turned the horses around and waited for the Indians to arrive.

The canoe was paddled by a brave and a squaw, and the center of their boat was loaded with many large baskets. The dugout came alongside and Dutch stood, signing with the Indians. They called themselves Walla Wallas, and had baskets of greens to trade. They said that they came each summer from a distant winter camp, to fish for salmon and trade what they had cultivated. Their baskets were filled with Wapato plants, more large onions and other greens.

Dutch quickly traded his last two twists of tobacco for two large baskets of greens. Then he asked about the petrified trees, and was told a long and colorful story about a tall mountain that exploded with fire and ice, freezing the trees in place. It was a good tale, told with much animation. The Walla Wallas were a friendly lot, so Dutch handed out a few trade beads. Just before the dugout departed, the brave invited them to come back the next year, as they always summered in the same place.

With the trade completed and spirits high, Dutch and his companions rowed back into the current and proceeded down the river. Around the very next bend they found a vista so breathtaking that they stood in a silent awe. The river basin had risen up to a gorge with sheer granite walls on both sides of the river. On top of those ridges were rolling hills with a seemingly endless forest of pine and cottonwood. And on the south shore, standing like a lone sentinel, was the east side of the snowcapped mountain they had seen from up-river.

The trio was filled with wonderment as this spectacular scenery drifted by with the current. Around each curve, the deep canyon provided fresh views. There were dozens of tall, magnificent waterfalls rushing off the granite cliffs, and large rugged river coves with sandy beaches. The shorelines were filled with lush green vegetation and a sea of colors from countless wildflowers. Above the raft, the sky was crowded with hawks and eagles and numerous other birds, all plying the crystal clear waters. Soon, on the north shore, a second, tall snow-capped peak came into view. Drifting through this gorge was like sailing in the palm of God's hand.

"Do these tall mountains have names?" Freddie finally asked.

"Aye," Dutch replied. "The tall peak before us is the one the Indians call Wy'east. But one of Captain Vancouver's men saw it and named it Mt. Hood, after some famous British Admiral. The northern peak Lewis & Clark called Mt. Washington."

"I have never seen mountains so high or a river so deep. This be the work of the Lord," Cora added, her voice soft with amazement.

Dutch stood at the helm, drinking in the panorama and wondering what words could possibly be used to fully describe such a place. The astonishing views lasted for many hours as the raft snaked its way past Mt. Hood and drifted through a rain forest of fir trees that stretched out as far as the eye could reach.

In the late afternoon, with the mountains and gorge now behind them, the troop guided the raft into a quiet cove on a large, treed island. There they unloaded the animals and made camp.

That evening, after the Bible reading, Dutch and King walked to the eastern shore of the island and looked back up the river. There in the golden light of the late sun sparkled the entrance to the gorge, with Mt. Hood standing guard. Dutch had found something he didn't even know he had lost, the majestic Columbia River Gorge.

Beyond the Horizon ————

While traveling the Gorge, the troop had not used their sail because the currents were too brisk and the winds too stiff. On the second day, however, they found that the flow had slowed and the winds were but a breeze, so up went the sail. The tarp sailcloth was quite small, but it provided enough power to push the raft along.

The river now reminded Dutch of the green flow of the Ohio with its lazy currents, many islands, and thick, lush shorelines. In the silence of the sail, the troop heard Whippoorwills, frogs and a myriad of songbirds. They were making good time and enjoying new discoveries around each bend in the river. They came upon many limpid rivers and streams and in the distance saw another snow clad peak that Captain Vancouver had named Mount St. Helens.

By midday, with the river turning northwest, they came to the confluence of a large river from the south. This waterway was wide and deep and seemed worth exploring but, for the first time, Dutch felt the tides of the Pacific, and he kept sailing on.

Soon, the river turned due north and the breeze fell off. Then, in the early afternoon, the tide turned against them, so they worked their oars for hours, making slow but steady headway. The river was wide and lazy, and at times they had difficulty finding and staying on the main channel. They rowed past many islands and coves, and saw a plentiful display of wildlife. There were deer and elk, innumerable flocks of waterfowl, and countless salmon leaping from the water. This land was rich, with a bounty like no others.

Nestled along the shores, they passed a few Indian villages and saw a few canoes fishing, but they didn't stop or make contact. Instead, in the hot afternoon sun, they sweated at their rowing stations. It was early evening by the time they finally made camp on another large, treed island.

The next day, the river twisted back to the northwest. With a good breeze and an outgoing tide, the raft sailed effortlessly down the broad river. They passed many other rivers that flowed into the Columbia, some of which were large enough to explore, but they never stopped, as Dutch was determined to find his homestead before the weather changed.

To pass the time, he stood at the rudder and told Freddie and Cora of the Lewis & Clark Expedition, and how that band of courageous men had traveled the river in only flimsy canoes.

"Were there no women with the expedition?" Cora asked, resting against her rowing yoke.

"An Indian woman named Sacagawea was with the troop," Dutch answered. "She helped guide the expedition all the way across the continent. She will be famous someday."

Cora gave Dutch a sly glance. "Maybe someday I will be famous, too."

"Reckon Mountain Jack was our Sacagawea," Freddie added.

"Aye, he found our way," Dutch replied. "Jack was a free and easy-going mate, until he scratched a sore with the mention of his dead wife. Then he lost *his* way. God forgive his black heart."

Again in the afternoon the breeze died down, the tide turned, and they had to row. But as the time slipped away, Dutch could feel the Pacific coolness on his cheeks and taste the salt air. They were getting closer, and the trio was getting excited to see their destination at last.

Late in the afternoon, with the river now flowing west, they camped once again on a large, treed island where they hoped to find some game and have seclusion from the Indians.

The next morning dawned with a thick layer of cool, gray fog hanging over the river. With a slack tide and visibility down to only a few hundred yards, the troop rowed the raft slowly, fixing keen eyes on the water. Soon, the current increased with an outgoing tide, and Dutch steered for the main channel and drifted. Like a blanket, the gray mist of fog hovered over the raft as the trio silently searched their way. They turned one slight bend and passed by what looked to be a small island. Then they heard the faint sound of a bell ring out.

The dog's ears perked up, and everyone strained to hear more.

"That's a ship's bell!" Dutch whispered from his helm.

A few moments later, they heard the clear sounds of a boatswain's pipe and the murmuring of voices.

Dutch let the raft drift closer to the north shore, and asked Freddie and Cora to row. They kept moving, hoping the fog would lift, but it didn't. Through the mist, Dutch caught a quick glimpse of a dark shadow, then lost it again in the rolling fog. They heard more voices, and suddenly like a ghost, a large ship materialized in the mist. The square-rigged craft was a brigantine with a raised forecastle and quarterdeck, and two tall masts with all sails furled.

"Stop rowing," Dutch said quietly from the helm.

As they drifted slowly closer, they noticed how the ship pulled at her anchor in the current. Dutch hesitated to approach the ship. If it was Spanish or Russian, that could mean trouble, as each of those countries claimed the river as their own. With any luck, though, it might be an American ship.

Dutch drew out his spyglass and put it to his eye. The ship was dark brown with white trim, and its hull was encrusted with barnacles. Clearly, it was a long way from home. Turning the glass skyward, Dutch saw, at the top of the tallest mast, a limp Union Jack. Moving the lens to the bow, he found that he could just read the ship's name through the gray haze: *Wind Song*.

"She is a British ship," he whispered, putting the telescope back in his pouch. "We will stop and see if we can trade for some supplies."

The raft drifted closer and Dutch finally called out, "Ahoy, *Wind Song*."

In the rolling fog, a surprised deck officer in a bicorn hat appeared at the rail and yelled down, "What be your business?"

"Can we approach and do some trading?" Dutch yelled back, watching more sailors come to the rail.

"Where are you from and what is your destination?" the officer countered.

"We departed the long narrows three days ago, and hope to be on the coast today," Dutch replied.

"You may approach and secure your raft to the ship, while I check with the Captain," the officer yelled back.

In the strong tidal current, Dutch maneuvered the raft alongside the ship's boarding ladder and secured it with ropes, fore and aft.

The crew of the ship gathered at the rail, looking down at the visitors with curiosity. The *Cora* was a strange-looking craft, with a deck full of livestock, saddles and a broken-down buggy. The dog paced the raft, barking up at the sailors. Dutch commanded him to be quiet, and removed the last sheepskin and one rack of horns from a saddlebag.

He handed the horns to Cora and said, "These British can be an uppity bunch, so I may need this rack of horns to sweeten the trade. We'll see how it goes."

Soon, the officer reappeared and called from the rail, "You many come aboard, but only you."

Dutch scrambled up the ladder with his bundled hide in hand. Once aboard, he counted twelve six-pound cannon on deck, and one swivel gun fore and aft.

The rawboned officer introduced himself with a scowl. "I be Mr. Jenkins, the mate. Follow me." Abruptly turning, he led Dutch down a hatch and through a few passageways to the Captain's cabin. He knocked firmly on the door, and a gruff voice granted permission to enter.

The stateroom was cramped and smelled stale, with a chart table, desk, bunk and two aft windows that offered views of the gloomy fog.

The Captain looked up from his desk with a teacup in hand. "I be Captain Wallace McBride. And you would be…?" The man had a Scottish brogue, and a voice that demanded respect. His face was weather-beaten and clean-shaven, with hazel eyes and brown hair.

"I be Dutch Blackwell, most recently of Boston, sir."

The skipper motioned for Dutch to take a seat in front of his desk. "You're a long way from home, lad. Would ya like a spo' of tea?"

"Aye, thank you, sir," Dutch replied, taking his seat.

"If you came from the long narrows three days ago, you must have had the wind to your back," McBride said, while pouring the tea.

"Aye, we did," Dutch replied.

"We've been trying to move up-river to trade with the Indians, but these damn contrary winds keep blowing the wrong way."

"It's the way they howl here in the summer time, sir. It will be another month or two before they shift around."

The Captain seemed perplexed by his guest's knowledge, "You've been here afore?"

"Aye, I was born around here, sir. I'm coming back to open a trading post on the river. But it's been a long journey across the divide, and I need supplies, so I stopped to see if you'd be interested in doing some trading."

The Captain slid a piece of paper across the desk and turned his inkwell to Dutch. "Aye, we might be able to help. Scrieve down your needs and I'll have the mate check our stores while we chat."

Dutch wrote out his list and handed it to the Captain, who read it. "Your needs are great. What will you trade for these supplies?"

Dutch stood and unfolded the sheepskin on top of the desk. "This be the skin of a rare Bighorn Sheep. It will bring over a hundred dollars in gold at Canton."

Both the Captain and the mate examined the skin carefully. "Never seen a fur like this before. It's splendid...but how do you know its worth in China?" the skipper asked.

"Almost four years ago, in Canton, I sold two albino sea lion skins for that amount of gold each. The Chinese know the worth of rare furs and will pay top dollar."

Mr. Jenkins's face twisted in disbelief. "How did a bloke like you get to China?"

Dutch smiled at him. "Aboard the British ship *Sea Witch*. I crewed on her for almost a year."

The Captain seemed surprised by this information. "Who was your skipper?"

"Captain Harrison, sir. He was a firm but fair commander, and when we got to England he offered me a berth on his next cruise, but I sailed on to Boston."

The Captain smiled. "Pleased to hear that, lad. Simon Harrison is a friend of mine." The skipper handed the list of supplies to the mate. "Find out what we can spare and report back to me." As the mate departed, the skipper set a bottle of French brandy on his desk. "Let me sweeten your tea a wee bit, and we'll drink to Captain Harrison's health."

Dutch and the skipper spent almost half an hour talking before the mate returned. During that time, Dutch learned that the *Wind*

Song had spent the summer fur trading up north, and had crossed into the Columbia River on its way to the Sandwich Islands. The crossing had been frightful, and now Captain McBride was worried about sailing back across the bar. He showed Dutch his map of the river entrance and asked him for advice.

Dutch was pleased to tell him what he knew about the treacherous bar conditions.

When the mate returned, he handed the paper back to the Captain, who read it again. "We can spare the flour, beans, salt pork and coffee, but not the sugar or potatoes. Instead, we can trade a barrel of molasses and a bag of turnips, along with the salt, pepper and vinegar. We have no whiskey or tobacco, as we have traded our supply away. But the mate doesn't believe your sheepskin is worth all these supplies. You'll need to add to your side of the trade."

For a moment, the cabin fell quiet to the sounds of squeaking timbers. Dutch thought out his options, then looked up at the mate. "The staples I seek wouldn't cost twenty dollars in St. Louis, and I'm offering a pelt worth a hundred dollars. Doesn't seem quite fair."

With an ice-cold stare, Mr. Jenkins replied, "You're not in St. Louis, lad, and this is not a supply ship. Sweeten the trade or be on your way."

Dutch stared levelly at the mate. "There is a woman on my raft. She has another item that may be of interest. Let her come aboard."

"A woman? Are ye pure mad?" the Captain exclaimed.

"Aye, we found her on the trail and she joined us. Let her come aboard, sir."

The Captain dispatched the mate to fetch Cora, while Dutch told him a little more of her story.

When she and the mate entered the cabin, Cora carried the set of horns. Dutch explained what value they would have as custom powder or drinking horns. The skipper saw some worth in them, but not enough. Dutch mused trading his white buffalo robe or the second set of horns, or the twenty dollar gold piece hidden in his boot. But he wasn't willing to pay that much. Finally, with a sour expression, he pulled his poke from his pouch and dumped all the coins onto the desk: three silver dollars, two dimes and a nickel. He pushed the coins across the desk. "This be all I have."

Captain McBride stared at Dutch for a long moment, then pushed back the money. "I never take a man's last shillings," he said, as his face relaxed into a grin. "Very well, lad, you have a trade. Mr. Jenkins, see that these supplies are brought on deck."

After the mate departed, Dutch introduced the Captain to Cora, and explained more of her tragic story. "She's a good cook and a good worker. She's also smart. She needs to return to America. Could you take her on and let her work her way home?"

"Nay," the skipper replied quickly. "A biddie aboard a ship is asking for trouble."

Cora turned to Dutch with a startled look and said, in her squeaky voice, "Mr. Dutch, I'm surprised at you. I have no notion of leaving you and Uncle Freddie. You are my family now."

Captain McBride grinned at Dutch and extended his hand. "The lassie is your problem, lad, not mine."

With the fog lifting, they returned to the deck and found their supplies heaped in a large pile. Dutch counted the items carefully as he handed them down to Freddie on the raft. Twenty-five-pound sacks each of flour, beans and turnips. Two slabs of pork, ten pounds each of coffee and salt, and half that of pepper. The last items he handed down were two heavy barrels, one of vinegar and one of molasses.

When he was finished, Cora climbed down the ladder while Dutch turned to thank the mate. He found him next to the rail, holding a small canvas bag. He handed the poke to Dutch and said, "With the Captain's compliments, from his personal stores." Dutch looked inside and found two bottles of brandy and a large tin of tobacco. With a respectful smile, Dutch saluted Mr. Jenkins and said, "My compliments to the Captain. May this ship have a safe passage home."

By the time the raft got underway again, the fog was lifting, with a slight breeze from the east. While Cora and Freddie slowly rowed, Dutch kept the raft in the main channel as they slipped by a few islands.

Pulling on her oar, Cora said tartly, "Uncle, your nephew tried to leave me behind on that British ship."

"Why?" Freddie asked of Dutch.

"She said she wanted to return to Tennessee. With winter soon upon us, I thought she'd be safer aboard the *Wind Song*, but the Captain would have none of it."

Cora stopped rowing for a moment, gazing at Dutch. "I'll make it home to Tennessee if the Lord so provides, but not on a ship like that. I saw how those lustful sailors looked at me."

"Well, I tried," Dutch replied, shifting the rudder slightly. "You'll find that the Pacific coast is hard country, and doubly hard in the winter."

"We've been through worse," Freddie replied, with pride on his face.

Dutch watched his two comrades slowly work their oars, and reflected on how the journey had changed them. The original grousing from his uncle had been replaced with determined self-respect, and Cora had grown from a fearful girl to a proud young lady. The only thing missing was Jack. For all Jack's faults and dark ways, Dutch still longed for his friendly manner around the campfire.

The main channel slowly twisted to the south shore, and they drifted past several islands. Suddenly, Dutch began to recognize some of the landmarks. These were the same waters where he and his father had killed the albino sea lions. This was a pristine place, without a hint of mankind's touch, ruled solely by Mother Nature.

By late morning, as they rowed close to the south shore, they came to a cove that looked out of place. Turning into the inlet, they came to a stop and gazed upon what remained of an abandoned fort that was returning to the land. Two log walls had been dug into the ground, but now the timbers tilted every which way, with blackberry bushes growing all around. In a clearing next to the fort sat a large pile of cut and honed timbers, ready for use but covered with thick vines and scrub brush.

"What is this place?" Freddie asked.

Dutch shook his head slowly. "I do not know. But we will return, when the raft is empty, and carry away the logs to build our chicken coop."

"Mr. Dutch, we ain't got no chickens," Cora objected.

"We will next spring. Until then, we will live in the chicken coop while we build the trading post," Dutch replied with a grin. "Now, let's move on. We are close to our destination."

Prompted by a stiffening breeze, the troop raised the sail and continued on their way.

The main channel twisted past more islands, then moved back towards the center of the river before changing course again and turning southwest. The river was now broad and wide, with many sandbars and island along its shores. Under a blue and warming sky, the raft sailed by a high, rocky point covered with trees – a point that Dutch knew well – and they continued on. Here, the Columbia estuary was expansive with tall mountains all around, extending for many miles to the Pacific.

As they sailed past the point, Cora pointed skyward and asked, "Mr. Dutch, what kind of bird that be?"

Dutch craned his neck. "That be a Blue Heron, the best fisherman on the river."

In midafternoon, with seagulls screeching and Dutch's heart racing, they furled their sail and drifted in front of a large, level peninsula. On one side of the headland was the river; on the other side was a large, gray-blue inlet that Captain Vancouver had named Young's Bay. Up from the rocky and sandy shore, a verdant plateau opened to a large, lush meadow. Above this clearing was a series of timbered mountains, with many creeks and rills draining into the estuary. This was a place of many memories for Dutch, some of which were happy and bright, although others were somber and dark.

In a jubilant mood, the troop rowed their raft to a small, sandy beach. With his boots worn to the nub, his buckskins only threads and his face full of whiskers, Dutch stepped on home land again. The date was September the fourteenth; he had completed his odyssey in just five and half months!

After a fine meal of salmon, beans and greens, Dutch poured some brandy into his coffee and passed the bottle to his uncle. He did same and offered some to Cora.

"I cannot refuse. This be a special day," she said with a smile, as Freddie poured a small amount into her cup. "By the grace of God, we have arrived here safely."

They made a toast to Jack and the Reverend, and said a silent prayer.

When they looked up again, they saw the *Wind Song* in the distance, sailing towards the Columbia Bar. They walked down to the point and stood in the late sun, drinking their fortified brew and watching the ship depart.

"Why did you select this place?" Cora asked.

Dutch looked fondly at her and replied, "I'll name this headland Joseph Point, after my father. Here we have mountains filled with game, grassy meadows for our animals, and a river full of fish. This place has much to offer, and each morning we can stand upon this strip of land and see what the tide brings in."

XI
The Overland Astorians

—ɯ—

 he Astor Expedition to the mouth of the Columbia River is
 sometimes referred to as "the Hunt Party" or "the Overland
Astorians." In 1810, John Jacob Astor, along with his Canadian partners, Alexander McKay, Duncan McDougall and Donald Mackenzie,
met in New York to sign the Pacific Fur Company's provisional agreement. Astor owned a one-half interest in the Pacific Fur Company;
the other half-interest was divided among his working partners, each
owning two-and-a-half to five shares. All of these working partners
would venture to the Columbia River, either overland or by ship.

Once the Pacific Fur Company was in operation, some of the
partners helped obtain ships and supplies, while others returned to
Canada to recruit bold men for this daring enterprise. Most of these
adventurous recruits signed five-year contracts with the company and
were hired as hunters, interpreters, trappers, traders, clerks, guides
and *Canadian Voyagers*. The original party also included one woman,
Marie Dorion, an Iowan Indian and wife of interpreter Pierre Dorion,
and their two young sons. During the journey, a baby would be born
to the Dorians and die near present day Union, Oregon.

Upon receiving the news that there was treachery among some
of his Canadian partners, Astor promoted one of his American
partners, Wilson Price Hunt, to be sole commander of the overland

expedition, with Donald Mackenzie, a Canadian, as his second-in-command. Wilson Hunt was a St. Louis fur trader with no outback experience. He made a number of decisions that were disastrous to the enterprise, the first being to double the size of the expedition from thirty to sixty men. This would require more months of recruiting, so he also took the unusual step of sending out the original party of thirty on the expedition just before winter. This overland group left St. Louis on October 21, 1810, and traveled up the Missouri River before setting up winter camp at the mouth of the Nodaway River in Northwest Missouri. During those winter months, the partners recruited the additional men needed. Finally, the sixty-person expedition broke the Nodaway camp on April 21, 1811.

The original plan was to follow the Lewis and Clark trail up the Missouri. But, after just a month on the river, Hunt learned that the Blackfeet Indians were on the war path and so, to avoid any possible trouble, he abandoned the river route and decided on a passage overland. After many delays, and problems trading his boats for horses, the expedition finally departed North Dakota in mid-July.

The party traveled west with relative ease through South Dakota and Wyoming, and accumulated 6,000 pounds of dried buffalo meat along the trail. Once on the Snake River, another fateful decision was made to leave the horses behind and build canoes. Hunt believed it would be easy to descend the Snake River all the way to the Columbia. But traveling down the river proved disastrous, as they encountered many waterfalls. At one set of rapids, two men were lost due to capsized canoes, and a great deal of their food and other supplies were lost, as well. The group soon discovered that the Snake River was unnavigable and their canoes were finally abandoned. The party divided into factions near present day Twin Falls, Idaho, and set out on foot for Astoria. One group traveled the south side of the Snake River, while another party walked the north side. A third party went their separate way. This hike across the arid wastelands of Idaho and Oregon would prove to be dreadful, as well, and the main party didn't arrive at Fort Astoria until February 15, 1812. Only 45 of the original 60 members of the expedition made the ten-month passage to the Columbia River.

Most Astorians survived the trip, but they utterly failed to blaze a dependable trail to Oregon, arriving there just barely ahead of a competing British expedition. However, when some of the Overland Astorians returned east, many months later, under the command of Robert Stuart, they made many historical discoveries. These included the South Pass through the Rocky Mountains, where hundreds of thousands of settlers were soon to follow along the Oregon Trail.

—ɯ—

The Alliance ———

With a gray haze clinging to the bay, Dutch was awake before first light. He started the fire, and then mixed up a batch of his biscuits, using Kate's sourdough starter. They had traveled for weeks without any flour, so he looked forward to the prospect of fresh rolls, bacon and sweet native blackberries for breakfast.

Setting the biscuits aside to rise, he put on the coffee pot. Then he and King walked down to the river's edge. The morning was like a jewel, with no hint of a breeze and the early light shimmering off the mist. With the gentle hues of blue and gray stretching from the sky to the surrounding mountains, he knew his future was before him. As he gazed across the water to Cape Hancock (Cape Disappointment), he wondered if the *Wind Song* had slipped safely over the bar the night before, or if she was anchored at Bakers Bay, waiting for the right sea conditions. In any event, he wished Captain McBride the best, as it was a long way home. One thought led to another, and soon he was musing over a long list of things that had to be done before the storms came.

"Mr. Dutch," Cora's squeaky voice said, "what are you doing up so early?"

Startled back to reality, Dutch turned to her sleepy face and replied, "Just watching the day begin. Couldn't sleep on a fine morning like this."

"Aye," Cora replied, fondly looking at the river. "This be a peaceful place to be, and it's so beautiful."

Dutch smiled at her. "In a few months, this will be a miserable place to be. The winds will blow up from the south, and the rains will roll in from the west. For months on end, this land will be rain-drenched and wind-ravaged, with nary a blue sky in sight. We have many projects to build before that happens."

Cora thought for a moment with a blank stare, and then turned to leave. She walked a few steps before turning back to Dutch, "If you need building projects, why not start with a proper privy? I'm weary of using the forest like a bear."

"Aye, that's a fine idea," Dutch replied, joining her on the walk back to camp. "Well, better get my biscuits on."

With birds singing and river ripples glistening, the trio sat on a long log, enjoying one of their best breakfasts in months. Every biscuit, berry and pork strip was consumed with joyful faces. Even King ate two biscuits and three pieces of bacon.

"The Columbia River is a familiar friend," Dutch said, pouring himself more coffee. "It was the past that drew me here, and it will be the future that roots me here."

"What is that future?" Freddie asked, finishing his food.

"It's whatever *we* want it to be. For me, it's the satisfaction of building a life here in the wilderness. For you, the future could be different."

"What if I long for my home?" Cora asked with a serious face.

"You are not trapped here. Many ships will touch our shores, and I will pay your way, if that is what you wish."

Freddie got up and poured more coffee. "Cora and I know nothing of trading and dealing with Indians. How can we profit from this?"

"You will learn, and we will share in all profits fairly," Dutch replied.

Freddie's face filled with a grin, and he raised his coffee cup high. "Here's to success, even if we don't understand it!"

Dutch smiled at him, and then lit his pipe with a punk from the fire. "Our first task is to dig Cora a proper privy. Then I'd like to row up to old Fort Clatsop and see if we can find some planks to build a decent table. But before we do anything, I thought you might like to say hello to your brother."

"My brother?" Freddie replied with a puzzled face.

"Aye, his grave is nearby. That's another reason why I picked this point. What say you, Uncle?"

Freddie's face turned sober. "Aye."

With Cora cleaning up from the morning meal, Dutch and Freddie walked out of camp, carrying only a small scythe and a hatchet, with the dog at their heels. As they moved through the thick underbrush, they used the tools to cut away a narrow path. Soon, they came to the bay and followed the shoreline south.

Young's Bay was large, four miles long and two miles wide. It was fed by many streams and by two major rivers that the Indians called Netul and Kilhowanah. The thickly timbered land above the shore was steep and hilly, with many rocky ridges. Dutch kept his keen eyes focused for one particular boulder whose shape was etched deep in his mind.

"Nephew, why did you trade for a barrel of vinegar?" Freddie asked, hacking at the trail.

"I knew this Swedish bloke back in Boston. He was always jawing about a homeland dish he called pickled herring. He claimed pickled fish could be cured to last for years." Dutch stopped his own hacking and turned to his uncle. "One day, he brought me a sample, and I found the taste to my liking. So why not pickled salmon?"

"How's it made?"

"Simple. It's just fish, sugar, salt, vinegar and onions. If the fish *can* be cured, then we will be eating salmon all winter."

"We can always smoke and dry the fish, like the Indians do."

"Aye, we will do that, as well," Dutch replied, swinging the scythe again.

A few moments later, he espied the rock he had been looking for, and they moved up a slight hill to where a huge vine-covered boulder protruded from the slope.

"This is the marker," Dutch said, pulling away the creepers. "My father and blood brother are buried here, in front of this boulder. Someday soon, I will chisel their names in the rock."

Dutch dropped to his knees and continued pulling away the ground cover and underbrush. Freddie joined him, and they worked at clearing the ground in front of the marker. When they were done, they stood and placed their hands on the stone and bowed their heads and said a silent prayer.

When Freddie looked up again, he asked, "How did this happen?"

Just as Dutch was about to respond, the dog ran back up the trail and made a tight circle, with a snarl on his lips.

"I'll tell you later. There be Indians about. We should get back to camp."

As they moved quickly back down the path, with King on point, Dutch cursed himself for not bringing his rifle. When the camp came into view, he peered through the foliage and saw three Indians sitting on the long log in front of the fire. As Dutch and Freddie slowed and walked into camp, Cora rushed up, her face a mask of fear.

"They just rowed up to the beach and walked to the fire. I can't understand a thing they are saying. They scared me to death!"

Dutch commanded the dog to stay next to Cora, and walked over to the Indians. They all wore basket hats, were small in stature, and dressed in rawhides with seashell strands around their copper-skinned necks. Their facial features were bold, with sloping foreheads, pigeon toes and bow legs as was typical of the local Indians. They carried no weapons other than the knives that dangled from their belts.

As they made eye contact, Dutch recognized the older brave in the middle, who was holding a basket.

The Indians looked at Dutch with suspicious eyes.

He made the peace sign and worked his hands as he spoke the Clatsop tongue. "Chief Coboway, nice to see you again. You are welcome in my camp."

The Indians were wide-eyed, clearly startled that he knew their language. "How do you know me?" the old Chief asked.

"My family had a trading post at the fort up the Netul River. I was but a young brave then."

The old man's eyes brightened as he recalled Dutch's family. He talked with fondness of Joseph and of his squaw wife, Raven. "They be fair traders, and brewed a fine beer. We enjoyed many hours together."

The Indians had seen their campfire smoke from the night before, and had paddled up the river to investigate, bringing a basket of oiled anchovies and greens as a gift. Coboway handed the basket to Dutch, who thanked him and promptly took the food to Cora.

"We have nothing to fear. These be Clatsops, and this basket is their tribute."

Freddie and Cora looked relieved.

"Uncle, fetch me a handful of blue and white beads and one rifle from the trading bag. We will talk awhile in their tongue. I will tell you later what was said."

Dutch returned to the Indians and took a knee in front of them. The Chief asked more about his family, and Dutch told him the tragic tale. "We were attacked at the fort by some renegade Chinooks and a Russian man. They tried to steal a season's worth of pelts from my family. They had rifles, war canoes and many warriors. The battle was long and bloody, but we escaped down the river and across the bay to an anchored British ship. During the fight, my father and brother were killed."

"Why did Joseph burn down my fort?" Coboway asked with a stern face.

"It was a diversion, as we were but four."

"The Chinooks have a new Chief now. He is called Comcomly, and he is very powerful. The Chinooks control the far side of the river, and Clatsops this side of the river." There was disdain in his voice when he spoke of the Chinooks. The two tribes had always been rivals.

Freddie approached with the rifle and beads, and gave them to Dutch, who said, "I'm going to introduce you. Look them in the eye without any fear."

"This is my Uncle Fredrick, the brother of Joseph. The squaw is Cora. She is from a land where people are brown."

The Indians looked at her with curiosity, and mumbled to each other with strange looks on their faces.

"We have come here to open a trading post." Dutch stood and approached Coboway, handing him the beads. "I remember, Chief, that you liked blue and white beads, so this is my gift to you."

Coboway was impressed and showed the tribute to his two companions. They all had smiles on their faces.

"How many rifles do the Clatsops have, Chief?" Dutch asked, holding up the rifle.

"Three long guns and pistol, but the hand-cannon no work," the Chief replied.

"I would like to trade you four rifles," Dutch said, holding up four fingers.

Coboway looked surprised by the offer. Rifles were the most prized items in any Indian village. "What is our trade?" he asked cautiously.

"Come with me to the river and I will show you."

All the Indians walked with Dutch down to the shore, where he had them turn and look back at the camp. "We will build our trading post on this ground. But this is Clatsop land, so you will trade this property to me for two rifles."

"You said four," the Chief answered, holding up four fingers.

"Aye," Dutch smiled and turned to the bay. "You will also trade us hunting, fishing and gathering rights on the bay and lands from the Kilhowanah River to the Netul River, and all the way south to the hump-back mountains."

Coboway and the braves murmured to each other. "So we could no longer hunt and fish these grounds?" the Chief asked with concern.

"Nay, your people will always hunt and fish here. But so can we, without any trouble from your tribe."

"You have hunted and fished these grounds before and we didn't stop you. Why do you trade for them now?"

"I want an alliance with the Clatsops. I seek their permission and protection. Many white men and ships are coming here, and I want to remain friends always with the Clatsops."

The Chief looked dismayed to hear that other white men were coming but, in the typical Indian way, he didn't ask a single question.

"I will trade you two rifles, with powder horns and bullets now, and two more next season, when the salmon return," Dutch said. "This will make the Clatsops a rich tribe."

The Chief's dark eyes peered at Dutch as if he were searching for an answer. "This will be for the council to decide. You bring the rifles and come to the village tomorrow. We will give you our answer."

"Aye," Dutch responded.

"Bring brown squaw. My people would like to see such a person."

Dutch agreed, and the Indians got into their dugout and paddled away. As they moved downriver, he wondered if Coboway might be holding a grudge because his father had burned down the fort. Only time would tell.

He walked back to camp and told his friends what had been said during the powwow. When Cora learned that she was to go to the village the next day, she was hesitant. But Dutch assured her that the Clatsops were only curious about her.

"They think me some kind of freak," Cora said with a frown, "when it's them that are queer."

As the friends crafted handles for the shovels and a pickaxe, they talked more about the local Indians and how to treat them if approached. "Show no fear, but don't be a bully," Dutch said, working a piece of oak. "The Indians may seem childlike, but they are the masters of this land. Chinooks live on the north side of the river. They are the biggest and most powerful nation. The Tillamooks live to the south of the Clatsops, and they are strong, as well. They all look the same, and speak the same language, but with time you'll learn who belongs to what tribe."

Freddie seemed confident that he could handle the Indians, while Cora rambled on about being enslaved again.

With a breeze in the trees, and the handles completed, the friends walked into the forest and selected a place for their outhouse. As Cora cleared a path back to camp, Dutch and Freddie started digging a large slit trench. The first few feet were easy going, but then they hit rocks and roots. After a few hours of backbreaking work, they had a large pile of stones and a ditch that was six feet deep and four feet long. On top of this trench, they built a platform of elevated split logs, with a notched toilet hole. When finished, the privy was useable but exposed to the elements. This they would correct, later, with a small shed.

Before leaving for the fort, Dutch told Cora that she should remain in camp with the dog. She was to use the sail and set it up as a tent, then gather as many berries as possible and keep a keen eye on the livestock and supplies. "There are cougars and bears in these mountains, so stay close to our animals. The dog will alert you if man or beast approaches." Dutch also left her one of his pistols and one of the extra rifles. At first, Cora seemed fearful of remaining alone, but Dutch reminded her that this was the way of the frontier. "You have to be careful out here. The wilderness can sneak up on you. Trust only in the dog and yourself."

After placing some tools aboard the raft, Freddie and Dutch rowed across Young's Bay and up the Netul River. As they paddled, Dutch told his uncle what he knew of the surrounding lands, and pointed out a few landmarks he remembered. The weather was bright, with only a hint of a warm breeze, and they made good time with an incoming tide.

A few miles upriver, they paddled ashore and, after securing the raft, walked the slight rise to the burnt-out remnants of Fort Clatsop. The old stronghold, nestled in a dell of tall fir trees, looked bigger than Dutch remembered. Some of the bastion's log walls were still stuck in the ground, but leaning every which way. On the south side, most of the fortress was nothing more than a pile of charred logs, but on the north side, two corners were still erect, with only a few logs collapsed upon each other. Everything was covered with thick blackberry vines and weeds.

"What are we looking for?" Freddie asked, staring at the scorched remains.

"Anything and everything," Dutch answered. "Nails are a big treasure, reusable logs and planks, parts of tables and chairs, and anything else we might find under the debris. My family left much behind the day we escaped from here."

They worked under the hot sun, clearing away the vegetation and rolling logs off of each other. Using an iron crowbar, the two men removed nails and saved whole wooden planks, stacking each one aboard the raft. Working on the two erect corners, they found pockets of collapsed rooms with pieces of furniture still intact, and heavy doors with wooden latches and leather hinges. There was also a good supply of cedar shingles nailed to what remained of the roof structure. Dutch unearthed a few porcelain cups, plates and tin utensils his mother had once used, now scattered around the dirt floor. They also reclaimed her rusty iron cooking pot, a skillet and a damaged coffee pot. Against one wall, they recovered empty clay jugs and two small crocks, a basket of dentalium shells, an iron-tipped spear, and Dutch's boyhood bow with a half dozen arrows. They also found some trading trinkets: beads, spools of twine, mirrors, iron tool-heads and a few knives. The old clothes they uncovered were mostly rotting rags, although they discovered his father's wool winter coat, wrapped in a seal-skin slicker, with both garments still in good repair. As Dutch searched the next room, he discovered a large leather pouch under a collapsed table. Inside was a fringed white buckskin frock, a necklace of beads, and moccasins adorned with tiny seashells.

Inspecting the garment in a shaft of sun light, Dutch's eyes filled with tears: this ceremonial dress had once belonged to his mother. Folding the frock neatly again, he returned it to the pouch and set it aside. Dutch was surprised the Indians hadn't found these treasures years before. But then, the fort had never seemed very important to the Clatsops.

As Freddie worked at pulling nails, he said to Dutch, "If we build a forge, I can straighten these spikes and make more nails from the rims of the iron wagon wheels."

"Aye." Dutch rolled a few more logs free. "And we can also melt down some of these rusty tools."

"How did you come to live in this fort?"

"We were staying down the coast when father heard about white men living here." Dutch stopped working and wiped his brow. "We raced up the coast as fast as we could to join them. But when we got here, they were gone."

"So what did my brother do?"

"Father made a deal with the captain of a British ship to open the fort as a trading post. At the end of the season, the ship would return for our pelts and carry our family to London."

Old Fort Clatsop gave up many treasures that day, and even told a few secrets. With the shadows lengthening, they paddled the raft for camp, with a cargo of logs, planks, parts of furniture and other personal items. As they alternately rowed and drifted with the current, Dutch told his uncle what remained of the story of his family's escape from the fort. The tragic tale was hard to talk about and filled with dreadful details. In the end, Freddie realized the full story of his brother's wretched death.

"It was the ship's cannons that finally drove off the renegades, but not before my father and brother were killed," Dutch concluded with watery eyes.

"Did you kill any of those Indians?" Freddie asked with a bitter face.

Dutch looked away, gazing out to the bay. "Aye, and the Russian as well. It be a memory I would like to forget."

After a few moments of silence, his uncle grimly replied, "I will help you chisel their names on that rock marker. They must not be forgotten."

Arriving back at camp, they were greeted by a happy dog. As the men unloaded the rescued treasures, Cora sorted through the curios while telling them of her day. There had been no trouble, and she had rearranged the camp to include a tent under the cover of a tall fir tree. She had also collected a basket of berries and proudly announced that she had killed two ducks with her slingshot. The men were pleasantly surprised by her hunting abilities.

Dutch approached Cora and handed her the pouch he had found. "This is for you. There is a dress inside that once belonged to my mother. Wear it tomorrow, when we visit the Clatsops."

Opening the leather bag, she removed the frock and unfolded it. "It is beautiful!" she said, with bright eyes and a smile. "I will cherish it forever, Mr. Dutch."

As the men continued to unload the raft, Cora folded up the dress and slipped the pouch over her shoulder, then went to work, plucking the birds for dinner. Once the men finished the unloading, they turned their attention to repairing a table and three wooden chairs.

That night, with a vermilion sun setting over the estuary, they sat at a proper table, enjoying berries, biscuits and the succulent ducks while talking of their future plans. It was joyful to have some small comforts again.

Early the next morning, the men went to work, building a shed for the privy. Reused logs from the fort were cut to length, notched and stacked upon each other. In the front of the crib, a doorway was cut to match the size of one of the salvaged doors. The privy was finished with a shed roof made of recycled cedar shingles, and the final touch; a basket of dried maple leaves. When it was completed, Dutch chuckled to himself; the first structure he built on the Oregon Coast was an ordinary outhouse.

With tools in hand, Freddie and Dutch walked back to the camp, and found it empty. Dutch called for the dog and Cora, but there was no response. Stoking the fire, he moved the coffee pot closer to the flames. Just as he was about to call out again, Cora and the dog appeared from bathing down on the beach. She was wearing the white fringed frock, necklace and fancy moccasins. Both Freddie and Dutch stood speechless, as her beauty took their breath away. Her chocolate skin seemed to glow in contrast to the paleness of her dress. And her freshly washed curly black hair shimmered in the sunlight. She looked magnificent!

"You're pleasing to the eye, dressed as an Indian," Dutch finally said as they approached.

"Your mother and I are near the same size, so the fit is good. When will we leave for the village?"

"After I bathe, and have something to eat, we will go."

With Freddie and the dog remaining in camp, Dutch loaded two trade rifles and a saddle bag filled with trading trinkets onto the raft. With Cora aboard, he untied their barge and they rowed down-river towards the Clatsop village. The river was running with the outgoing tide and the sky had gone from crystal blue in the morning to a hazy overcast at noon. Dutch smelled rain, and made up his mind to keep a keen eye on the weather.

"The Indians will want to touch you. Don't be alarmed. They are only curious, so show no fear."

"That be a rude habit they have, and I can't understand a word they say," Cora replied pulling her paddle.

"Stay close to me. I'll translate whenever I can. If we get separated, stand with a stoic face." Dutch froze at his station, with his head high. "For some reason, Indians respect those who are indifferent to them."

Moving across the raft, he gave Cora a handful of small seashells. "Use these to pay tribute to anyone who is especially friendly to you. The dentalium shell is sometimes used as money, so it's highly prized."

Cora gazed at the mollusks in her hand with wonderment. "They look like animal fangs."

"Aye," Dutch replied, moving back to his rowing station.

Just off the Columbia's south shore, they rowed the raft for about six miles and then turned up a lazy green river. Not far up this estuary, they came to a sandy cove where many canoes rested on the beach. They put ashore.

Chief Coboway and a few braves greeted them warmly on the beach and showed them the way.

Once over a small, sandy ridge, they came to the Clatsop village. The tribe was sprawled out on a level plain with many hip-roofed cedar lodges. These dwellings had no windows, only doors, and some of the lodges were forty feet long and twenty feet wide. All had smoke rising to the sky from smoke holes in the roofs. The alleys in between the shelters were crowded with Indians of all sizes and ages. Squaws worked at tanning hides, while men made repairs to their lodges, and children played with barking dogs. The village had a rhythm to it.

As Dutch and the others walked along the pathways, his mused that the village seemed smaller then he remembered. Then he noticed the pox scars on a few faces. The white man's scourge, small pox, had ravaged the village. A few of the Indians followed the party all the way to the Chief's lodge. With many villagers gathered around, Coboway introduced his guests to his people. Questions were asked, and some of the squaws touched Cora gently. Dutch answered in their tongue, which surprised most onlookers. He told them Cora was from a faraway place where all people were black or brown. One young brave, with a bear-tooth necklace, shouted that he had seen another person like her in a Tillamook village. "How long ago?" Dutch asked. The brave answered that it had been two seasons ago, and said that the man was the Chief of the Tillamooks. Dutch translated so Cora could understand.

When she learned there was another Negro in the neighborhood, she smiled broadly and asked, "Will you take me to see this man?"

"Maybe," Dutch replied. "His name is Marcus. He was a friend of my father's."

After a few more questions, Chief Coboway put up his hand to stop the many inquiries. Then he and Dutch went inside his lodge to meet with the council. As they departed, Dutch said to Cora, "Stand stoic. You are in no danger."

Walking inside the smoky lodge, Dutch found five tribal elders sitting cross-legged around a large fire pit. They were all dressed in their finest buckskins and adorned with bone piercings and beaded necklaces. As he handed the trade rifles to the council members, he gazed upon the spacious room, built of thick cedar planks and filled with native treasures. Chief Coboway's lodge was the grandest of them all. Taking a cross-legged seat next to the fire pit, he made the peace sign and greeted each elder by name, as he was introduced. Dutch felt at home around the council fire and he relished looking upon the Indian faces. Coboway told the elders about Dutch's family and how he had been born to an Indian woman in a Tillamook village.

The council grunted and smiled at the story. Then an old brave, with three eagle feathers in his hair, asked, "Why do you ask for land that is not ours?"

Dutch looked the elder in the eye and worked his hands and tongue. "This is your land, given to you by the Mother Spirit. Hold tightly to your land. It is the legacy to your wealth."

"What kind of wealth do we have?" one elder scoffed.

"The Clatsops are rich. You have animals in the forest, trees on the mountains and fish in the sea. Others are envious, so hold tightly to your land."

"If this be so, why should we give you land for your trading post?" another elder asked.

"Fine question," Dutch replied. "I wish to trade for the land, not have it given to me. And I will act as your advisor when the other white men come."

The oldest of the elders, a man with many wrinkles, said, "Tell us of the white men that are coming."

Dutch told them what he could of the Astor expedition and about supply ships that would soon come. He guessed the Astorians would build their trading post on the north side of the river, close to the Chinooks, while his post would be on the south shore, close to the Clatsops.

"Will you trade us whiskey?" Coboway asked.

"Nay," Dutch answered. "But I will brew a batch of Spruce Beer, come next season."

There were many other questions about the rifles, the trade agreement and, most of all, about the other white men coming. As they talked, Dutch continued to stress his desire for peace with the Clatsops. There was some bickering between the elders, but in the end they agreed to the terms of the trade.

Standing, Dutch read aloud from the agreement he had written:

For the sum of four rifles, two now and two next season, the Clatsop Tribe deeds to Dutch Blackwell, for now and forever, the point of land known as Joseph Point and the hunting and fishing rights on the bay and the lands between the Kilhowanah River and the Netul River, and all the way south to the hump-back mountains.

When he finished reading, the elders grunted their approval and Chief Coboway made his fish mark on the parchment. With the alliance sealed, Dutch opened his saddle bag, and handed the Chief two powder horns, two pokes of bullets and a small bag of flints. With the elders smiling, he sat down again and filled his pipe with tobacco, which he lit, and passed around to the council. As they all smoked and talked, he traded a third powder horn for a fine sea otter pelt and some fish hooks and a file for a nice beaver skin. Dutch volunteered to fix the broken Indian pistol, and the council accepted his offer. It was good to be amongst the coastal Indians again.

With Coboway on his heels, and his saddle bag over his shoulder, Dutch returned outside and found Cora surrounded by giggling children and happy squaws. With adoring eyes, these women and children were treating her like an Indian princess. They loved her beauty – and her squeaky voice, as well.

"These be nice people," she said, beaming, as Dutch approached.

"Did you hand out the shells?"

"Aye," she replied. "Gave them to the children."

Dutch tilted his face skyward. "The winds have picked up, and the weather is changing. We better get started back."

The Chief and a few braves walked Dutch and Cora to the beach and said their farewells. Under cloudy skies, they rowed out of the cove and turned into the lazy green river. A few minutes later, they paddled onto the Columbia River, just as a light drizzle started to fall.

Working her rowing station, Cora asked, "Why do all the Indians have sloped heads?"

"It's a sign of beauty to them," Dutch replied, pulling his paddle. "When a child is born, it sleeps with a cedar board tied to its head. Over the years, the board flattens the child's forehead."

Cora made a sour face. "That sounds dreadful. They look so deformed."

Dutch smiled at her. "One man's deformity is another's beauty."

They arrived back ashore just as the rain started in earnest. After securing the raft, Dutch and Cora rushed into camp to find Freddie and the dog standing under the cover of the tent flap.

"Did it go well?" his uncle asked.

"Aye," Dutch replied, moving under cover and removing the pelts from his saddle bags. "Got us the deed to the land and our first two skins."

Cora held the otter fur to her face. "This is so soft, and it smells so fresh! What is it worth?"

"Sea otter skins? A hundred dollars each. Beaver pelts are ten or fifteen dollars each."

Cora's and Freddie's faces lit up. Now they understood the true value of this enterprise.

The Chinooks ————

The next few weeks were filled with the urgency of the changing seasons. Dutch, Freddie and Dolly, the mule, traveled back up the Columbia River to the abandoned fort and salvaged every cut and hewn log they could find. The heavy timbers were mule-dragged to the shore and then tied together and floated downriver to camp. As they worked the site, they found a few other treasures: a half-filled keg of nails, the rusty blade of a two-man ripsaw and a pair of soggy boots still in good repair. In two long days, they gathered all the cut logs on the river and then did the same at old Fort Clatsop. By the time their work was completed, they had nearly a hundred and fifty logs in camp for their construction needs.

Their first project was to build a forge with an open shed roof. While the men dug the fire pit and set the posts for the roof, Cora and her mule gathered shore stones for the furnace. These rocks were carefully stacked, then mortared with a mixture of bog mud and squaw grass. As Dutch finished the forge walls, Freddie and Cora crafted a bellows made from salvaged wood and a deer hide. In the late afternoon, the roof was finally finished and a small curing-fire built inside the furnace. With the project finished, the trio admired their labors, with smiles on their faces.

"Sweat is the sweet taste of success. Now on to the chicken coop," Dutch said with a sense of pride.

The first task at the furnace was fixing the Clatsop pistol. This was accomplished by straightening the hammer and adjusting the trigger. The forge was the first factory in Oregon Territory. In the coming months, Freddie would prove himself to be a skilled blacksmith and a savvy trader with the Indians.

There was no rest for the friends. After dinner, the evenings were filled with making and mending clothes, fixing tools, sharpening blades and building furniture. The early morning hours found the men hunting, while Cora searched the forest and bogs for camas and other edible roots. They bathed and washed their clothes once a week and the men shaved as often. The friends seemed to be in perpetual motion, moving from one task to the next.

The point of property on which the trading post was to be built was a sparsely treed site of over an acre in size. The gentle, sloping meadow behind this point added five acres more. This pasture had a stream running through it that was fed by two brooks and many fresh-water springs.

Before starting the next project, they marked with stones the position and size for the trading post, a smokehouse, a garden area, and a large barn with a corral. Next to this barn, the chicken coop would be built. The structure was simple enough: a log room twenty feet across and fifteen feet deep, with a dirt floor, a single door, and a shed roof with a smoke hole. The trio would live inside the coop while the barn was built. Living in this cramped shanty would be a challenge, but far preferable to a breezy tent.

With the days shortening and the nights cooling, they completed the chicken coop in late September. The log walls were chinked with moss and mud, and the table and chairs were moved inside and placed next to the fire pit. Bed frames, with rope mattresses, were made to keep the trio off the damp ground. Shelves and wooden pegs were installed, and trail bags hung from the rafters. The final task was to cut a few cords of firewood to be stacked under the roof eaves. When completed, the coop was dark and crowded, but weather-tight.

It had taken just over a week to build the coop, and now the trio turned their labors to the barn. This was to be a bigger structure, with four stalls, a tack room and hay storage in the rafters. On a bright October day, the first log puncheon was rolled into place and leveled. A second soon followed, parallel to the first, but eighteen feet apart from it. With these two long logs half buried in the ground, the level foundation for the barn was set in place. Using the mules, Dutch and the others dragged logs into place, notched and rolled one upon the other. It was a process of pulleys and planks and the sheer strength of all involved.

At each notched corner, the joinery was strengthened with oak bungs. Those inserted pegs would help keep the barn from twisting in big storms. Slowly, the walls took shape, and soon the gambrel roof rafters were in place. The barn roof was large, and they had run out of recycled shingles, so Freddie and Dutch went into the forest and chopped down a large cedar tree. Using the cross-cut saw, they cut lengths from the trunk, and then used the mules to drag the logs back to camp. These lengths were cut to size, and split shingles made.

With the shingles drying in the sun, Freddie worked his forge, making roofing nails and hammering out iron hinges for the barn door. As he worked the bellows, Dutch and Cora rowed across the bay to an open stretch of ground and cut dried sea grass for their animals. They rolled the blonde grass into bales, tied the bales with twine, and loaded them aboard the raft. It would take many loads before the barn was filled with enough winter hay to carry them through to spring.

October could be a fine month on the river, with warm days and cool evenings. The late summer and early autumn was also the time when the Indians fished on the ocean side of the Columbia. Once a few big storms had rolled through, the large schools of salmon entered the river and began moving upstream to spawn. When that happened, the fishing fleet would fill the estuary in all directions.

One bright day, while the trio was hammering cedar shingles into place, Dutch looked out from the rooftop and saw an Indian canoe crossing the river, headed their way. He was the first down the ladder and, with rifle in hand, walked to the beach with King on his heels. Freddie and Cora soon followed, also with their weapons.

The shovel-nosed canoe was large, with an Indian standing at the bow. Behind him, an entourage of eight warriors paddled the boat. As they approached, weapons could be seen and a chant heard.

After commanding the dog to sit, Dutch turned to his friends. "They be Chinooks. A fearless and fearful lot, but we should be in no danger."

A few moments later, the large canoe came to rest on the beach. The standing Indian was the first to come ashore. He was short, with bowed legs, and he wore a leather patch over his right eye. An iron war axe dangled from his belt, and he had three feathers in his pulled-back, braided hair. He was dressed in fringed deerskin, and had an elk hide around his shoulders.

As the other braves stepped to the sand, with weapons in hand, Dutch made the sign of peace to the Indians and said, in their tongue, "The Chinooks are welcome in my camp."

The one-eyed Indian appeared surprised by his words, and asked, "How do you know our tongue?"

"I was born in a Tillamook village."

The three-feathered brave looked at Dutch with distrust. "I am Comcomly, Chief of the Chinooks."

Dutch smiled at him. "Chief Coboway told me of you. He is my friend."

While the warriors stood gawking at Cora, the Chief looked about the camp and asked, "Why you here?"

"Building a trading post," Dutch replied in both words and sign.

This news brought an angry look to the chief's face. "This is Indian land. We control all the river trade," the Chief said sternly.

"This was Clatsop land," Dutch said firmly. "I traded many rifles for this land. We have an alliance."

One pudgy brave, holding a rifle, asked, "Why would our brothers, the Clatsops, make an accord with you?"

Dutch turned to the Indian and glared at him. "Chief Coboway is my faithful friend, and I told him about the other white men that are coming here. I will council the Clatsops on how to deal with these new arrivals."

"What other white men?" Comcomly asked, scowling.

Dutch pointed to the east. "Many men will soon be here from where the sun rises. They will open a trading post here, as well."

The Chief's eyes got wide, and he shook his head angrily. Reaching for his war axe, he waved it over his head and shouted, "The Chinooks control this river, not the Clatsops! You must leave these lands and go away forever."

King snarled at his quick movements and let out a loud growl. Freddie and Cora had no idea what was being said, but they felt the Chief's threating look, and grasped their weapons more tightly.

Dutch raised one hand and turned to his friends while speaking English, "These boys don't much like us, but don't worry." He then turned back to the Chief and said in his tongue, "You must take this up with Chief Coboway, as Clatsops control this side of the river."

The Chief frowned at Dutch and then moved towards the dugout, still waving his axe. As his warriors loaded into the boat, the Chief turned and shouted, "You must be gone by tomorrow or we will drive you away."

"Only the Clatsops can drive us off this land," Dutch yelled back, while the royal canoe paddled off.

As the trio walked up the slight rise to camp, Dutch explained what had been said and what was demanded. "I am surprised by the Chinook threats," Dutch concluded. "The coastal tribes are mostly a peaceful people."

"What should we do?" Cora asked.

Dutch smiled at her. "Let's finish the roof. No one is driving us off our land."

That evening, Dutch and Freddie paddled the raft up to the Clatsop village and returned the repaired pistol to Chief Coboway. He was delighted to have the weapon back, and offered the men a basket of greens and a fat fish. While accepting the gift, Dutch told the Chief of the Chinook threats. He didn't seem concerned and only replied that the Chinook were a greedy people.

Early the next morning, with a thick layer of clouds hanging over the estuary, Dutch took his coffee and walked to the point. Using his telescope, he searched the waters to see what the tide had brought in, and spotted three canoes crossing the river, heading his way. True to his word, Comcomly was returning, this time with two additional war canoes packed with warriors.

Returning to camp to fetch his rifle and shout the alarm, he then returned to the beach to watch the Indians approach. Soon, Freddie and Cora were at his side, with their rifles in hand.

"The last thing we want is a fight," Dutch said, with the lens to his eye.

"So what do we do?" Freddie asked.

Dutch handed the telescope to his uncle and thought for a moment. "We have a slight breeze from the east, so let us build a bonfire here, using our green cedar scraps. That will make a smoky flame, which should drift down the river to the Clatsop village. Then we will see how strong our alliance is with Chief Coboway."

The comrades raced back to camp, grabbed as much cedar as they could carry, and brought it to the beach. With the Chinooks still well off-shore, Dutch lit the bonfire and fed the cedar scraps into it. As flames took hold, dark smoke filled the sky and began to drift slowly downriver. As the three canoes drew closer, they slowed, then drifted to a halt some fifty yards from shore. The comrades standing around the bonfire with their weapons in hand saw that the Indians seemed confused. Soon, the would-be invaders started chanting and banging on their war drums.

"They sing us a war chant to frighten us off," Dutch said, adding more wood to the fire. "Uncle, you and Cora should dance around the fire while I play my flute."

"What good will that do?" Cora asked.

"If we seem indifferent to their threats, they may go away."

Dutch sat on top of a large rock and started to play his flute. As his music filled the air, Freddie and Cora danced, arm in arm, around the flames, smiling.

This gaiety lasted for only a few songs before the morning air echoed from a musket shot. Flinching, Dutch turned to the Indian canoes and spotted a warrior shooting at a seagull that was perched on a nearby rock.

The bird was undisturbed. Another brave took a shot at it. He also missed, but this time the bird flew away. The Indians were attempting to show off their proficiency with the rifles, and they weren't very good. As the bird flew overhead, Dutch stood, raised his rifle to his shoulder, took aim, and squeezed the trigger.

Fizz...Bang!

The bird dropped from the sky and splashed into the water, not twenty feet in front of royal dugout.

As the smoke from his rifle drifted with the breeze, Dutch glanced downriver and saw more canoes heading their way. Reloading his rifle, he pointed and yelled, "The Clatsops come."

The Chinooks looked their way and started pounding the drums again. Freddie and Cora added more wood to the fire, while Dutch retuned to playing his flute.

A few minutes later, the waters in front of Point Joseph were filled with Indian dugouts. The Clatsops were armed with rifles, spears and arrows. They drifted near the Chinook boats without a word being spoken.

As the sun finally broke through the clouds, the friends watched Chief Coboway's canoe come alongside Comcomly's bigger dugout. The two chiefs were out of earshot, but they talked for several minutes with great animation. Finally, the Chinook Chief yelled commands, and his fleet turned and headed back across the river.

All on shore were greatly relieved to watch the warriors paddle for home. Chief Coboway rowed his canoe close to the beach and yelled, "We saw your smoke, and heard the Chinook songs. I reminded Comcomly which side of the river he was on. You should have no more trouble." With that, Coboway made the sign of peace, and the Clatsops paddled for home.

The standoff was over, and the alliance had held! The comrades celebrated their victory with a fresh pot of coffee and satisfied smiles. In the near future, Dutch decided, he would visit Chief Comcomly and pay him a tribute. He wanted the Chinooks as friends, not foes.

In the middle of the month, just as they finished the barn, the rains came. It was only a drizzle, at the start, but on the second day a major storm blew in from the south, accompanied by lashing winds and drenching rains. With the heavy barn doors installed, and the loft filled with grass, the trio moved the animals inside the barn and secured them in their stalls. The log walls still needed to be chinked and a corral built, but for now the animals were safe and dry.

After Cora had moved her mule into its stall, she dropped to her knees and felt the mule's underside. "My Jenny is pregnant," she called out.

Dutch and Freddie moved to join her and watched as she continued to examine her mule. Everyone was astounded by the news, as they had all been careful to keep the animals separated on their way across the continent. Now, both Willow and Jenny were with foals.

"Jack's horse again. What the bloody hell can a man do?" Dutch said, shaking his head.

"Well, if there's enough desire, there's always a way," Freddie replied with a grin.

Cora stood up with a smile. "Reckon we'll need a bigger barn."

Winter Trap Lines ————

The storms didn't stop them from their work. Inside the barn, the men made a watering trough for the animals from cedar planks, and then moved it outside to collect the falling rain. They also begin splitting cedar posts and rails for the corral fence.

Their next project was the smokehouse. A wigwam was made, using posts and large cedar boards, close to the river shore. Inside they dug a fire pit and installed canvas flaps around the roof's smoke holes. When finished, the Indian smokehouse was designed so that it could also be used as a steam bath during the winter months.

With the big storms came the large schools of salmon. The day after the storm blew through, the river filled with native fisherman. From the shore, the trio watched as hundreds of canoes of all sizes and shapes began plying the waters for fish. Some of the Indians used spears; others used lines and hooks. Still others used native-made nets.

"I've seen the river so full with fish that you could walk on their backs from shore to shore," Dutch said with a grin, watching the fishing fleet.

"How will we fish? From the raft?" Freddie asked.

"Aye. Forge a large gaff hook attached to a long handle for me. I'll make a couple of willow poles for us, with sinew line and hooks. With any luck, we should be able to fill the barge with fish."

"What will we use as bait?" Cora asked.

"Tomorrow morning, we will drift and paddle with the outgoing tide down to Cape Hancock. There, at low tide, we will find mussels in the rocks, and clams in the sand. That will be our bait. Then, with the flood tide, we will drift and fish all the way back home."

There are few fish as majestic as the Pacific Salmon. They hatched in the fresh waters of the western inland lakes and streams and then, as small fry, swam all the way to the ocean. After a life cycle of three or four years at sea, they returned to spawn in the very same waters where they were born. An individual returning salmon could weigh over seventy pounds. These large fish were as powerful and wild as the Columbia River itself.

The next morning, under a warming sun, the friends gathered two large baskets of mussels and clams on the low-tide beaches of Cape Hancock. They soon had more than enough for bait, and for their dinner table, as well. Drifting back across the river with the flood tide, Freddie was the first to hook a fish, but the salmon was so large and powerful that it snapped the fishing pole in half and got away. Quickly, the trio changed fishing tactics. Freddie held his baited hook just under the water, close to the raft. Dutch watched as fish approached the bait, and snatched them out of the water with the gaff hook. Once it was on deck, Cora would kill the flapping fish with a wooden club, and wrap it in wet canvas. Catching these silver rockets with only a gaff was like catching lightning in a bottle. Within a few hours, the friends had over thirty fish rolled up in canvas. This 'snatch and kill' technique proved to be their best way of fishing from the raft.

Once back at camp, the fish were cleaned and half were filleted and smoked, while the other half were thoroughly salted and stored overnight to draw the moisture from the flesh. The next day, the salted fish were skinned, and then soaked in fresh water for another night. On the third day, the red flesh was cut into strips and soaked in a brine of vinegar, sugar and onions. Within a few days, the brine would cure the salmon, keeping it fresh and firm.

This fishing, cleaning, smoking and curing went on for the next several weeks. When the season ended, the trio had hundreds of pounds of dried and smoked fish stuffed inside the saddle bags that hung from the rafters in the chicken coop. They also amassed three five-gallon casts of pickled salmon. As to the flavor of this new culinary invention, both Freddie and Cora raved about the sweet taste of the fish. Dutch's only comment was that it needed more onions.

By the time the corral was finally finished, November began to blow in, with one storm right after another. Accompanied by bone-chilling winds, the rain came down sideways for three solid days, driving the trio inside the cramped chicken coop. Huddled around the fire, they listened to the weather and talked of tasks that needed to be done.

"Mr. Dutch, when will we meet the Negro Chief of the Tillamooks?" Cora asked, sipping a tin cup of tea.

Dutch removed a burning stick from the fire, and used it to light his pipe. "We can't float there with the raft, or walk there with these storms, so I reckon it will be next season."

Freddie got up from his chair and poured himself a cup of coffee. "Our supply of cut timber has dwindled to near nothing."

"Well then," Dutch said, looked up calmly from his seat, "we will have to start cutting trees down in the forest."

Just then, a gust of wind blew around the coop, rattling the rafters. "With storms like these, it be too dangerous for working in woods," Cora answered, looking up at beams.

"The ditch we dug for the trading post puncheons is just a sea of mud. Maybe we should hold off construction until the weather improves," Freddie suggested.

"Aye," Dutch replied. "But I can't hold off much longer getting our winter trap lines set, and to do that we'll need a canoe."

Freddie twisted to face his nephew with a surprised look. "Carving out a dugout could take weeks."

With the rain tattooing on the roof, Dutch replied, "When the storms clear, Cora and I will visit Chief Coboway with some pickled salmon and see if he will swap me a boat in exchange for our last trade rifle."

Freddie frowned in the firelight. "That will leave us only two rifles and two pistols for the winter. And why do you take Cora?"

"The Clatsops are sweet on her. They treat her like an Indian princess."

"I ain't no princess," Cora scowled from the doorway as she pulled on her rain slicker. "I'm going to the privy. When I get back, how about a Bible story?"

At the first break in the weather, Dutch and Cora visited the Clatsop village. The Indians were pleased to see their neighbors again and asked many questions as they walked towards the Chief's lodge.

Hearing the commotion, Coboway came outside and greeted his friends warmly, inviting them into his home.

The large, smoky lodge was filled with the Chief's family. With pride, Coboway introduced each clan member to Dutch and Cora. In all, eleven relatives and three slaves lived with the Chief and his wife. Clearly, there was good reason why his lodge was so large; it was filled with sixteen people.

After the introductions, Dutch and Cora were invited to sit by the fire. As soon as they were cross-legged on the ground, Dutch presented a small crock of fish to the Chief, and asked him to taste his new invention.

Coboway opened the clay lid and sampled a morsel of the pickled salmon. Almost instantly, his face lit up with an approving grin. After a second taste, he passed the crock around to his family, with strict instructions to take only one taste each. "Your fish is sweet and good," he said with a smile, watching as his family sampled from the jar. "Your squaw must teach our squaws how to make such a food."

The last to taste the fish was his wife, Ona, who then returned the crock to Coboway. As he placed it on the ground, Dutch handed him the rifle. "I need to trade this rifle for a good canoe. Do you know of one for trade?"

The Chief motioned for one of his sons, and asked him to fetch a squaw by the name of Talipa or Gray Fox. As they waited, Coboway told the story of the death of this squaw's husband. He had drowned crossing the bar, two years before, leaving his family in a bad way, with no braves in his lodge, and three young children to feed. Talipa had done her best to find another husband, but sadly she had not succeeded. She and her family were poor, but she did own a sturdy canoe carved from white cedar. "I have paddled this dugout many times," Coboway said with an earnest face. "You could do no better."

When the gaunt widow came into the lodge, Dutch could see the sadness in her eyes. Her hair was matted and unkempt, her buckskins dirty, and she stood next to the fire with a long face and her head low. When Coboway had explained the offer of the rifle for her dead husband's dugout, she hesitated for a moment, and then said in a low voice, "It is food I need, and a brave to hunt with me."

The Chief looked up at her. "With a rifle in your lodge, braves will soon come."

Talipa lifted her head and looked at her Chief with a thoughtful expression. His wisdom was sound; all braves coveted rifles. Abruptly, she agreed to the trade.

Dutch stood and gave her the weapon, along with a powder horn, a bag of bullets, some flints and handful of colorful beads. For a long moment, she stood looking at the items she held. Then she beamed, "I will see that the canoe is loaded onto your barge."

After her departure, the Chief told Dutch that Talipa had gone from poor to rich with this single trade. "Soon, there will be many suitors at her lodge; I will see that she marries well again."

Dutch and Cora remained with the family for over an hour. Ona served them oiled anchovies and spiced hot water while they talked more. Once the pipe was smoked, some of the relatives asked questions about Cora's tribe. Dutch translated each word and made sure the Indians understood all of her answers. It was a lively discussion of both the black and red cultures.

Finally, as they stood up to leave, Ona gave Cora a basket of crabs, and the Chief gave Dutch some whale oil. The Clatsops were a fine people, with many traits in common with white society. They respected wealth, looked out for each other, and were governed by wise leaders. Dutch was pleased to call the Clatsops his friends.

The very next day, under threating skies, Dutch and Freddie paddled up the Kilhowanah River in their new dugout to set their winter trap lines. The shovel-nosed canoe was sixteen foot long and nearly three feet wide. Made from white cedar, it was a sturdy boat with a flat bottom and a shallow draft. The slightly raised bow was carved and painted with images of fish. Propelled by oak paddles, the craft moved almost effortlessly up the lazy green river.

Soon the river was no longer affected by the tides, and the water turned crystal clear. Turning the boat into a small narrow stream the men maneuvered around some rocks.

"Have you ever trapped beaver before?" Dutch asked, rowing from the rear.

Freddie chuckled as his pulled his paddle. "I'm a city boy. The biggest varmint I ever trapped was a rat!"

"See the tooth marks on those trees? Let's stop here and set our first trap," Dutch said pointing to shore.

The dugout nosed onto a rocky beach, and the men got out of the boat. Opening a trail bag, Dutch removed one of his iron-jawed traps. "The beaver is a timid animal, but very intelligent. They have few natural enemies so they can live for up to twenty years, and grow to over a hundred pounds. Find me a thick stick, about four feet long, and we'll plant the trap right here, in this little feeder stream."

Dutch took his moccasins off, rolled up his pant legs and waded out into the water. He searched the clear streambed for just the right place for the trap. Freddie joined him, with a long stick in hand. Dutch handed the trap to his uncle and then removed a small bottle from his pouch. Removing the cork, he poured a small amount of a dark, oily, stinky solution onto the jagged jaws of the trap.

"My God," Freddie said, wrinkling his nose. "What the hell is that stuff?"

Dutch smiled at his uncle. "It's oil that comes from the sex glands of a female beaver. This vial is from my trapping days in upstate New York."

"Wow, is that stuff rancid! Never smelt anything like it before."

"It be like perfume to the boy beavers," Dutch answered with a grin, putting the cork back in the bottle.

Dutch carefully open the jaws of the trap and set the release trigger, then slowly lowered the iron snare into the rocky creek in about two feet of water. Attached to the trap was a length of chain with a large iron ring on the end. He deliberately positioned the chain and then, using a large river rock, hammered the stick through the ring, anchoring the trap to the streambed. By the time he was finished, only about six inches of the stick showed above the water flow.

"The beaver is a curious animal," Dutch said, looking up from his work. "When he swims by and sees this stick, he will stop and investigate. Then he will smell our perfume, and we will have him in our snare."

"And when we come back to check our lines, the sticks will show us where our traps are," Freddie replied with a confident look.

Dutch smiled at his uncle. "Now you're thinking like a trapper."

The men set six traps that day, in six different streams, all in areas that showed signs of beaver activity. They would take turns, in the coming months, checking their traps weekly and adding fresh scent as needed. They hoped to snare half a dozen beavers each month.

On the paddle home, sticky rain started. It was slow and gentle at first, but it brought with it the promise of another storm.

Not long after reaching the tidal waters, Freddie stopped rowing and dried his face on his sleeve, then turned to Dutch. "This big timber country takes my breath away. But, Nephew, this is a lonely place. At night, I long to have someone under the robe with me. Is it right to take a squaw?"

Dutch was astonished by his question. "I reckon most trappers take Indian women as their wives, and it's a good way to build alliances with the tribes."

"Have you taken a squaw?"

"Not yet. Maybe someday, if the right maiden comes along."

"How about Rose, back in St. Louis? She gave me a poke for two bits, once. But she was as cold as ice."

Dutch hesitated. Talking sex with his uncle was uncomfortable. "Come spring, we'll go across the river to the Chinook village. Maybe you will find a woman there."

Freddie smiled at his nephew and nodded in agreement. Then he turned back and started rowing again, saying nothing more for the rest of the trip.

That night, with the eye of another storm over the estuary, Dutch tossed and turned in his bed. He heard the rolling thunder and the fury of the winds, but it was his uncle's words that filled his thoughts the most. He was a lonely man, in a lonely place…but was taking an Indian wife the right answer? For the first time, Dutch's gut filled with doubts. Was he destined to be just another trapper, alone and lost in a vast, unforgiving wilderness?

In the darkened room, one of his hands grasped the medallion around his neck. What of his infatuation with Mary Rose? She was the only woman who had ever turned his head. Was his fate to take an Indian wife instead? Listening to the rhythm of the rain, he reminded himself of what his mother had once told him: "Love comes from trust, not desire."

XII
The Great Race

—ɯ—

*J*ohn Jacob Astor invested an amazing four hundred thousand dollars as capital for the Pacific Fur Company. For a business-man, who was known as a miser, this was a phenomenal amount of money, but the trading post on the Columbia River was vital to Astor's dreams of 'world domination' of the fur trade. His American Fur Company already had a near monopoly in trafficking and trad-ing furs around the Great Lakes regions and east of the Missouri River. Additionally, Astor purchased most of his trading supplies in London, and had many other business interests in England, as well. If he could now gain a foothold on the Pacific Coast, John Astor would become the first international trader of peltries.

In the far north and west, however, he faced stiff opposition from two major competitors. The Hudson Bay Company was incorporated in 1670 with a royal charter from King Charles II. The charter granted the company a proprietorship over the Indian trade, especially the fur trade, in the region watered by all rivers and streams flowing into Hudson Bay in northern Canada. This area was called Rupert's Land after Prince Rupert, the first director of the company and a cousin of King Charles. The Hudson Bay drainage basin, so described, encompassed an area one-third the size of modern-day Canada.

Company forts were established along the bay's coastline, and the Indians brought furs to those locations to barter for goods such as knives, muskets, kettles, needles and blankets. By the end of the eighteenth century, the Hudson Bay Company had expanded into the interior, with a string of trading posts that grew up along the great river networks of the west, foreshadowing the modern cities that would succeed them.

Astor's other rival was the North West Company. This consortium of smaller competitors controlled 80 per cent of the Canadian fur trade around the Great Lakes and across the northern tier of the United States. From its earliest days, the company had faced a serious geographical challenge. Most trade goods came from Britain and were shipped, comparatively inexpensively, to Montreal. The difficulty was the long, formidable overland journey from Montreal to the Northwest.

In order to make the passage within one season, the Company employed a two-stage transportation system. Each spring, huge birch-bark canoes carried trade goods from Montreal to Fort William, at the western shore of Lake Superior. There they would be met by other brigades coming down from the northwest. Cargoes were exchanged, with furs moving east and trade goods traveling farther west and north. The men and their laden canoes then returned from whence they had come.

The unit of trade with the Indians was one prime beaver pelt. Its general value was one ounce of gun powder, or 8 knives, or 2 hatchets, or 1 blanket. For a dozen pelts, an Indian could receive a musket. Trading trinkets with the northern Indians was difficult but highly profitable.

Astor was not the only one coveting the Pacific Northwest trade routes, as both the Hudson Bay Company and the North West Company wished to stake a claim on the territory for themselves, and in the name of the British Government. The great fur race was on!

—m—

The Astorians ————

Faced with howling winds and blowing rain, the friends felt the last harsh breath of 1810 as they crouched on straw mats deep within a cedar womb. The dark space was lit only by bright coals deep within a fire pit. Dutch dipped a tin ladle into a wooden bucket and slowly poured water upon the surrounding hot stones. The liquid sizzled, and steam choked the small wigwam with a hot, foggy mist. Dressed only in their small clothes, the trio huddled in the vapor-filled smokehouse, celebrating the approaching New Year.

"What's your best memory of 1810?" Dutch asked of no one in particular.

"That's easy," his uncle replied. "It was finding you, back in St. Louis."

"What of you, Cora? What is your best memory?"

"When you told me I was free! That word rolled around my mouth and tasted so sweet. I was walking in tall cotton all day."

The dark, hot, foggy room only revealed the vague shapes of the three friends.

"What do you expect from 1811?" Dutch asked, with sweat dripping down his forehead.

"I hope to meet the Negro Chief of the Tillamooks," Cora answered, drawing a wet cloth across her face.

"Find me a good woman," Freddie replied.

With the rain song tapping on the roof, Cora asked, "And what of you, Mr. Dutch?"

Eyes closed, Dutch lifted his head into the foggy mist. "May the New Year bring us happiness and health… and our supply ship."

A gust of wind whistled around the wigwam, rattling the cedar planks as the rain continued its loud dance upon the boards. "We'll need provisions soon," Freddie said, pouring water over his head. "We have no flour, bacon or beans, and our coffee is near gone."

With beads of sweat dripping from the point of his nose, Dutch turned to his uncle. "Living on the frontier is learning to live without." In the dark, he fumbled for his leather pouch and pulled out a bottle and a tin cup, which he held out in the dim light of the coals. "Here's the last of our brandy. May we enjoy it tonight while we say farewell to 1810."

In the darkened shelter, the three friends passed around the cup and savored every drop of the last of their liquor, while talking of years gone by. When finished, their bodies dripping with sweat, the trio dashed out of the wigwam and plunge themselves into the cold waters of the river. Invigorating moments later, they ran for the chicken coop where dry clothes and a warming fire awaited them. This steam and cold therapy was born from Indian traditions and served the friends well.

With tempests blowing in, one after the other, the trio had spent the last few weeks of the year locked into a routine of tending the animals, mending personal items, hunting, checking trap lines and repairing their wind-ravaged structures. In between the many storms, the men worked up in the forest, falling and bucking timber, then dragging the logs back to camp. Ever so slowly, their pile of construction timbers started to rise again. With the addition of the new canoe, they also dismantled the raft, and set aside its logs and spikes for their future needs.

Their trap lines had proven productive, and they were taking two or three beavers a week. The tasty meat was added to their cook pot, while the skins were scraped clean, then tanned in the barn. As Dutch watched the pile of hides grow, he wished he had packed-in more traps, as the beaver seemed as plentiful as the seagulls.

Late in January, a strange event happened: the sun reappeared, with a few clear, cool days. For three days in a row, the men worked in the forest from sunup to sunset. Early in the morning of the fourth clear day, Dutch announced that the tides were right to do some winter clamming.

"How do you know the tides are right?" Freddie asked, with his morning brew in hand.

"The Indians have no calendars," Dutch replied, "but they know the tides down to the half-hour. They do this by watching the moon on clear nights. That is what I have been doing. We should have a fine low tide, late this morning."

Chewing on some dried salmon, Cora asked, "So we will cross the river again?"

"Nay, we will paddle out to the south spit, where the river meets the ocean, and dig in the sand for clams. Then, with the flood tide, we will fish our way back home."

"Are there still salmon in the river?" Cora asked.

Dutch poured himself a cup of coffee. "Maybe, but on a fine winter day like this, we will fish for sturgeon, using clam necks as our bait."

"What is a sturgeon?" Freddie asked.

"It's a fish the Indians highly covet. Sturgeon meat is white and very tasty. One large fish will bring us many meals."

Freddie smiled broadly. "I'd rather fish than work in the woods, any day."

After securing the animals safely in the barn, the friends loaded the canoe with a large basket, a shovel, the gaff hook and two willow fishing poles. The little canoe shoved off with the sounds of a cocky crow overhead. Cora and the dog sat in the center of the dugout, while the two men paddled from the bow and the stern. It was a brisk, bright morning with hardly a breeze in the trees, and the little pirogue cut through the shallow river swells almost effortlessly. They paddled close to the south shore and soon passed the river that led to the Clatsop village. There they found a few other boats fishing, and waved at the Indians as they rowed by.

It was a fine morning to be on the river, with some of the surrounding mountains still grasping wispy clouds high in the treetops. Far across the glistening river, on the north shore, they espied the tall craggy cliffs of Cape Hancock and the sandy and green islands of Baker's Bay. On the south shore, they paddled by many sandy alcoves and rocky shoals teeming with numerous kinds of water fowl. The estuary was alive with spectacular views everywhere they looked.

Soon, their ears filled with the sounds of the crashing surf, and they beached their boat high up on the dry sand of Point Adams. While the dog barked and chased birds, they walked a few hundred yards from the south shore across the sandy spit to a long beach

Brian D. Ratty

that faced the vast Pacific Ocean. As they stood on high ground, looking at a beach littered with driftwood, Dutch pointed to the tall, crashing waves where the river met the sea. This boiling surf of white foam stretched all the way to Cape Hancock and far out into the ocean. "This be the most dangerous river bar in the world. It is a wonder that any ship can cross the river here." He turned and pointed down the littered beach. "See that tall, rocky point, way off in the distance? That is Tillamook Head. Many miles beyond that point is the Tillamook village where I was born."

"That's where the Negro Chief is?" Cora asked, as the sea breeze lifted her hair.

"Aye," Dutch answered, moving down to the beach. "Let's walk to the wet sand, and I'll show you how to dig for clams."

With the tide low, the beach was deep with wet sand. The friends moved to the surf line, where Dutch started stomping his feet. Within a few seconds, he pointed to many divots in the sand. He slid the blade of his shovel next to one indentation and shouted, over the sounds of the pounding surf, "These little dimples are the clam shows. Dig quickly, with your back to the ocean." Dutch pushed his shovel deep into the seashore and lifted out a blade full of wet sand and let it drop onto the beach. Inside this wet lump was a plump clam. Dutch picked up the mollusk and showed it to his friends. The crustacean had a brown, oblong shell about eight inches long, three inches wide and over an inch thick. On one end of the sharp shell was a long white neck; at the other end, a white tail. "The Indians call these 'digger-clams' because they can burrow deep into the wet sand. The squaws dig them with sharp sticks, but I prefer a shovel."

As Cora held the crustaceans in her hand, it spit at her. She let out a loud scream and dropped the mollusk to the beach. "It pissed on me!"

Dutch smiled at her and picked up the clam. "It was just sea water. Uncle, you dig the next one."

Within the hour, the wet beach held many holes, and the friends had a basket filled with the tasty digger-clams. As they moved back up the beach, Dutch called out for the dog. The trio stood on the high ground, with smiles all around, watching King run back up the sand, chasing sandpipers.

Once on the other side of the spit, they were soon paddling for home. When the canoe reached deep river water, they drifted with the tide, fishing for sturgeon.

"Could we paddle this dugout all the way to the Tillamook Village? Core asked, while cutting up bait.

"My father had a sea-going canoe," Dutch replied, baiting his hook. "It was twice the size of this boat, with a sail and outrigger to stabilize it in the ocean swells. Nay, this boat be too small and narrow for the sea."

With pole in hand, Freddie turned from the bow. "This big timber country is so bountiful, I doubt many Indians starve out here."

"Aye," Dutch replied. "But now, most of the braves leave the hunting and fishing to their squaws or their slaves."

"Why do the Indians keep slaves?" Cora asked

"Because they are lazy and complacent," Dutch replied. "Sometimes, when you have too much of a good thing, you don't realize its true worth."

They did briefly snag a sturgeon that day, maneuvering it close to the canoe before it finally snapped the willow pole. In the limpid waters, they got a good look at the fish. It was a monster, almost half the size of their boat. The prehistoric-looking fish had a powerful, slender body with a large, jagged backbone that looked much like armor. It was an ugly fish, but they were sorry to lose it, as they guessed it weighed well over a hundred pounds. To catch a sturgeon in the future, they would need a thicker fishing pole and a wire line. As a consolation for the lost fish, however, they enjoyed a feast of digger-clams.

February was a horrible month, filled with wind-driven rains and raging storms. The days were short and wet, while the nights were cold and dark. The trio burned nearly two cords of firewood in that month alone. But, rain or shine, there were chores to do, and something always needed fixing or mending.

The first breath of March proved promising, with warmer winds and brightening skies. With the soggy ground finally starting to dry, the men re-dug the narrow trench for the trading post's forty-two-foot log puncheons. It took the better part of two days to get the foundation logs level, plumb and square. Once the footings were in place, the log wall timbers could be notched and rolled into place. The basic layout of the single-story log cabin was simple enough: the trading post side of the cabin was a large room with a stone fireplace, two windows facing the river and two doors, one in the front of the structure and one inside, connecting to the adjacent living quarters. The domicile side of the cabin was twenty feet wide and twenty-four feet deep, with a stone fireplace, cooking and eating areas, and two small bedrooms at the rear of the room. The main room of the living quarters also had two windows facing the river, with a third window looking out to the barn and corral. In addition, there was a front door and a back door. Once completed, the trio would be freed from the chicken coop and much more comfortable.

With warming weather for a few days in the middle of March, the friends planted an early garden. Freddie built a wooden plow with an iron blade, then strapped it to one of the mules. For hours, the trio labored in the dirt, removing stones and tilling in compost. With the soil finished, they planted a few rows of turnips, Spanish onions, carrots and potatoes. In the milder months of April or May, they would plant tomatoes, corn, cabbage, and radishes. Their garden plot was small, but would have sun most of the day. They remained hopeful of a bountiful harvest.

Standing with a shovel in hand, Cora looked out at their planted rows and asked, "Will anything grow in this cool, damp climate?"

"Don't rightly know," Dutch replied. "Never seen a garden in the coastal plains before.

Freddie scoffed, "Even a city boy knows that our plants will be an open invitation for all the vermin in the forest. Doubt we'll see much from this garden."

"King will be on guard, and soon we will have wire for a fence," Dutch replied, and looked up at the sky. "It's gonna rain. Guess we won't have to water today."

As was his habit each day, rain or shine, Dutch walked out on Joseph Point to see what the tide had brought in, and so it was in the early morning hours of March 24, 1811. Using the telescope, Dutch scanned the distant mouth of the river first, and through the gray haze he found nothing moving on the water. He then checked Baker's Bay and panned to the nearby Chinook village. Nothing. He was about to turn the lens to the Clatsop village when a faint shape above some trees caught his eye. He had scanned this area before without noticing it, but now his attention was drawn. What was he seeing? It looked like a man-made cross. No, concealed behind a timber island was the very top of a tall ship's mast! Was this their supply ship?

Dutch blinked his eyes and looked again. Then, with great elation, he rushed back to the chicken coop and announced his discovery. "This could be our supply ship, so we need to erect a flag pole."

"Why a flag pole?" Freddie asked, slipping into his boots.

Dutch moved to one of his trail bags and started to rummage through it. "So the ship's Captain knows where we are."

"This ship could be just another trader," Freddie cautioned, putting on his coat.

"Aye," Dutch replied, with the flag finally in hand. He unfolded the cloth and held it up.

"What kind of flag is that?" Cora asked, wide eyed.

Dutch smiled at her. "We be under the protection of the King of the Netherlands now."

"Holland?" Freddie said with a confused look. "Isn't that some tiny nation at war with France?"

"Aye, but they are friends with the British. My partners are members of the Dutch East Indies Company. They will be sending in our supplies and taking out the pelts."

Under a threating sky, the men went up into the forest and selected a straight alder for the pole. They cut and bucked up the tall tree, then dragged the thirty-five-foot mast back to camp. At the very top of the pole, they fastened a small pulley and inserted a length of rope for the halyard. Next, they made a wooden cleat for the base.

The rest of the day was spent digging a six-foot hole in the rocky ground for the shaft to rest in. Once it was deep enough, they manhandled the pole into the pit, and pulled the shaft upright. Carefully positioning it, they back filled the hole with rocks and dirt. Then they ran the four-by-six-foot flag up and tied it off.

When finished, the mast was an odd-looking sight. The flag was too small for the tall timber and, with its three parallel fields of red, white and blue, looked out of place. As Dutch stood looking up at the flapping flag, he felt a twinge of guilt. Was he betraying his adopted country?

Early the next morning, the trio walked to the point and took turns looking across the river with the telescope. What they saw were two small boats slowly rowing upriver along the north shore.

"What the hell are they doing out there?" Freddie asked, with the glass to his eye.

"They be sounding the river," Dutch replied with his coffee cup in hand.

Cora scratched her head. "What are they listening for?"

Dutch smiled at her. "They are not listening for anything. They are checking to see how deep the water is. They use a weighted rope with knots every six feet. A big ship needs ten fathoms of water to sail safely. I reckon it will be a while before the ship sails again."

"What's a fathom?" Cora asked.

Dutch stretched his arms out on each side of his body. "Six feet to a fathom. Ten fathoms equals sixty feet of water."

"Should we paddle out and introduce ourselves?" Freddie asked, handing back the telescope.

"Nay," Dutch replied. "The map I gave my partners showed a deep water channel on the south shore, not the north shore. I think this ship might be Astor's."

"Shit," Freddie said, scowling. "I was looking forward to fresh biscuits and whiskey again."

Dutch smiled at him. "Uncle, our ship will be here soon enough. Let's see if we can get a few more logs into position. I would like the trading post done by the time our supply ship arrives."

Over the next few days, the friends watched each morning as crews from the ship continued sounding the waters. It wasn't until June 5th that the ship set sail again. But instead of heading east, up the river, the vessel turned south and crossed the river. Once on the south shore, it turned again and headed east, with white, billowing sails.

The friends stood on their beach and watched as the ship cruised straight for Joseph Point. As it got closer, they could make out the American flag and read the ship's name: *Tonquin.* Soon, sailors came into view, and Dutch pointed out how deep in the water the three-masted ship was. "She be filled to her decks with all the things needed for a trading post."

While King stood proudly on a large rock, barking, the *Tonquin* slackened some canvas and sailed right past the point, just a few hundred yards away. Faces could be seen clearly and voices heard as the ship glided by. One sailor in the sailcloth yelled, "Is that a woman there on the beach? We ain't seen a woman in months."

"Aye," Dutch replied with a wave of his hand. "You must be Astor's men."

Standing at the stern rail were three men dressed in waistcoats, pointing at their encampment. A man in a tricorne hat shouted, "Who the hell are you?"

Dutch cupped his hands and shouted back, "We be your competition."

Faces turned to frowns and a few of the men made lewd jesters. "We'll see about that. This be American land," one man shouted back. Within a few moments, the ship disappeared around another river bend.

The comrades were no longer alone on the Columbia River.

As the friends walked back to camp, Freddie asked, "Do you think we will see them again?"

"Aye" Dutch replied, "We be like a scab to the Astorians. They will return and try to scratch us away. That should be interesting."

That afternoon, Chief Coboway and two tribal elders paddled up to their beach for a powwow about the new arrivals. They had learned from the Chinooks that the Astorians were planning a trading post fort on the shores of a small cove not far from Joseph Point.

Coboway said with great animation, "You told us they would build across the river. Now they are on our land!"

"I reckon I was wrong," Dutch replied.

"So what is your council now? Should we drive them off?" another elder asked.

Dutch shook his head. "Nay. They have many rifles and big cannons. I will speak to them and see if they will buy the land from you. Give me a few days and I will return to your village and make council with all the elders."

Chief Coboway looked at Dutch with a sour face. "My people are frightened with all the new white faces, and Comcomly is talking about an alliance to drive off all the white men."

"Even if you turn the river red with blood, more will come," Dutch answered, working his hands as well as his lips. "The white man is more numerous than the stars in the sky, and more dangerous than all the bears in the forest. It is peace with a profit you should seek."

The old Chief shook his head in sad agreement and turned to leave. As the Indians got to their canoe, Coboway glanced back to Dutch and said, "I will hope for peace, as the Chinook chief wants all the whites dead and the brown girl as his slave."

As the Clatsops paddled away, Freddie and Cora wanted to know what had been said. Dutch told them of the conversation, leaving out only the Chief's parting remarks. Dutch hadn't lived his life with fear, and he refused to face the future with fear.

Two days later, the men looked up from rolling another log into place and found a ship's longboat paddling their way. The white boat was being rowed by six sailors and had two men in waistcoats and tricorne hats at the stern.

Grabbing their weapons, the men and the dog walked to the beach to greet their visitors.

As the boat approached, one of the men at the tiller shouted, "Ahoy there! Can we come ashore?"

"Aye, you are welcome here," Dutch replied.

The two gentlemen from the stern were first off the boat. Then the sailors got out and dragged the longboat to high ground. The two men advanced towards Dutch and Freddie with outstretched hands and smiles. One man was big and burly, with sandy hair and green eyes. The other was short and stout, with blonde locks. The big fellow was first to speak, with a heavy Scottish accent. "I be Duncan McDougall, Chief Factor of the Pacific Fur Company, and this is one of my partners, David Stuart."

The men shook hands while Dutch replied, "I'm Dutch Blackwell, and this is my uncle Fredrick. The dog there is called King. You must be Astor's men."

Duncan took his hat off and scratched his head. "How do you know who we are?"

By now, all the sailors were crowded around, listening.

"We have been expecting Astor's brigade for months," Dutch replied, leaning on his long rifle, "although we thought they would come overland. I was to join the Astor troop in St. Louis, but, when I got there, Mr. Hunt was still in Montreal recruiting. So we crossed over on our own."

"Two men crossed the continent alone!" Duncan replied with surprised face. "How long did that take, and how do you know Astor?"

Dutch smiled at the big fellow, "Five an half months from Boston. Use to work for Astor in New York."

"Then ya have a contract with him?" the short fellow asked, also with a Scottish brogue.

"Nay, I'm a free trapper. Got my papers signed by Astor himself."

"What's with the Dutch flag? This be American land," Duncan said, glancing up at the flag pole.

"The truth be, this side of the river is Clatsop land and the north side is Chinook land. We purchased this peninsula from the Clatsop for two rifles. As for the flag, I made a deal with a trading company out of Amsterdam. We own this trading post together. Soon, our supply ship will arrive."

Duncan and David looked at each other with bewildered faces, as some sailors muttered amongst themselves. The news of a competing trading post was a cause for much concern.

"Well, Mr. Blackwell, will you show us your post?" Duncan asked with a forced grin.

"Aye," Dutch replied with a smile. "And I would offer ya some whiskey, but we ran out, months ago."

Mr. Stuart told the sailors to stay on the beach, and the four men with the dog walked back towards the compound. They stopped at the uncompleted trading post and talked of its construction and position on the point. "It be exposed to the south winds, but it gives us a good view of the river," Dutch told them. Next, they strolled into the barn, where the two gentlemen were surprised to find Cora tending the animals. Dutch introduced her and she bowed to them, and then said, with pride in her squeaky voice, "My mule Jenny and the packhorse are pregnant, so they have been given lighter work."

The two Astorians seemed astounded to find a Negro girl and four animals on the river. "We could use a mule to help build our fort," Duncan said, looking Dolly over.

"The timbers are heavy and hard to move," Mr. Stuart added.

"We've been using the mules like that," Freddie replied. "But it's a tricky thing, dragging timbers on the forest floor."

Duncan turned to Dutch. "We would trade you some whiskey, if your uncle and his mule could help out. It be the neighborly thing to do."

"Where are you building your fort?" Freddie asked.

"Just two or three miles downriver. You could walk to it from here," Stuart answered.

"We'll think on it," Dutch said, moving away from the stalls.

In the tack room, the Astorians asked about the broken-down buggy, and started talking about building a road from their fort to Joseph Point. "We could use the road to exchange goods, and, if need be, as an escape route if we have any trouble," Duncan said, with his hands on the bent axle.

Then Mr. Stuart noticed the tall stack of cured pelts. "Did you trade for these?" he asked Dutch.

"Some we traded, some we trapped."

Stuart pulled a large sea otter pelt from of the pile. "We'd trade two jugs of whiskey for this pelt."

"Bet you would," Dutch replied with a grin, "seeing how it's worth a hundred dollars in Canton."

"How do you know the market for sea otter pelts?" Duncan asked.

"I was born not far from here. My mother was part Indian. We traded for years, up and down the coast," Dutch replied, moving towards the open barn doors.

As the men followed, Dutch pointed out the chicken coop, but he didn't take them inside. They talked more about the surrounding waters, fishing, hunting and trapping. The Astorians seemed impressed with Dutch's knowledge, and he explained further his many years of living with the coastal Indians.

"We met that Chinook Chief, Comcomly," Stuart said. "He seemed like a nice enough bloke. He has many wives and daughters."

Dutch flashed his guests an apprehensive look. "He should be feared and respected. At times, the Indians seem childlike, but that is only a deception. They are the masters of this land and should not be totally trusted."

Duncan seemed surprised by the commentary, "We have traded with the Chief and had dinner in his lodge. We found his hospitality warm and friendly."

"Don't be fooled," Dutch replied. "Your first concern should be making peace with the Clatsops and paying them for the land. It would cost only two rifles and could assure a peaceable enterprise."

"We've never paid for Indian land before," Duncan quickly replied.

"Suit yourself," Dutch said, moving towards the beach. "There's thousands of Indians around here, and if they get the notion to fight, you won't have enough muskets or cannons to drive them off."

"I'll think about it," McDougall said, approaching the beach, "while you think about loaning us a mule. In any event, come by our encampment tomorrow afternoon and I'll introduce you to our troop."

"Aye, we'll stop by, tomorrow," Dutch replied.

Just before the Astorians got into their longboat, Duncan whispered to Dutch, "Probably not a good idea to bring the darkie with ya. A woman like her could bring out the devil in a man."

Fort Astoria ─────

That afternoon, with the dog on his heels, Dutch saddled up Scout and rode him into the woods, searching for a trail that might lead east to the new fort. They looked for the better part of an hour but only found a steep rocky terrain surrounded by a dense, dark forest. Dutch was about to give up when he came upon a stream with a gentle current from the east. Turning into the water, they splashed upstream following, the meandering creek. Not far up the flow they came to a well-used game trail that curved around a steep mountain. After riding this trail a few miles, he found himself in a clearing on the other side of the peak, with a fine river view of the small cove where the ship *Tonquin* was anchored. It was still another mile down to the beach, but Dutch had found the back door to Fort Astoria. Resting in his creaking saddle, Dutch guessed the fort was only three miles from Joseph Point, as the river flowed, but almost six miles around the mountaintop. With some hard work, a road could be made linking the two trading posts, but Dutch pondered the wisdom of such a task.

The next day, Freddie and Dutch paddled upriver to the little deep-water cove. Most of the shoreline above where the fort was being built was rocky. But on the west side of the inlet was a sandy beach littered with supplies. They rowed past the *Tonquin* and found the longboat alongside, taking on cargo from the ship's hold. As they approached the beach, they noticed two eight-inch cannons on top of a bulwark, pointing out to the river. Next to these guns, a crew was building a tall blockhouse. Just up from this tower was another crew, working on the vertical timbers of a classic log-style stockade. Dutch was astonished by how much work they had accomplished in a few short days.

Under a clear, warm sky, their canoe glided to the sandy beach, where Dutch got out and pulled the boat to higher ground. As they stood looking at the assortment of supplies, they noticed other Indian dugouts resting on the sand. Turning to move up towards the fort, they were greeted by Mr. McDougall.

"Welcome to Fort Astoria, gentleman. Follow me and I'll show you around."

As the men walked up a slight rise to the construction site, Dutch saw dozens of Chinook Indians milling around.

"Never a good idea to have this many Indians about," Dutch said to Mr. McDougall. "They tend to be thieves."

"We keep a sharp eye on them," he replied nonchalantly.

The men were soon inside the log walls, where they found three log cabins being built. "The longest building is the barracks for the men," Mr. McDougall said. "The other long building is the trading post and warehouse, and the smaller cabin is the partners' quarters."

As they continued to walk towards the rear of the fort, Dutch asked, "How many men do you have working here?"

Duncan kept moving while replying, "Thirty Astorians, twelve labors from the Sandwich Islands and twenty-four sailors. We lost seven men crossing that bloody Columbia River bar."

Dutch was surprised at the size of the contingent, and by the number of deaths crossing the bar, but he knew that the mouth of the Columbia River was one nasty stretch of water.

Just outside the rear walls, the men came upon a sea of tents where the Astorians camped. Under a tall spruce tree, they found three men in waistcoats sitting around a table, with pewter mugs in hand. Mr. McDougall performed the introductions. David Stuart, from the day before, was sitting next to his brother, Robert Stuart. Across from them was a bearded chap named Alexander McKay. All these men were Canadians and partners in the Pacific Fur Company. They were also well-seasoned traders, and their reception of Dutch and Freddie was noticeably cool.

"We expected to find our overland regiment already here, and instead we find the likes of you. Do you know when the brigade might arrive?" David Stuart asked.

Dutch shook his head. "I have no idea. I thought they would be here late last year."

"You agreed to join Astor's expedition but then you deserted him, is that correct?" Mr. McKay asked with a chilling demeanor.

Dutch turned to McKay and looked him in the eye. "At St. Louis, I was told it would be months before the expedition would be ready, and I wasn't wasting a summer in that town. Nay, I had no contract with Astor and, being a free trapper, I just moved on."

"I understand you came overland in just five and half months from St. Louis," Robert Stuart said.

"Nay," Dutch replied, twisting to face him. "We trekked from St. Louis in four months; it took me six weeks just to get to St. Louis."

David Stuart's eyes got big. "So you crossed from Boston in five and half months?"

"Aye, we did," Dutch answered, with a proud smile.

"How is that possible?" Robert Stuart asked.

"Along the way, we met a mountain man who showed us the Sweetwater Trail. We crossed the divide in a place called the South Pass, and then dropped down to the Snake River. The rest of the journey was just a long dry horseback ride."

All the partners looked at each other with astonished faces.

"Join us for a drink," Mr. McKay said, sliding across the table two mugs. "We'd like to hear more of your story."

Robert Stuart poured the whiskey while Dutch and Freddie came to rest in chairs. When finished pouring he looked up and said, "I'll be heading east in the next few months, to report back to Astor. Did you make any maps of this South Pass? And would you share them with us?"

"Reckon that wouldn't be a problem," Dutch replied, tipping his mug to the group. "Cost you a few jugs of whiskey, though."

Robert smiled. "That we have plenty of."

"Do either of you know the local language?" Mr. McDougall asked.

Freddie puffed up and replied, "Aye, Dutch was born amongst these people and knows their language well."

With the spirits flowing, and mutual respect building, Dutch and his uncle learned a great deal in the course of the afternoon. The Astorians were well organized and well supplied. They had a blacksmith, a carpenter and a boat builder who would soon put together a small coastal schooner, the frame of which they had carried from New York. They also had a cooper who would make barrels for shipping back the skins. The finished garrison would have a troop of twenty or more men, all of whom would be engaged in trapping or trading. The partners were naïve and uninformed about the Indians, and were already trading whiskey, rifles and trinkets with the Chinook. They felt confident that their fort would ward off any threat. They also implied that they had a secret weapon.

After a few drinks, Dutch told the partners about the back-door trail he had found to Fort Astoria. Then he agreed to help the Astorians up in the forest. "Freddie and his mule will be here early tomorrow morning to help drag out your timbers. But I'll need to trade his efforts for supplies."

The partners talked amongst themselves for a moment and then agreed to trade a jug of spirits and one sack of flour, beans or coffee for each day of labor. The partners also agreed to pay the Clatsops two rifles for the land.

"We want no trouble," Duncan said. "Will you take me to their village and make the introductions?"

"Aye," Dutch agreed.

He and Freddie stayed for supper and had a wonderful meal of bacon and beans with freshly baked bread. They also met other men in the troop. George Bell, the cooper, was a delightful man with a keen sense of humor. Henry Clay, a tall, lanky fellow, was one of the hunters, and he put on a demonstration with his double-barreled smooth-bore rifle. His skills with a gun much impressed the Chinooks, who watched closely.

Dutch and Freddie also met Captain Jonathan Thorn, the skipper of the *Tonquin*. He was an abrasive and arrogant person, and Dutch wondered why Astor had hired a man who seemed to have no regard for anyone but himself.

In the warm glow of sunset, Duncan walked his guests back to the beach, where he gave them a jug of brandy and five pounds of flour.

"I know your stores are depleted. This be advance payment for your work."

The Astorians proved to be a good lot and, with the sky darkening, Dutch and Freddie paddled for home with the familiar warmth of whiskey in their bellies. It had been an eventful afternoon.

For the next week, Dutch and Freddie took turns working the mule up in the woods with the Astorians. It was hard, back-breaking work, but the rewards were plentiful: jugs of liquor, and sacks of food.

A few days after Dutch and Freddie's visit to Fort Astoria, Duncan McDougall and Henry Clay walked over, and Dutch paddled them to the Clatsop village with two trade rifles. It was a bright spring day and, as they rowed downriver, Dutch talked more about the Clatsop culture.

"Coboway is a noble Chief. If he respects you, you will have no problems."

"He will have to earn my respect." Duncan scowled, paddle in hand. "If not, we have ways of keeping the Indians in line."

Dutch said nothing more, surprised by his harsh words, and troubled by his attitude.

The canoe turned in at the small river and was soon resting on the beach next to the village. The men were warmly welcomed and shown to the main lodge, where Chief Coboway and the elders waited. Dutch introduced the Astorians and then translated the negotiations.

After a few remarks from the elders, Mr. McDougall stood and talked at length about how powerful his Chief John Astor was, and how many trading posts he owned. He told the council that Fort Astoria was strong, with many men, rifles and cannon. He said his Chief Astor wanted only peace with the tribes, and then he offered the two rifles in trade for the land. The elders seemed inclined to accept his offer, but Duncan kept on talking.

"Translate this word for word," he said to Dutch with a serious expression. "As I walked through your village today, I noticed some faces with pox scars," he said, while reaching into his pocket and pulling out a small glass bottle with a cork top. "My Chief Astor gave me this little vial of death. The clear liquid inside is smallpox. If for any reason the Clatsops cause trouble, I will open this bottle and spread the pox all around your village. Do you understand?"

Dutch was stunned by his comments and hesitated to translate them, but he finally did, word for word.

The elder's faces turned ash, and their mouths dropped open. The lodge went quiet for the longest moment. The word *smallpox* hung over the elders heads like a shroud. Finally, Chief Coboway turned to Dutch and asked, "Did you know of this evil vial?"

"Nay."

"Is it true that his Chief has such powers?" Coboway asked, with a frightened glare.

Dutch hesitated again. How could he answer such a bold-faced lie?

McDougall turned to Dutch with a frown. "Well, mate, are you with us or against us?"

Dutch scowled at him, shaking his head, and turned back to Coboway. "Aye, the white Chief has such powers, but he won't use the pox if there is no trouble."

"Do you have such powers?" one elder asked of Dutch.

"Nay. I would never harm my friends the Clatsops."

Duncan McDougall had frightened the council deeply. In the end, they reluctantly agreed to the payment of the two rifles, but John Astor made no friends among the Clatsops that day.

After the meeting, down on the beach, Henry Clay put on another demonstration with his musket. His marksmanship mesmerized the many Indians who watched. Henry was a crack shot, and could reload both barrels in under a minute. It was only later that Dutch learned that these gun exhibitions had been preplanned by Duncan to remind the Indians of how proficient the white man was with a rifle. Further, McDougall had made the same speech about his vial of death to Chief Comcomly and the Chinooks. It was his brilliant but despicable strategy for keeping the Indians at bay.

In the middle of May, Willow gave birth to a chestnut colt with a blonde mane and tail. It was a miraculous event to watch, and the trio spent the whole day fussing over mother and son. Dutch named the foal Buck, after Mountain Jack's sorrel. He was the most winsome little spindly legged colt the friends had ever seen, and even King followed him around like his shadow. Willow turned out to be a fine mother, and Dutch was sure that, given time to grow, Buck would have his mother's strength and his father's speed.

Towards the end of month, Fort Astoria was finally completed, and Mr. McDougall sent out invitations to all of the chiefs for a gala flag-raising ceremony on the last day of May. Dutch and Freddie were also invited, but Cora again was not acknowledged.

The day of the event was cloudy, with a threat of a storm, so the men saddled up Scout and Dolly and rode the back-door trail to Fort Astoria. When they arrived, they found the stockade filled with Astorians, sailors, Pacific laborers and dozens of Indians. The freshly finished fort sparkled under the gray sky. It looked ominous, with its swivel canons and guards in the tall log blockhouses, along with now four eight-pound cannons out front. The fort was a visible testament to the power and might of John Astor.

In the center of the parade ground, inside the log walls, a long row of tables had been set up, laden with food and drink. One table had different cheeses and breads, with an assortment of dried fruits. On another table were platters of sliced ham and venison, with baskets of seafood. On the last table were jugs of whiskey, brandy and wine, as well as bottles of beer.

It was a wilderness spread the likes of which Dutch and Freddie had never seen before. Helping themselves to mugs of brandy, they walked about the fort. Inside the trading post, they found Chief Coboway and two elders, all dressed in their finest buckskins, looking at the trade goods.

As Dutch and Freddie approached the group, the Chief held up a white porcelain pot and asked, "What is this used for?"

Dutch smiled at him. "It is called a chamber pot, and the white-man puts it under his bed so that, when Nature calls, he can shit in it."

The Chief looked bewildered. "That would stink up the lodge. Why not just go outside, like any other civilized person?" Putting the pot down, the Chief continued with a sly look, "I talk with Chief Comcomly today. I told him you have a vial of death, as well, and that is why he couldn't scare you off your land. You should have no more trouble with the Chinooks."

Startled that Chief Coboway had used the lie to Dutch's advantage, he said, "You have much wisdom, Chief."

With a wily smile, the chief replied, "I am wise enough to know that the vial of death is only a fable for squaws to talk about."

When the men went back outside, Dutch told his uncle what had just been said, but to his surprise, Freddie told him that he had understood much of the conversation. "My ears are becoming to understand their words."

That afternoon, they talked to all of the partners and learned much news. Mr. MacKay was soon leaving aboard the *Tonquin* to travel north and trade with the Indians. The ship would return in the autumn to pick up the fort's pelts and then sail for Canton. While he was gone, the Stuart brothers were leading a party upriver in search of a place to build another trading post.

Later in the afternoon, the guests were invited outside to the cannon rampart, where Mr. McDougall gave a short speech about the new stockade. "I dedicate this fort to the men of the Pacific Fur Company, and to the United States of American. May Fort Astoria always be a safe harbor for those in need." Then, as Duncan slowly raised the American flag, a flutist played *Yankee Doodle Dandy*. Afterward, all the cannons were fired, "Fire one…fire two… fire three… fire four." The big guns' loud reports echoed across the water like thunder, and all the guests watched in awe as the cannon balls dropped harmlessly into the river, sending up tall white plumes of water. The noise, the smoke, and the display of power were all intended to remind the Indians that Fort Astoria was not to be trifled with.

After the ceremony, Dutch and Freddie filled their plates with food, and enjoyed the fort's hospitality. By the time they had eaten, much drinking was going on and many of the Indians were already drunk, so Dutch and Freddie decided to leave.

As they were cinching up their saddles, Mr. McDougall approached. "Thanks for coming, mates. I hope you enjoyed the ruckus. With the fort done, I'm going to put a few of the islanders to work on making the back-door trail into a proper road. Freddie, maybe you could fix that wagon axle, and then you boys would have a better way of getting here."

The men agreed and shook McDougall's hand. As they pulled themselves into the saddle, he added, "Don't be strangers. The coffee pot is always on, and we have plenty of brandy to sweeten the brew."

The Mary Rose ————

On the fourth of June, the *Tonquin* sailed past Joseph Point. The friends stood on the beach, waving goodbye, and watched it slip across the river to Baker's Bay. They were sorry to see it go.

With the weather warming and the garden showing good color, the trio made a renewed effort to complete the trading post. The walls only needed a few more rows of timbers. Then planks would have to be sawn for the floor, before work could begin on the rafters and roof.

On the eighth of June, Freddie looked up from positioning the final wall log and saw a ship entering the river near Cape Hancock. Was the *Tonquin* returning? He shouted out his discovery and then scrambled down a ladder.

The friends grabbed the telescope and rushed to the beach. It was a fine bright day, with a light breeze from the west, and Dutch stood with the lens to his eye.

"Why would the ship be returning?" Cora asked.

The ship in question was still many miles off, and Dutch could only make out its silhouette, but it didn't seem as big as the three-masted *Tonquin*. This vessel appeared to have two masts, and was rigged with square sails on the foremast and fore-and-aft rigging on the mainmast.

With the telescope still to his eye, Dutch replied, "It isn't the Astorians. It's a brigantine."

The ship turned for the south shore and reefed some sails. As this maneuver was carried out, Dutch caught the first glimpse of the ship's flag: horizontal stripes of red, white and blue. He removed the lens from his eye, smiling. "It's our supply ship, the *Mary Rose*! I would know her jib anywhere."

It took the ship over an hour to come to anchor in front of Joseph Point. Soon, the longboat was being rowed towards the beach. The first to step off the launch was the ship's skipper. And to Dutch's great surprise, it was Captain Eric Jacobson.

Dutch greeted him warmly, with an outstretched hand. "Pleased to see you again, sir."

The Captain grasped his hand, smiling as he replied, "Looks like the Indians didn't get your scalp, lad." The square-jawed skipper wore a blue sea-coat with gold trimmed epaulets, and polished knee-high boots. His deep-set hazel eyes held a piercing stare, and his deep voice bespoke authority.

Another officer approached with the Captain. The first mate was a chisel-faced fellow named Patrick Person. Eight other sailors pulled the longboat to higher ground and quickly gathered around their officers.

Dutch introduced his friends. "This is Fredrick, my long-lost uncle. I found him in St. Louis. The girl here is Cora. We found her wandering a wilderness trail. The dog over there is King, after King George. He don't much like strangers, so give him a wide berth."

All the jack-tars looked, wide-eyed, at Cora. "Is she your slave?" one of them asked.

"She's a real beauty," another added.

"Nay," Dutch replied, "she be no slave. She is our friend and has our protection."

Captain Jacobson twisted to face his sailors, and scowled. "Belay that talk. This be none of your affair." Then he turned back to Dutch with a grin. "Your map saved the day when we crossed that damn river bar. I've never seen whitecaps so tall or waters so violent. Once we'd slipped past Cape Hancock, we saw your flag, right where you said it would be. Will you show us around your compound?"

"Aye," Dutch replied. "We had hoped to have the trading post completed by the time you arrived but, what with us helping out the Astorians, and all our foul weather, we ran out of time."

"So you crossed with the Astor Expedition?" Mr. Person asked.

"Nay," Dutch replied. "It was their maritime contingent. They've built a stockade just around the next river bend. The overland group has yet to arrive."

Captain Jacobson was curious about this news. "So you and your uncle and this girl crossed the continent on your own?"

Dutch smiled proudly. "Aye, but we had the dog, as well as the help of a mountain man. Come. Let me show you our camp."

With the sailors remaining on the beach, the officers followed Dutch and his friends up the slight raise to the compound. They stopped first at the uncompleted trading post, where Dutch and Freddie explained their construction and future plans. The Captain and mate seemed unimpressed, and talked about the lack of storage space.

"You have dirt floors and no room for our cargo," Captain Jacobson said. "Our hull is filled to the deck with supplies. We must take this into account."

The large barn made a better impression. They were delighted to see the stack of pelts already secured, and asked questions about local conditions. They were also pleased with all the livestock. As they stood by Willow's stall, watching her nurse Buck, the skipper commented, "That colt be a fine-looking fledgling, and a good addition to our enterprise."

"My mule Jenny is in the next stall, about to have her foal," Cora said proudly in her squeaky voice.

The two officers glanced at each other with surprised faces; this was the first they had heard Cora speak.

"Your voice has the pitch of a boatswain's pipe, ma'am. Quite… unusual," Mr. Person said with a smile.

"Thank you, sir," Cora answered, with a curtsey.

Outside, they inspected the garden and commented on the size of some of the plants. They were impressed that the dog had been able keep the local varmints away.

Next, Dutch showed them the inside of the chicken coop. There was a bitter smell in the room, as some of the dried fish hanging from the rafters had started to mold. The officers seemed dismayed with their living conditions.

"You wintered inside this one log room?" Jacobson asked.

"Aye," Freddie replied. "It was better than a tent."

"Did you bring me my chickens?" Dutch asked. "I've been dreaming about eating fresh eggs again."

"Aye, and goats and pigs," the skipper replied. "This room will be a proper place for your animals, as it already smells like the hogs."

Once outside again, they slowly walked back towards the beach. "We have brought you many things that will improve your lot," the Captain said. "But before we can unload the cargo, we will have to build a floating dock. It would take far too long to off-load the ship using just the longboat. I want us to be trading up the coast by the end of the month, Dutch."

Back on the beach, the officers stepped into the longboat and prepared to shove off. "I'll send the launch for you folks at eight bells," Captain Jacobson said, moving to take the tiller. "You can come aboard and have dinner with my officers, and we can start planning our endeavors."

"No need for your launch, sir," Dutch replied. "We will paddle out to the ship in our canoe at four o'clock."

As the sailors pushed off in the longboat, the Captain replied, "But leave the dog on the beach. My ship is not a place for a mutt like him."

While walking back to camp, Freddie said, "The Captain seems like a hard man. He barks out orders and has few good words to say."

"He's like the British, arrogant and unpleasant," Dutch replied. "But it takes a strong-spirited skipper to survive these waters."

Cora was silent and long-faced, all the way back to the chicken coop. Once inside the small, smelly room, she finally said, "The Astorians shun me, and now the Dutch officers invite me to supper. I've never taken a white man's fancy meal before. I fear they will think me a stupid fool."

"I know that feeling," Dutch replied with a smile. "Wear my mother's dress and say very little. Once at the dinner table, watch me carefully and do what I do. Your beauty will beguile the officers."

The first mate greeted the guests on deck as they pulled themselves up the boarding ladder. With a small crock of pickled salmon in his hands, Dutch was the last up, and stepped aboard just as the final bell of eight rang out.

The ship's deck held a dozen cannons, with two swivel guns fore and aft, and was littered with wooden crates containing the barnyard animals the Captain had talked about. They were noisy and smelly, but a wonderful sight to see.

The sailors on deck craned their necks and twisted their heads to get a glimpse of the visitors. Many flashed wanton looks at Cora, but not a word was said.

Mr. Person showed the trio aft, through a hatch and down a gangway to the Captain's cabin. The compartment looked larger than Dutch remembered it, with a spectacular river view through the stern windows. The chart table, in the center of the cabin, was covered with a cloth and set up for eight people. Next to it was a credenza, containing numerous bottles of sprits and crystal glassware.

Captain Jacobson greeted his guests coolly but did comment on how beautiful Cora looked, dressed in Indian buckskins. He showed his visitors around the opulent cabin while his steward, a seaman named Jensen, pour out drinks of brandy, whiskey or rum. Above the skipper's berth was a likeness of Mary Rose, but Dutch didn't comment on it. He did finally set the crock of pickled salmon on the sideboard and told the Captain about the gift and its recipe. After the drinks were in hand, the skipper and Mr. Person moved to the credenza and sampled the fish with their fingers.

"The fish is firm and savory. When did you cure this batch?" The skipper asked, reaching for a second morsel.

"Last October," Dutch replied. "Unlike smoked or dried salmon, I believe that properly cured salmon can last for years, just like pickled herring."

Mr. Person chewed on his second bite with an approving smile. "The Scandinavians love their pickled herring and consume it like candy."

"That's the idea," Dutch said, taking a small piece for himself. "I will send you back with a few casts of the fish. If they survive the journey, and if you can find a market for pickled salmon, then we shall add to our profits."

The Captain liked the notion, and the men talked of salmon fishing until they were joined by the third mate, a young ensign named Mr. Fisher. He had been summoned to give the guests a tour of the ship. Cora and Freddie were excited to see the *Mary Rose*. Leaving their drinks behind, the trio followed the young ensign to the quarterdeck, where they met the second mate, who had the watch. With the young ensign in the lead, the trio walked the vessel from stern to stem. As they moved along, he expounded on the workings of the ship. At the end of the tour, Freddie and Cora gleefully stopped to inspect the livestock on deck.

At the rail, the young ensign turned to Dutch and whispered, "I have something for you, Mr. Blackwell." He reached into his pocket and produced a small envelope. "It's a letter from Mary Jacobson. She and my younger sister Lily are dear friends, and I promised her I would deliver this personally to you."

Dutch took the letter and glanced at his own name, written in a delicate hand. His heart fluttered at the mere thought of Mary Rose.

"If you have a response," the ensign continued, "give it to me and I will see that Mary receives it. This be her secret," he cautioned. "Her father would not approve."

"Aye." Dutch stuffed the envelope in his pouch. "Thank you, Mr. Fisher."

Returning to the Captain's cabin, Dutch found that two new individuals had joined the group, dressed in waistcoats. Ralf and Robert Reed were brothers, and carpenters by trade. The Captain explained that they were hired by the Commodore to help with the post construction. While the ship was trading up north, the brothers would remain behind, finishing up whatever was needed. At the end of the season, the *Mary Rose* would return to the Columbia, dropping off Dutch and gathering up the brothers and the post's pelts, then sail for China.

Over another round of drinks, the Captain and his men planned the shore activities for the next few weeks. Half the crew would work on building a floating dock and unloading the ship. The other half would work in the forest, felling and bucking timber. A great many cut planks would be needed for the dock and cedar shingles for the post roof. The Captain delegated the Reed brothers to help Dutch and Freddie with the construction of the trading post. "Everyone will work," the skipper ordered sternly. "There will be no slackers. I want to be trading up the coast by months end."

The meal that evening was a fine beef brisket, served with vegetables, fresh bread, cheeses and wine. Dutch couldn't recall when beef had tasted so good. The table talk was lively as well, with tales alternating between the ship's crossing from Amsterdam and the trio's overland odyssey to the Pacific. Through the fog of chatter and booze, however, Dutch's mind kept circling back to the envelope in his pocket.

After the dinner, the friends paddled home in the moonlight and staggered to the chicken coop. Cora had said few words during the evening, and had watched Dutch closely during the meal. She had done just fine, and Dutch complimented her.

With a long face, she replied, "The Indians treat me like a princess, while the officers see me as some prize. I felt out of place."

"We are in a strange land, surrounded by strangers," Dutch replied earnestly. "We are all out of our element here."

Cora forced a small smile. "I guess I just long for my own people."

Moments later, Dutch excused himself for the outhouse. Walking toward it in the moonlight he had his first chance to read Mary's letter.

I think of you often, Mr. Blackwell. You are the only free spirit I know. My life is filled with books, rules and schedules, with never any time for myself. Please tell me of your life and your journey across the great American divide. May you be safe and healthy.

Your Friend, Mary

Dutch's heart shivered as he read Mary's words. She thought of him often… and called him a free spirit! She cared about his health and well-being!

But who was he kidding? She lived in another world. Mary saw him only as a romantic frontiersman and, although there was tenderness in her words, he would answer the letter in that same frontier spirit. That was the way of things, at least for now.

Mr. Person supervised the construction of the dock, while Mr. Jensen, the second mate, worked a similar gang up in the woods. Soon, Joseph Point rang out with the song of many hands working.

Chief Coboway and a few elders paddled out to the point on the third day to investigate the construction. On the beach, Dutch introduced his visitors to the Captain and First Mate. They were both dismissive toward the Clatsops, as cool as a winter breeze. With Dutch translating, the Chief invited the Captain and the mate to his village, but the skipper refused the offer, telling him that he had no time to dilly-dally. Translating, Dutch told the Chief that the skipper would make such a visit after the trading post was completed. He did his best to convey only friendship toward the Clatsops.

As the Indians wandered off to watch the work, Dutch turned to Captain Jacobson and said, "Your dismissive attitude towards the Indians could get us all killed. They are not fools."

The skipper scowled. "I've been dealing with savages all my life, from head hunters on Borneo to Aborigines all over the Pacific. You treat them like children and they will knuckle under."

Dutch shook his head slowly, "You know nothing about the culture of these people. They are not children. The coastal Indians can be fierce, harsh and cruel, so I advise you to think before you act."

"May I remind you, I'm in command," the Captain answered angrily. "Things will be done my way."

Dutch felt rage boil up inside of him. Under the skipper's piercing stare, he turned sharply and walked away. As Dutch got to know the Eric Jacobson better, he noticed the man had a melancholy streak, a condition which frightened Dutch.

The Reed brothers made many suggestions concerning the finishing of the trading post. The simple hip roof was redesigned into the more complicated gambrel style, which would allow for storage over the trading post and for three bedrooms over the living quarters. While Dutch and Freddie installed plank flooring on both floors, the brothers handcrafted windows, using glass that had been shipped from Amsterdam. They also built the stairways and hung the heavy doors, using iron hinges from the ship's supply.

As the men worked together, Dutch learned that Ralf and Robert Reed were cabinet makers by trade, and carpenters by necessity. But their real passion was for boat building. Dutch told them of the shallow-drafted keelboats on the Ohio River, and how he wished for such a craft to cross the many shallow inlets and bays on the coast. They told him of a type of flatboat sailboat that used a special centerboard that allowed the keel to be lowered when under sail and then raised when crossing shallow waters. That type of schooner would make a much expanded trade territory possible, so it was agreed that, once the trading post was completed, the brothers would build such a craft. The boat would be ready for Dutch when he returned at the end of the season.

The dock was constructed from four twenty-foot long floating log rafts, secured to each other with iron cables. When completed, the dock reached from the beach to the deep-water channel. Once it was in place, the longboat towed the ship close to the end of the dock, where fore and aft anchors were dropped. The ship remained unattached to the wharf, connected only by thick boarding planks. Soon, the contents of the hold were being off loaded and taken ashore.

XIII
Nootka

—⚏—

$\mathcal{N}$ ootka Island played a pivotal role in the fur trade. It was first discovered by Captain James Cook in 1788. It is a large island, 290 miles in length and 50 miles in width. The archipelago was the home to a large number of Indian tribes making up three separate nations. Captain Cook had sailed his ship, *HMS Resolution,* to the northern waters in search of the allusive Northwest Passage. It was here that he traded with the local natives for sea otter pelts, which were later sold in China for a great amount of profit. It is said that Nootka Island was the birthplace of the maritime fur trade.

Realizing the potential profits of the trade, other seafaring nations sent expeditions to the island. Between 1774 and 1788, Spain sent several ships north from their newly established Spanish territory of Mexico. One expedition built a fort at Friendly Cove and claimed all of the Pacific Northwest, including Nootka, belonged to Spain. The British strongly disagreed, and sent Captain George Vancouver to explore, map and circumnavigate the island.

Due to the abundance of the coveted sea otter, Nootka Sound became a hotly contested prize between the English and Spanish. In the winter time, Friendly Cove was a safe haven for ships, from many nations, making repairs and finding relief from the stormy seas. Soon a serious confrontation loomed, when Spain seized two British owned trading vessels and sailed them to Mexico. In the end, cooler heads prevailed and the situation gave birth to the Nootka

Convention. This political accord was certainly worthy of the "Age of Enlightenment," as it marked the first time England and Spain did not come to blows over conflicting imperial interests.

Within twenty years, Spain would relinquish their claim to Nootka and the British would rename the archipelago Vancouver Island.

—⚏—

Tragic Tale ————

Before sailing north for the trading season, Dutch and Freddie had gone into the forest and filled large burlap sacks with fresh new buds and needles from a young spruce tree. The bags were taken back to the barn and the bows boiled in water for many hours. After the buds were brewed, the liquid was strained into three forty gallon wooden casts. Warm fresh water was added to each cask, as well as five pounds of sugar and half a pound of yeast. The barrels were covered with wooden lids and allowed to steep further in the warm barn. During this brewing time, Cora searched out and cleaned every clay jug and glass jar they had hoarded over the past year. Once the spruce beer was totally fermented, it would be bottled and traded to the Indians.

"One beaver skin is worth a half gallon of brew," Dutch said stirring the second cast. "Two beaver or one otter is worth a gallon. But never allow the Indians to drink the beer inside the post. They must take it outside. If they return the empty jug or jar, give them a fish hook."

Cora put her finger in the cask and tasted the young beer. "This brew is horrible!" She said with a curled nose. "Why do the Indians like this swill?"

Dutch smiled at her, "Once properly cured, the beer will be tasty with a good kick. Sailors have been drinking this brew for centuries, it helps ward off scurvy."

"I'll stay with my brandy," Cora replied with a grin.

"We have a copper still now, we can make our own spirits," Freddie added.

"Uncle, while I'm gone I'd like you to distill two hundred pounds of sea salt. We will need it come salmon season. Hire one of the Clatsops to guide you down to where Lewis and Clark made their salt."

"Aye," Freddie replied with a bright face. "I would like to see their salt works."

Two days later, on the twenty-sixth of June, Dutch sailed with the *Mary Rose* and stood at the stern rail with a long face watching Joseph Point slip away. With a dark premonition stuck in his head, he would miss his mates and his dog. There was much to do in the next few months and with the help of the Reed brothers, he hoped to find his camp safe and successful upon his return.

With screaming seagulls overhead, the ship crossed an amendable Columbia River Bar and sailed up the coast. Their first stop was Grays Harbor, but when they reached the bay they found contrary winds and tides that prevented the passage. Captain Jacobson ordered the ship to layoff the harbor until conditions improved. During this time, Dutch took his noon meal with the Captain and the first mate Mr. Person.

"So what do you know of Grays Harbor?" The skipper asked of Dutch while eating bread and cheese.

"According to Grays Journals, the bay is large and fed by many rivers and streams. There are numerous tribes and villages along the shores, but the water is shallow with many shoals. Once inside the harbor we should head north. According to his chart, that is the deepest approach."

"What of the Indians, and how do we trade with them?" The mate asked.

"We will find the Quinault tribe on the north shore," Dutch replied drinking wine from a crystal glass. "I will invite the Chief aboard and pay him a tribute. Once we have respect for each other, the trading can start."

"What kind of tribute?" The Captain asked.

"I will give him some gunpowder or a blanket, some trinket he'll value," Dutch replied.

With a frown, the skipper scoffed, "Nonsense, what a waste of our wares. We are not afraid of these Indians and won't give away free merchandise."

"It is my way… we will pay the tribute," Dutch replied with a firm voice. "And while I understand these are peaceful people, we will do our trading from the longboat which will be tethered to the ship. I will do the dickering and set the values. At no time will we allow Indians on the deck, other than the Chief himself and a few elders. The fore and aft swivels should be loaded and manned at all times, as well as a few muskets in the shrouds."

The Captain's hazel eyes glared as he wiped his lips with his napkin, "I've traded with natives all over the world and I've always allowed them aboard the ship. Trading from the longboat is a waste of time." He poured himself a glass of wine. "I won't shillyshally with these people, let them board the ship and we will trade for their pelts and move on."

Dutch returned the skippers glare with a determined face, "The Commodore asked me to teach you the ways of trading with the coastal Indians and this is my method. If you wish to do it your way sir, fine, then I'd be obliged to be taken back to the Columbia. I won't risk my life with arrogant shipmates and decks filled with strange Indians."

The cabin went quiet for the longest moment, only the lapping of water could be heard. "Leave us Mr. Person," Jacobson finally said with a sharp tongue.

"Aye sir," the mate replied getting quickly to his feet.

Once Mr. Person was out the door, the skipper turned to Dutch with a fuming face, "No man talks to me with such contempt, and never in front of my officers. I should place you in irons or have you flogged. I am the Captain and aboard my ship it's always *my* way."

Dutch slowly poured himself more wine without responding to the Captains outburst. After taking a drink he smiled and replied, "Crossing the continent, I faced mobs of buffalo, hordes of Indians and battled river privates. They didn't frighten me and neither will you. I am not a member of your crew. I am an equal partner in this enterprise, so show me respect or return me to my outpost. The decision is yours… sir."

The Captain pondered his response with angry eyes, but then conceded to him. "We'll try it your way and see how it works. But never speak to me with contempt again; you will not challenge my authority."

Later that afternoon, the ship slipped inside Grays Harbor and with the longboat sounding the way, moved slowly towards the north shore. The crystal clear bay was large and the surrounding mountains were studded with forests of spruce, hemlock, cedar and fir. Dutch stood at the stern rail and marveled at this green gold.

With the sunset approaching, the *Mary Rose* dropped anchor in front of a large native village. Not long after, the ship was visited by the Quinault Chief and two elders of the tribe. Dutch greeted them at the rail and accepted two large baskets of crabs they brought as gifts. The Indians spoke the Chinook Jargon and were quite friendly. Dutch gave the Indians a tribute of a colorful blanket for the chief and fishing hooks for the elders, he also passed around tin cups of rum and they talked about making trade the next day. From this conversation he learned that the ship *Tonquin* had been at the same anchorage only the month before. The tribe had tried to do trading with the ship, but had found her Captain surly and too hard to bargain with. "This Captain was a foolish man," the Chief said. Dutch and the Chief soon agreed to the terms and methods of trading for the next day. With an amber sun about to slip behind the horizon, Dutch thanked the Indians and lit his pipe and passed it around. The Quinault's seemed to be honest people, and eager to make fair trades.

Early the next morning, under the watchful eye of the Captain and crew, Dutch and the mate stood in the longboat with the trading supplies spread out on the planks. They had blankets, knives, hatchets, axes and other iron tools. There were also trinkets of colorful beads, sewing kits, bolts of cloth, copper kettles, iron pots, gunpowder and trade rifles. What was missing, much to the chagrin of the Captain, were jugs of whiskey and rum, which Dutch had refused to trade. The water around the ship soon filled with canoes and as the dugouts approached the longboat, one at a time, Dutch greeted the Indians with the sign of peace. After some pleasant bantering, he inspected the pelts being offered and set the value of the skins. Then the dickering would begin using well established Indian etiquette. Negotiations were made with a nod of the head, the flash of the eyes and the swipe of the hand, always palms down until the final offer was made and then, with agreement, it was palms up. It was a slow process, but soon the number of pelts grew upon the deck. He made a few trades for sea otter pelts, but for the most part, the skins that day were beaver, fox and cougar. Dutch enjoyed trading and talking with the Indians and he learned much of Quinault tribe.

Late that morning, as the sun was burning through the mist, a birch canoe approached the longboat. The craft was quite out of place, as all the other canoes were the typical log dugouts. Paddling this boat was an older brave with a dark complexion and a copper skinned squaw. As they came alongside the brave said in English, "I be Jasper Ramsay, and this is my woman Bright Eyes."

Dutch was surprised to hear his words. "Are you an Indian?" he asked.

"Nay," he replied smiling, "I'm British. Came out here years ago and have never left. Is your ship heading north?"

"Aye," Dutch replied, "How did you get here?"

"I jumped ship in Montreal and started walking west, didn't stop until I got here. I have some otter pelts to show you, but they aren't for trade right now," Jasper said handing the skins to Dutch. "Last month the Captain of the *Tonquin* hired my oldest boy, George, as his interpreter. He sailed away with the ship, and now I hear he is being held captive by the Clayoquot tribe on Nootka Sound. If you secure his release, I will pay you handsomely with prime pelts like these."

Dutch examined the pelts closely; they were indeed prime skins. "What of the ship?"

"Indian fisherman came through a few days ago. They know only of my son and nothing of the ship. Will you help me?"

Jasper and his woman looked at Dutch with earnest eyes, searching for any signs of hope. He handed back the pelts, the couple reminded Dutch of his own parents. "Aye, I'll keep an eye out for your boy. But I've never heard of the Clayoquot Indians before."

Bright Eyes answered in her native tongue, "They are a hostile and treacherous tribe and not to be trusted. Bring my son home and you will be much rewarded."

"Give me a description of George and I'll try to find him," Dutch replied confidently.

As Jasper told Dutch the likeness, he removed a necklace made from dozens of small colorful dentalium shells. "Wear this around your neck, if George sees it, he will know you speak for me." Dutch slipped on the pendant and shook hands with Mr. Ramsay. As they paddled away, he shouted, "I'll do my best, you can count on that."

Late in the afternoon, with fifty-six pelts on the deck, the ship slipped her anchor and moved to the south shore where the next day the trading would resume. That evening Dutch told the Captain and his officers the story of Mr. Ramsay and the fine pelts he was offering for the return of his son. They were all sharp eared that night, and talked at great length about the fate of the *Tonquin* and the marooned interpreter. All agreed that great caution would be needed when approaching the Clayoquot Indians. Captain Jacobson patiently listened to his men talk and then reminded everyone that their mission was trading, not rescue. "My ship will not be put in danger for a few otter skins."

Two days later the ship departed Grays Harbor and sailed north for the Strait of Juan de Fuca. After spending three weeks trading with the tribes of the Puget Sound the *Mary Rose* sailed for Vancouver Island. Dutch's methods of trading had proved productive and the ship had collected near four hundred pelts in their first month of the season. Both Mr. Person and Ensign Fisher had proven themselves good traders and were beginning to understand Indian sign. But the Captain had remained dismissive towards the natives and his arrogance was becoming quite annoying to Dutch.

With timbers creaking and sails billowing, the ship moved up the coastline of Vancouver Island trading with the many Indians they found inside the pristine bays and inlets. The culture of these island natives was quite different, as these people were great artisans building tall colorful totem poles, and large pole lodges, but they were also more warlike.

Midway up the island the ship sailed just off Woody Point near Nootka Sound, where the Clayoquot Indians lived. The Captain hesitated approaching the main village and talked of moving further up the coast. "I want no trouble," he said standing next to the helmsman.

"Arm the crew and move to the village sir," Dutch replied with a telescope at his eye. "I will go ashore and talk to their Chief and determine his mood."

"I will not put my ship at risk," the skipper answered sharply.

Dutch removed the spyglass from his eye and handed it to Ensign Fisher. "We need to learn the fate of the ship and the boy, it is our duty. The story we were told may be only a rumor. The Ensign and I will go ashore, with six armed sailors, and see if the Chief will smoke the peace pipe."

"I will not allow my ship to be stranded overnight near this village. I don't trust these Indians."

"Nor do I sir," Dutch replied. "I will return before sunset and we can sail out into the open sea. The darkness will cloak us from any pursuit. It be the right thing to do, sir."

Captain Jacobson glared at Dutch with a strange stare. "The ship will weigh anchor at twilight, if you have not returned, we will leave you behind. Do you understand Mr. Blackwell?"

"Aye," Dutch said looking at his pocket watch. "Mr. Fisher let us prepare to go ashore."

Once inside Nootka Sound the Captain maneuvered the ship into a small cove that was close to the Clayoquot village and then came about and dropped anchor. With the bow of the ship facing open water, the skipper was prepared for a hasty departure. He also ordered the canons loaded and the crew armed. The longboat was launched and six volunteer crewmembers were loaded aboard carrying pistols and rifles. Mr. Fisher and Dutch were the last to take up their positions in the skiff.

Looking down at the men bobbing in the water, the Captain said from the rail, "Twilight Mr. Blackwell, not a moment later."

Taking the tiller in hand Dutch looked up at the skipper and replied, "Aye Captain, throw me down a tarp, maybe I can smuggle out the interpreter."

Mr. Person threw down a canvas tarp and the longboat rowed away. As they moved across the water Dutch could see many Indians watching their approach from a sandy beach filled with canoes. Just up from this beach was a rocky point that was heavily forested. He moved the tiller in that direction. "You men stay close to the boat, Mr. Fisher and I will walk to the village. If we run across the missing sailor, I'll have him circle around to the point and you can hide him under the tarp. Stand prepared to shove off at any moment."

The longboat slid onto a gravel beach some hundred yards from the village. After Dutch and Mr. Fisher were ashore, the sailors got out and guarded the boat. Walking towards the village, Dutch told the Ensign the general description of George Ramsay. "If we see him, we cannot bring attention to him. I will just talk loudly to you about circling around to the boat. Hopefully the Indians will not understand my words, but George will."

As they approached the hamlet they were greeted by a large number braves. All of them carried war clubs, hatches or rifles. They were a fearful looking bunch, with soiled faces and unusual looking basket hats. But Dutch also noticed that many of the men had fresh wounds and scars from a recent skirmish. He greeted them with the peace sign and asked to see their Chief. The Indians had a hateful glare, but agreed to take them to the Chief.

As they walked through the village the crowd grew larger with many woman and children. The settlement was large with dozens of lodges and hundreds of people. Finally the procession stopped at a large pole house and they were joined by the Chief. He was a short pudgy fellow with a ruby scar on his right cheek. His name was War Cloud and he wore a robe made of bird feathers. Dutch spoke to him in the Chinook Jargon and he responded with a chilly demeanor. Dutch turned to Mr. Fisher and said loudly in English, "George, circling around to the longboat and you will be safe." Then turning back to the Chief he removed a sheath knife from his pouch and handed it to him. Using the Chinook Jargon he continued, "This be my tribute to you Chief. May we make trade with your tribe?" War Cloud grunted and handed his gift to one of his wives. As the Chief responded, Dutch scanned the many faces watching, while rubbing Mr. Ramsay's necklace. As they discussed the terms for trading, Dutch kept turning to Mr. Fisher while loudly saying, "George, circling around to the longboat and you will be safe." The Chief was a determined negotiator and kept dickering about the values that would be paid. All the while the sun was beginning to set. Finally they reached an agreement; the Indians would come aboard the ship the next day and trade with very favorable values for their pelts. War Cloud and the crowd seemed please and as Dutch filled his pipe with tobacco, he asked the Chief if any other ships had stopped by the village in the last few moons. With a sly look on his face he responded, "No." Dutch lit his pipe and the two men smoked together, all the while the sun was slipping behind the horizon. The Chief invited the two men to stay and celebrate the trading agreement, but Dutch refused telling the Chief that his Captain was tyrant and would not allow him to stay on the beach after sunset. He seemed to except this excuse and with a wave of his hand, the crowd parted so they could leave.

"See you tomorrow Chief, we look forward to much trade."

The men rushed back down the beach with one eye on the setting sun. Once at the longboat they learned that George was in the bottom of skiff, covered with the tarp. As the boat shoved off, with the sailors franticly rowing, they heard the boatswain's pipe and the rattling of the anchor chains. Approaching the ship they made it to the boarding ladder just as the sails were unfurled and the *Mary Rose* started to move with the breeze. George Ramsay was the first aboard, followed by Dutch and Mr. Fisher. As the sailors came up the ladder, war drums erupted on the beach and in the faint twilight Indians could be seen rushing to their canoes.

"An old man saw me run for the rocks, he must have alerted the Chief," George Ramsay said looking out at the village.

It took a few minutes to recover the longboat and then the Captain called for more cloth. As the ship slowly picked up speed, many canoes closed the distance and the Indians begin firing their rifles.

Kaboom, Kabbom.

The two aft swivel cannons responded to their gunfire. The skipper ordered rifleman to the rail and they fired as well. Soon the surrounding water filled with gun smoke and the battle raged on for a few more volleys. The Captain ordered all lights extinguished and the deck fell into darkness. *Kaboom, Kabbom,* the swivel guns sounded their angry breath one last time. Within a few minutes the ship was on the open ocean with no sign the Indians or their land in the night wake. The danger was over.

The only illumination on the darken quarterdeck, came from the oil lamp in the binnacle next to the helm. The men gathered around this glow with the harsh light distorting their faces. All eyes were on George Ramsay.

"I saw my father's necklace when you entered the village, then I heard your English words. Thank you for rescuing me!" George said with the compass light washing his young face. He was a lanky lad with dark hair and bright eyes.

"What of your ship?" Captain Jacobson asked.

The lad shook his head with a sad face. "It is no more, sir."

"What the hell happened?" Dutch asked.

In the dim light, George's knees buckled and then he recovered, warily telling his story with a firm voice. The month before, the *Tonquin* had dropped anchor just off the Clayoquot village and George had gone ashore to arrange for trade. When he returned he warned Captain Thorn that the Indians might be hostile. The next day the skipper allowed the natives aboard his ship in great numbers. The Captain knew nothing about trading and there were many disputes. When War Cloud and Thorn got into an argument over the value of some otter pelts, the Captain threw the skins at the Chief and ordered him off the ship. This insulted the Indians and they all took leave. "I told the Captain we should weigh anchor and move on, but he would not listen." The next morning a large group of Indians returned with their squaws, but without the Chief or any weapons. Captain Thorn thought this was a sign of peace, so the trading resumed. The braves came aboard with their pelts, leaving the squaws in canoes. But the Indians were only interested in trading for knifes and hatchets. Soon all the natives were armed and they attacked the crew. The battle lasted for hours and the deck became slimy with blood. Some of the crew jumped into the water, but the squaws paddled over and clubbed them to death. Captain Thorn and Mr. MacKay were bludgeoned and all the other officers were killed. With only five crewmembers still alive, they barricaded themselves in the Captain's cabin, driving off the remaining Indians by killing them as they tried to come down the narrow passageway. It was a horrible bloody battle and the deck was littered with dead and dying men. The wounded and dead Indians were thrown overboard, while the officers and crew were laid out on the deck and covered with sailcloth. The men knew the Indians would return the next day so George and three others lowered the longboat into the night water and rowed away seeking the protection on nearby Island. The fifth man was badly wounded and crawled to the powder magazine. The next morning when the Indians returned to loot the ship, he lit the magazine on fire and the whole ship exploded killing over a hundred Indians. "An old squaw later told me that it rained body parts and wood that morning, turning the bay blood red." The longboat was soon discovered and the four men captured. They were all killed, except George, because War Cloud wanted him as his slave. George concluded his story with a simple truth, "Twenty four men are dead, because an arrogant Captain didn't know what the hell he was doing."

Not a word was said from the stunned men, who listened to this tragic tale. Dutch glanced at Captain Jacobson a few times during the story, but he always looked away. On the chart that night, next to the Clayoquot village, Dutch wrote Blood Bay.

The Mary Rose continued sailing north up Vancouver Island trading with the local inhabitants. With the addition of George Ramsay the trading sessions went faster and the total number of pelts grew to over eight hundred by the end of July. After the tale of the *Tonquin* Captain Jacobson's attitude towards the natives was much improved. He held out respect for the locals and deferred all trading decisions to Dutch and George.

In August the ship sailed for the Queen Charlotte Islands and spent a few weeks plying the northern waters. By the end of the month the ship turned for home with over a thousand hides stored below deck. As they sailed south, Dutch took the time to write a response to Mary's letter. His answer was five pages long and filled with well-chosen words, vivid descriptions of crossing the divide and living in the wilderness of the Pacific Northwest. He portrayed himself as a frontiersman, living from one adventure to the next. The note was chatty, friendly and without any romantic overtones. When he completed it, he secretly gave the letter to Mr. Fisher. "Tell Mary that I have thought of her often and hope she is doing well. Thank you Mr. Fisher for your troubles."

On their way back down the coast, the ship put into Grays Harbor again and returned George Ramsay to his parents. It was a heartwarming reunion and true his word, Jasper rewarded Dutch with a dozen prime otter skins. During the cruise, Dutch and young George had become good mates and he gave the lad a trade rifle as payment for all his help during the season. He also gave the family back the necklace with a warm invitation to come by the trading post anytime they were in the area. The Ramsay family was a fine clan.

With Grays Harbor in their wake, a few hours later the ship stood off Point Adams at the mouth of the Columbia River. What lay before them was a narrow trough of calm water with boiling whitewater and towering waves on each side for as far as the eye could see. It was an ominous sight and most timid sailors would move on, but not Dutch and Captain Jacobson. They were in a good position with the wind at their backs and the tide ebbing. It was time to cross the bar.

Wilderness Abode ————————

Once committed there was no turning back. The narrow channel they sailed was only sixty yards wide with twenty foot curling swells on each side of the trough. They approached the five mile crossing from southwest and under cloudy skies, pointed the bow of the ship right at Cape Hancock. The skipper stood on one side of the helmsmen shouting out commands while Dutch stood on the quarterdeck rail watching and yelling out warnings. The breakers were so tall that they were curling with white water high above the ship's deck. The sounds of the pounding surf filled the air, drowning out the shouts from the Captain. Once Point Adams slipped by the ship, the trough changed course to north-northeast. Just as the twisting and pitching ship changed to this new course a thirty foot sneaker wave crashed over the bow, drenching the deck with sea water. Two sailors were almost thrown overboard and many more were tossed about. The ship listed heavily to one side with her sails almost dipping into the river. Quickly, with timbers creaking and seawater swirling, the ship righted itself and the helmsmen gained control again. After a few more turbulent miles the ship was inside the estuary and changing course again for the south shore. It had been a hair-raising crossing and now with a hazy sun in the sky, the ship was safely inside the bar. The river was filled with Indian canoes fishing and the helmsman had to maneuver around these boats. The salmon were in!

"Mr. Person," Captain Jacobson shouted from the wheel, "Check the ship for any damage."

"Aye, aye," responded the mate.

"Mr. Blackwell," the skipper continued, "this river of yours is like crossing into hell."

Dutch moved to the helm with a smile on his face. "Most timid Captains just moved on, that be why it took so many centuries to discover the Columbia."

The helmsman turned to Dutch with fear still in his face, "I wouldn't want to do that ever again. I thought that sneaker had us."

The skipper replied, "In a couple days you'll have to do it again. Then we will be finished with this miserable flow."

As the ship passed a canoe pulling in a net filled with salmon the Captain pointed and said, "Look at the size of those fish! I have never seen such large fish in all my travels."

"Aye," Dutch answered, "They be silver gold."

A few moments later the mate was back on the quarterdeck carrying a wet beaver pelt. "A split spar on the bow, other than that the ship is fine, sir. But seawater seeped in through the deck and the cargo got flooded. We will have to pump out the bilge and dry out the pelts. Then we should build watertight crates before we leave for China."

"I don't want to linger here," Jacobson said sharply.

"Molding skins will have no value in China sir," the mate replied.

Dutch looked carefully at the pelt, "That's why the Astorians brought along a cooper. He has been building barrels ever since the *Tonquin* departed.

"Aye, we will have to do something," the skipper relented. "Maybe with the demise of their ship, we can buy the casts from the Astorians."

As the ship moved slowly towards Joseph Point, Dutch begin noticing things that were new or out of place. The outpost looked finished, and to his surprise, there were now three window dormers built into the riverside gambrel roof. And next to the dock, he could see a small lacquered sloop bobbing in the water. Everything around the point looked fresh and manicured, even the flag pole had been white-washed and its tricolored flag looked peaceful and inviting. It was good to be home.

The ship was maneuvered into position at the end of the dock and the anchors were dropped. Dutch gathered up his belongings and was the first to depart the ship. Waiting at the bottom of the ramp was King. When he saw Dutch his snoot turned to a smile and he started howling with joy. Once on the dock, Dutch knelt to him and man and dog were reunited. Cora was next, dressed in a buckskin frock and with a bright smile on her face. He gave her a hug and she told him that his uncle was out working the trap lines and would be back shortly. The Reed Brothers also greeted the ship and after shaking hands with Dutch they pointed out the sloop they had built.

"The tapered hull is flat bottomed and twenty six foot long with an eight foot beam. The forward cargo hatch can carry a half-ton. The small cabin has two berths with an oil cook stove and there is a hand pump for the bilge. Behind the cabin is the cockpit with a solid oak rudder and a built in compass under the starboard seat. The daggerboard is five foot long and when the keel is dropped down, it protrudes under the boat by almost four feet. The main mast is twenty four feet tall and well balanced with the hull. The boat makes good time under sail and is very maneuverable. She is built with the finest oak and hemlock lumber we have ever used."

Dutch was impressed with the design of the sloop and the craftsmanship of the brothers. "It's a fine looking boat boys, thank you for your hard work." He turned to Cora and continued, "We'll sail down to trade with the Tillamooks and we'll name her *Raven,* after my mother."

The Captain and mate joined them on the dock and the party walked ashore to have a look at the trading post. Once inside the large trading room, they found the walls filled with shelving and the floor filled with bins and tables containing the trade goods. Everything was neat and in its place. At one end of the room was a large stone fireplace with a split-log mantel. Next to it were counters for examining the hides. Across the room was a doorway that opened to the living quarters, and a staircase that led to the second floor. As the men walked around the well-lit room looking at the merchandise,

Cora informed them they had over three hundred pelts up in the attic. "The spruce beer was very popular."

The Captain turned to Dutch with a surprised face, "You wouldn't trade spirits from my ship but you do from your trading post?"

"Aye," Dutch replied, "It is a brew the Indians love. I'll wager there is a jug of spruce beer in every Clatsop lodge. They use it as a tonic, to help ward off scurvy."

"I've heard of spruce beer," Mr. Person added. "It's old time elixir used by sailors."

Opening the door to the adjoining room, Dutch and the dog walked into the living quarters and his mouth dropped open with astonishment. Under a tall ceiling, on the left side of the back wall, was another large stone fireplace also with a split-log mantel. In front of the stone hearth were two new chairs and a bench. On the right side was the iron cook stove that had been brought over from Amsterdam. Next to the stove were small tables for food preparation and on the wall, cupboards with blue cloth drapes. On the right wall, under the riverside windows, was a varnished split-log table with six chairs. At the rear of the room was a log staircase that led to the upstairs bedrooms. Cora and Freddie had added some personal touches as well; a jar of colorful wildflowers on the table, his old bowler hat and Lakota peace lance were on the mantel and gone were candles replaced with oil lamps; civilization had arrived on the Columbia River! Dutch stood in silent wonderment taking in his new abode. Ralf Reed approached him, placing his hand on his shoulder, "Cozier then the chicken coop, hey mate?"

Dutch turned to him with a smile and replied, "I be all snug and dry in this cozy room. But how did you accomplish all this in such a short time?"

Ralf was joined by his brother Robert who answered the question. "The Astorians helped out. They loaned us some of their Islanders in trade for a few tools we will leave behind. They are a good lot and we enjoyed many evenings with them."

With Cora showing the Captain and mate around the main room, the brothers took Dutch upstairs and showed him the bedrooms. His room was the largest and looked out a window with a river view. There were shelves on the wall, even hooks for hanging clothes and a small mirror on the back of the door. The brothers had also built a larger rope bedframe, upon which laid his white buffalo skin and on the floor he found the crate of books he had ordered. The two back bedrooms were good sized as well, each had a window that looked out at the barn. They also had beds, mirrors, hooks and shelves. There was also an upstairs door that opened to the trading post attic. Inside this large room, Dutch found piles of pelts, stacks of merchandise and shelves filled with an assortment of provisions. He was overwhelmed with the brother's work and couldn't find enough good words to say. The new living quarters was like a wilderness palace and he thanked the Lord for the deliverance of the Reed Brothers.

Dutch was reunited with his uncle a few hours later and two men walked the grounds catching up on the news. The trap lines were still proving productive and Freddie had added six new traps to the line. He also had distilled the sea salt and stored it in burlap bags in the barn. The garden was doing well, with copious crops of turnips, onions, carrots and potatoes. "The Indians tell me it was an unusually warm summer," his uncle said showing Dutch a basket of the harvest.

"Did the Chief's come by to trade?"

"Coboway a few times, but Comcomly had yet to stop by."

"Any trouble when I was gone?"

"Only once," Freddie said. "A drunken Chinook had staggered over from the fort and tried to have his way with Cora. She drove him off by throwing hot coffee on him and kicking him in his groin. Then King joined in and chased him out. We've never seen the bloke again."

"Bully for Cora, she's got grit," Dutch replied proudly. "What of the Astorians?"

The overland party still had not arrived and the partners were quite concerned. With the fort now complete, some Astorians had moved up river and a British bloke named David Thompson, with a number of Canadian Voyageurs, had arrived in July. As they talked of the Astorians, Dutch told his uncle about George Ramsey and the tragic tale of the *Tonquin*.

"I fear Mr. McDougall will take this news poorly," Freddie replied with a sad face. "Their provisions are dwindling and the pelts need to be transported before the winter sets in."

"Aye, Captain Jacobson and I will go there tomorrow. Maybe we can help."

That evening the reunited trio invited the Captain, mate and the Reed Brothers to the living quarters for salmon bake, with garden potatoes and sourdough biscuits. Dutch loved working at the new stove as it reminded him of the many meals with Kate and Sandy back at the pub. It was a gala welcome home party with much wine and vivid stories.

Early the next morning Duncan McDougall stood on the beach, next to the fort, saying farewell to some trappers in a canoe when Dutch and Captain Jacobson paddled up. He was not surprised to see his old friend, as everyone on the river was talking about the return of the brigantine. He greeted his visitors warmly and Dutch did the introductions. After some pleasantries the men strolled to the fort and went inside. The main yard held many skins, drying in sun, and the sounds of the blacksmith shop filled the air. Entering the trading post they found a clerk working at a tall desk and two Astorians restocking shelves. The men moved to the fireplace and poured themselves some coffee, while Dutch asked everyone in the room to gather around. Once he had their ears he said in a firm voice, "We be the bearers of dreadful news...and I want to tell this story only once." He then told the room the tragic story of the *Tonquin*. As the story unfolded, Dutch watched the faces of the men as they listened in silent disbelief. They all showed pain and anger, while Duncan seemed frozen in place, his eyes staring at this coffee mug, and with no expression on his face. Dutch concluded the story with George Ramsey's comment about the arrogant American Captain. "We are sorry for your losses and we extend our condolences," he concluded. The trading room went silent for the longest moment.

"Is there another ship on the way?" The Captain finally asked.

"Aye," the clerk replied, "but not until next spring."

Finally Mr. McDougall blinked, "That damn Captain Thorn, may his bloody soul rot in hell. That was a good ship with good mates!"

"We need barrels," Dutch said to Mr. McDougall. "We can trade you enough provisions to get you through the winter."

"And we can take your pelts to China as well, and forward the proceeds to Mr. Astor in New York," Captain Jacobson added.

Duncan glared at his visitors for a long moment with anger still on his face. Then he realized that life marches on. "The pelts we can store here until the next ship. The provisions we will need." He turned to his clerk and continued, "What is the count on our barrels?"

The skinny bookkeeper went over to his desk and returned with a gray ledger. Thumbing through the pages he said, "As of yesterday, Mr. Bell has built 156 large casts, eighty of which are filled with the forts pelts."

Mr. McDougall sipped his coffee for moment and then replied, "We will trade you 56 kegs with watertight lids for two hundred pounds each of flour, beans, coffee, sugar and a hundred gallons of whiskey or rum."

Captain Jacobson smiled at Duncan and then extended his hand, "You're a man that makes quick decisions, I like that. I'll check with my First Officer to see if we can fill you needs, if we can, you can consider it done." The men shook hands on the deal.

For the next week, Joseph Point rang out again with activity. Part of the crew worked at transferring provisions to Fort Astoria in the longboat and returning with empty barrels. But 56 kegs were not enough storage for all the cargo, so other parts of the crew and the Reed Brothers went into the forest and built wooden crates. These coffin like containers were made out of cedar and all the joints were pitched to keep them watertight. As all this activity was happening, Dutch and Freddie took the new sloop out on the river and using a rope net, with cork floats, they gillnetted over two thousand pounds of salmon. The *Raven* proved to be the perfect fishing platform.

By the end of the week all the cargo was aboard and lashed down in the forward hold. The final count was fourteen hundred and ninety two skins. A third of which were sea otter pelts. The trading season had been good, and the Captain and crew looked forward to a profitable passage to China and then home to Amsterdam. The last items to go aboard were four kegs of pickled salmon and two casts of salted fish. They could have sent more, but they had run out of vinegar and salt and used up most of their supply of sugar and Spanish onions.

As the casks were being hoisted aboard Captain Jacobson turned to Dutch and said, "I hope your fish travels well. If it turns rancid it well stink up my ship."

Dutch shook his head with a smile, "Tell the Commodore that if he finds a market for the fish, send me lots of vinegar, sugar and salt next year."

"And onions?" the skipper replied.

"Nay, with the new sloop, I'll sail up river and trade with the Walla Walla's. They have the biggest and sweetest onions I've ever seen."

Under a cloudy sky, with a brisk east wind, the *Mary Rose* slipped her moorings and moved down river on the morning of October 12, 1811. The friends stood sadly on the dock watching the ship cross the river and then turn west at Point Hancock. Soon she slipped from view, and disappeared into the jaws of the Columbia River Bar. Little did the comrades know that they had just unwittingly opened the way to one of the greatest salmon fisheries in the world.

The Tillamooks ──────

After the departure of the *Mary Rose* the weather remained warm and bright. Before the doldrums of winter set in, Dutch had planned two trips. The first was to visit the Chinooks and pay tribute to Chief Comcomly.

With Cora and King watching the outpost, Dutch and Freddie loaded some trade goods into the sloop and sailed across the river.

As they came near the Chinook village they saw the royal canoe returning from Fort Astoria. Waiting on the shore was a large number of villagers welcoming home Comcomly. Once the Chief was on the beach, Dutch turned the sailboat towards the hamlet. The Indians stood watching the strange little boat furl its sails and glide effortlessly to the beach. With all eyes on Dutch, he was first out of the craft carrying an earthen jug and colorful blanket. With the Chinooks gathered around their Chief, he approached the stoic faced Comcomly with a friendly smile and the sign of peace.

"I'm pleased to see you again Chief," he said in their Jargon. "This blanket, with its rich colors, reminded me of the Chinook people and I give it to you as my tribute."

The one-eyed Comcomly grunted, but still had a frown on his face. Handing the blanket and jug to him, Dutch continued, "The jug is filled with spruce beer. It is a fine brew, and I give this to you as well."

The Chief closely inspected the wool blanket in the sunlight and then handed off the afghan to a young squaw standing next to him. He removed the cork from the jug and took a big drink of beer. Wiping his lips, a broad smile chased his face. "Your tribute is accepted, we be friends. Is that brown skinned squaw still in your camp?"

"Aye, she is."

"Good, you stay with us tonight. You can meet my daughters and maybe we can trade squaws. Will you give me a ride in your winged canoe?"

Comcomly and his oldest son were loaded into the sailboat and Dutch and Freddie sailed them around the river for over an hour. A fine time was had by all, and by the time they returned to the shore, father and son had consumed the jug of spruce beer.

That evening was a strange mixture of merriment. Eels were cut up and severed raw, with mushrooms. Spiced hot water, spiked with rum, was passed around. At the bottom of every tankard a dead lizard was found. The sensuous dancing was performed by three of the

Chief's daughters who lathered their naked bodies with seal oil and then danced around in provocative ways. The smoky lodge soon filled with the odorous smell of sweat and oil and the sounds of the drums marched well into the night. Freddie flirted with all the daughters and at times danced around the fire with them. The shindig didn't break up until dawn the next day. During this time, Dutch was able to keep his wits and learned much from the Chief. The Chinooks were the bullies of the river and Comcomly received a tribute from all the tribes that came to Fort Astoria to trade. He controlled his side of the river with an iron fist and held contempt for the Clatsops easy going ways. The Chief had four wives and many children. And much to Dutch's surprise, one of his older daughters was about to marry Duncan McDougall. This would make Comcomly the father-in-law to the Chief Factor of the Pacific Fur Company. It was to be a grand alliance for the Astorians and the Chinooks. Now Comcomly wanted to trade another daughter to Dutch for Cora. Then he would have an accord with both trading posts and could profit from all the Indian trading on the river. He was an ambitious man and Dutch answered his overtures with great caution, telling him that Cora wasn't a slave, but an emancipated woman. The Chief had a hard time understanding how any squaw could be liberated. That just wasn't the Indian way!

At first light the next morning, Dutch and his uncle staggered to their sailboat and got underway. Once the daggerboard was down and the sail up, Freddie slumped in cockpit and put his head in hands. "My brain is throbbing and my ears are ringing. Why do we do this to ourselves?"

"It was the mushrooms Uncle. The Indians use them as an aphrodisiac. They can cloud a man's judgment. Did you find a woman you liked?"

"Hell I don't know," Freddie responded still holding his head. "They all smelt so bad and the drums were so loud… maybe taking an Indian squaw is bad idea!"

When the men returned to the post, they found Cora at the stove cooking up bacon and eggs. "Good morning boys, would ya be hungry?" She asked with a bright face. Both men sadly shook their heads no. "We need some sleep," Freddie said heading for the staircase with Dutch on his heels. Cora moved to the table to eat her breakfast and looked up at the men slowly climbing the stairs. "You boys won't be worth spit today; but then, you have to pay the devil back."

Dutch stopped half way up the rise, "Tomorrow we will sail to Tillamook Bay. I'll make preparations this afternoon, until then some peace and quiet please."

The trip across the river had been easy, now the new boat would face the real challenge, crossing the Columbia River Bar. With Freddie and King tending the store, Dutch lowered the daggerboard and with Cora trustingly at his side, they headed for Cape Hancock. Cora had never sailed before and she was very curious about the boat. As they moved down the river Dutch explained to her the different parts of a sailboat; mainsail, jib, keel, port, starboard. She seemed to grasp the concepts and Dutch let her take the tiller to feel the boat under sail. "This be much better then paddling," she said with a smile as the sloop sliced across the calm waters.

As they approached Baker Bay, Dutch adjusted the sails and took the tiller. It was a perfect morning to cross the bar, with a warm breeze from the east and a tide that was near ebbing. But still the swells at the mouth of the river were deep and long. Once Cape Hancock was on the port side, Dutch turned the boat to the southwest and sailed into the tall swells. The sloop bounced about like a cork, with curling waves all around. Fearful of capsizing in a gusting breeze, Dutch spilled the wind from the mainsail and let the jib do the work. Thank God for the daggerboard, it was a perfect balance. Deep inside the trough of the waves they lost sight of land and Dutch kept his eyes glued on the horizon. Within the half-hour they were in the shallow swells of the Pacific Ocean.

With the peaceful crossing complete, Dutch twisted to Cora and found her eyes bulging and her chocolate skin near white. "Are you queasy?" He asked noticing her hands trembling.

She just stared out at the ocean for the longest moment. "No, I'm not!" She finally replied with a fearful voice. "But I thought for sure the sea was swallowing us up."

Dutch chuckled, "Do you remember the bible story of David and Goliath?"

"Aye," she replied in a shaky voice.

"The ocean is like Goliath, big and strong. We are like David, fast and smart. We will always win if we keep our wits about us."

Cora glared at him, with color returning to her face. "Next time I'll walk."

With a sea breeze on the nape of his neck and nostrils filled with salt air, Dutch turned the sloop and followed the shoreline south. As he approached Tillamook Head he moved to deeper waters offshore. It was a pristine day to be sailing and his mind filled with many memories of traveling on the ocean with his family. With many birds filling the sky, Cora asked their type as they flew by. They saw pelicans, terns, cormorants and hundreds of seagulls. They talked about the vast expanse of the sea and size of the forests on the shimmering tall mountains. "It is all so big," Cora said with wonderment, "It makes me feel so small."

"We are in the palm of God's hand out here," Dutch replied from the tiller.

A few hours later they approached the mouth of Tillamook Bay. Dutch remembered clearly the landmarks to the entrance. He laid-off the opening and studied the capricious tides before committing to the crossing.

"This little strip of white water has protected Tillamook Bay for centuries," Dutch said watching the swells. "The Indians paddle their canoes across the bar all the time, but Captain Gray and his sloop, *The Lady Washington*, was the first ship to sail into the bay. My father was with him that day."

"It looks dangerous," Cora answered.

Dutch tightened the jib line and came about. Then he let the mainsail billow again. "It's time to battle Goliath," he said as the little sailboat headed straight for the waves. With Cora's hands wrapped around the rail posts, Dutch found the narrow channel, with curling breakers on both sides, and shot through the gap racing towards the mouth of the bay. Within a few moments the sailboat was inside the calm estuary.

"We win again," Dutch said with a smile. "Let's hope the Indians are as welcoming as the weather."

Cora didn't respond, her hands still tightly holding the rails.

The main Tillamook village was a mile inside the bay and on the north shore. Dutch cranked up the daggerboard and turned the boat, heading east for the settlement. He had no idea of what reception they would receive. Would his family be remembered? Was Marcus still Chief? Would they be hostile or friendly? Approaching native villages was always a cautious gamble.

Rounding some tall rocks in the estuary the hamlet came into view and they passed a few canoes plying the waters. Dutch waved at the fisherman and shouted out friendly greetings in the Tillamook tongue. Some of the dugouts answered his call with a friendly welcome.

By the time the sloop rested on the beach, in front of the village, there were many Tillamooks waiting. After lowering the sails, and retrieving a blanket from the forward hatch, Dutch and Cora got out of the boat. As they approached the crowd of natives Dutch was reminded of the tribe. The Tillamooks were shorter than most coastal Indians and their sloping foreheads seemed steeper as well. They adorned themselves with buckskins, seashells and bone piercings. Once in front of the gathering, Dutch asked if Marcus was still Chief of the Tillamooks. The people seemed stunned to hear his native words and gazed upon the brown squaw.

Finally an elder stepped forward and asked, "Who are you and why are you here?"

"I am the son of Joseph Blackwell," Dutch retorted. "I was born in this village and given the Indian name of *Dutcu*. My mother was called Raven, a Tolowa woman. We have come to make trade."

"I remember your clan," One of the braves shouted from the ranks.

The elders face relaxed. "I be Timber Wolf, your mother was once my slave. Long ago I taught your father how to build canoes. Where are they now?"

"Sadly they have passed over to the spirit world," Dutch answered. "Will you take me to your Chief so I can pay him my tribute?"

With the crowd following, Timber Wolf led Dutch and Cora through the village. The settlement seemed smaller then Dutch had remembered, and he noticed many of the villagers had pox scars on their faces. Arriving at the Chief's lodge, Timber Wolf scratched the open door and went inside. Moments later, Cora and Dutch were invited in by an older squaw wearing a fringed deerskin frock.

Entering the darkened room it took a few seconds for their eyes to adjust. The lodge had no windows, just a smoke hole in the ceiling and the light spilling in from the open door. In the shadows they found Timber Wolf and Marcus Lopez, the Chiefs Christian name, squatting by a small fire. As they came near, the two men stood. Marcus was a head taller than Timber Wolf and his curly black hair was salted with gray. His midnight skin was much darker then Cora's and it glistened in the dim light. He was a big man with giant hands.

Timber Wolf introduced Dutch to the Chief and Marcus gave Cora a wanton glance.

"I am the son of Joseph Blackwell," Dutch said in his language. "Black Fox we have met once before, long ago, when I knew you as Marcus. I bring you this blanket as my tribute and ask if we can make trade with the Tillamook people."

"I remember your father well; we were shipmates once," The Chief said taking the blanket. "Sorry to hear he is dead. Come sit by the fire and we will talk. Is the Negro squaw your slave?"

Dutch and Cora came to rest on log next to a small fire with Black Fox and Timber Wolf crouching across the flames. Dutch told the story of Cora and how she had been a slave to a Cherokee Indian. "I freed her, and she is now a liberated woman," Dutch said proudly.

As they talked, Dutch translated the conversation so Cora could understand. During this time Dutch learned that since Captain Gray, no other ship had ever entered the bay. There had been other traders, but they had come in with their longboats. He also learned the disturbing news that small pox had visited the tribe only the year before. The Tillamooks called it the white-man's sickness. As they continued, the Chief's two wives served food and spiced hot water to the visitors. When Cora asked a question in her squeaky voice, the two squaws snickered and made funny looks at her. Dutch didn't like the ridicule. Marcus didn't seem to notice her voice and rudely flirted with Cora openly. It was finally agreed that they could trade with the tribe the next morning, and as they got up to leave, Black Fox invited them to stay the night. Dutch noticed the hateful glares of his wives faces and refused his offer. "Thank you Chief, but I wish to show Cora your beautiful bay before we leave. We will return tomorrow morning and do the trading." The squaw's looked relieved as the visitors moved to the doorway.

With Cora outside, the Chief whispered to Dutch. "I want the Negro girl as my wife; I will trade you ten beaver skins for her."

"You already have two wives," Dutch replied. "Is that not enough?"

Marcus smiled broadly, "She would be my queen and number one wife. I would attend to all of her needs, she would have no chores."

The Chief was smitten and Dutch replied, "I will tell her of your offer."

That afternoon, Dutch sailed the sloop to the other end of the bay and anchored for the night. With small pox still on the beach, he had no intention of spending the night on the shore. That evening, after dinner, Cora and he sat in the cockpit drinking coffee and watching the sunset.

"Black Fox offered me ten beaver pelts for you and Chief Comcomly offered me one of his daughters. You are becoming a valuable asset," Dutch teased with cup in hand.

"The Negro Chief was rude to his wives and very demanding. He reminded me of my father, always yelling at my mother."

"He told me you would be his queen, with no chores to do."

Cora smiled and took a sip from her cup. "A Negro Indian queen, now that would be a sight to see. Nay, Black Fox is not for me."

"How about Freddie, he is lonely."

Cora grinned, "Your uncle is a good man, but he is also white and old. Nay, if I take a husband, he will be young and daring like you, and a Negro like me."

Dutch gazed at Cora and quipped, "Race is a tricky thing. Take me, I be just a breed, more white then Indian, but my heart is more Indian then white."

"Would you take an Indian wife?" Cora asked with an earnest face.

"Aye," Dutch replied quickly, "if she was beautiful and smart like my mother."

With darkness approaching the two friends talked until the sky filled with stars.

With dark clouds building in the south, the next morning Dutch and Cora did a brisk trade with the Tillamooks. They worked from the boat, on the beach in front of the village, trading all kinds of tools, trinkets, blankets and rifles. Their most popular items were fish hooks, nets and sharping files. The villagers were friendly and some of them told stories about the old days when Joseph and Raven lived amongst them. Dutch enjoyed talking with the natives and soon the wares dwindled while the pelts became plenty. By late morning the trading was over and Dutch prepared the boat to get underway.

Black Fox had been on the beach most of the morning, flirting with Cora and mingling with his people. He now approached the boat and said, "You can stay the night in my lodge."

Dutch pointed to the southern sky, "Those clouds have been building all morning. A storm is coming. We must leave before it hits."

Marcus looked disappointed and turned to Cora and said in clumsy English, "You come back, stay with me. I treat you like queen."

Cora smiled at the Chief and then helped Dutch push the boat into the water. As they climbed aboard Dutch called out, "We will return next season at this time."

Black Fox and a few other villagers stood on the shore watching as Dutch raised the jib and pushed the boat to deeper water with an oar. Within moments, with the keel down, the sloop listed in the breeze and with the sails billowing, moved quickly down the estuary.

It had been a profitable trip as Dutch had counted fifty four prime pelts in the forward hatch. When they reached the bar, Dutch turned the boat into the surf and escaped the bay in the same narrow channel he had come in on. Once on the other side of the white water he turned the boat for home.

With the sky darkening, they reached the Columbia bar late in the afternoon. As the sloop came to within a few miles of Point Adams, Dutch caught a glimpse of a large ship entering the river. The three-masted schooner was many miles ahead of them and was soon swallowed up in a rain squall. Dutch kept a keen eye on the weather and searched for the main channel. As he approached the bar, he turned the boat for Cape Hancock. With lightning and thunder in the distant southern sky, they sailed for the unpredictable crossing. As they entered the curling swells it started to rain in earnest. Dutch dispatched Cora below to work the hand pump and keep the bilges dry. With a freshening south westerly wind Dutch found the correct approach and maneuvered the sloop away from some shallow shoals. Within a half hour the sailboat was safely inside the river. It had been another terrifying passage across the Columbia Bar.

With the rain letting up, Cora stopped pumping and joined Dutch on deck. "Never again," She said to Dutch with a fearful face. "This be my last sail on this or any other boat."

With his wet sealskin slicker around his shoulders and his hand on the tiller, he smiled at Cora. "Fear of sailing is like the pain of child birth, it is soon forgotten."

Cora glared at him. "Only a fool would believe that."

Within the hour the sailboat was moored at the end of the dock at Joseph Point. Freddie and King greeted the boat to hear news of the trip. Cora was first off and knelt on the wharf and kissed the timbers. Freddie smiled at her and playfully asked, "Did you find your sea legs?" Cora stood with a frown on her face and started stomping off towards the living quarters. Turning her head she said, "You can have my sea legs; I won't need them anymore." The men chuckled at her exit and moved to the forward hatch to unload the pelts. As they worked, Dutch told his uncle of their successful trading sessions with the Tillamooks.

"Did you see a ship enter the river just before us?" Dutch asked.

"Aye, it was a Yankee trader, I think it dropped anchor up by the fort."

With the men about to carry away their cargo, a small canoe approached the dock with Mr. Bell paddling. "Ahoy Dutch, Duncan needs you urgently at the fort. He asked that your ride over with your carriage."

"Why?" Dutch shouted back.

"I have no idea mate," the cooper answered while turning his canoe around.

Once their goods were safely inside the trading post, Dutch and Freddie went to the barn and hitched up Dolly to the cart. As Dutch stepped aboard his uncle said, "It's going to rain again, and it's getting dark. If you stay for drink, you'll have to stay the night."

Dutch buttoned his rain slicker and replied, "Nay, I'll be back before its dark." Then whipping the reins he moved out of the barn. His mind was filled with questions, why had McDougall summoned him and what of the ship he had seen? Once on the backdoor road, he clucked Dolly and increased the gait. As the road came out of the dark forest, on the other side of the mountain, Dutch looked down in the dim light and found a ship anchored in the cove. A few minutes later he rode through the open back gate to Fort Astoria. Tying Dolly at the hitching rail in front of the trading post, a man approached him from the yard.

"Would ye be Mr. Blackwell?" he asked with a New England accent.

"Aye," Dutch replied.

"Good, I be Captain Hawks, skipper of the *North Star* anchored out in the cove. Your name has burned my ears for over ten thousand miles. You be some kind of a famous frontiersman."

"What are you talking about?" Dutch asked with a curious face.

"Let's go inside, I have a package for you."

The two men climbed the stairs and opened the door to the trading room. Inside the darkening room Dutch found Duncan McDougall and the clerk talking together. There was another person, standing by the fireplace with their back to the room. Resting on the floor next to this person was a sea trunk and a carpet bag.

"I have found the allusive frontiersman," Captain Hawk shouted to the room. "Now I can deliver his package."

Duncan and the clerk looked up, while the person at the fireplace turned to the room, removing a large felt hat. In the dim backlight of the flames, Dutch noticed long flowing raven hair. Then his eyes focused on the face. His mouth dropped open and his heart raced, it was Kate Wilson from Boston!

"What the hell," Dutch shouted rushing across the room. "Where did you come from?"

Kathleen quickly moved to him and threw her arms around him and they embraced in bear hug. As they separated Dutch said, "I just sent you and Sandy a letter on a ship bound for Amsterdam."

Kate's face looked tired and gaunt, but her sweet brown eyes flickered in firelight. She stared at Dutch for the longest moment and then finally said, "Sandy is dead."

XIV
Stunned

—ɯ—

*K*ate's sad words rolled off her quivering lips and stung Dutch like daggers. Her face, washed by the firelight, looked sullen, and her brown eyes were teary,

"How and when?" Dutch whispered.

Kathleen kept her hands on his shoulders. "June, last year," she said in a small voice.

They hugged again, the sounds of the crackling fire loud in their ears, time seemed to stand still.

Duncan's deep voice broke the silence, "It's getting dark, mate. You better get started back."

Dutch pulled away from Kate, ignoring his warning. "When did you leave Boston?"

Her sad face seemed to be etched in stone. "Last October."

Captain Hawk chimed in, "We were badly mauled rounding the Horn and had to put into a Spanish port for repairs. After the damn Spaniards fixed the ship, their government seized her. We were marooned in that filthy port for months."

"You're the only family I have now," Kathleen said, staring into Dutch's eyes.

"What of your son?" he asked.

A slight scowl chased her lips. "A week after Sandy died, I received a letter from the Navy, informing me that he had jumped ship somewhere in the Pacific. He is now listed as a deserter. Can I stay here with you?"

Dutch's heart filled with a sweeping tide of emotions. "Of course you can. But this is a savage place. Are you sure this is what you want?"

"Aye," she replied without hesitation. "I'll cook and care for you. It will be just like old times."

"Good," Duncan said, moving towards the baggage on the floor. "I'll help you load her things aboard the carriage."

Dutch gazed at her sad face and then moved to the luggage. He handed Kate the carpet bag and grasped one of the handles of the sea trunk. The two men lifted the heavy box and headed for the door. "My god, what do you have in here? Rocks?" Dutch asked as they crossed the room.

Kate's smiled as she put on her hat. "Everything that remains of my life is in that trunk."

With Captain Hawk on their heels, they went outside and loaded the baggage into the rear of the buggy. With that accomplished, Kate turned to the Captain with an outstretched hand, "Thank you, sir, for delivering me safely here. I hope I wasn't too much of a bother."

In the waning light, the skipper shook her hand. "Best damn cook I've ever had aboard ship. I'll come back at the end of next season and see if you want to return to Boston."

"Where will you winter, Captain?" Dutch asked.

"Nootka. We lost a bloody year because of those Spaniards."

Dutch helped Kate into the carriage, then walked around and climbed aboard, as well. Turning back to the two men on the porch, he said, "Thanks, Duncan, for your kindness. Captain, I hope to see you next year." Then he slapped the reins and rode out of the fort.

Under a thick, black layer of clouds, Dutch found the twilight dark and gloomy. Once he turned onto the back-door road, the darkness of the forest made it even more difficult to see. He trusted that Dolly knew the way, but still he looked around keenly, constantly alert.

The ride was quiet for the longest time. Then, just as it started to rain again, Kathleen broke the silence. "Did I do the right thing, coming here?"

With his gaze fixed on the obscure road, Dutch replied, "Reckon there be no right or wrong about it. You are here now, and you be a fine addition to my little family."

"Family? What family?"

Dutch glanced at Kate in the gloomy shadows and saw her confused expression. "Found my long-lost uncle in St. Louis, and a Negro girl wandering a wilderness trail, and of course there's King."

Kate grasped his arm gently. "I had no idea. I'm sorry to be putting myself upon you."

Dutch twisted her way. "How could you have known? You'll be no trouble."

The carriage splashed across a creek, and soon they were out of the dark forest and into open meadow. Dutch pointed down the slight rise. "That be our compound. I call it Joseph Point, after my father."

A few moments later, in the last glint of twilight, the buggy pulled into the darkened barn. Dutch dismounted and came around the carriage to help Kate down. When he looked up, he spotted Freddie rushing from the house in the glow of a lantern. When he entered the barn, he held up the oil lamp and saw Kate standing in the shadows. "What the hell!"

Dutch made quick introductions between Kate and his confused uncle. Then the men unloaded the buggy, unharnessed Dolly and placed her in her stall. With rain falling in earnest, the three ran from the barn, with the men sharing the weight of the heavy trunk.

Once inside the living quarters, they were greeted by King. He had Kathleen's scent in his snout in a flash, and started howling with joy as he jumped up on her. Cora, working at the stove, looked up at the commotion with a surprised face.

The men put the heavy trunk down at the foot of the stairway, and Dutch said to the room, "This is my dear friend Kate. She has come to stay with us, and has brought me tragic news of a dear friend who died."

Cora came over to Kate, extended her hand with a welcoming smile and a small curtsey. Freddie also welcomed her. Within moments, Kathleen stood next to the glowing fire with a glass of brandy in her hand. Dressed in a wrinkled blue gingham dress, with a sad, tired face, she spotted the bowler hat on the mantel.

Picking it up, she forced a smile. "How sweet. You wore my gift across the continent."

"Aye, it gave me good service," Dutch replied.

Kate took a sip of her brandy and told them of her misery in the past year.

"Sandy had not been the same since Dutch departed on his pilgrimage. He moped around the pub, complaining that he was getting too old for the business. I got him to hire some new help, but it just wasn't the same. He was still always grousin' about this or that. Then, one morning, when I went to wake him, I found him dead. The Doctor said it was his heart, and that he went peacefully in his sleep." Kate wiped a tear away with a hanky and continued. "Well, a few days after his funeral, this lawyer comes into the pub with Sandy's Last Will and Testament. I had no idea he had such papers. Anyhow, he left me the pub, and half of all his money. The other half he bequeathed to you, Dutch. *Money?* I thought. *What kind of money could Sandy have?* It was just like him, to leave me one last surprise. A few days later, when I was cleaning out his room, I started finding all sorts of money hidden away. There were gold and silver coins from all over the world, stashed deep in his boots, in his socks, under the rugs and stuffed under his mattress. When I counted up the money, he had just over a thousand dollars. That's why my trunk is so heavy. Sandy's legacy is inside."

Dutch nervously paced the floor, hanging on her every word, while mumbling to himself, "Sandy, I don't want your money."

With the storm raging outside, Freddie sat on one of the chairs in front of the fireplace, enthralled with Kate's story. Cora sat on the other chair, staring at the crackling fire, with a coffee mug in hand.

Dutch stopped and turned to Kate with a look of disbelief. "You traveled around the Horn with a thousand dollars? You're lucky to be alive! Most jack-tars would shank ya for that kind of money."

Finally, a small grin crossed her lips. "Not to worry Dutch. It was just your half. Anyhow, after I learned that my son had jumped ship, I decided to sell the pub and come out here to be with you. I got five thousand dollars for the pub, which is a great amount of money. So I invested the proceeds with your old friend, Tony the Spaniard, and paid Captain Hawk three hundred dollars to bring me out here."

"Three hundred dollars for passage? That's outrageous," Dutch retorted with a sour look. "What kind of outfit is Tony into?"

"He be getting into the steam tugboat business. He hopes to have a dozen boats working the harbor in the next few years. I own a good share of his enterprise."

Dutch's spirits brightened. "He's an honest bloke and, while I know nothing of steam engines, he surely would. Good for you. You have some security now."

Kathleen went on to explain how hard it had been to find a ship bound for the Pacific Northwest, and then convincing any captain to take a woman on such a voyage. "In the end, it was only my purse that talked," she concluded.

The conversation soon moved to the kitchen table, where Cora served up venison stew with fresh-baked bread. While taking their meal, they exchanged stories of their travels to the Pacific Coast. After dinner, Kate went to her trunk and retrieved a fat rawhide bag, which she dumped open on the table. "From my figuring, there be five hundred eight dollars and fifty two cents here." The bag's contents were mostly coins, silver and gold, and a few printed bank notes from all over the world. Everyone gleefully searched through the pile of money, calling out the different countries of origin.

"I never wanted this money," Dutch said, examining a German coin. "Where the hell do you think he got all this, Kate?"

Kathleen was finally smiling, and it was nice to have her joyful again. "I have no idea, most likely from tips and cutting cards with the customers. He was always a lucky bloke."

The banter went on to near midnight. By the end of the evening, Kate and Cora were fast friends, while Freddie had been mostly quiet and subdued. After letting the dog out one last time, Dutch and his uncle carried the trunk upstairs and put it in Cora's room, where Kate would stay. It had been an evening of many surprises, both tart and sweet. As for the money, Dutch had little use for it.

The next morning, Kate joined Dutch for his stroll to the point to see what the tide had brought in. With coffee mugs in hand, they walked under a cloudy sky.

"Your compound is big and impressive. Not what I expected to find," Kate said.

"Aye, it's a good place to be. Last year, we were living in a chicken coop."

Once at the beach, Dutch pointed out the local geography and talked of the different tribes. They used the telescope to search the river. Kate had many questions about the estuary, the weather and the fur trade. She was apprehensive about living amongst the Indians, but Dutch assured her that his alliance with the Clatsops was their shield against any trouble. "If you treat the natives with respect, you will get respect in return. They be like any other people, just finding their way in life."

As they walked back to the post, Dutch asked, "What do you think of my little family?"

Kate smiled. "Cora is a fine lass and I enjoy her, squeaky voice and all. But her stew last night was lacking. Will she be offended if I take over the cooking?"

"Nay, she is happiest tending the animals. What of my uncle?"

"He seems a little quiet. I think he might be jealous of me being here."

Dutch put a hand on Kate's shoulder, turning her to face him. "He's a hard worker, has learned the local language, and is one of the best blacksmiths I've ever seen. But he's lonely. Last night, I think you swept him off his feet."

Kathleen chuckled. "I hope not. If I wanted boots under my bed, they would be yours, not his. But there be too many years between us. So let's just leave those years in place."

As winter took hold, the troop found itself locked in a daily routine. Kate fit into the family like a glove. She cooked all the meals and kept the house. There was no grousing from anyone, her food was always savory and the living conditions favorable. Cora tended the livestock and mended fences, when she wasn't working in the shop. She enjoyed the barnyard and had named all of the animals, right down to the scrawniest chicken. Dutch and Freddie hunted almost every morning and tended their trap lines at least once a week. They also maintained the buildings and the dock. The rest of their time was consumed with trading with the local Indians. Even though the spruce beer had run out long ago, business remained good, with many inland Indians making the long trip downriver. Upstairs in the attic, their stack of pelts grew like moss on a tree.

Early in November, there was a break in the weather. Dutch took this opportunity to bring Kate back to the fort in the canoe. It was a cool, bright day on the water and, as Dutch paddled upriver, he pointed out different landmarks and made comments about the wildlife.

Kathleen traveled in the front of the boat, dressed in a heavy wool coat, with a bonnet on her head. With the sun on her face, she gazed out across the river, one hand shading her eyes. "It is so big, and void of man's handprint, that it's a little frightening. One could get lost here."

"Aye, that is why I love it. A man has elbow room here," Dutch replied pulling his paddle.

Kate twisted her head and looked back at him with an expression of awe. "This is what you meant when you talked about God's fingerprint."

The boat slid to the beach, next to the fort, and they walked up the slight rise and entered the compound. McDougal had asked Dutch to make two duplicate maps of the South Pass and the Sweetwater Trail, so that his men might find the way when they returned east. Dutch had been promised some trade goods for his efforts.

Climbing the post porch, they entered the trading room and found Duncan talking to one of his clerks. The Astorian warmly greeted his visitors and offered them coffee. With mug in hand, Kathleen searched the shelves and bins for whatever she needed, while the men went over the two new maps.

As they talked, Dutch learned that three Astorians had recently deserted. Duncan had dispatched other men to head them off from returning east. "I can't abide deserters. They set a bad example."

A few minutes later, with the maps safely folded inside his pouch, McDougal said, "Take whatever you want, folks. These maps will be very useful for our journey home."

Kate turned his way. "Where are your spices? I need nutmeg, garlic powder, some oregano, and any other spices you might have."

Duncan looked at her with disbelief. "We've got salt and pepper. That's about it."

Kate shook her head, "How about a double boiler? Would you have such a pan?"

Duncan scratched his head. "I have no idea what that is, ma'am."

Dutch chuckled at the conversation and inserted, "Kate, this be Astoria, not Boston."

In the end, Dutch and Kathleen paddled home with a bolt of cloth and two jugs of brandy.

Surprise ————

With short days and long nights, the howling winds swirled up the coast with one squall after another. The estuary sky turned almost black, and the surrounding mountains were lost in the clouds for weeks. Dreadful weather or not, the family still had chores to do, and the men still hunted, worked their trap lines and maintained the compound.

Kathleen was a great addition to the family, and in the evenings she provided a new energy to the Bible readings. She worked diligently with Cora, helping her to improve her reading and writing skills. Then Dutch or Freddie would read from one of the books that had been shipped in from Amsterdam. These new stories added a fresh excitement to the long, dreary, dark nights.

With Kate cooking, all the holidays were observed with special foods and lively celebrations. For Thanksgiving, she made a rich seafood stew, and for Christmas she butchered one of the hogs and made a ham dinner fit for a king. Because she had no fresh supply of spices, she ventured up into the forest and along the bay shores, collecting local mushrooms, roots and weeds that she dried and added to her cook pot. It was a time of warm harmony, and Dutch noticed that his uncle was always smiling and hovering around Kate in her kitchen.

As was their tradition, the group spent New Year's Eve in the smokehouse, dressed only in their small clothes. With rain dancing on the cedar boards, the friends huddled around the coals of the fire pit, sipping from mugs of fortified coffee. With the red-hot rocks steaming, Dutch raised his cup. "Here's to 1812. May she be as good as 1811."

Kate wiped her face with a wet cloth. "1811 wasn't so good for me, other than finding my way here. May 1812 bring us all promise."

With a drop of sweat on the point of her nose, Cora answered, "I found me my Negro chief, this year, and wonder if I should have taken him up on his offer."

Dutch chuckled. "He offered ye a good bargain. You could be his queen."

Kathleen was surprised to hear of the Negro Tillamook chief, and they talked about his offer. It was a joyful conversation, and they teased Cora about being a Negro Indian queen.

"I'm still waiting to find my queen," Freddie said, taking a drink. "Maybe, this new year, I will find her."

"Would you take a squaw?" Kate asked.

"Only if I have to," Freddie replied in a sad voice.

With the storm still raging, the family finally exited the smokehouse and ran for the chilly waters of the Columbia. After some exhilarating screams, they were back inside the living quarters, shivering by the fire. At midnight, Dutch and Freddie went to the front porch and fired off their muskets. Their report was answered by festive rifle fire from the fort.

During the winter months, Dutch and Freddie rode over to the fort a few times to check on the Astorians and to catch up on any news. After sending a few of their troop upriver to explore the many rivers and streams, the Astorians' numbers had dwindled to only a dozen men. And still there had been no word of the overland party.

Duncan McDougal returned their visits a few times, always arriving at the Point around meal time. He had learned of Kate's good cooking from Captain Hawk, and now he was eager to partake of her tasty meals.

On January 18th, eleven Astorians from the overland party finally arrived at Fort Astoria. Dutch and his uncle rode over to meet the men and hear the news of their crossing. Donald McKenzie, the commander of the troop, a seasoned trapper and frontiersmen, talked of the troubled passage. What Dutch had done in less than six months had taken them almost a year and a half. He told of the Blackfoot Indians being on the war path, and how they had traded their keelboats for horses to avoid any trouble. After many delays, and months later, they crossed the plains on horseback. Along the way, they killed hundreds of buffalo, jerking thousands of pounds of meat.

When they finally arrived on the Snake River, they released their horses and built canoes. "The idea sounded simple enough. We would float down the river all the way to the Columbia," he said, his face gaunt. But the river, just as Mountain Jack had said, was unnavigable. They lost two men to the currents, and a few supply canoes. Finally, they gave up on the river and started walking west.

Soon thereafter, with winter on their heels, the troop broke up into four parties. McKenzie and his men walked the south shore of the river, while William Price Hunt commanded a troop walking on the north shore. Some other men stayed behind to trap the Snake waters, while still others made their own way west. It was a miserable crossing for all. Without any food, they ate the pelts they carried and even devoured their own moccasins. Barefoot and near starvation, they finally came to the Columbia, where they traded rifles for three canoes. "We hunted for a few days, and ate our fill of fish before we descended the river," he concluded. "This was a journey from hell."

Dutch and Freddie spent the day at the fort, getting to know the other men and hearing the different stories of survival. That afternoon, as they rode back to their compound, they thanked the Lord Almighty for Mountain Jack's wisdom and experience.

The William Price Hunt troop of thirty men, one woman and two children arrived at the fort on February 15th. Over the next few months, most of the overland Astorians would straggle into the fort. In the end, of the sixty men who began the journey, only forty-five souls would make it to Astoria.

Shortly after the arrival of the large troop, Duncan McDougal paddled over to the point with William Hunt. The Astorians found Dutch and Cora restocking shelves inside the trading post.

"Dutch, I want you to meet Mr. Hunt. He's the overland Chief Factor of the Pacific Fur Company," Duncan said with a friendly smile.

Dutch and Hunt shook hands; his grip was as limp as a willow, and his eyes were gray as the winter sky. As Cora poured coffee, the men talked about the miserable passage. It was the same story of missteps and poor judgment. "At Fort Osage, Captain Clemson gave me your letter, Dutch," Hunt said with a cool glare. "Astor had an agreement with you, and he demands loyalty. You should have waited."

Dutch walked to his pouch, where it hung on a wall peg, and removed a parchment, which he handed to Hunt. "I have no trust in Astor. He tried to have me killed. The last time I saw him, I damn near cut off one of his ears, but he did sign this letter, declaring me a free trapper."

Mr. Hunt angrily glanced at the paper and handed it back. "He didn't expect you to be the competition. There isn't room for two trading posts on this river. Therefore, we are going to buy you out or drive you off."

"We have a good offer," Duncan quickly added. "We will buy ya out, lock, stock and barrel, and make you a partner in the company for your efforts."

"Or have our friends the Chinooks drive you off the land," Hunt added sternly.

Dutch stared at the Astorians for the longest moment, then turned back to his pouch and returned the letter to it. "You come into my shop and make threats? I'm disappointed, Duncan." Turning back to the room, he continued, "This is Clatsop land, and I have an alliance with them. Chief Coboway knows that your mystical 'vial of death' is just squaw talk. If he tells the Chinooks the truth of it, you will have an Indian uprising on your hands. No, gentlemen, I will not be driven off my land or bought out by Astor. And the Clatsops will stand with me."

Hunt glared at Dutch with open hostility.

"We had to try, Dutch," Duncan finally said. "We want no trouble with the Indians. But some of the partners believe you're a scab that needs to be picked."

Dutch smiled. "Many have tried, and I'm still here."

With much of the tension drained from the room, Cora sweetened the coffee with brandy, and the Astorians continued to talk about what was going on at the fort. They were running low on supplies and, with the many new mouths to feed, food was an issue of great concern. A supply ship was expected soon, and the partners had sent a small party of men to camp out at the top of Point Hancock. If they saw a vessel approaching, they were to set fire to the forest as a beacon. It was a desperate measure, but the Astorians were in a desperate way. Hearing of their needs, Dutch offered to loan them some supplies. "We can spare some flour and beans."

"I've can give ya two balls of goat cheese," Cora added with a sincere look.

Duncan looked surprised by their kind offer. "Frontier life is a funny thing," he replied. "We came here with anger on our lips, and leave here obliged to you."

With the longer days and improving weather, Dutch took Kathleen out sailing on the estuary. They dug for digger-clams on the south spit, gathered mussels from the rocks on Point Hancock, and fished the river for spring Chinook salmon. He also took her to the Clatsop village, where he introduced her to Chief Coboway.

The Indians were surprised to see that he had yet another woman with different-colored skin. The people were curious about her but respectful, and paid her tribute with a basket of anchovies. She, in turn, handed out fresh-baked sugar cookies, which was a treat the Indians had never tasted before. They spent a delightful afternoon with the Clatsops.

In April, three groups of Astorians journeyed back up-river. One group was heading to St. Louis with a metal box containing dispatches for Astor. Another party was setting out to recover the supplies left behind by Hunt's troop on the Snake River, while still another group paddled up the Willamette River to open a trading post. The Astorians were at full strength again, and on the move.

One morning in May, Dutch stood on the point with his telescope and watched a ship enter the river and sail for Baker's Bay. Later he would learn it was the fort's supply ship, *Beaver.* The Captain, Cornelius Sowles, was a timid sailor who refused to move down-river. The coastal schooner the Astorians had built was used to move the supplies from the ship to the fort. This was a long, slow process, and it took weeks before the *Beaver* could set sail again.

During this time, Mr. Hunt returned the supplies he had borrowed, and causally commented that he would soon be sailing with the ship. "There is a northern Russian island called Sitka. We hear they have thousands of seal skins to trade. I will return in the fall."

Dutch was pleased to see him go. Of all the Astorians, Hunt wasn't his favorite.

In the middle of June, the supply ship from Amsterdam finally arrived. It was a sloop named the *Sea Urchin*, under the command of Lieutenant William Hart. The first officer was a young, lanky fellow named Ensign Evans. The ship boasted eight six-pound cannons and two swivel guns fore and aft. She had a crew of fourteen sailors and had departed Amsterdam on New Year's Day. The ship had made the passage around the Horn late in the season, then sailed for the Sandwich Islands, where she spent a few weeks taking on supplies and making repairs.

Dutch and his uncle stood on the floating dock, watching the heavily burdened sloop maneuver the approach and then drop anchor, fore and aft. Once the snap lines were in place, they were invited aboard the ninety-ton ship and shown to the Captain's cabin.

Seated at his chart table, Lieutenant Hart wasn't much older than Dutch. With a firm handshake and a friendly smile, he invited the men to take a seat. "Your river chart was invaluable for crossing the Bar, this morning. It's nice to meet you, Mr. Blackwell," the Captain said.

"Our river bar is like our weather, unpredictable as hell," Dutch replied, taking his seat.

The two men talked about the ship's crossing and the cargo they carried. The *Sea Urchin* was a seasoned ship and had seen duty all over the world. Mr. Hart had started his career aboard the ship when he was just sixteen, and had worked his way up the ranks. He seemed like a fine fellow, and Dutch invited him and the mate to dinner that evening.

"How is the Commodore?" Dutch asked.

Hart pushed two envelopes across the table. "The Commodore sends his greetings and a few dispatches."

Dutch reached for the parchments and replied, "Had the *Mary Rose* returned to port before you sailed?"

"Nay, she was expected in a few weeks. How was your season with her?"

"Fine," Freddie inserted. "She sailed from here with near fifteen hundred pelts aboard."

As his uncle and the Captain talked of the previous season, Dutch opened the smallest envelope and read a short message from the Commodore. It instructed Dutch to spend the summer aboard the *Sea Urchin,* showing the Lieutenant and his crew his methods of coastal trading. The Commodore also wrote of the strong market for otter and beaver pelts. He closed with a warning: "War clouds are building. Keep alert!"

With a sour look, Dutch shook his head slowly; another bloody war! He had looked forward to remaining on the river for the season, not wasting his time teaching pilgrims the way of the wilderness. But that was not to be.

The second envelope was a Bill of Lading that listed all the cargo the ship carried. Dutch glanced through the stack of papers and put them back into the fat envelope.

"Guess I'm spending my summer with you, Captain. Sorry for that surprise," Dutch said, with a disappointed expression.

Lieutenant Hart got up from the table with a grin and walked to the cabin door. "I have a surprise for you, Mr. Blackwell." He opened the door and shouted down the passageway, "Mr. Evans, bring in the prisoner!"

With curiosity, Dutch heard a door open, and a few footsteps. His gaze was glued on the open doorway as a short sailor appeared, wearing tattered trousers, a dirty waistcoat, and a tricorn hat on his head. His gaze was downcast as he entered the cabin.

The captain reached up and peeled off the prisoner's hat. Long golden locks fell out from beneath the cap, and the Lieutenant gently raised the prisoner's filthy chin to the room. "A few weeks out of Amsterdam, we found this stowaway. She would not tell us her name, but says she knows you, Mr. Blackwell."

With the cabin dead silent, Dutch's heart sank. The girl was Mary Jacobson! With a muddled mind, Dutch blurted, "Do you know who the hell this girl is?"

Lieutenant Hart stared at Dutch. "That's for you say," he replied, clearly confused.

Like some dock tramp, Mary stood in the doorway in her dirty clothes, her blue eyes pleading for anonymity.

"Well, Mr. Blackwell, do know this woman?" the Captain demanded.

"Aye," Dutch replied, moving towards her. "Her name is Mary. We took a meal together in Boston, a few years back. I will take her off your hands, Lieutenant."

"Good. She be a distraction to my crew," the relieved captain said. "Mr. Evans, we will be dining ashore this evening. Set the watches and prepare to begin unloading our cargo tomorrow morning."

After retrieving a small valise from a dingy cabin, Dutch and Freddie quickly ushered Mary off the ship. As they walked down the dock, Dutch handed his uncle the satchel and said, "Tell Kate there will be three extra for dinner. Move your traps into my room. Mary will sleep in your room. She is going to need a bath, so have Cora ready the copper tub. We will walk awhile and be in shortly."

With his mind swirling with questions, Dutch and Mary strolled down to the point. Then, standing in the sunshine, they began to talk. She told him that she had been unhappy at home, finding her life filled with studies and social events she detested. "I'm not like my sisters, who love their clothes and soirees. I long for adventure, not being a lady of means." In a voice full of rebellion, Mary told of how her father persisted in ridiculing her and making unreasonable demands. "He treats me like a child and wants absolute control of my life," she said, her eyes dancing with anger.

Dutch couldn't believe he was standing next to her.

She went on to explain that she had overheard the Commodore talking about sending the *Sea Urchin* to the Columbia, and had made her plans to stow away. Mary told her mother that she was going to stay with relatives in a nearby city, and on New Year's Eve she disguised herself as a wharf ruffian and snuck aboard the ship. "When the crew finally found me in the forward hold, they had no idea who I was. All I told them was that we were friends. Dutch, please don't betray me."

For most of the passage, Captain Hart had kept her locked in the cabin boy's nook and, while she took her meals with the officers, she was never permitted to roam the ship. When the *Sea Urchin* arrived in the Sandwich Islands, she was allowed onto the beach to bathe and wash her clothes, but that had been about the extent of her freedom.

"Your family will be worried sick," Dutch said. "You will have to return home on the *Sea Urchin* after she unloads."

Mary reached out and put a hand on Dutch's cheek, looking him straight in eye. "No! I didn't come this far just to turn tail for home. I left a letter in my father's desk that explains my actions." Mary removed her hand from Dutch's face and gazed at him with pleading eyes.

"You told him that you were coming to see me?"

"Aye," Mary replied quickly. "He knows the truth and might follow me, but I hoped we would have the summer for you to show me this wilderness first."

"This is no place for silly infatuations."

Mary's smudged face turned to stone. "I am not a foolish girl. Something special happened when we met and, like this land, I thought it was worth exploring."

Dutch reached out and grasped one of her hands. "It is worth exploring. Your tenacity is impressive. How old are you?"

Mary squeezed his hand. "I be nineteen soon. I'm no longer a girl, Dutch. I'm a woman. You will have to deal with that."

Dutch nodded with a grin. "Fine, but let's get you cleaned up first. I have some amiable folks for you to meet."

Summer of Splendor ————

By the time they returned to the trading post, Kathleen and Cora were filling the copper bathtub with hot water by the stove.

Dutch introduced his visitor. "This be Mary Rose. She is an old friend from Boston. Kate, you may recall me talking of her. She will be staying with us awhile."

With a warm smile, Kathleen extended her hand to Mary, saying, "I remember you told me she was a beautiful young lady, not the stinker that stands before me."

Mary shyly shook her head. "It's been weeks since my last bath, and months of wearing the same tattered clothes. I apologize for my appearance."

"No need for regrets, dearie," Cora said in her squeaky voice with a smile. "We'll get you cleaned up like a newborn."

The women shooed the men and the dog from the living quarters, with firm instructions not to return until suppertime.

They set to working the trading post, while Dutch explained to his uncle what the hell was going on. "She be like the forbidden fruit to me, enchanting and tempting. But her presence could destroy all that we have worked for."

Freddie listened to his nephew ramble on about Mary for the better part of the afternoon, his constant chirping only stopping when a few Indians came by to make some trades.

Finally Freddie said, "You've done nothin' wrong, Dutch. She came here of her own accord. Just keep it that way, and she'll soon be gone."

Captain Hart and Ensign Evans walked through the post door, late in the afternoon. In their neat, clean uniforms, they walked around the trading room, inspecting the many items and asking about values. As they moved along, Dutch talked of the pelts the local Indians traded. "Sea otter is the most valued, but beaver, elk, cougar and fox skins all have worth, as well. Keep a keen eye out for any pelt that has unusual coloring. The Chinese pay top dollar for unique skins."

"How many pelts did you take in, during the winter?" Captain Hart asked, examining a copper kettle.

"We have near three hundred, up in the attic," Freddie answered proudly. "Some we trapped and some we traded. They be all prime furs."

Kate opened the door from the living quarters and announced that supper was ready, and then turned back to her stove. As the men walked towards the residence, Dutch continued, "If we have a good season up north, by the time you sail, you should have fifteen-hundred skins aboard. That should please the Commodore."

Once inside the living quarters, Dutch introduced the women to the officers. Kate was stirring a pot at the stove, while Cora poured wine at the table.

"Smells delicious, ma'am," Captain Hart said to Kate. "What's cooking?"

Kathleen smiled. "An old goulash I call pig-knuckle stew."

The men took their seats at the split-log table and reached for goblets of wine. Dutch looked about the room. "Where's Mary?"

"She'll be down shortly, Mr. Dutch. We had to mend her up a proper dress," Cora replied.

Dutch heard footsteps and saw Mary descending the log staircase in a light-green dress with a white bodice. Her figure was full, and her freshly washed, pulled-back golden hair glistened in the light. With all eyes watching she arrived at the foot of the stairs and turned to the room, her face was small, earnest and youthful with her full red lips curled in a smile.

Dutch could not believe his eyes; her beauty sucked the air from the silent room. Both officers quickly got to their feet as she approached the table.

"Nice see you again, ma'am," the overwhelmed Captain said.

With his gaze glued to Mary, the Ensign stiffened and bowed slightly. "Sorry if we offended you in any way, Miss. We had no idea you be a lady."

Cora poured her a goblet of wine, and everyone took their seats again. Captain Hart asked Mary a few questions about herself and her family, but she answered coyly. The conversation soon turned to the upcoming fur season, and the women learned for the first time that Dutch was planning to sail north with the *Sea Urchin*. All three of the ladies glanced at him with sour faces, but didn't say a word. Dutch returned their glares with a nod, and the men continued to talk of the business at hand.

With a second glass of wine in hand, Kathleen served the stew with warm, fresh bread and goat cheese. It was a tasty meal, with lively conversations about everyone's tribulations upon arriving on the Columbia River. Freddie told stories of Mountain Jack, while the officers talked of rounding the Horn. During this table chatter, Dutch kept sneaking glances at Mary, and pinching himself. Was she really here?

The meal ended with a glass of brandy and plans for unloading the ship.

Finally, getting up from the table, the Captain and Ensign politely thanked their hosts and returned to the *Sea Urchin* in the waning evening light. As Dutch and Freddie returned from showing their guests out, Kate lit a lamp and placed it on the table. "I think we should have a talk, Dutch," she said with a stern look. The women had been mostly quiet during the meal, and now they wanted to talk. The men took their seats again.

Kathleen poured herself more brandy at the stove and then joined everyone. "Mary told us the truth of it. She be a runaway, with her father more than likely close behind, so you can't spend a summer away, leaving us to deal with him."

Cora twisted to Dutch. "That wouldn't be right. He be *your* partner. Anyhow, you promised to take me back to the Tillamooks, this summer."

Mary stared at him, as well. "I came all this way to explore your land. Won't you give me the summer to find my way?"

"Mary is a fine lady, Dutch," Kate quickly inserted. "She just needs some time to figure things out."

Dutch was surprised to hear their reactions. "Back in Boston, I gave the Commodore my word to show his men the way of coastal trading. If I don't go with these greenhorns, their lives could be in peril."

"I can go with them," Freddie asserted with a determined look. "I know the signs and the Indian way of barter."

In the lamp light, Dutch looked carefully into his uncle's face; he had come a long way. "Are you sure of this? There could be great danger in this enterprise."

Freddie looked around the table with a face full of confidence. "Aye, I'm sure. I know the value of tribute, and the character of the Indians. There will be no trouble."

"Good," Kate replied with a smile. "And we will have Dutch around, all summer."

It took the ship's crew five days to unload and store nearly sixty tons of cargo. The trading floor overflowed with goods, while the attic was crammed with foodstuffs and extra supplies. Even the loft of the barn was packed with casts of molasses, lamp oil and gunpowder. God forbid if there was a fire; the whole damn compound would explode.

Just before the *Sea Urchin* departed, Dutch gave Captain Hart a chart of the northern waters that showed where some of the Indian villages could be found. He stressed again the importance of staying safe and trading fairly. "The Indians are the masters of their lands. Always pay a tribute and show respect."

With a favorable tide and winds, the ship departed on the morning of June 20th. All the women had come down to the dock to say farewell to Freddie. Now they stood with sad faces, watching the *Sea Urchin* proceed down river. "I hope he doesn't get seasick," Kate said, shading her eyes with her hand. It wouldn't be the same without Freddie around.

Kathleen and Cora were more than pleased to have another woman in the house. There was something special about Mary; she was easy as a spring breeze. Cora made a fringed deerskin frock for her, and a pair of moccasins, while Kate sewed up other garments from cloth she found in the trading post. Within a few days, Mary had a handmade wardrobe which she wore with great pride.

Soon after Freddie's departure, Dutch loaded up the canoe and, with Mary paddling up front, headed for his trap lines. It was a brilliant summer morning, with hardly a hint of a breeze. Mary had spent her life around boats, and she took to the Indian dugout with ease. As they crossed Young's Bay, Dutch told her of the land and pointed out Humpback Mountain in the far distance.

She stopped paddling and twisted his way in her buckskins. "Have you ever climbed those peaks?"

Dutch sliced his paddle in the water. "Reckon not. Been too busy surviving."

Mary's gazed at him reproachfully. "That's a shame. This endless land needs exploring." Twisting forward again, she dug her paddle deep into the water.

As they moved up the Netul River, they passed the ruins of old Fort Clatsop, and Dutch talked of Lewis and Clark. It was a story Mary vaguely remembered reading about. "They were all brave men," Dutch concluded, working his paddle, "and worthy of their place in history."

Once on the trap lines, Mary waded into the shallows with Dutch and watched carefully as he checked and set the traps. The snares produced two beavers, that day, which Dutch gutted creekside with his sea-knife. She was enthralled with the furry little animals, and asked many questions. Once the last trap was checked, they hunted the upper reaches of the river. Dutch rambled on about different animal signs and their particular habits, but no game came under his rifle that day.

On their way back down the river, they caught two fat rainbow trout, then pulled ashore, where they ate the fish Indian-style. As they sat around the small camp fire, Mary commented that it was the tastiest fish she had ever eaten. After that, with a slight breeze rustling the trees, they paddled for home. Dutch silently thanked the Lord for sending Mary to him. It had been a splendid day.

The very next day, an hour after the rooster had crowed, Dutch and Mary saddled up Scout and Willow, and rode south for the Humpback Mountains. They traveled the shoreline of Young's Bay and then up the Kilhowanah River. As they moved along the trail, they talked of the countryside, home and family. Once well above the tide water, they forged across the river and headed south. The meadows they crossed were filled with thickets and downed snags, with many creeks and rills flowing across the land. It was a demanding trek, with no single game trail leading the way.

Finally, they came upon a pathway that meandered through a stand of timber so tall and dense that sunlight could not reach the forest floor. As they moved through the ferns of this virgin rainforest, Dutch talked of the towering redwoods, and told stories of his family when he just a younker. "We lived on a small stream the locals called Skunk Creek. The Indians believed it was a place of evil spirits, so they never bothered us."

Mary asked many questions, and heard more about his family's life on the frontier. She spoke of her childhood, as well, but her life was a stark contrast to Dutch's early years.

Late in the morning, they emerged from the dark forest and found themselves looking up at the tall twin peaks. Hobbling their mounts, they trekked up the steep western pillar on foot. As they ascended the pinnacle, they found new views at every turn. Within the hour, they stood silently on top of the last boulder, gazing at a spectacular view of the Pacific Ocean. The cobalt blue horizon line was so vivid that they could make out the curvature of the Earth and hear the distant crashing surf. With the sun on their faces, Dutch pointed north to the Columbia River Bar and to the south, Tillamook Head. He put his arm around Mary's shoulder and proudly pronounced, "We now stand where no man has ever stood before."

Mary turned to him, overwhelmed. "I knew if I came here, that I would fall in love with this land."

Dutch stared into her beautiful blue eyes. Then, with her golden hair dancing in the breeze, he kissed her. Her welcoming full lips tasted sweet and were as soft as a cloud.

When they slowly parted, Dutch whispered, "I have a confession. I've killed men before, but I've never kissed a girl before."

Mary studied his dimpled, chiseled face and put two fingers on his lips. "No more confessions. All our yesterdays are forgiven. All we care about is our tomorrows." Then she brashly pulled him close, and they kissed again.

Holding hands, they turned around on the mountaintop, gazing out at the glorious views. They talked of the green sea, of tall trees in the east and of the vastness of the ocean in the west. This virgin land showed God's fingerprint with every view.

Just before descending the mountain, Dutch kissed Mary one last time and said to her, "You are right. This land, like us, needs to be explored."

The dog had taken to Mary, as well. During most meals, he curled up under the table next to her and waited patiently for any scraps she might hand down. During the Bible sessions, King curled up by the fire, always with one eye on Mary. If she had to use the privy, King would be the first out the door.

One evening, after Cora and Mary had retired, Kate and Dutch sat at the table, drinking coffee. "Your dog is quite fickle. He followed me around when I first got here, and now his affections are with Mary." Kathleen smiled. "He is as smitten with her as you are. That's a blessing, Dutch. She is an exceptional lady. But take your courtship slow. Enjoy this time together."

That night in bed, just as sleep arrived, Dutch's father spoke in his ear. *God will bless this union.*

The next few weeks flew by in a blissful blur. Dutch took Mary hunting, and showed her how to use a rifle and dress out game. She proved to be an enthusiastic fledgling, a steadfast shot with expert butchering skills. They went sailing on the estuary, taking day trips to Point Hancock, the south spit and Baker's Bay. It was a time of discovery, not only of the land, but of each other, as well.

As June blended into July, they rode to Fort Astoria, where Dutch proudly introduced her to some of the partners. During this visit, Duncan introduced his new wife, a Chinook squaw named Rainbow. She was one of Chief Comcomly's daughters, and she wore a buckskin frock decorated with seashells, with a robe of bird feathers around her shoulders. Her figure was full and her copper-skinned head was sharply sloped.

The two women were fascinated with one another, Rainbow had never seen a white woman or anyone with golden hair before, and Mary had never met a squaw. Dutch translated a lively conversation. There was much giggling and laughter as the two ladies chatted with one another.

With the trees rustling, they rode for home on the back-door trail. Mary asked why Duncan had married an Indian. Dutch explained that there was a long tradition of trappers marrying squaws to strengthen their alliances with the tribes.

Mary giggled and replied, "I am surprised you haven't married a Clatsop woman to strengthen your alliance."

From his saddle, Dutch turned to Mary with a smile. "Been waiting for a maiden from a more powerful tribe."

Mary looked confused. "What tribe?"

Dutch reined in Scout, and Mary rode up next to him. With a bright face, he replied, "The Amsterdam tribe."

It took a moment for his meaning to sink in. When it did, Mary's face lit up like the sun. "Mr. Blackwell, are you asking me to be your wife?"

"That be the truth of it, if you'll have me," Dutch answered, with a serious look.

They climbed down from their horses and into each other's arms. After a long kiss, Mary looked into his face and softly replied, "I'll always be yours."

Subterfuge ————

That evening, Dutch and Mary told Kathleen and Cora of their engagement. "When the *Sea Urchin* returns with Freddie, I'll ask Lieutenant Hart to marry us," Dutch said with passion in his voice.

Kate smiled at the couple as they sat holding hands at the table. "You two were meant for each other," she said, passing around a platter of food. "But Mary is still a runaway, and her father might be close at hand. If he appears, Dutch, there is going to be trouble."

"He will not talk me out of this," Mary said firmly.

Dutch smiled fondly at her and got up from the table to fetch the coffee pot.

"While we wait, we can sew you a proper wedding gown," Cora said with a bright face.

As Dutch returned to the table with the pot, he looked at Kate. "August is upon us, and I'll need to spend some time at the salt works before the salmon season. Reckon I'll take Mary and sail down to the salt-cove. We'll camp out on the beach."

Kathleen's expression turned sour. "I reckon not, Dutch. It isn't proper for an unchaperoned lady to camp out on a beach with a man. This might be the wilderness, but there are still rules of proper courtship."

"It wouldn't be right, if her father got here and Mary was gone," Cora added.

Sadly, Mary nodded her head in agreement. "They are right. I'll stay here. Cora can show me how to trade with the Indians."

"And I'll teach her to cook," Kate said with a smile.

A few days later, Dutch loaded the copper still into the boat and sailed for the Clatsop village. There he hired a brave called Falcon, who had worked with Freddie at the salt works the year before. Under a clear sky, the two men sailed for the cove, some twenty miles down the coast. They spent ten long, lonely days distilling the sea water into two hundred pounds of sea salt. When they finally sailed for home, Dutch was excited by the thought of being reunited with Mary.

However, when he arrived at the Point, only King was waiting for him on the dock. As he tied up the sailboat, he noticed that the canoe was missing. "Where did the girls go, boy?" he asked, kneeling in front of his happy dog.

King's smiling snout and wagging tail gave no indication of trouble. Dutch and his dog walked to the house, but it was empty. They checked the trading post, and found Cora sweeping the floor. From her, Dutch learned that Kathleen and Mary had taken the canoe across the river to dig for clams.

Two lone women on the river wasn't a good notion, and he started to worry.

It took almost an hour to unload the salt and store it away in the barn. As Dutch worked, he fretted about the women being gone. There were many dangers lurking in the forest, and the ladies were only city girls. He cursed himself for not being with them.

Finally, in the early afternoon, their canoe came into view. As they paddled up to the dock with bright faces, Dutch scolded them. "Where the hell have you been? I've been worried sick about you!"

Mary handed him a large basket of clams. "This is not the welcome I expected."

"We were in no danger," Kate added, handing over a basket of greens. "I had one of your hand cannons with me."

Dutch knelt to the dock and held the boat as the two women got out. "You should have taken King."

After Dutch had tied up the canoe and risen to his feet, Mary approached him with an alluring look. "We are pleased that you are home. No more fretting."

Dutch's anger melted away like snow as she kissed his cheek.

Over the next few weeks, Dutch and Mary made day trips up-river, trading with the numerous villages along the shores. These were special times, as they could talk about life, the Indian cultures and anything else under the sun. He also discovered that, while he had been at the salt works, the three women had become as thick as thieves. Cora had taught Mary some Indian signs and how to trade with the locals. Kathleen now accepted Mary as one of her brood, and the two had formed a mother-and-daughter bond. Dutch was pleased that Mary felt at home on the river.

On the last day of August, they made a day trip up-river to a village of Multnomah Indians. There, they spent a few hours trading trinkets from the boat. Early in the afternoon, they sailed for home. It had been a wondrous day, and the Indians had traded some beautiful hand-crafted gems that Mary now cherished. "Feel the craftsmanship of this purse, and look at the details of the beading!" she exclaimed.

Dutch held the bag and agreed, then tacked the boat with the wind again.

The miles melted away as the couple talked of the accomplishments of the many inland Indians. Late in the afternoon, however, the tide turned against them, and the wind died out. Dutch reckoned they were only a few miles from home and decided to row into an island lagoon to wait for an evening breeze.

Once the anchor was set, Mary put on the coffee pot, and the couple soon sat in the open cockpit, drinking the brew. Dutch removed the tiller handle and set it aside, then went below and retrieved two beaver pelts they could use as cushions. The water of the little cove was as still as glass, and birds filled the island trees, singing their summer songs. It was a beautiful place, and time slipped by as they talked of their future together. With the late afternoon sun chasing the horizon, Dutch kissed Mary and told her of his love.

She pulled him close and shyly whispered, "Have you been with a woman before?"

Dutch looked into her blue eyes and shook his head slowly. "Nay."

A grin curved Mary's lips. "I am surprised no Indian maidens have been with you."

Dutch felt embarrassed. "A Lakota medicine man offered me his granddaughter, once, but I resisted – something I cannot seem to do with you."

She boldly pulled him close and kissed him. "That's alright… I'm a virgin, as well. We have saved ourselves for each other."

"It's my unworldliness that worries me," Dutch answered, feeling his face turning red.

Mary smiled coyly and put a hand on his cheek. "We can discover each other without any shame. You stay here."

She moved to the cabin hatch and went below. Moments later, she reappeared with a blanket around her shoulders. She moved to Dutch and let the comforter fall to the deck. Her naked body was beautiful, backlit by the setting sun. Dutch sat gazing at her, his eyes filled with glory. He stood and they came together in a loving embrace. "Here's a blanket for you," Mary whispered with a bashful smile.

The next thing Dutch recalled clearly, they were wrapped in their blankets, watching stars race across the night sky. For each shooting star, there was a kiss.

At the muffled sounds of water lapping, Dutch's eyes snapped open to a predawn twilight. Resting next to him, with her head on his shoulder, was Mary. The blanket they slept under was covered with dew.

He looked at Mary, nestled in his arms. It had been a night of splendor he would never forget, but now it was the morning of reality. Gently, Dutch nudged her, saying softly, "Mary, it's time to wake."

She slowly opened her eyes and blinked a few times. When she saw Dutch's hovering face, a smile chased over her lips. "Good morning. What time is it?"

"It be dawn. We slept here all night. Kathleen is going to be worried, and mad as a hornet."

Mary raised her head up and looked around the boat with sleepy eyes. "There be no shame in it. We did nothing wrong."

Dutch pulled their blanket back, and Mary turned her naked body to him. Putting one hand on her face, he kissed her soft lips. "Good morning, my love. We better get a move on."

Within the half hour, they rowed out of the cove and onto the river. Mary hoisted the sail and then nestled close to Dutch at the tiller. As the island slipped away in their wake, Mary looked back and said, with a fond smile, "We should name that cove Discovery."

It was a brilliant morning on the river. The clear blue sky was filled with birds of all sorts, while the surrounding green mountains tightly clasped white wispy clouds. With the sail billowing, the westerly breeze was just fresh enough to keep the boat slicing through the calm teal waters.

As they sailed around Tongue Point, they got their first good view down-river. After passing Scowl Bay, Dutch noticed a ship anchored off the dock at Joseph Point. Mary took the tiller and Dutch stood, using his telescope to get a better view. "Your father has arrived. That be the *Mary Rose*," he said, collapsing the spyglass. "I would know her jib anywhere."

Mary smiled up at him. "You would, eh? Well, it seems that Judgment Day is upon us. Do not allow Father to dissuade us in any way. Promise me, Dutch."

Mary's face had turned serious, and Dutch could see fear in her eyes. "I promise."

They sailed past the *Mary Rose*, reefed the sail, and then rowed to the dock and tied up. They were surprised to find the silver-haired Commodore waiting on the wharf. It was just 8 AM when they stepped ashore.

"Grandfather, what are you doing here?" Mary asked as she rushed to the old man and gave him a hug.

He glared at her angrily. "Your Father is in my cabin, waiting. Dutch and I need to talk, while you make peace with him."

Just then, Kathleen rushed down to the wharf with a sad face. As she approached, she snapped, "They got here yesterday. I promised them you would be back before sunset. When you didn't arrive, things got ugly. That Captain is a tyrant. Where have you been?"

Dutch calmly stared at her, and then at the Commodore. "We lost the wind and fell asleep, last night, anchored in a cove. There is no shame to it. Nothing happened."

The Commodore nodded at the ship. "Mary don't keep your father waiting." Then he turned to Dutch. "We have to talk, here and now. Kathleen, please give us this time with no interference."

Kate looked at the old man for a moment with a frown, then turned away. As she walked back down the dock, she shrugged. "I'll be inside the house, Dutch."

Without a word, the men walked down to the Point and stood in the morning sun, looking out at the estuary. The old man was a distinguished-looking gent, with his tall, lean body, weathered face and rust-colored eyebrows. "There can be nothing between you and Mary. Do you understand?" he finally said, still staring out at the river.

"Commodore, look at me," Dutch replied in a firm voice.

The old man turned to him.

"Mary will be my wife. She has agreed. There is nothing you or her father can do about that."

The old man's sad eyes looked away. "Impossible."

"Nay, it isn't" Dutch retorted. "I know you consider me just a lowly frontiersman, but Mary loves me, and this land and I love her. We will wed."

The Commodore's brown eyes glared back at him. With a gloomy face, he finally said, "I will tell you why you are wrong. My full name is Horace Joseph Clarke. Does this name have any meaning to you?"

Dutch looked confused. "Nay, other than that my father was called Joseph."

The Commodore nodded his head slowly. "I will share my secret. Just before the Revolutionary War, when I was but a young ensign, my ship put into Boston Harbor. It was my first visit to the colonies, and I wandered the town, taking in the culture. In one of the shops,

I met a beautiful young lady named Martha. Her husband Samuel was off fighting the Indian wars. God forgive us, we fell in love. The liaison only lasted a few weeks before my ship departed. Many years later, I received a letter from Martha, informing me that she was dying and that I had fathered a child. She had named the boy Joseph Blackwell."

As the old man spoke, Dutch recalled finding a similar letter in his father's effects. That was where he had seen the name Clarke before. It took a moment for the full weight of the words to settle upon his shoulders. "So that makes you my grandfather?"

"Aye," the old man replied, with his eyes afire. "Now you know why you cannot wed my granddaughter. Your children could be idiots."

"When did you know all this?"

"I suspected it at our luncheon in Boston."

Dutch felt such sudden pain he might die of it. Staring back at Horace, not knowing how to respond, he turned slowly and walked back up the rise that lead to the compound.

From the shore, the Commodore called, "I hope you will keep this confidence."

Dutch made no reply. Instead, aimlessly, he wandered the grounds, trying to sort out what he had just learned. He was kin to Mary, blood kin. His name wasn't Blackwell, Freddie was only his half-uncle, and his grandfather lived! Dutch's gut felt as if it had been kicked by a mule. How could his devotion to Mary be ripped away with a few simple words?

Soon, he found himself standing inside the barn. What was he to do? He had given Mary his word, but marrying blood kin was a sin. He closed his eyes and said a silent prayer. When he finished, his father's voice was in his ear. '*You don't know the truth of it. Stand by your woman.*'

With those words swirling in his head, a feeling of determination swept his body. He turned from the barn and walked to the house, where he found Kate at her stove.

"Has Mary returned?"

"No," she answered sadly. "They are all still on the ship."

"She is going to need you, Kate. Come with me. We are going aboard, as well."

Dutch and Kathleen marched down the dock and up the boarding ladder without a word. Once on the deck, they were greeted by Mr. Person. With a smile and an outstretched hand, the mate said, "Nice seeing you again, Mr. Blackwell."

Dutch shook his hand firmly. "Where's the Captain?"

"He be in the Commodore's cabin with Mary."

Dutch turned for the quarterdeck, with Kate on his heels. They moved down the aft hatch and through a dark passageway, and soon found themselves standing in front of the cabin door. Without knocking, Dutch pushed open the mahogany hatchway and entered the compartment.

The two aft windows washed the stateroom with morning light, but the tension in the air hung over the cabin like a shroud. The Commodore sat behind his chart table, with a coffee mug in hand. Captain Jacobson stood next to him, wearing an angry expression. Across from them was Mary, slumped in a chair. Her eyes were red and puffy, and it was clear that she had been crying.

Dutch glared at the Captain. "Nice seeing you again, Eric. Are you finished interrogating your daughter?"

Mary twisted to look at him, her face sad. "Grandfather says he has dissuaded you. Oh, Dutch, you promised."

"How dare you barge in here? This is family business. Get the hell out of here," the Captain shouted.

Dutch turned to the two men. "Blood kin or not, I will wed Mary. We just won't have any children."

Eric's face turned from anger to bewilderment in an instant. "What the hell are you talking about?"

Dutch twisted back to Mary. With Kate standing next to her, he knelt and continued, "If we have no children, they can't be idiots."

The room went silent. Mary cocked her head with an odd look. "What you are talking about?"

Dutch stood and turned to the old man in frustration. "So Horace hasn't told you the truth of it? Well, Commodore, do I tell them or do you?"

Horace looked down at his coffee mug. "I was hoping you would keep my confidence," he muttered.

"Not when your secret is ruinous to Mary," Dutch replied sternly.

"What the hell is going on? What secret?" Eric demanded.

The old man lifted his head and gazed sadly at Mary. He hesitated a moment, and then, with his fingers nervously tapping the top of the chart table, he repeated what he had confided to Dutch.

As the story unfolded, Captain Jacobson slumped in his chair, staring at the deck. Mary and Kate listened to the Commodore, glued to his every word. Once he had concluded, he said, "That be why this union is impossible. Your children could be dimwitted."

Mary started to sob, and Kate put her arm across her shoulder. "But if they have no children, there would be no risk," she said sharply to the Commodore. "And please stop referring to 'idiots' and 'dimwits.' They are all God's children."

"The problem is not with you, Mary," Dutch said, standing over her. "It's about me and my bloodline."

"Stop!" Captain Jacobson shouted angrily. He raised his head and looked around the cabin, his face ash-gray. "Mary is *not* blood kin to Mr. Blackwell," he said getting up from his chair and moving to the liquor cabinet, where he poured himself a mug of whiskey.

Mary stopped sobbing and dried her tears.

The Captain turned back to the room, his face sullen.

"Mary, you were born on a stormy November night in the German town of Hanover. You're Mother and I were traveling, and didn't expect our baby for another month or more. When she suddenly went into labor, the innkeeper sent for a midwife. When she arrived and saw how difficult things were, she sent for a doctor." He took a drink from his mug. "The baby was coming so early and the labor was so violent, we didn't know what to do. The doctor never came, and my wife's agony grew worse. Hours later, she gave birth to a little boy. After the delivery she passed out from exhaustion, not realizing that our little boy had been stillborn. There was nothing we could do for him. The doctor finally arrived. He had been delayed with another difficult birth, only a few blocks away – a tragic event where the mother had died. With a long face, the doctor examined my wife and our dead baby. He told me our child had died because he had been born prematurely, and that my wife was lucky, for she would recover. I wept like a baby, and told the doctor how devastating this loss would be to my wife. He took pity, and told me that the mother who had died earlier had no family, and that her newborn was to be given to an orphanage. He suggested an exchange, and I immediately agreed. When my wife finally awoke, she had a beautiful baby girl wrapped in her arms. That girl was you, Mary."

The room fell silent again. All that could be heard was lapping water, moaning timbers and a few muffled footsteps from the deck above.

"I suppose I am not entirely surprised," Mary said in a shaky voice. "I've always been so different from my family... What do you know of my birth mother?"

Eric took another swallow of his drink. "Nothing, really. Only that the doctor said she was a young tart who found herself pregnant and died in childbirth. My dear wife, the only mother you ever knew, never learned of the exchange. I hope you will keep our secret."

Dutch's mind was reeling, but the overwhelming emotion that he felt was relief. With a smile like a sunrise, he turned to Mary and pulled her to her feet. "We can have as many children as we like. There is nothing to fear."

Her face remained sad as she looked him in the eye. "You would marry the daughter of a whore?"

Dutch pulled her close. "Your mother's sins are not yours!" Then he put two fingers on her lips. "All our yesterdays are forgiven," he said, quoting her own words. "We care only for our tomorrows." He kissed her, and then, as they separated, Dutch turned to Horace and asked, "Will you marry us, Commodore?"

"Are you certain that you want to join such a secretive family?"

"Nay," Dutch replied with a smile. "But I am entirely certain that I want to stand next to this woman for the rest of my life."

"Where and when?" the Commodore asked.

"Tomorrow at sunset, on the quarterdeck of this ship," Dutch replied, hugging Mary.

Kathleen cleared her throat, "Actually, Dutch, we should wait for Freddie's return. He is your family, as well."

Everything changed, that morning. The Captain and Commodore had both relieved their consciences, and were ready to bless the union of Mary and Dutch. The *Sea Urchin* was due back within a fortnight, which gave Kathleen time sew up a proper wedding dress. As they awaited the return of Freddie, the crew of the *Mary Rose* unloaded the cargo they had brought, as well as the water-tight barrels they had used last season for shipping the furs.

When the Commodore gave an accounting of their first season, Dutch was surprised to find that his share of the profits, less expenses, was just over four thousand dollars. That money had been deposited in his name with the Bank of Amsterdam. He also learned that both the salted and pickled salmon had made the long journey without spoiling, and had found a good market in Europe. Their enterprise on the Columbia River had a bright future.

At sunset on September 14th of 1812, on the crowded quarterdeck of the *Mary Rose*, most everyone on the river gathered to witness the nuptials. Dutch, wearing his store-bought clothes and cougar necklace stood nervously with his uncle and the dog by his side. As he waited, he heard a loud cry from above and craned his neck skyward. A bald eagle soared just above the mainmast. His father's words rang out in his ear; *You be in loving hands now, with nothing to fear. I will see you in heaven, by and by.*

Dutch smiled up at the bird and nodded his farewell.

From below decks, the women appeared. Mary looked radiant as a morning glory, wearing a soft cream buckskin dress adorned with seashells and a rainbow of trade beads. Her golden locks were braided with flowing ribbons, and delicate wildflowers were tucked into her hair. She moved to stand next to Dutch, with Kate and Cora smiling at her side.

The couple looked out at the gathered sea of faces. They could feel the crowd's goodwill and eagerness for the wedding festivities to follow. Indian canoes filled the waters around the ship, and Duncan McDougall and many other Astorians were in the crowd. The crews of the two ships filled the decks and hung from the shrouds. The Captains, dressed in their finest navel uniforms, stood by stoically to witness the event.

Finally, with Bible in hand, the Commodore turned to the guests and raised his hand for quiet. Then he turned back to Dutch and Mary, opened the Bible, and asked, "Mr. Clarke, are you prepared to take this woman as your own?" Dutch was stunned that his grandfather had given him his last name. "And, Miss Jacobson, are you prepared to take this man?"

The couple answered in unison with bright faces and a loud "Aye."

Horace continued, blessing their union. "Dearly beloved, we are gathered here today..."

With the sun setting over their shoulders, the pair exchanged their vows and kissed.

When their lips parted, Dutch turned to the audience and proudly proclaimed, "Ladies and gentlemen, may I present my wife Mary, Mrs. Dutch Clarke."

Last Reflections

—⁂—

*D*utch looked up from his third mug of coffee and found over a dozen people gathered around the Swede's table. They were all working blokes, with weedy beards and scruffy clothes. "And that's how my name changed and I got me a bride, all on the same day," he concluded. The eager faces of the men listening all seemed to be enthralled with his story. Dutch pulled out his pocket watch and clicked it open, and was surprised to find that it was early afternoon. "My jaw is tired. I'm afraid I've rambled on far too long. Please forgive me, mates."

There was a murmur from his audience. Then the Swede's powerful voice asked, "What happened to the Astorians?"

Dutch looked around at the men in the barroom, and found that all of their gazes were still fixed upon him. "Well, a few months after our wedding, the news of the war of 1812 reached the river. Soon after that, a large group of Canadians from the North West Company paddled up to the fort. They told the Astorians that British warships were on route to seize the fort. The Astorians squabbled amongst themselves about fighting off the British, but then decided to sell out to the North West outfit. So, without firing a shot, the British and Canadians took over Fort Astoria and renamed it Fort George. In just a few short years, Astor had lost hundreds of thousands of dollars. More tragically, his enterprise had cost the lives of sixty-one brave souls. Years later, there was a saving grace for Astor. His men had built Fort Astoria, and that helped to prove that America had a legitimate claim to the Columbia River. History will write of him as a hero, but I will always regard him as just another scoundrel."

As Dutch tapped the ashes from his pipe into an ashtray and filled the bowl with fresh tobacco, the blond-haired lad across the table asked. "When were you here last?"

Dutch lit his pipe with a wooden match and exhaled white smoke. "In 1815, my wife became pregnant with our first child. That's when we knew we had to return to civilization. But where would that be? In the end, we flipped a coin: heads Boston, tails Amsterdam. Tails won. That was forty-five years ago."

"What of Kathleen and Freddie?" someone else shouted.

Dutch puffed his pipe, and a fond look came over his face. "Sweet Kate moved to Holland with us. She remained our dear friend, confidant, and the nanny to our six children until she died, just a few years ago. Mary and I took her back home to Boston and buried her next to her husband and Sandy, God rest their souls. Freddie stayed with the trading post for a number of years. He married a Clatsop squaw named Sunrise. They both died in the tragic fire that burned down the post in 1826. They are buried out on the point, next to my father and blood brother."

"What of your enterprise?" the redheaded lad asked.

"After the fire, we got out of the fur business. The beaver was about played out and the sea otter was long gone. Instead, we started shipping salmon and lumber back to Europe, and bringing out industrial and farming supplies. The enterprise is still operating, although the Commodore and Eric are gone."

"What of the dog?" the bartender shouted across the room.

Dutch turned his way with a smile. "He ran off, after the wedding. Reckon he was jealous of my affections for Mary. Anyhow, we like to think he took up with a she-wolf and that his pups are still roaming the woods." Dutch glanced at his pocket watch again, then stood and moved away from his chair. "I've got to get going, mates," he said to the room.

"What happened to the Negro girl?" the Swede asked, also getting to his feet.

Dutch looked across the table at him and nodded his head slowly. "Mary and I sailed her down to the Tillamook village. In the end, though, she got cold feet and couldn't see herself as an Indian queen. So we brought her back home. A few weeks later, Captain Hawk and his ship anchored off our point. He had entered the river to see if Kathleen wanted to return to Boston. She didn't, but Cora did. I paid him three hundred dollars to get her back to America. The last I heard, she had married a Negro preacher, and they were helping Negro slaves escape to the north on what they called an underground railroad." Dutch looked around at the faces in his audience and concluded, "You know, boys, another war is brewing."

The Swede extended his massive paw with a smile. "Best damn rainy-day yarn I've ever heard. Thanks for sharing it with us, Dutch." As the two men shook hands, the saloon doors opened, and in walked Mary. She was dressed in a long, tailored tweed coat, with a yellow bonnet covering her hair, and she carried a closed umbrella. The years had been good to her. Mary's radiant beauty filled the barroom, and heads turned. She caught Dutch's eye in an instant, and he turned from the table and started moving towards her.

The saloon went silent. The men were astonished to find such a lovely lady amongst them.

"Where have you been?" Mary asked with a note of concern. "You left for your walk hours ago."

Dutch approached her, put an arm around her shoulders, and turned back to the room with a smile. "This be my Mary, boys. Ain't she a peach?"

The men applauded, with bright smiles.

Mary turned to her husband, flushed with embarrassment. "Dutch, the carriage is waiting out front."

He stared back at her fondly. "Just give me another moment." That said, he moved to the bar, opened his purse, and removed two twenty-dollar gold eagles. Dutch handed the money to the bartender and whispered, across the counter, "I be buying the drinks for my mates. These boys were good listeners."

The astonished barkeep looked down at the two gold eagles, not believing eyes. Then he looked up with a grin, nodding his approval.

As Dutch turned back to leave with Mary, one of the men shouted, "Where are you off to?"

Taking hold of his wife's hand, Dutch turned his weathered face to the room. "We'll pay our respects to some departed family, and then we'll walk to the Point and see what the tide has brought in."

END

Maps

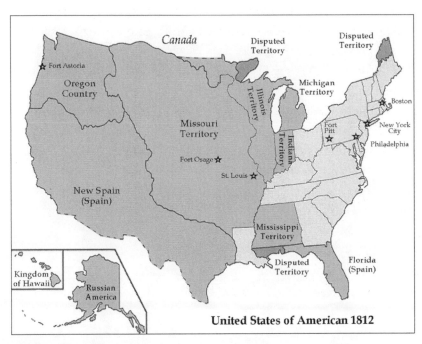

United States of American 1812

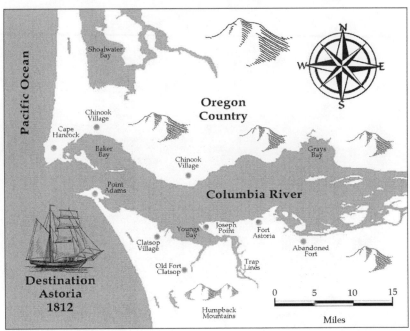

Destination Astoria 1812

Acknowledgments

—⟋⟋⟍—

I'm not much of a touchy feely kind of guy. I bristle when people talk about the concept of 'it takes a village.' My heroes are loners, strong-willed and determined folks who stand on their own two feet. You know, the John Wayne type. Nevertheless, if you're an author, it *does* take a village to write a book! I'm grateful to have family and friends who gave of their time to help me research, read, correct and polish my manuscript. Without their generous input, my storytelling would be a dismal failure.

Writing historical fiction is a rewarding enterprise for anyone who loves history. Once the general story line is set and a rough outline has been written, the leg-work begins. For Destination Astoria, my wife and I traveled the North Coast and the Columbia River basin, preparing the research for this story. We explored historical societies, interpretive centers, county and local libraries. We connected with various museums, including The Garibaldi Maritime Museum, where the legend of Captain Robert Gray was the inspiration for my last two novels.

We walked the old pioneer trails and investigated enthralling stories of the frontiersmen who came before us. We learned details of the Astorians, the British, and the War of 1812. These discovery trips opened many doors and helped start my two year writing process. Once the raw chapters were finished, they were sent out to 'the village'.

My editor, Judith Myers, has collaborated with me on all four of my novels. She has a magic touch with language and is a joy to work with. One way or another, her indispensable and savvy advice always made my words read better. Judy has given me new insights into the power of the written word.

Kate Miller provided a second look at my punctuation, and enthusiastic feedback on my story development. Her comments and thoughtful observations were deeply appreciated. My thanks to Ron Booton who has a keen eye for word aberrations and offered many thought-provoking remarks that helped polish my story.

Horse expert, Roz Kelly, gave me guidance on the finer points of equitation. She knows horses, and how to gracefully care for these majestic animals. Her advice was invaluable.

A special thanks to 'Commander' Rick Jacobson for the loan of his flintlock pistol, and to Bruce Boylen for all his work getting the old pistol ready to photograph. Thanks to Carrie Bergin of the Yankee Trader, for the generous loan of great antique props to complete the front-cover illustration. Kudos to Beach Books, Karen Emerling for her advocacy of local authors.

My wife Tess has always been the first to read my stories, and has provided non-stop encouragement and unwavering support. Her constructive feedback keeps me focused, and her heartfelt enthusiasm keeps me hopeful. Her deep faith, along with her grace, humor and loving kindness, has co-authored my life.

Yes, it took a village of wonderful, caring people to help me finish this book!

Having expressed my gratitude to all those who helped with this project, I must state that it is still my name on the title page, and I am responsible and accountable for every word.

Other Books

Other Books by Brian Ratty

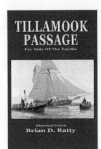

Tillamook Passage

Book Length: 324 Pages
Historical Fiction
Audience: Adults 18 and up
ISBN 978-1-4634-0615-8
Soft Cover: $19.95
Hard Cover: $24.95
eBook: $3.99

Winner: Eric Hoffer Award

Dutch Clarke—The War Years

Book Length: 512 Pages
Historical Fiction
Audience: Adults 18 and up
ISBN 978-1-4343-953 3-7
Soft Cover: $19.95
Hard Cover: $24.95
eBook: $3.99

Forward Magazine Book of the Year

Dutch Clarke—The Early Years

Book Length: 376 Pages
Action – Adventure
Audience: Young Adults & up
ISBN 978-1-4490-1451-1
Soft Cover: $19.95
Hard Cover: $24.95
eBook: $3.99

Forward Magazine Book of the Year

Available From:
Amazon.com — Barnes & Noble.com — DutchClarke.com

Made in the USA
San Bernardino, CA
18 June 2014